OTHER BOOKS BY HEATHER GRAHAM

OTHER BOOKS BY JON LAND

*Published by Forge Books

THE RISING

Heather Graham *and* Jon Land

A TOM DOHERTY ASSOCIATES BOOK
NEW YORK

THE RISING

A Forge Book
Published by Tom Doherty Associates
175 Fifth Avenue
New York, NY 10010

www.tor-forge.com

Forge® is a registered trademark of Macmillan Publishing Group, LLC.

ISBN 978-0-7653-7112-6

Our books may be purchased in bulk for promotional, educational, or business use. Please contact your local bookseller or the Macmillan Corporate and Premium Sales Department at 1-800-221-7945, extension 5442, or by e-mail at MacmillanSpecialMarkets@macmillan.com.

First Edition: January 2017
First Mass Market Edition: December 2017

Printed in the United States of America

0 9 8 7 6 5 4 3 2 1

For Tom Doherty and Bob Gleason
Vision doesn't age

ACKNOWLEDGMENTS

All books are a team effort and we're incredibly grateful for the team behind this one. The list starts with Tom Doherty, as great a publisher as he is a friend, who gave birth to *The Rising* when he took us to lunch and said, "The two of you should do a book together." Bob Gleason, the best editor in the business, took things from there on a team led by Linda Quinton, Phyllis Azar, Patty Garcia, Elayne Becker, Ryan Meese, Lucy Childs, Aaron Priest, and Natalia Aponte whose input was crucial in helping this book reach its full potential.

We are especially indebted, as well, to Jeslyn Farrow Russo for sharing her remarkable grasp of the Bay Area and Northern California, including St. Ignatius Prep where her son Xavier starred on the same football team as our book's hero, Alex. Jeremy Wall provided crucial input on the technical side of things, a big shout-out to Dennis Pozzessere for his knowledge of all things Alcatraz, and our deepest thanks to everyone at NASA for all their encouragement and support, both technical and otherwise.

No man or woman is an island and no writer is either, even when there are two of us. And we also want to thank all those from the production and sales side of things who believed in this project from the very beginning.

As for us, we now turn our attention to the next book in the series (tentatively titled *Blood Moon*), but for now there's this one to enjoy. So let's turn the page and begin.

Sometimes even to live is an act of courage.

—Seneca

THE RISING

FROM AN ANONYMOUS JOURNAL

You don't know who I am, and you don't need to. This isn't my story.

It's Alex's.

I can't explain all of it; it's better if I just tell it the way it happened and let you make up your own mind. I'm writing this down and I don't believe all of it myself. Like it's all some crazy dream or maybe somebody slipped something into my soda and I imagined the whole thing.

I never wanted to become a hero and don't consider myself one now. I look back on all of this a lot, looking for something I could've done differently, but there's nothing. My decisions weren't really conscious ones; I did what I had to do in each respective moment and regret none of those decisions. So if I had it to do all over again, would I?

The answer is simple: I didn't have a choice then, any more than I've got one now. None of us does.

Know what, though? When I look back and think about all I left behind, everything, really, I still know I could never have left Alex alone. He needed me, and if you believe in the cosmic nature of fate, maybe that's what had brought us together in the first place.

I don't regret any of it. Some things are bigger than

you, me, and the whole world. And this was about the whole world. Literally, as crazy as that sounds.

I want to lay it all out for you, so you'll understand even if you don't totally believe it. I don't blame you, either. Maybe I'm really writing this for myself, to help me understand. Sure, I was there to watch it all unfold, but looking back, I've started to doubt my own thoughts and memories. So I need to get this all down to make sure I don't lose it, because this isn't just a story.

It's a warning.

There's a reason why people once thought the world was flat or ended at the ocean. It made it easier to convince ourselves we were in control of our own planet and destiny, neither of which is even close to the truth. That's what I learned from Alex and what I need to tell you, what you need to hear. Sure, we know the Earth isn't flat now and stretches well beyond the oceans. But the truth I've learned is born out of a new reality that's just as extreme and unimaginable.

We want to think this is our world.

It's not.

We want to think we're safe.

We're not.

Like I said before, though, this isn't my story. It belongs to Alex. If there's any hope for us left, and I mean all of us, amid the terrible truths I've come to know, amid the rising of a dark, new world around us, it rides with him. This is his story.

Because he's the survivor.

PROLOGUE
PATTERNS

Northern California, eighteen years ago

Only those who risk going too far
can possibly find out how far one can go.

—T. S. ELIOT

Thomas Donati chased his NASA supervisor down the hall of the secret underground level, cutting him off just before he pressed the "up" arrow for the elevator. "You need to take a look at these figures."

"I have," Orson Wilder told him.

Donati reached out and flipped around the pages Wilder was still holding. "Right side up this time."

Wilder sneered, then nodded grudgingly as he reached around Donati and pressed the "up" arrow once and then a second time when it failed to light. "What am I looking for?"

"Signs."

"Signs?"

"Of a potential cosmic convergence of unprecedented proportions. Here, let me show you. . . ."

The elevator door slid open and Donati followed Wilder into the cab. "This earthquake in Tibet, a rogue wave wiping out an entire island in the South China Sea, the inexplicable malfunction of our interstellar monitors located in the northeast Pacific Ocean."

Wilder pulled away as far as the cab would allow, suddenly discomfited by Donati's proximity. "We have people you can bring this to on the extraterrestrial-communication side."

"This isn't about communication, no," Donati insisted. "Communication would fascinate me, not scare me."

Wilder looked down at the wad of papers. "So this scares you?"

Donati nodded. "Taken individually, no. Taken together in the aggregate, yes." He whipped a marker from his pocket and drew a circle on the elevator wall. "Picture this as the Earth. Here are the locations of the stimuli I just mentioned." Donati proceeded to draw X's to accompany his continued narration. "Tibet, the South China Sea, the northeast Pacific Ocean. A neat line," he finished, drawing his marker across the elevator wall to connect them, "perfectly following the curvature of the Earth." Donati popped the cap back onto his marker. "You asked me if I'm scared? I'm terrified. The prospects of this make me feel like I'm walking a tightrope with the lights out."

"Colorful metaphor."

"Accurate, in this case. We're talking about seismic levels of quantum disruption accompanied by radical spikes in the discharge of electromagnetic radiation. You see what I'm getting at here?"

"No, not really," Wilder said impatiently.

"Our lab exists on the same plane as these apparently random events. Our work could be causing disruptions leading to ripples in the time-space continuum. Or . . ."

"Or what?"

"The pattern could indicate contact from the other side of the doorway we're trying to open, a precarious proposition, indeed, no matter how exciting it may be. Now do you see what I'm getting at?"

The elevator stopped. The door opened. Neither man made any motion to step out.

"All right," said Wilder, "what would you recommend?"

Donati hesitated before responding. "Shutter the lab."

"*Our* lab?"

"Until we have a better idea of what we're dealing with."

Wilder thrust the pages out between them. "What does this have to do with that, even remotely? And I couldn't shutter the lab even if I wanted to."

"Why?"

"You know full well why."

"I guess I don't."

"You think we're the ones in charge here, making the decisions, pulling the strings?" Wilder shook his head slowly, better to make his point. "Not even close. It's the people pulling *our* strings who call the shots from behind a curtain that would make the Wizard of Oz proud."

Wilder started to step from the elevator, but Donati latched a hand onto his forearm, restraining him. "They don't know what we're dealing with here; *we* don't know what we're dealing with here."

"Are you trying to scare me, Doctor?"

"Inform you."

"And now you have." Wilder looked down at the hand still clamped to his suit jacket. "So if you don't mind . . ."

But Donati left it in place. "Shut the lab down, Orson. There's one more indicator I left out."

"And what's that?"

"The last energy readings for the quantum field

displacement grids registered at an eight-point-five on the eigenstate of the wave function."

"So?"

Donati's eyes bore into Wilder's. "So our generators are only capable of producing slightly over seven."

He released Wilder's arm but the facility's director made no effort to leave, holding a hand before the door so it wouldn't close again. Wavering for sure, until his expression hardened anew.

"I'll take this under advisement, review your findings in more detail, Doctor."

Wilder had stepped out of the cab when Donati's voice chased him back around. "Just keep this in mind." He had his marker back out and ready by the time Wilder turned, adding a fourth X to the neat line around the Earth. "This is us, right here. I can't explain what's happening any better or clearer than that. I just know you need to shutter the lab until we understand this phenomenon better."

The elevator doors started to close and this time it was Donati's hand that stopped them.

"Under the circumstances—" Orson Wilder began.

But the sudden shrill screech of the emergency alarm blaring throughout the facility cut him off before he could continue.

ONE

ALEX

The Present

A hero is no braver than an ordinary man,
but he is braver five minutes longer.

—RALPH WALDO EMERSON

1

COIN FLIP

"All right, visiting captain, the call is yours."

Alex Chin watched the referee toss the ceremonial coin into the air, watched it spiral downward upon the St. Ignatius College Prep turf field set on a hill overlooking the Pacific Ocean in the Sunset section of San Francisco.

"Heads," he heard the captain of the Granite Bay Grizzlies say.

"It's tails," the referee said, stooping to retrieve the coin. "Home captain?"

"We want the ball," Alex said, long hair matted down inside his helmet.

His gaze drifted again to the man in the wheelchair situated just off the sideline. He was clapping up a storm with the rest of the jam-packed crowd on the home side, gathered to watch the Central Coast sectional championship game between Alex's St. Ignatius Wildcats and the Grizzlies of Granite Bay, a public high school near Sacramento.

Tom Banks was as close to a legend in these parts as there was, quarterback of the last Wildcats football team to make a run at the state title until a vicious hit out of bounds put him in a wheelchair for the rest of his life. His son Tommy played linebacker for the team now and had cracked the starting lineup earlier in the season. Alex had heard Tom Banks hadn't been back to this field in all the years since his injury, tonight marking a quiet, unceremonious return just to watch his son play. The first time Alex had heard his name was when his own parents brought it up as a rationale to keep him from playing football.

As a result, Alex had joined the freshman team four years ago without saying a word to Li and An Chin, except to make up lies about where he was and what he was doing when he was really at practice. They didn't find out until the local paper ran a story about the Wildcats promoting a freshman to start at quarterback for the first time in the school's storied history. They'd been oh-and-four when Alex took over but then won five out of their last six games to finish at five hundred. The team upped that to seven wins Alex's sophomore season, then eight his junior, before going undefeated this fall and earning a home play-off game.

Alex and the other two Wildcat captains switched positions with their Grizzly counterparts at the fifty-yard line to mimic the direction in which each would be going to start the game. The Cats were representing the Western Catholic Athletic League, and the Grizzlies, the Sierra Athletic Conference, with the winner advancing to the Division 3 state championship. St. Ignatius had taken the ball, instead of deferring possession until the second half, because they'd scored all eight times this year when they received the opening kickoff.

We want the ball.

Right now, though, Alex stooped and picked up the game ball the ref had laid down in the center of the Wildcat logo smack dab in the middle of the field.

"That's not yours, son," the referee scolded.

But as his fellow captains rushed into the pile of teammates cheering and jumping in a tight mass on the side-line, Alex tucked the football under his arm and jogged out toward the end zone near where Tom Banks sat alone in his wheelchair.

"That's unsportsmanlike conduct!" he heard the ref call after him. "Fifteen-yard penalty, son!"

Alex still didn't stop, didn't even look back.

"This game's for you, sir," he said, handing Tom Banks the ball. "We're gonna finish what you started."

He watched Banks tuck the football under his arm the way he must have when he, like Alex, was an all-state quarterback. The man's eyes teared up, the two of them looking at each other until Alex threaded a hand through his face mask to wipe his own. Then he ran off to a rip-ple of applause through the crowd, toward the sounds of Coach "Blu" Bluford yelling for him to get with it, the game was about to start, and what the hell was he think-ing, anyway?

Alex knew his parents were up there somewhere, soon to be holding their breath as always in fear of his being injured. They may not have yelled at him the way Coach was yelling right now, once they found out he was play-ing football, but they'd been pissed too.

"Why can't I play?" he'd challenged. "It's my life."

"You don't understand," his mother said.

"We are doing this for your own good," his father added.

"You have to trust us."

"No," Alex said adamantly. "I want to play football. I'm *going* to play football."

He remembered how his parents had looked at each other in that moment. Not angry, not disappointed, more like . . .

Scared.

Alex threw himself into the lurching pile of teammates pounding each other, swarmed by them and he felt the energy radiating like the air on the hottest day summer had to offer. The referee blew his whistle to summon the teams out for the kickoff, the crowd rising to its collective feet, stomping on the bleachers.

"What are we?" Alex shouted from the center of the swarm.

"Glue!" came the deafening response.

"What are we?"

"Glue!"

"What are we?"

"Glue!"

"Then let's stick together and play some football!"

And with that Alex led the kickoff team out onto the field where the referee was waiting for him, tucking his yellow flag back into his belt.

"So was it worth it, son, was it worth fifteen yards?"

Alex turned toward Tom Banks, now cradling the game ball in his lap.

"Absolutely," he said to the ref. "No question about it."

2

GO, TEAM, GO!

"So, Samantha," Cara, the head cheerleader, said to Sam Dixon after the Wildcats had gone up seventeen to ten in the second quarter, "you make up your mind yet?"

"Yes, call me Sam."

Cara rolled her eyes. "That's a boy's name."

"It's been a boy's name for the whole twelve years we've been in school together," Sam told her. "And it's what you've always called me until, like, yesterday."

Cara rolled her eyes again. "Really? Fine. Whatever. Just tell me if you're going to help us out or not."

Sam was spared an answer when the upcoming kick-off forced Cara back to the rest of her squad.

"I'll take that as a yes," she yelled over her shoulder above the cheering crowd, smiling. "I know you won't disappoint the CatPack. We're your friends."

Sam lifted her backpack from the concrete and laid it on the bleacher seat next to her in the very front row. Earlier in the day, Cara had stuffed Monday's AP bio exam, pilfered over the Internet somehow, into one of the backpack's side pockets after a request, more of a demand, that Sam provide the answers over the weekend. The cheer squad liked calling themselves the "CatPack." But Sam preferred to think of them, less affectionately, as "Cara and her Clones." And now they wanted to be spared the bother of studying for a test none of them stood any chance at all of acing, maybe not even passing. They didn't even belong in AP bio and Sam had no idea how they'd managed to qualify, wanted to tell Cara maybe the CatPack should just transfer into a different class.

But she hadn't and now the test for which Sam was supposed to provide the answers made a slight bulge in that side pocket of her backpack, overstuffed to the point of being stretched at the seams.

You make up your mind yet?

The truth was she hadn't, and Sam turned back to the game to distract herself. She understood the concept of football. She just wasn't sure that she liked the game. It was everyone trying to get the ball over the goal line—and willing to crunch, bang, and shove one another to do so.

But Alex played football, and while Cara (of course) was dating Alex, it didn't stop Sam from admiring him from a distance. In Sam's code of honor—perhaps a foolish one at times—friends didn't betray friends. In this group, she'd seen a lot of cheating and lying, and she kept her mouth shut when someone had said something in confidence. She wasn't sure that paid, really.

Sam was sitting down low in the stands, in the closest seats to the field, the only reserved ones, because Cara had secured the ticket for her. A nice gesture, Sam thought, until Cara had stuck the stolen test into her backpack along with the ticket.

"We're counting on you, girl." Cara winked and bounced off with her tumbling hair glimmering over her shoulders in her prissy cheer uniform.

Sam hadn't had any intentions at all of going to the school's first playoff game in fifteen years, but now she had a ticket and, well, her own reasons for going. All of which were spelled *A-L-E-X*.

The thing was, Sam liked being friends with Cara, even though they weren't friends anymore, not really. Sam holding on to what they used to have because some part of her still craved it, and Cara holding on for reasons akin to the test now stuffed in Sam's backpack to claim her expert scientific eye. That must've been the main reason Cara seemed so happy when Sam landed the internship at NASA's Ames Research Center, home to the Astrobiology Institute, located down in Silicon Valley. She should've just said she wasn't about to answer the exam questions ahead of time and chance being caught as a cheater herself. Risk maybe her whole future, because she didn't want to be the outcast she often felt like, because she was afraid of running afoul of Cara and the Clones, who could make her life a living high school hell.

Well, screw the CatPack.

Easier said than done, of course. The school belonged to this group, who loved parading about in their clingy uniforms, the halls lacking only red carpets rolled out ahead of their strut.

Yeah, screw them.

The cheer ended and Sam watched Cara shoot her a look that stopped just short of a smile, more a warning than a glance. *Help us or else.* Sam always helped because she didn't want to find out what "or else" entailed.

Sam imagined herself dressed in a CatPack outfit, bouncing about and playing to the crowd.

No, actually, she shouldn't imagine the sight because when she did, she'd see herself jumping about while trying to keep her glasses on at the same time—a book or her iPad stuck in the extra pocket she'd sewn into her short, short skirt falling out with each bounce. These girls didn't care one iota, smidgeon, gram, molecule, or some infinitesimal quantum particle about anything in any way involving a worldview. Their lives were limited to the confines of the school and the city where they were treated like royalty simply because of who they were. Never mind the fact they hadn't contributed or discovered a damn thing, never anything of worth to anyone beyond themselves.

Sam, on the other hand, had just made an amazing discovery she couldn't wait to share with Dr. Donati, her supervisor at Ames. Not that Cara and the Clones would understand, much less care. But Donati surely would, because the pattern she'd uncovered was undeniably there.

Sam wanted a career in NASA. She wanted to become an astronaut and go into space as part of the next phase of the manned program. She wanted a different kind of crowd than this to applaud, as she made her way to the capsule of some futuristic spaceship.

Now flying for the USA, Samantha Dixon!

Just as she finished that thought, the crowd jumped to its feet, cheering. Sam returned her gaze to the field to find Alex Chin strutting away from a ball carrier he'd deftly avoided for a twenty-yard gain on a quarterback keeper, to the high-fives of his Wildcat teammates. She felt her own heartbeat slow again, after fearing herself caught in a fantasy.

But she wasn't a cheater in the fantasy. There was no place for cheaters at NASA.

APPLICATION FOR SPACE PROGRAM SUMMARILY DENIED.

Sam saw that in her head now, her whole life ruined by one stupid mistake because she wasn't brave or strong enough just to say no. Maybe she could tell Cara she'd lost her backpack, and thus the test.

Maybe she should just tell Cara to go to hell. A year from now, she'd be at Harvard, or Brown, or MIT, or Stanford. But they didn't accept cheaters, either, much less give them the financial aid Sam needed with her overgrown-hippie parents too busy making pesticide-free products to make any money. Setting up "grow" communes for anyone who paid them a small deposit, with the balance almost never paid in full. No money, but a fridge full of tomatoes and a nook full of homemade jellies and jams. *Wonder if one of my schools of choice might accept those in lieu of tuition?* Strange how all Sam could think of was growing up while her parents never seemed to have grown up at all. Her father still called people "dude."

Really?

Now they had taken to growing medical marijuana, having secured their grow license for a local dispensary. It had made her very popular in school once word got out, since any number of kids who'd never said a single word to her thought it would be no problem for her to clip a few buds off the plants for them. Sam reminded them that constituted a crime; "Just say no," the saying went, and that's what she did.

To distract herself as much as anything, Sam turned her attention back to the game, seeking out Alex, who was calling the signals from behind center. At least when she tutored him, she got paid. Even though she would've done it for free. And there was at least one good thing about being at the game tonight, at field level, no less: she got to watch Alex play, the crowd cheering as he threw a perfect strike over the middle for a thirty-yard gain that put the Wildcats in easy range of the Granite

Bay end zone. The crowd leaped to its feet en masse, pounding the stands so hard the ground actually shook. In front of Sam on the sidelines, the CatPack bounced as if their sneakers were equipped with springs, pompoms shaking in rhythm.

That's when she felt a man squeeze into the flat bleacher seat behind her. Sam smelled something like motor oil combined with fresh tire rubber and figured he must be an auto mechanic. But a quick glance revealed him to be well dressed all in black, the hands pressed atop his knees looking so clean the skin seemed sprayed on. Their eyes met but the man's didn't really regard her, and Sam turned away fast, trying to figure out why she suddenly felt so unnerved.

3

THE SECOND COMING

"Hey, stay down, fool! Come after me, and that's how you land!" Alex Chin taunted, as the running back he'd drilled into the turf from his free safety position on defense was helped back to his feet and moved woozily toward the sideline. "Yup, yup, time to leave the field and don't bother coming back!"

The other team's trainer came out onto the field to help number twenty-four, as Alex summoned the defense back into the huddle. They were taking the game—but he didn't like the way it was going, just one score up late in the fourth quarter after a glut of penalties called on the home team had kept the game close. Maybe the ref was still pissed at Alex for stealing the game ball prior to kickoff.

He hadn't thrown his flag once for all the hits after the whistle Alex had taken while in at quarterback. Alex had the feeling that the coach of the visiting Granite Bay Grizzlies had put a bounty out on him or something—*free pizza for whoever knocks Alex Chin out of the game.* Even on defense, the fullback hadn't just tried to block him on the last play; he'd tried to elbow-jab him in the back between the ribs. The blow had stung and stolen his breath, but Alex showed no response at all, didn't even complain to the ref. There were better ways to get even.

"This is our house," he told his teammates, back in the defensive huddle. "Fourth quarter and they're still trying to play dirty. Let them. One stop to go for the CCS championship. We own this field. Let's send them home! Let's go to state! What are we?"

"Glue!"

The defense clapped in cadence and fanned out to take their positions, then rapidly shifted about as Alex called out defensive signals. Pretty much the only television he'd been watching lately had been the opponents' game films, something he was much better at studying than his senior year subjects. Every time he resolved to pay more attention to this or that subject, there was an offensive tendency to be studied or defensive weakness to be exploited. That was the thing about calling signals on both offense and defense. You had to know your opponent on both sides of the ball, instead of just one.

"Forty-three Juke!" Alex called out, as the quarterback backpedaled from center into the shotgun set. "Forty-three Juke!"

He could tell from the tight end going into motion that Granite Bay was going to run a screen to that side, hence his defensive signal to shift the Wildcats' outside linebacker into a slot where he could disrupt the play. Alex rotated toward that side at the snap, saw the screen taking shape, and outside linebacker Tommy Banks, all 150 pounds of the legendary Tom Banks's son, propelling himself toward an offensive lineman who looked twice his size, moving out to block.

Alex heard the bone-jarring impact as he rotated into position and charged the line, the crackle of helmets and shoulder pads crunching against each other. Tommy Banks disappeared under a sea of churning feet and black pellets kicked up from the turf field, as Alex knifed in through the gap Tommy had created and tackled the running back, who'd caught the screen low, for a five-yard loss. Then he bounced back up and moved straight to Tommy, who'd just made it up to his knees.

"That's what I'm talking about, four-two!" he said, helping the smallest kid on defense back to his feet. "That was on you, all you! You made your dad proud, you hear me? You made your dad proud!"

And the crowd erupted in cheers again, for Tommy Banks this time as he jogged back a bit dazedly to the huddle with Alex's hand wrapped around his shoulder.

"Let me see something," Alex said, turning the kid's face toward him with both hands on his helmet.

"You're not gonna kiss me, are you?" Tommy mused through the blood from a cracked lip.

"Another play like that, and I just might. Follow my finger," Alex instructed, holding up his middle one to make sure the crunching tackle hadn't left Tommy's eyes glassy.

"Very funny."

Alex glanced at the scoreboard, which showed the Cats up seven points with twelve seconds to go and the Grizzlies forty yards from the end zone.

"Third down, boys," he said in the huddle. "Stop them two more plays, we go to state. One deep-zone blitz to go. Let's do it!"

The standing-room-only crowd began hooting it up as soon as they broke the huddle and spread out into position across the line of scrimmage. They got really loud when the Grizzlies' quarterback brought his team up to the line and tried to shift the offense from the unexpectedly aggressive man-up coverage he was facing. The whole offense looked rattled. The quarterback took the snap, fumbled it, and covered up fast, no choice but to use his final time-out.

"There you go, there you go!" Alex said, slapping the pads of his teammates. "Almost over now, almost done!"

Having no idea in that moment how right he was about to become.

4

STRANGER IN A STRANGE LAND

It felt weird, Sam thought as both teams gathered on the sidelines during the time-out, not to have her nose in a book. She was currently re-reading Heinlein's *Stranger in a Strange Land*, one of her all-time favorites along with *Fahrenheit 451* by Ray Bradbury and pretty much anything by Isaac Asimov. She loved reading science fiction dating all the way back to H. G. Wells and Jules Verne, never ceased to be amazed at the ability of those authors to foresee the future.

She'd read the books and saw herself doing something similar for NASA. Not just foreseeing the future, but planning and helping to bring it to pass.

Unless she was suspended for cheating on an AP bio exam. Unless she got caught supplying Cara and her bouncing cheer buddies the answers to the test they'd stolen.

Sam wanted to take it out of her backpack pocket and tear it up then and there. Otherwise, she might very well find herself explaining to her boss at NASA why she'd been expelled from high school instead of expounding on the discovery she couldn't wait to share with him.

The information was on her iPad, currently stuffed into the backpack pressed against her on the bench. The findings she'd come across could have been coincidence, but she doubted it. And, assuming there was some validity in those findings, what exactly did they suggest?

Maybe nothing.

Maybe lots.

She wouldn't know until she shared the information with Dr. Donati. The findings may well not amount to much, even if they were accurate. But Sam had never been shy about showing initiative with anything related to science and she wanted NASA to see her as the kind of free, creative thinker they so valued.

But how much would they value a proven cheater?

Again she thought about tossing the stolen exam in the trash and again she stopped short of doing it. Fixating on that again, both the game and the findings stored on her iPad flitting at the edge of her consciousness. All of a sudden, the hero of *Stranger in a Strange Land*, Valentine Michael Smith, seemed eerily easy to relate to. A human raised by Martians who finally comes home to Earth to find it's not really home.

A stranger in a strange land, indeed, just like her.

Sam didn't feel she belonged here right now any more than Valentine when he first came to Earth. And he never stopped being a stranger, she remembered, as the teams broke from the sidelines and gathered in their respective huddles.

Time for just one more play, Samantha thought, rising to her feet with the rest of the crowd and smelling the odd motor oil–like scent again as the man behind her rose too.

5

IMPACT

Fourth down and half the field to go now. Alex bobbed up and down in the ground mist gathering on the dew-rich field, the halogen lights strung from poles overhead slicing through the gathering fog to create a haze-like effect that covered only the field. As if the stands were walled off. As if the world extended no farther than this.

With time stopped, Alex glanced toward the sidelines, reminding himself to enjoy the moment, savor it, because being on top of the world wasn't something that happened every day—never, for most people. But his gaze again drifted to Tom Banks, who was nervously clutching his football like it was a newborn baby.

The "Second Coming," the most seasoned of Wildcat football fans called Alex, Banks being the first.

Granite Bay came to the line of scrimmage and Alex called out the defensive signals, reading the formation to identify the coming gadget play, a flea flicker or something, with the receiver in motion lagging behind the play to accept a toss from either the running back or tight end. The Grizzlies needed this score just to tie, but he'd seen stranger things happen and crept closer to the line of scrimmage, ready for the snap.

It came without the quarterback noticing Alex sliding

to the left to shoot the gap between offensive linemen moving out to block, reaching the running back at the same time as the ball. Alex hit him with enough force to jar the ball loose and send it floating through the air.

Straight into the arms of Tommy Banks, who caught it clean and seemed to freeze.

Game over, Alex thought, *just go down and cover up.*

Then instinct took over and Tommy started running instead, twisting toward the sideline en route to the end zone, near which his father was seated. The quarterback and one of the linemen had a direct bead on Tommy, their angle certain to cut him off before he turned upfield.

Sam watched a kid who looked too small to be playing for the Wildcats chugging down the sideline. They were on defense a minute ago, meaning he must've gotten the ball after an interception or a fumble. A pair of Grizzlies, Bears, or whatever they were called converged for the tackle from two different angles, certain to sandwich the smaller kid between them. Then, though, a blur of motion zoomed into the picture, another Wildcat slicing to cut the tacklers off.

Alex.

Go out of bounds! Alex thought, but Tommy clearly had other thoughts as the quarterback's and lineman's focus was entirely on him, all their pent-up frustration over the impending, now inevitable loss about to be unleashed in a single violent moment. Tommy would never see it coming, the tackle sure to crush him. Alex could see it all happening on a Jumbotron in his head as if it were a done deal. Only it wasn't, and he still had as good an angle on them as they had on Tommy.

Alex charged across the field, looping ahead to cut off the would-be tackle, stop Tommy from getting crunched just as his father had a generation before. Running as fast as he'd run in his entire life and catching a glimpse of Tom Banks cringing in his wheelchair.

Sam was on her feet with everyone else in the stands, practically bouncing up and down. The bleachers reverberated in a tinny echo she could feel at the core of her eardrums. Hardly a football fan, she couldn't help rooting for the kid who looked too small to be out there streaking for the end zone, with Alex slicing in to throw him a block.

And that's when she felt something brush against her. Thought nothing of it until the smell of motor oil flooded her nostrils and left her looking at the man who'd forced himself into the seat behind her sliding toward the aisles holding—Sam's gaze dipped downward, to the open empty pocket of her backpack—her iPad in his grasp.

"Hey, somebody stop him! Stop him!" she cried.

But the crowd was roaring too loud for her to be heard and Sam pushed her way after him, past the students crowded into the front row.

"Hey!" she yelled again. "Stop!"

He started up the aisle toward the exit, not turning to regard her.

"Somebody, stop him!"

But the crowd was so loud now Sam couldn't hear her own words. She reached the aisle to find her way blocked by students positioning themselves to rush the field in celebratory fashion. Sam did her best to fight through them, nobody giving an inch and seeming to form an impenetrable wall between her and the guy who'd stolen her iPad.

He was getting away!

She glimpsed him descending the ramp that would free him from the stands, the distance between them continuing to grow with Sam still fighting to follow, when she heard a sickening crunch and the crowd went quiet.

The moment before impact, Alex Chin saw the blur of two onrushing forms aglow in the light cast by the halogen bulbs towering overhead. Tommy Banks never heard them coming over the crowd noise, clueless to the bone-rattling crunch he was about to suffer as he veered away from the sideline with the end zone in sight.

Alex excelled at all things football with the exception of blocking, since he was never asked to do it. So when he threw himself airborne in the last instant before Tommy got sandwiched, it felt awkward and wrong. The last sight he remembered was a glimpse of Tom Banks in the wheelchair—upside down because of the way Alex's body had canted.

Sam felt the air go out of the stadium, the crowd seeming to hold its collective breath. She stopped fighting against the swell of humanity to turn in the direction everyone else was already staring, a single focused gaze aimed straight at a form down on his back in a Wildcats uniform, lying so that his body straddled the sideline. Motionless.

It couldn't be, Sam thought.

But it was.

Alex.

* * *

He'd slammed into both Granite Bay tacklers a mere instant before they reached Tommy, bent in half at impact until it felt like his lower body was separated from his upper. Alex felt his spine rattle, seeming to crack low and high at the same time and sounding like a gunshot inside his head. The field felt spongy beneath him and he didn't realize he'd hit it until he heard the blaring echo of the referee's whistle blowing.

That was all Alex heard because the crowd had gone totally quiet, so quiet he could actually hear the air seeming to whistle inside his helmet.

Why aren't I getting up? Somebody, help me up.

Then Alex realized it wasn't just that he couldn't get up, he couldn't even *move*. Started to suck in a deep breath when he realized he couldn't breathe, either. It felt like his helmet was a plastic bag fastened over his face to shut out the air. He heard the referee's whistle blowing louder, figured it was drowning out his cries for help and then realized he hadn't uttered any.

Somebody, help me!

Alex thought the words but couldn't speak them. Around him, the jam-packed stands were nothing but a soft blur, the blackness of the night sky descending until it swallowed him.

6

FROZEN

Sam had forgotten all about the man who smelled of motor oil and her stolen iPad. She'd heard about moments when time seemed to freeze solid, but had never experienced one until now. That's what watching Alex lying still on the sideline felt like, a snapshot instead of a video. The crowd remained dead silent, standing as if still preparing to celebrate while assuming a position more like a prayer service.

Whomp!

That's what the collision sounded like. She'd heard it, even though she'd been facing away from the field trying to follow the path of the thief.

Sam watched trainers from both teams and the Wild-cats' team doctor sprinting onto the field toward Alex. An ambulance parked off the far sideline of the field at every game spun its flashing lights to life in anticipation of a hospital ride, needing no signal to head out to the downed player.

"Cara!" she called out to the blond-haired shape with pom-poms dangling by her hips on the sideline, then louder, "Cara!"

Cara didn't turn, as transfixed by what was taking place on the field as she was. Alex down on the ground, engulfed by kneeling and crouching forms. The kid for whom he'd thrown the block standing in the end zone, no one acknowledging the score. He looked lost, as frozen as she felt.

Sam returned her gaze to the sideline, saw Cara talking on her cell phone. To her mom, maybe, or someone else who'd been watching the game on television. Sam waved, trying to get her attention but to no avail, Cara jabbering away, managing a smile.

A smile? Her boyfriend was lying broken on the field. So where'd the smile come from?

"Who is it?" a teacher named Danika Tomkins asked, suddenly alongside her. "Is it Alex?"

"Yes," Sam managed, even though the downed form was now blocked from view by a sea of figures hovering over him. "I think so."

In fact, she didn't think, she knew, but couldn't bring herself to say it, hoping against hope she was wrong. Her whole world was about being right all the time, every answer on every test, and now she desperately wanted to be wrong.

"Oh," Ms. Tomkins managed. "I hope he's . . ."

Her voice trailed off, drifting away with the breeze. Lost along with everything else besides the ambulance backing into position near Alex beneath the spill of the lights breaking the night.

Sam remembered her iPad in that moment and swung again for the area she'd last seen the foul-smelling thief. But he was gone, long gone, and Alex still wasn't going anywhere.

7

AMBULANCE RIDE

"This boy needs some help now!"

Alex dimly thought he recognized the referee's voice in the same moment he heard the steady beeping of the ambulance as it reversed. He could breathe again, he realized, but each contraction of his chest felt labored and wrong.

His vision misted over and when it cleared he looked up to see Tom Banks hovering over him. Only, he wasn't in the wheelchair anymore; he was standing up.

You want your ball back? the football star who'd been injured in this very same stadium asked, extending it toward Alex.

"Can you move your fingers?"

But it wasn't Tom Banks asking him that question now, it was a man wearing the blue uniform of a paramedic as he squeezed on a pair of exam gloves he'd plucked from a cargo pocket on his pants.

"Can you move your fingers?" the paramedic asked him again.

Alex didn't have the strength to try.

"Can you feel your legs?"

The world felt too soft and cushiony for him to bother. He felt warm hands feeling about his neck and upper back and then easing his helmet off to let his long sweat-tangled hair dangle free. He'd seen so many scenes like this unfold, mostly on television but also live, never for one moment considering it could be him.

And now it was, following literally in the footsteps of the legendary Tom Banks. That thought spurred him to look to see if he still had the ball Banks had given back to him while again standing up on working legs. There was no ball or Banks, of course.

There was nothing at all.

The paramedics and ambulance were gone, the stands that had turned dead quiet were gone, even the field was gone. In their place were machines, vast tentacled steel monsters moving about with surprising agility. The field seemed to tremble under their weight, impressions that looked like miniature sinkholes left in their wake as their clanking steps kicked up swarms of the black pellets lending the artificial turf its cushion.

Alex looked up and saw one of the machines looming over him in place of the EMT, retractable arms extending from slots in what might have been shoulders and positioning themselves beneath him.

Don't touch me! Get away from me!

Alex tried to cry out but couldn't find the breath he needed. The machines were everywhere, just like in the pictures he drew in his sketchbook, currently tucked between the mattress and box spring in his bedroom, its pages full of black ink and pencil drawings of things his mind showed him. Alex never knew when one of the spells would overtake him. Usually it was when he was listening to music or trying to do homework. He'd go into a weird state that felt like daydreaming and when he snapped alert again, another page had somehow been filled by hands so lacking in talent that he'd nearly failed art.

"The hospital's been alerted to have a neuro team standing by," he heard a voice he didn't recognize say.

The field, the stands, and everything else were back, the machines gone.

"Can you hear me, son? Just nod if you can."

Alex could but didn't. The activity around him settled into a restive frenzy, teammates kneeling in a semicircle with some praying, the world gone hazy and captured in soft focus in the spill of the bright light pouring downward. He felt himself being strapped to a board, then lifted onto a gurney and hoisted into the ambulance's rear.

Alex felt a clog in his throat and for a moment, just a moment, thought his breath was being choked off for good this time. Then he realized it was fear, a cold dread arising from the reality just beginning to dawn on him through the haze.

Alex started to choke up, felt the tears first welling in his eyes and then spilling downward. From the ambulance's rear, his gaze locked on the scoreboard, frozen with two seconds left in the game, the Cats with the ball and just one victory-formation kneel-down from winning the Central Coast sectionals. And they'd be moving on to the Division 3 state championship round after an undefeated season, thanks to their All-American quarterback, now lying broken in the back of an ambulance.

Just before the ambulance doors closed, Alex spotted Cara Clarkson, his girlfriend—most of the time, anyway—standing frozen on the Wildcat head emblazoned on the fifty-yard line. She used the sleeve of her cheerleader uniform to wipe away her tears, her pompoms shed halfway between the sideline and midfield.

Alex, she mouthed. *Alex . . .*

"My parents," Alex heard himself say, as the ambulance tore off with siren wailing once it reached the street fronting the high school.

"Take it easy, son," a paramedic said, hooking up an intravenous line to his arm.

"My parents," he repeated, thinking how they'd never wanted him to play football in the first place, how he'd started practice freshman year without telling them, that work parlayed now into a host of scholarship offers.

And suddenly that's what Alex was thinking about— all those scholarship offers, including the one he'd settled upon. Alex's father, Li Chin, taught mathematics at San Francisco City College, where he'd recently been awarded tenure. His mom, An, had some fancy title but was little more than a glorified cleaning lady where she worked. Money was tight and had only gotten tighter in the wake of the economic downturn that had seen both of them suffer, first, wage freezes and then a modest reduction. Alex needed football to pay for college, and now who knew if football would still be there for him?

That thought started the tears flowing again, his stomach twisting into knots. Alex couldn't just lie here helpless. He had to know, had to try.

He willed life into his feet, pictured them moving. At first it felt like his brain was disconnected from his body but then he felt them wiggling. Imagined he knew the feeling a baby gets when it takes its first step.

Recharged, he willed the same life into his fingers, then his hands. Watched them spasm briefly before beginning to obey his commands.

"Easy there, son," the paramedic warned. "Stay still now."

But he could *move*. He wasn't paralyzed.

"Alex *Chin*," the paramedic was saying now, reading off a clipboard as if surprised by what it said.

I'm adopted, you idiot, Alex almost said, used to the double takes people gave him when they saw his name before they saw him.

The Chins had adopted him as an infant, never once making him feel different or out of place in their home. If anything, as a young boy he thought there was something wrong with him. Why else would he have sandy blond hair and blue eyes? He'd stand in front of the mirror and pull his eyes to the side, hoping to train them to stay that way so he could look like he was supposed to, like his mother and father. As a result, he'd learned tolerance early and never judged anyone based on anything other than who they were as people, just like he hoped people would judge him. The only time he ever got into fights was in elementary and middle school when somebody made fun of his parents.

It was the one thing he couldn't tolerate, the one thing he'd never grown thick-skinned about. He didn't mind when somebody called him Alex *Chink*. But once they made fun of his mother or father, all bets were off and somebody was going down.

That thought brought a slight smile to his face, though his eyes were still wet with tears. At six-foot-one, he towered over Li and An Chin, both naturalized American citizens who nonetheless bore the brunt of prejudice and wrath against China. Alex had long grown used to the caustic stares cast his family's way, like they were doing something wrong by being together. So when he first started playing football, he'd launch himself at opponents with a fury bred of the anger left over from those looks, those stares, those lingering glances. He couldn't hit bigots and the small-minded, but opposing players on a football field were something else again.

The siren had stopped sounding. The ambulance bucked to a halt and the rear doors thrust open to reveal the familiar California Pacific Medical Center sign. Alex closed his eyes and when he opened them again, figures draped in light blue medical scrubs were walking on either side of the wheeled dolly into the hospital.

I'm all right, he wanted to tell them through the clog in his throat, *I'm okay.*

One of the figures walking alongside the gurney was a woman with long hair the same color as his and he wanted to tell her how pretty she was. But a dark figure standing at the head of the hall leading to the emergency room's exam area claimed his attention before he could grope for the words. The figure was crazy tall and ridiculously thin, draped in black everywhere except his flesh, which was sallow and sickly pale. A patient, surely, the pallor of his skin due perhaps to the effects of chemotherapy or treatment for some other lingering disease.

The gurney squeaked against the tile and spun round the corner at the head of the hall, seeming to pass straight through the tall man. Alex tried to raise his head to see if he was still standing there, forgetting all about the headboard strapping him in place. That point of the hallway came into view again when they turned the gurney toward an empty examination room and eased Alex toward it.

But the tall man was gone.

8

WAITING

"You don't have to stay," Cara said in the hospital waiting room.

Sam kept the biology textbook cradled in her lap. "I want to."

She felt Cara reach over and squeeze her arm.

"You're a good friend, Sam, I don't deserve you."

You don't deserve Alex, either.

"What was that?"

"Huh?"

"I thought you said something."

Sam shuffled her legs and tucked the textbook under her arm. "Nah. Just clearing my throat."

"'Cause the thing is, I feel really bad."

Sam hoped Cara was going to tell her to forget about supplying answers for the science exam still tucked inside her backpack, that it had been a mistake and she should shred the pages, burn them, maybe.

"I'm not sure how much longer I'll be dating Alex," Cara said instead.

"*What?*"

Cara gazed about the hospital waiting room, as if to make sure nobody had heard the exchange. "Shhhhhh! And don't you say a word. Swear you won't say a word. I haven't decided yet," Cara said.

"What do you mean *you* haven't decided?"

"You know Ian Sandler, right?" Cara asked.

Ian had graduated the year before them. Sam wasn't sure what he was doing now.

"What about him?" she asked Cara.

"His dad has an in with the Warriors."

"With who?"

"The Golden State Warriors. You know, local pro basketball team."

"No, I don't. You're kidding, right?"

"Kidding about watching my dream come true? No way, girl. Hey, we're seniors now and things change. Alex is going off to do his thing and I've got to do mine." Then, after a pause, "You'll see."

"What's that mean?"

"You know."

"I do?"

Cara frowned, as if it were obvious. "Things will get better. As soon as you get to college. High school's not worth the stuff that gets stuck to the bottom of my boots. That's why Ian's so important to me."

"You mean his dad is."

Cara rolled her eyes. "Whatever, girl, whatever." Her stare tightened. "So can you keep it secret?"

"Haven't I always kept your secrets?"

"I thought it might be different with Alex."

"Why?"

"You know."

"There you go again telling me what I know."

"Well, *I* know you're crushing mad on the boy. I can see it every time you look at him. Hey, I don't blame you. All those tutoring sessions, all those hours spent looking at him. How can you help yourself? The kid's totally gorgeous."

"Not gorgeous enough, apparently."

Cara shook her head, as if Sam were just a dumb kid who didn't understand. "Grow up, girl. Graduation is all about change. I'm just starting the process earlier."

"With Ian."

"And the Warriors, maybe; yeah, you bet." Cara drew a little closer. "And look at the bright side."

"What?"

"You know."

"Again telling me what I know?"

"Yeah, that you'd like Alex to ask you out. And once I tell him we're done, he'll be able to."

Sam looked down. "He doesn't look at me that way. I'm just his tutor."

"How do you know how he looks at you?"

"Because I keep him looking down at his books, that's how."

Sam could tell Cara knew she was lying, at least not telling all of the truth. She'd had crushes since she'd been around eight and had never acted on a single one of them. Preferred instead to stare wantonly and longingly at her chosen object of desire, secure in the notion that the relationship would stretch no further.

And here she was a senior in high school and she'd never had a boyfriend, not even close.

Unless you counted Phillip Steeg and you couldn't really count Phillip Steeg because their date had consisted of eating cookies in his tree house when they were both twelve years old. He'd leaned over to kiss her and ended up slicing her lip with his braces. Sam kissed him back anyway, following the taut look in his eyes as he pulled away.

"Whoa," he said, "that was nice."

Sam nodded; it had been nice for her too. Because she'd been thinking of Alex as she kissed him.

Cara's iPhone started buzzing and she checked the text that had just come in. "Huh?" she asked, having forgotten what Sam had just said.

"Never mind."

"Okay."

"So you're not worried?"

"Oh, about Alex? Of course I am. But he'll be fine."

"You can't know that."

"Yes, I can. I'm psychic. I can tell the future. Like the whole CatPack acing the AP bio exam next week. Right, Sam?"

9

DIAGNOSIS

Alex saw his parents slip into the curtained-off cubicle in the midst of his initial examination, their heels clacking against the floor ahead of them. He smelled the light, sweet familiar scent of his mother's perfume, making him feel better immediately.

"The preliminary news is promising," a doctor with a shock of ash gray hair reported, as he continued his poking and prodding. "He has full use of his limbs, no sign whatsoever of paralysis, and no evident spinal compression or swelling."

He heard his mother sigh, his father mumble something in Chinese under his breath, sounding like anything but a now tenured professor at San Francisco City College.

"I've scheduled a CT scan just to confirm the initial diagnosis," the doctor continued, "and we're going to keep Alex overnight for observation. But if everything checks out, he should be able to go home tomorrow."

Alex's father was nodding up a storm, the way he always did when stressed. His mother was steadying herself with short, shallow breaths, the picture of calm and repose.

"Will I be able to play next week?" Alex asked, finding his voice.

The doctor seemed reluctant to meet his gaze. "Let's just take one step at a time, shall we?"

"Yeah, but could you just tell me what you think?"

"I think we should take one step at a time, starting with that CT scan."

"So you're not sure."

"Alex," his father began, but his mother silenced him with a tight squeeze of his arm.

"That you'll be able to play football next week?" the doctor resumed. "No, I'm not. Not yet, not until we've had an opportunity to do a full work-up and see how you respond in the next twenty-four hours."

Alex turned away, looking back at his parents. They seemed smaller to him today. And how was it he'd never noticed how tired his father looked or the patches of gray beginning to dot his mother's hair at the temples? Could have been the hospital's harsh fluorescent lighting. Could have been. Or . . .

Or *what*?

Or his parents were getting old, worn down by life in large part because of all the sacrifices they had made on his behalf. He'd never been much of a student, having gotten through St. Ignatius's top-flight, demanding curriculum the past year thanks to the tutoring administered relentlessly by Sam Dixon to keep him from failing out. Alex had always figured his parents forked over the money to her out of guilt, blaming the mismatched household for his problem with keeping hold of lessons in his mind. Indeed, while American families were wiping Chinese hospital infant wards clean, it was almost unheard of for a Chinese family to adopt a Caucasian boy. His parents had always been vague on the specific circumstances of the adoption and Alex never pressed them, accepting their droll tale to spare them the toil of sharing any further truths. It was what it was and that was good enough for him.

Because the truth of the matter was, Alex Chin was positive he loved his parents more than other kids loved theirs. Other kids, after all, didn't have to contend with what he did, like the time an old-fashioned traveling carnival set up shop in Golden Gate Park.

10

THE BIG TOP

As a little boy, Alex recalled the carnival as an annual attraction, but it hadn't returned to the sprawling grounds, larger than New York City's Central Park, in years. Those lavish grounds included a flower conservatory, a botanical garden, and a Japanese tea garden along with several museums, stadium facilities, and various venues for cultural events of all sorts. Alex wondered why the carnival had stopped coming and couldn't recall where on the site it had actually been situated, as if what had transpired the last day his parents had taken him there had stricken the setting from memory.

He was eight at the time, already taller than An and fast catching up with Li, the family renting the bottom floor of a two-family tenement at the time. They were hustling through a fairgrounds called the Big Top that proclaimed itself to be the world's largest traveling amusement park. Rushing to get in line just after sunset for the carousel, which Alex desperately wanted to ride. His parents pulling him along and Alex fighting to keep up.

It must have appeared differently to some other carnival patrons, who thought they were witnessing a kidnapping. The police were called. Black-and-white police cars descended on the carnival, an army of San Francisco cops rushing toward the perceived criminals. Back then, and now, to an extent, his parents reverted to Chinese when anxious and nervous, and the sight of the police converging did something to them Alex had never witnessed before.

"Hurry!" he heard his mother blurt to his father. "They must know! We must run!"

So the Chins panicked. Grabbed hold of Alex and tried to run toward a darkened gap between the tilt-a-whirl and a stretch of rigged games. Ran right into a cop with a hand on his pistol. The cop grabbed Li Chin and jerked him aside. Next thing Alex knew his mother was pleading, practically begging the cop with hands clasped in a position of prayer before her, all in Chinese; and blaring only a single phrase to his father Alex could make sense of:

Wŏmen de mìmì . . .

"Our secret."

Another cop dragged her away, forcing her to stumble and lose her balance; she fell to the concrete, now layered with stray candy wrappers, peanut shells, and popcorn shed by the wind.

It was at that moment that Alex became a football player, launching himself headlong into the cop with a throaty scream. He hit the man square in the knees, all eight years and seventy pounds of him, toppling him upon an oil-stained patch on the makeshift midway and pummeling him in the chest with his small fists.

Alex didn't remember much after that. Other cops pulled him off and held him while he cried and screamed. Things got settled, apologies were made, and the Chins left with free passes to all the rides for the remainder of the carnival's stay in town. They never used them, not that year or the next or ever. The Big Top carnival returned to Golden Gate Park for years afterward, but Alex had never returned, even at the urging of his friends. The mere thought of it always brought a lump to his throat, reminding him how much he loved his parents then and how much he loved them now.

Wǒmen de mìmì, Alex remembered his mother saying for the first time in a very long time. *Our secret . . .*

Which was what, exactly?

11

FOREIGN LANGUAGE

"Everything will be all right," his mother said, comfortingly, squeezing his hand. "You must have faith."

Alex pulled his hand away, his mind veering to a different secret his parents had been keeping. His head had begun to throb, but he pushed his thoughts through it.

"Like you have in me?" he said, words seeming to echo in his head.

His mother and father exchanged a befuddled glance, Alex suddenly able to think of nothing else but opening his mother's drop desk drawer in search of a pencil a few days before. Feeling it balk at his initial tries before he jerked it toward him to reveal a clutter of brochures jamming up the slide. He grabbed the pencil he'd come for, just then noticing the brochures were all for prep schools featuring fifth-year post-high-school programs.

"I saw what you were hiding in your desk," Alex heard himself say to his mother from the emergency room bed, as if it were someone else's voice.

"Alex, this isn't the place or time to talk about this—" his mother said, about to go on when his father squeezed her arm and she went quiet again, embarrassed by the presence of the doctor inside the cubicle.

He wanted to stop himself but couldn't. "There's nothing to talk about. I'm going to college. I'm going to play football. *Next year.*"

"Alex," his mother continued, pulling free of his father's grasp. "Your grades . . ."

Leaving it hanging out there, like she didn't need to say anything more.

"They suck." His head began to really pound, a pain that radiated all the way down his spine, almost as if it were bouncing off his bones. "But the colleges offering me scholarships don't care, so why should I? Why should *you*?"

Now it was his mother taking his father's arm in both of her hands. He seemed to stiffen under the grasp, never taking his gaze from Alex.

"Because," his mother started, her voice ringing with conviction, "you should go to a better college, not just one that wants to give you money. The Ivy League, even."

The doctor cleared his throat, as if to remind them he was still there, but Alex responded anyway.

"The Ivy League? You call that football?" He stopped, the pounding in his head intensifying.

His mother whispered something that made his father stiffen even more.

"We'll talk about this later."

"No, we won't. We don't need to talk about it. And I'm playing football next week. Do you hear me? I'm playing football next week."

Alex's head felt ready to explode, as if someone were taking a brick to it from the inside, trying to crash their way out through his skull.

"My head," Alex said suddenly, the doctor looking up from a check of the nerve endings on his feet. "Oh man, my head . . ."

The doctor returned to his side, checking his pulse. "Try to breathe normally."

"Hitse marwa vesu luvi," a voice in the room said.

"Alex?" asked his father.

"Hitse marwa vesu luvi."

Alex heard the voice as if it were someone else's, the words making no sense to him. Just jibberish, not unlike when his parents spoke Chinese late at night when they were afraid he might overhear whatever they were discussing.

"Hitse marwa vesu luvi!"

The voice louder now, more demanding and demonstrative.

"Son?" came the doctor's voice. "Can you hear me, son?"

Alex could hear him just fine. But he wasn't in the exam room. He was somewhere else, somewhere different and dark. Running, bouncing. At least it felt as if he were running, and it was the world that was bouncing around him. He watched it shift and shake, gazing upward toward the sky. Except the sky was a ceiling, and he heard rattling sounds and the desperate wheezing of someone struggling for breath.

Not him. He was breathing just fine, thank you. All that conditioning, all that roadwork. He could run five miles on a cool day while barely breaking a sweat.

How could he be looking straight up? Why did he feel so small, so weak?

"Hitse marwa vesu luvi . . ."

"Alex?"

A hand squeezed his arm.

"Alex?"

Someone calling his name.

"Open your eyes, Alex. Look at me."

"Hitse marwa vesu luvi!"

His voice again, the words having no meaning to him.

"Alex!"

His arm was hurting now; someone was squeezing it so tight. Alex opened his eyes.

And saw the sallow-faced man at his bedside. Ridiculously tall, his head almost even with the ceiling, as if he were made of rubber and someone had stretched him out. His thin, knobby, skeletal fingers dug into Alex's arm until the nails cut through his skin and the fingers sank inward, disappearing.

Alex gasped, a bright flash erupting before his eyes, the monitoring machines hooked up starting to beep and screech.

"Alex!"

When his vision cleared, the tall man had turned to wisps of black air wafting upward, the doctor standing where he'd been, clutching Alex's arm with all of his fingers still showing. His parents jabbered away in Chinese, their words making no more sense than the strange language he'd heard himself speak.

"Let's get you that CT scan," the doctor was saying, his gelled gray hair looking chiseled onto his scalp. "Stat," he added to a nurse standing nearby.

TWO

VISITORS

There is nothing permanent except change.

—HERACLITUS

12

A SPARK

Sam stepped out of the California Pacific Medical Center elevator early Saturday afternoon and nearly collided with Cara, who was in the midst of a text.

"Oh, hey," she said, barely slowing her thumbs.

"How's Alex?"

"Great. Fine." She hit SEND and spoke over the whoosh that followed. "How's the test coming?"

"About that—"

"Don't disappoint me, Sam," Cara said, a sharp edge creeping into her voice. "Don't disappoint *us*. I told everyone in the CatPack not to bother studying because I knew you wouldn't let us down. You're not going to let us down, are you?"

Sam felt her convictions turn to Jell-O as she stepped out of the elevator. "No."

Cara hugged Sam lightly. "E-mail me later and tell Alex I said hi."

"You just saw him yourself."

The cab doors started to close. "You know what I mean," Cara said, looking down at her phone again.

Sam turned and walked away, shaking her head. She found Alex's single room all the way down the hall on the right and entered through the open door after knocking.

"You're kidding, right?" Alex asked, propped up in

the hospital bed with a disbelieving glare fastened Sam's way.

"How do you know I didn't just stop by to see how you were doing?"

"Because I recognize the textbooks through your backpack. How do you squeeze so much in that thing?"

"Practice, just like you."

"Speaking of which . . ."

"What?" Sam asked him.

"My parents told me they saw you here last night."

"I didn't want Cara to be alone."

"I heard she left after a few minutes, which would be more than she just spent with me."

"It was after we heard you were doing okay, that you could move your limbs and everything."

"I'm sure that was a great comfort to her."

"Trouble in paradise?" Sam asked, playing dumb as she unslung the backpack from her shoulder.

"Maybe that hit last night knocked some sense into me. Was she always like this?"

"Only since first grade."

"You think I'd be used to it by now."

"Resigned, at least." Sam eased the physics textbook from her backpack and laid it down on Alex's bed. "Ready to get some work done?"

"I got wrecked last night, in case you didn't know. I can't work today. I've got a headache."

"You felt well enough to visit with Cara."

"That's what gave me the headache. And I'm doped up." Alex rolled his eyes, made himself look woozy. "See?"

She regarded the pouch feeding liquid into his arm. "Normal saline solution to keep you hydrated. Sorry."

"Like you know everything."

"More than you," Samantha said. "That's why I'm the tutor. Do you remember where we left off?"

"My head hurts. I can't do this today. I had a CT scan."

"That's no excuse."

"They shot me up with something."

"It's called contrast medium dye," Samantha told him, brushing the wavy brown hair from her face. "It makes the scan clearer."

"Know what it showed?"

"Something bad?"

"Nothing." Alex smiled. "Turns out my head's empty. No brain at all."

"Good thing you have me then," Samantha said, taking off her glasses.

Alex looked at her closer. Since they'd gone to separate elementary and middle schools, he'd only known Sam since their freshman year at St. Ignatius but never really spoke much to her until she was assigned as his tutor. Now she looked different to him, as if he were seeing her for the first time. Just as his parents had looked smaller in the hospital lighting the night before, Sam looked . . . Well . . . *Better*. She looked better. Prettier.

Samantha started to put her glasses back on.

"Leave them off," Alex told her.

"Then I won't be able to see."

"Maybe that's my plan."

She left them off. "What'd the CT scan show?"

"I told you."

"I mean really."

"Doctor won't tell me. He says he wants to wait for my parents to get here."

"Oh," Sam said, looking down.

"Maybe it's just routine, the way they do things in this place."

"Maybe."

"But you don't think so."

Sam started flipping through the textbook. "I think we should try to get some work done."

"Where's your iPad?"

"Stolen."

"Get out."

"At the game last night. See what happens when I come to watch you play?"

"Guess I owe you a new one."

She hadn't told her parents yet. No reason to worry them about it since there was no money with which to buy a new one right now anyway. The thing was practically new, six months old at most. Maybe they'd taken out some kind of warranty on it or something. But what warranty included theft? And how much medical weed did they need to grow to buy a replacement?

A lot, Sam figured.

"What kind of kid steals an iPad?" Alex was saying. "Everyone's got a tablet of their own."

"It wasn't a kid," Sam told him. "And stop stalling."

"Stalling?"

"So you won't have to work. The doctor gives you a clean bill of health, only you get benched for being academically ineligible."

"Yeah, that would suck, but I can't help it if I'm stupid."

"You're not stupid."

Alex looked down, then up again. "My parents think I am."

"That's ridiculous."

"Is it? Then why do they want me to do another year of high school?"

"Do they?"

He turned toward the window, as if seeing something beyond it Sam couldn't. "I haven't really discussed it with them."

"Then how do you know?"

"I found brochures for a whole bunch of schools. My mother told me I'm not ready for college yet, at least not the kind she wants me to go to."

Sam hesitated. "I thought you said you didn't talk about it."

"It was last night in the emergency room. I shouldn't have brought it up, but I did." Alex's eyes turned almost shy. "Do you think I'm stupid?"

"No."

"The truth, Sam."

"No. *N-O.*"

"If I'm not stupid, why do you need to spell it?"

"Stop it, Alex."

"What?"

"That."

"*What?*"

Sam picked up the physics textbook and smacked Alex in the arm with it.

"Ouch." He grimaced.

"That didn't hurt."

"How do you know? It's not your arm."

"Because it's solid muscle. I think you broke the book," she said, laying it back down on the bed.

"As opposed to opening it, you mean." Alex winked. "And that's *physically* impossible.

"Very funny."

"I thought so. So you were at the game last night," he said, his tone changing a bit.

"Cara scored me a front-row seat," Sam told him, leaving it there.

"That ended up costing you—what?—five hundred bucks?" Alex asked, with a gleam in his eyes.

"Something like that."

"I'll buy you a new one with my signing bonus once I get drafted. Of course, that's a few years off." Alex propped himself up in bed, frowning. "Can I ask you a question?"

"That's what I'm here for."

"Not about school stuff. You ever do something and not remember doing it?"

"All the time. Like putting the milk back in the fridge and then rushing back downstairs thinking I left it on the counter."

"I'm talking about more than that. Say, drawing. Like in a sketchbook. Pictures of things you've never seen before."

Sam smiled, but stopped just short of chuckling. "That's called imagination."

"What if you don't remember drawing them?"

"You draw?"

"I didn't say that. Never mind," Alex said, clearly flustered.

Then a stabbing pain bit into the center of his skull and left him wincing. He thought he might be slipping into one of his daydreams where he'd wake up with ink staining his fingers, but his head just kept throbbing.

"What's wrong?" Sam asked him.

"I told you my head hurts."

"I thought you were lying. We'll pick this up later."

"No, you're here," he groused. "Let's just get it done."

He'd slept fitfully the night before, his first ever spent in a hospital. His parents had stayed until he began to nod off but once they left, the hospital sounds and a dull light flickering in the hallway kept him from ever really fading out. And each time he managed to slip off, his sleep was marred by strange dreams that were more like movies unspooling in his mind. Visions of being chased by something that remained at the edge of his consciousness. And once when he woke up, with a jolt that rattled his spine and brought fresh pain back to his skull, a shape stood in the doorway.

It was the tall man, looming so big that the top of his head stretched beyond the frame, his sallow face bathed in inky black splotches from the hallway's irregular lighting.

Alex had closed his eyes and then opened them again. Nothing but hallway loomed beyond. The tall man dressed all in black was gone.

At his bedside now, Sam was still flipping the textbook's pages in search of the right chapter. He found himself viewing her differently again, seeing more than just the glasses and perpetually overstuffed backpack. Samantha looked kind of like an athlete, even though she had given up gymnastics years ago. Shapely, with enormous hazel eyes and a head full of unruly brown hair she let wander every which way it wanted. Never wore makeup but looked great in the jeans she had on today, though her big-framed, tortoiseshell glasses kind of hid her warm, friendly eyes.

"Why don't you get contacts?" Alex asked her suddenly.

"Astigmatism. And I tried. Couldn't get used to them. Don't you remember I told you that?"

"When?"

"The last time you asked."

"Hey, you gotta cut me a break." He tapped the side of his head. "Got my bell rung, remember? Who knows what damage has been done."

"Just wait for the CT scan results."

"I had a CT scan?" Alex posed playfully. "I must've forgotten."

13

DR. PAYNE

"What time are you supposed to be up at Ames?"

"How do you know I'm due there at all?"

"Because it's Saturday. You always work there on Saturdays. I don't want to keep you from your job."

"It's only a job if they pay you."

"Like tutoring me?"

"I'm underpaid, believe me."

"You could always quit."

"Not until I get you through the state championship," Sam followed.

"Cara offered to tutor me, you know. She said it would be a good opportunity to spend more time together."

"What'd you tell her?"

"That I wanted to pass my classes." Alex narrowed his gaze. "What is it you're not telling me?"

"Nothing."

"Then stop looking away. You always look away when there's something you don't want to tell me."

Sam swallowed hard. "Like you do when we get to a subject you don't like?"

Alex propped himself up further, wincing from the sudden burst of pain in his head. "Test me. Go ahead, I dare you. . . . Wait, tell you what. You ask me a question. I answer it right, and we call it a day. Deal?"

"Deal." Sam leaned in closer to him. "What causes a spark?"

"Ha-ha! When a negative charge plows into a positive charge. Boom! Nailed it!"

Sam closed the physics book. "Yes, you did."

"Hey, don't sound so happy about me getting an answer right. Tell you what. I'm supposed to get out of here in a couple hours. Come over tonight and we'll pick up then," Alex told her. "Like around eight. Deal?"

"Deal."

And that's when the gray-haired doctor entered the room, looking grim and dour. Sam read his name tag: LOUIS PAYNE, MD.

A doctor named "Payne"? Really? thought Sam.

"We need to talk, Alex," Dr. Payne said. And then, with a sidelong glance cast toward Sam, "Alone."

14

HOME SWEET HOME

"Alex is angry with us," An Chin said, facing Li across the kitchen table.

"We should have discussed prep school with him before," her husband said, sighing.

"We decided to wait until after football season, remember?"

Li shrugged. "A mistake now. Clearly."

"Prep school is not a mistake."

"But him finding those brochures—what would you call that?"

"We were only exploring options."

"It's Alex's life."

"And he's our son. Is it so wrong," An demanded, "to want what's best for him?"

"Only if he embraces it, only if we make the decision together, with him instead of for him." Li Chin reached out and took An's hand in his. "And that's not the only thing we haven't told him."

An Chin looked away.

"We need to tell him," Li Chin said, cradling his wife's hand in both of his.

"No," she said, stiffening, staring down at the table as if her eyes might bore through it.

"There is a time and place for everything. It has come."

"No!"

"We must learn our lesson. All this with the boarding schools—it's a sign. We can no longer hold back the truth from him."

"He's better off not knowing," she asserted.

"You mean, *you* are better off, my love."

Li Chin gazed at the sealed cigarette pack sitting just to his right. Old habits died hard. He hadn't smoked since the day Alex became theirs. This pack of Marlboros was the very last one he'd bought, but never opened. He'd abandoned the habit as a gesture of thanks and goodwill to the higher powers he didn't necessarily believe in but respected all the same. He was a practical man, subscribing to the old Chinese proverb that to believe in one's dreams is to spend all of one's life asleep. Alex was his excuse to abandon the cursed habit. As a ritual, though, every time tension rose between him and his beloved An, Li Chin would lay the old unopened pack, smelling musty and stale even through the plastic, nearby, as if to defy temptation.

"He deserves the truth, my love," Li said, stroking his wife's hand now.

"He'll never understand."

An's car keys, as always, rested on the kitchen table before an empty chair no one ever used; it was just the three of them, after all. She'd made a habit of resting them there so she'd always know where they were, after misplacing them time and time again. Looped through the ring was a tiny wooden statue of Meng Po, the ancient Chinese goddess who brought light to darkness.

Keep it close always, to bring you the light, her father had told her before she left China for the last time. She'd never seen him again.

He had carved the statue himself and drilled a small

hole at its top so it could be placed on a key chain. It had been his final gift to her and hugging him with the statue squeezed in her hand was her final memory of him.

One last thing, he'd told her when they finally eased apart. *This Meng Po is also the guardian of secrets.*

So Li had his pack of cigarettes, An had Meng Po, and every time stress brought them to this very table, they reached out to take their respective talismans in hand in the hope the objects might provide reassurance where words had failed.

"He's an adult now," Li persisted, squeezing his ancient pack of cigarettes so hard the plastic crackled. "He deserves—"

"Don't tell me what he *deserves*!" An laid Meng Po back on the table, her various keys jangling against each other. "It's just . . . well, it's too soon."

Li looked at the sealed pack of Marlboros, then back at An. "It's been eighteen years."

"You want us to tell him the whole truth?" she said to Li, stroking what remained of the tiny statue's battered finish with her thumb, almost affectionately. It had been chipped and marred by too many key scrapes when the chain was stuffed in a pocket or purse. Much the worse for wear now, its once smooth wood no more than a memory, just as her father was. "That he's not really ours?"

Li closed his hand over the pack of cigarettes and drew it toward him.

"That his papers were forged by the same people who create fake documents for Chinese who sneak into the country illegally," An continued. "That buying the adoption documents that made him ours cost our entire savings at the time, and that we've lived in fear of being blackmailed or having the authorities uncover the fact that we never adopted Alex legally."

"I fear that phone call, I fear that knock on the door as much as you," Li said, coming up just short of tearing the cellophane from the old pack of Marlboros. "But I don't fear telling Alex the truth while that truth is still ours to control. He must hear it from us, my love."

"You mean as opposed to a phone call or a knock on the door?"

And before Li Chin could answer An's question, their front doorbell rang.

15

ARTIFACTS

"Is this about the CT scan?" Alex asked Dr. Payne after Sam had left.

"I'm afraid it was inconclusive," the doctor told him, not sounding very convincing. "Too much swelling to get a definitive diagnosis."

"So I need to get another one."

"Standard procedure."

"Like you not telling me something. Is that standard procedure too?"

Payne sucked in a deep breath and let it out slowly. "We should wait for your parents."

"I'm eighteen. That makes me an adult and means we don't have to wait for anything."

"I still think we should wait for them."

"Well, I don't."

Payne nodded grudgingly. "The CT scan showed a shadow."

"A shadow," Alex repeated, wishing in that moment he'd listened to the doctor and waited for his parents. Big tough football player feeling like a little boy again. "What's that mean?"

"Maybe nothing."

"Maybe . . ."

"Probably. We just need to make sure."

"Am I going to play football again?" Alex heard himself ask Payne, as if somebody else were posing the question. "Just tell me that."

Payne shrugged, the gesture abandoned in mid-effort. "Let's wait and see what the second scan shows. Try not to worry until then."

Right, Alex thought, *good luck with that.*

For the second time in twenty-four hours, Alex eased himself onto the CT scanner's table, the cold metal's chill slipping right through his hospital johnny. Knowing the drill now, he made himself as comfortable as possible and waited for the technician to slide the table robotically forward into position.

"You ready, Alex?" a voice called over a speaker.

Alex nodded. The nurse had backed behind a screen, no longer visible. He realized the technician might not be able to see him.

"Ready!" he called.

"Okay, here we go."

And the table began to move, positioning his head directly beneath the X-ray tube and over the detector panel. Alex watched the lights in the room dim and closed his eyes, trying to keep his breathing steady.

"Try to relax, Alex. Just breathe normally."

Is it that obvious how nervous I am? Alex would've asked if he'd been allowed to talk.

"Time to get started," the technician announced, and the irregular whirring sound began.

Alex closed his eyes as the machine began its work. He wished he had a happy place to go to in his mind, but he'd never needed one before and the only thing he could think of was the football field, which hadn't proven to be so happy the night before. Think of that and all he could picture was the bone-crunching impact that had put him here.

"Stay still, Alex."

He hadn't realized he was moving.

"Stay still. Take a deep breath and hold it."

Alex obliged as the table started to move through the scanner, accompanied by a humming sound that seemed to make the inside of his head feel warm. It stopped and he let his breath out before taking and holding another to avoid "artifacts" on the images, as a different technician had explained during his initial CT scan. This one would probably take about ten minutes, just like that one had. Only, he felt different this time, something fluttering inside his head as if a bird were trapped there flapping its wings.

"Seku nura fas turadi."

"Please don't talk."

"Seku nura fas turadi."

That indecipherable language again, sounding like it was coming from someone else when Alex knew it was coming from him. And then the room was suddenly filled with the machines from Alex's daydreams, moving this way and that. But this time he was wide awake, as the horde seemed to spot him and glide over en masse.

"Can you see them?" he cried out.

"Please, keep still. We're almost finished."

"Can you see them?"

"See what?"

How could the guy *not* see them? The machines were *everywhere*!

"Bassa, bassa, bassa—"

"Alex!"

"—bassa!"

The bulbs lining the scanner's internal chamber burned out in a rapid series of pops and crackles that sounded like misfiring firecrackers. The stench of scorched metal flooded Alex's nostrils and he opened his eyes to the sight of glass spraying in all directions.

"*Alex!*"

He felt as if his brain were outside his head, roasting. He remembered hearing at some point that the brain itself didn't feel pain. Well, it certainly felt heat, and Alex realized he couldn't move. Again. Just like last night on the field. Same, exact sensation that had stolen most of his breath and the rest of it now.

Pop, pop, pop!

Now the room's overhead lights were igniting, erupting, blowing apart with not even their filaments left behind. Alex's brain whistled in his head, a teakettle signaling it had come to a boil, when big hands grabbed hold of his legs and yanked him free of the machine.

The hands tried to restrain him once he was out, but Alex brushed them off, shaking free as easily as he dodged multiple tackles en route to the end zone. He looked down to see an orderly bigger than any lineman he'd ever faced lying on the floor, trying to push himself up.

Alex stretched a hand down to help him and ended up toppling off the table, hitting the floor hard enough to rattle his brain and send a fresh surge of pain through his head. A burst of light like a flashbulb went off in front of his eyes and he felt a pressure in both ears until one popped and then the other, leaving behind a persistent throbbing.

"Alex! Alex!"

He heard Payne's voice and looked up to see the doctor standing between him and the giant orderly Alex had dropped like the tiniest of running backs.

"Don't move," Payne was saying.

"I . . . can't," Alex said fearfully, his whole body feeling like it was frozen in place.

16

HOME INVASION

"Take anything you want," Li Chin said from the armchair in which the men had placed him. "Anything we have is yours—just don't hurt us."

The four of them had barged in as soon as Li cracked open the front door of their Millbrae home. The door had rocketed backward, slamming into Li and knocking him off his feet. An rushed from the kitchen when she heard the sounds of a struggle to find two of the men lifting her husband into a chair. Before she could scream, another of them was upon her, hand clamped over her mouth. He jerked her into the matching armchair and dragged it closer to Li's.

"Please," Li repeated. "Anything we have is yours."

But the men seemed utterly disinterested in the contents of the house, their focus purely on them.

"We only want what your wife took from us," the man standing in front of the others, in the shadows splayed by a single lamp, said. "From the laboratory eighteen years ago."

"I took nothing!" An insisted, her voice cracking. "I was a good worker. I was promoted to supervisor!"

The man took a single step closer to the Chins, his cold, emotionless gaze bearing down on An as the lamp flickered, his face framed by the shadows it cast. "You took what is ours and we have come to get it back."

"I was searched every day when my work was done. We all were."

"Except one day."

A cold dread hit An in the pit of her stomach. She tried to swallow and failed.

"You took something from the lab that day," the man continued. "It belonged to us and we have come to take it back."

The speaker turned to the other three men, seeming to pass some unspoken signal. The four of them looked virtually indistinguishable from one another. Not identical by any means, but in possession, eerily, of the same blank, nondescript features, hairstyles, eye color, and musculature, and carried themselves with a demeanor detached and utterly lacking in emotion. Their matching dark suits seemed stitched to their skin, so molded as to appear an extension of it.

But it was something else that both Li and An had noted they found most unnerving of all: their eyes never blinked, at least those of the three silent ones who'd centered themselves behind the speaker in a semicircle, enclosing him in their shadows, which fell over the Chins too in the light cast by the single lamp the men had left on.

"We have taken nothing, from you or anyone else," Li Chin said, sounding more indignant than frightened.

"You took something that belonged to us eighteen years ago," the same man said. "Where is the boy you call Alex?"

THREE

AMES

Truth makes many appeals,
not the least of which is its power to shock.

—JULES RENARD

17

INTERN

"Dixon! Dixon, where are you?"

Sam looked up from her desk at the Ames Research Center, where she was analyzing the latest research on habitable planets as part of NASA's Kepler mission. "Right here, Doctor. And I was hoping I could—"

"Where? I can't see you." Her supervisor, Dr. Thomas Donati, spun toward her, still wearing the mirror goggles he'd forgotten to remove upon finishing the latest view provided by the spectron holographic microscope. "Someone's turned off the lights again."

She moved to him and eased the specially formulated goggles up to his forehead, where they pinned the hairs that had escaped his gray ponytail in place.

"Yes, there we go. Much better, much better indeed. Extraordinary day, truly extraordinary. You know why, Dixon?"

"I know you're going to tell me."

"Because we're *alive*. Life is the greatest miracle of all, as well as the least appreciated. But not here; here we've learned to appreciate the sanctity and singular rarity of life, have we not?"

Samantha started to answer, but Donati rolled right over her words.

"I'd say 'intelligent' life but I realized a long time ago

that there's not enough of that to uncover even here on our planet. You know why?"

Again he resumed before she had a chance to answer.

"Because man chooses to think small, more than satisfied with what the five percent of his brain shows him about the world around him. We, on the other hand, are explorers—are we not, Dixon? Without ever leaving this center we explore new worlds and new possibilities. Breakthroughs, Dixon, every day a breakthrough no matter how small it might be. Because like life itself there is no such thing as a *small* breakthrough. What are you working on?"

"The Kepler research."

"Put it aside, put it aside. There's something I must show you, something you must see. Follow, Dixon, and do your best to keep up. Don't lag."

Sam rose from her chair. "If there's time, Doctor, I'd like to—"

"You're lagging, Dixon. Focus, hear me? Focus!"

Sam fell into step behind him.

The Ames Research Center, one of ten field centers operated by NASA, offered one of the most competitive internship programs in the country. Science geeks from miles and states around applied for admission, and Sam couldn't believe her luck when she got the e-mail informing her that she'd been accepted.

And she was assigned to her first choice: the Astrobiology Institute, which specialized in advancing the technologies for long-term manned space flights to make them friendlier on the body. Under her assigned mentor, Dr. Thomas Donati, she'd actually been working more in another area she'd found even more fascinating. Ames had assumed the leading role in the fledgling field of synthetic biology. The new NASA Synthetic Biology (Syn-

Bio) initiative at Ames harnessed biology in reliable, robust, engineered systems to support NASA's exploration and science missions. Dr. Donati's specific role was to develop technologies aimed at manufacturing regolith-based composites to be used as bio-based building materials in space. His department was developing Syn-Bio technologies to enable environmental closed-loop life support systems to create novel solutions for the purification of air and water and the production of methane from waste carbon dioxide.

Donati's team, of which Samantha was a part three afternoons a week and Saturdays, was also investigating the utility of SynBio for 3D printing to produce bio-based products, biomining to obtain minerals from planetary surfaces or recover valuable elements from spent electronics, as well as the production and purification of pharmaceuticals that might be necessary to maintain crew health on long-duration spaceflights. A science geek's dream.

And Samantha's work under Donati had been so stellar that he had recently recommended she be included in a team devoted to the conceptual study of astrobiology and exobiology that covered all issues pertaining to Earth's place in a universe that almost surely contained other life forms. Much of the real work at Ames was top secret, taking place in a combination lab and think tank to which her security clearance didn't yet permit access.

Because she was always in a lab, of course, she'd heard things. She knew that along with Donati's bioresearch, his division also studied what they referred to as wormholes or black holes in space—shortcuts through the millions of light-years that it could take man to get from one spot to the other. A problem of space travel remained time—it was no good to get someone somewhere if they'd been dead of old age hundreds of years before they arrived. And, just as the Earth rotated around the sun, and the sun found its place in the galaxy, other masses moved in space.

All that movement, Sam had learned, meant that there were "doors" that only opened at certain times and then closed again until maybe the next thousand years or so went by. So it was crucial for scientists at Ames and elsewhere to study and understand the doors to ensure that future space travelers didn't find themselves sucked into the true darkness of oblivion—a tremendous amount to comprehend, for sure.

Sam loved everything that she learned, and she knew she'd found her calling at NASA. For the first time in her life she was judged entirely on her brains and productivity, with no weight given to popularity and social standing. At Ames she was finally one of the cool kids, giving her a whole new perspective on how little all that meant in the great scheme of things. Because that very scheme of things, you learned at Ames, wasn't just about this world.

It was about thousands of others, potentially.

And that had a tendency to change your view of the microscopic part of the universe taken up by high school. Sam wondered what aliens might make of Earth if all they got to see was a school, even one as well regarded and run as St. Ignatius. She imagined they'd be so horrified as to question how the human race had lasted as long as it had.

The vastness of Ames, employing over two thousand people who were spread out over six separate facilities in its Silicon Valley site thirty miles from her home in Moss Beach, had enthralled instead of intimidated Sam. She saw in it not so much a village-size community as a uniquely compartmentalized world where nothing was too impossible to consider. No theory was discounted out of hand, and even lowly interns like Sam were encouraged to provide input and formulate honest responses to data affecting their particular department. Speaking of which . . .

"Doctor?" she called, almost running to keep Donati's pace.

"Not now, Dixon," he said, from slightly ahead of her. "We're headed to the future and I don't want to get sidetracked along the way."

18

PATTERNS

It took Donati's own top-level security card to access the extraterrestrial monitoring station through a sliding door where automated machines collected and collated millions of bits of data every day, most of which were ultimately discarded for being planetary echoes, star bursts, and other easily explicable events.

But today must have been different.

Inside the sprawling station, Donati stopped at one of the primary computer terminals displaying two versions of a bar grid projecting subspace electromagnetic chatter that could indicate some type of advanced or rudimentary form of communication.

"See? Can you see?"

Samantha couldn't.

"The difference is what I'm talking about, the difference in the grids! There's movement, consistent movement, not just a blip."

Sam looked closer at the dual bar grids and, yes, there was a deviation from the standard level indicating the norm. No more than a hair—well, a micromillimeter, actually—but definitely a jump recorded steadily over a six-hour period earlier that day.

"There was a similar bump yesterday," Donati explained. "But I discounted it, taking it for a blip. I hate blips, all the false hope they give us. But it repeated today and didn't fall off. See? Can you see?"

This time Sam nodded, wondering maybe, just maybe . . .

"I'm going to isolate its source," Donati continued, "even if it takes me all of the night, all of tomorrow, all of the next week. Here I'll be, ready for the breakthrough to break through. I had to tell somebody. This is too big to keep to myself. I could fall, bang my head, lose my memory, and then no one would ever know it wasn't just a blip this time. That somebody out there's talking. There was something similar, indicators anyway, before— about eighteen years ago—but that's, well, another story. The source, Dixon, we must find the source! Are you with me?"

With him? This was Sam's ultimate dream, to be involved on the forefront of something this exciting. But she was supposed to tutor Alex tonight; not that he'd care if she had to postpone the session until tomorrow. Still, they'd made plans and the truth was—

"Eighteen years," Donati repeated, breaking her thought. "Wonder if there's significance in that, a cycle or something. Know what I mean?"

"Like the time it might take a signal to reach Earth from another solar system."

"Good thought but, no, not in this case. What we may be looking at here is more a harbinger. Define it for me, Dixon."

"Something that foreshadows a future event."

"Not exactly in this case, but close enough. A precursor for something else, now and eighteen years ago. There's that number again. Significance, we must find the significance. Tell me you're not as excited as I am, Dixon!"

"I am, but . . ."

"But? There are no 'but's in science, Dixon. Haven't I taught you anything?"

"Lots. Everything."

"Lots, yes. Far from everything. You know what they call a scientist who knows everything?"

"No."

"God, Dixon, they call him *God*. Do I look like God to you?" he asked, turning away.

"Doctor?" she offered instead.

Donati swung, as if jarred from a trance. "What?"

"I was just going to say I have something else I have to do tonight. Not all of it; I mean, I just need to be gone for a few hours. I'll come back the second I'm done."

"A few hours," he repeated, sounding more disappointed than perturbed. "And if you happen to miss history unfolding in that time, don't blame me."

"I won't. I'm sorry. It won't happen again."

"See that it doesn't. Because I have a warning for you, Dixon, an important one: science waits for no man."

"Then I guess it's a good thing I'm a girl," Sam said, finally finding the courage to broach the subject she'd been rehearsing for days. "I need to tell you about . . . something I've uncovered. I wasn't sure I should, but now I wonder if it might be, well, connected."

"Wonderful! Connected to what?"

"This anomaly you found. Because I think I've found some too, an interconnected series of them."

"Series of what?"

"Anomalies. Otherwise inexplicable individual phenomena until they are considered as a whole."

"What phenomena?"

Sam thought of her stolen iPad, containing her findings, her proof. "It's all on my iPad."

"So show me."

"I can't. Somebody stole it last night."

Donati nodded, eyes narrowing. "Got your cell phone?"

Sam fished it from her pocket. "Why?"

"Because it's more powerful than the *Friendship Seven* that took John Glenn into orbit and even *Apollo Eleven* that brought man to the moon. Know what us scientists did in those days before e-mail?"

"What?"

"We talked. So talk to me, Dixon, explain it to me absent an iPad or supercomputer."

"All right." Sam tried, collecting her thoughts. "The largest avalanche in history occurred just last week in Nepal," she told Donati, imagining the photos and overhead shots revealing the indescribable destruction. "Three towns were buried, thousands missing or dead. An estimated billion tons of snow and ice released from their perch to form a rolling wall that buried a hundred square miles."

Donati nodded. "I'm glad I don't ski. What else?"

"A lake in Spain."

"I don't swim, either. So what?"

"It exploded."

"What exploded?"

"The lake. Well, not really exploded. More like combusted. A limnic eruption in which dissolved carbon dioxide, or carbonic acid, stages an escape from the waters that contain it, normally under intense pressure. In this case in an inordinately deep lake high on the flank of an inactive volcano in the Costa Brava region, complete with that pocket of magma leaking carbon dioxide into the water. A large cloud of carbon dioxide in the form of carbonic acid burst out of the water and suffocated around seventeen hundred people in nearby towns and villages. Spread for miles. No one in range was spared, livestock included."

Sam seemed to have Dr. Donati's complete attention now. His normally distant expression had tightened, as if the relentless energy driving him had throttled back a bit.

"Suffocated, you say. And why is this important, Dixon?"

"I'm getting to that," Sam said. "Two weeks ago geothermal satellite readings confirmed one of the largest sea earthquakes ever recorded, in the Sargasso Sea, that released a tsunami wave—"

"Wait, did you say *tsunami*?" Donati interrupted.

"Yes," Sam confirmed for him, "also believed to be the largest ever seen. It swallowed three islands, all uninhabited."

Donati's eyes bulged. He pulled at his graying ponytail with one set of tightly wrapped fingers. "What else?"

"A wildfire in South Dakota's Badlands National Park."

"Not tremendously unusual."

"But witnesses said this one started on its own."

"Spontaneous combustion," Donati drawled, as if it hurt to get the words out.

"Boy Scouts on the scene said the ground just started burning, followed by the trees. I know it sounds crazy, but—"

"Not at all," Donati said, seeming to picture it in his mind. "A fissure or crack going deep down beneath the surface."

"But the fire—"

"Caused by immeasurable heat originating at the Earth's core, pushed upward by the pressure to vent." His eyes seemed to catch fire. "Where's this iPad?"

"I told you, it was stolen."

"By who?"

"Some guy at the football game last night."

"A student?"

"No, a guy. A man. I didn't recognize him."

But he smelled like tire rubber and motor oil, Sam had to stop herself from adding.

"Can you erase the iPad's contents remotely?"

"I'm not—"

"There must be a way. Call Apple. Find out. Now. Immediately."

"I haven't finished yet. The thing is, these four incidents are—"

"Connected, Dixon?"

"I was going to say they occurred from a time standpoint in chronological order from west to east following in perfect synchronicity corresponding to—"

"The curvature of the Earth," Donati completed in a hushed voice, his gaze so distant now it made Sam think he was staring through the wall and not just at it.

"How did you know that, Doctor?"

He fixed his gaze upon her, as if realizing Sam was before him for the first time. "Know what?"

"What you just said?"

"About what?"

"Following the curvature of the Earth."

His eyes narrowed, taking on an intensity Sam had never seen in them before, along with something . . . else. "You didn't hear me say that."

"I didn't?"

"None of it, Dixon, not a single word. In fact, you never uncovered these findings and we never had this conversation. In fact, you weren't even here today."

"I wasn't?"

"I don't even recognize you, know your name. Where'd you get that ID? Security, security!" Then Donati's voice lowered. "You have your data backed up?"

"Well, I," Sam started, embarrassed, "I thought I had backed it to the Cloud but I must've messed up."

"Messed up?"

"When I tried to retrieve my research at home last night, it was gone. All of it."

"Never mind," Donati interjected. "I don't want to hear it anyway, don't want to know. We never had this conversation. In fact, you never came into work. Called in sick with a cold, right?"

Samantha feigned a sneeze.

"Thought so, Dixon. It's going around. Home with you now, home with you right now. Like you were never here, because you weren't. Be gone with you. Go!" Donati closed his eyes. "When I open them, you'll be gone. Poof! Like magic."

Sam backed up, angling for the exit.

"Dixon?" Donati said, eyes still squeezed shut. "I can't see you, Dixon!"

She didn't answer, almost to the door now.

"Dixon?"

She was through the door when she heard Donati's voice again, realizing in that moment what else she'd seen in his eyes:

Fear.

19

EMERGENCY RESPONSE

Dr. Donati entered his office and locked the door behind him. Then he braced a chair against the latch to further impede anyone from opening it. He visualized masked, dark-clad storm troopers bursting in with weapons fixed on him before he could complete the call he needed to make.

Among NASA's various duties and responsibilities, both defined and undefined, was watchdog. Combing the reams of collected data to evaluate potential threats, hostile and otherwise, looming beyond this world. It was a nebulous duty with no clear chain of command or reporting procedure, with the exception of a single telephone exchange activated by pressing a three-number sequence followed by the star key.

Donati had been involved in the formation of such a procedure, at least peripherally, eighteen years before, but had never had reason to use it. It had been christened "Janus," after the Greek god who presided over both war and peace, beginnings and ends, since any otherworldly discovery that could help the world could also destroy it, and vice versa.

But no such duality existed in the pattern of events Samantha Dixon had uncovered today, any more than it had in the similar pattern he'd uncovered eighteen years before.

How could I have missed it?

Perhaps because he wanted to, Donati thought, as he pressed out three numbers and touched the star key.

The line on the other end didn't ring. There was a click, followed by dead air.

"Donati, Thomas W.," he said, knowing the words were being processed for audio recognition to confirm his identity and thus the potential veracity of the warning he was about to issue. "NASA, Ames Research Center. Designation Peter-Victor-Charlie-seven-four-one-X-ray."

Donati stopped, nothing but more dead air greeting him through the silence.

"I'm calling a Janus alert. Probability high." Then, after taking a deep breath, "Threat level extreme," he added.

Because it was happening again.

They were coming back.

FOUR

ASHES TO ASHES

No one can confidently say
that he will still be living tomorrow.

—EURIPIDES

20

PAYNE AND PAIN

Dr. Payne stared at the phone, willing it to ring. The results of the second CT scan on Alex Chin, which had ended with every circuit and chip in the machine being fried, were displayed on the computer screen before him. Identical in all respects to the first scan that had been done, with one exception.

The area, the spot in question, was even more pronounced, as if it were . . .

What?

. . . growing? No, Payne thought, that wasn't it at all. It wasn't growing so much as, well, *spreading*. His initial thought was some kind of lesion tied to the blow the boy had suffered on the football field. Or, perhaps, that blow had aggravated an existing flaw or hot spot that had been there since birth. He was no expert, no neurosurgeon, and, truth be told, he needed a true expert, a specialist not to be found on staff here at the California Pacific Medical Center. So he'd e-mailed the results of both scans to a former teacher of his who was an expert in the field of brain function and abnormality with a request to call him back as soon as he'd reviewed the findings.

The phone rang and Payne jerked the receiver from its hook, fumbling it to his ear.

* * *

Alex had been undergoing tests for hours now, a steady, nonstop stream of them ever since the CT scan machine seemed to blow a gasket. The experience clung to his mind, rattling him no end.

It was my fault. I did it.

Of course, that was ridiculous. Of course, it had no basis in fact. But that's what Alex felt and it was a feeling he couldn't shake no matter how hard he tried, any more than he could shake the memory of the tentacled machines wheeling themselves about the room even though they'd never been there at all.

Every test they did when he was first admitted following his exam in the emergency room was repeated, and now additional ones had been ordered.

His father wasn't answering his phone; his mother wasn't answering her phone.

He wanted to go home.

He wanted to play football again.

But, for the moment, anyway, neither was happening and Alex found himself filled with fear that Dr. Payne hadn't reappeared because he had nothing good to say. He'd hinted as much earlier. Now the doctor's suspicions must have been confirmed and he was waiting to reach Alex's parents before delivering the news.

Maybe, though, he couldn't reach them, either. Or maybe they weren't answering Alex's calls because they were trying to figure out how to tell him.

Whatever the case, Alex could no longer just lie here and wait. The room didn't even have a television, and he was pissed he'd missed a visit from Coach Blu and some of his Wildcat teammates who'd shown up just after he was taken to have the repeat scan done. So he'd go back to his own room and wait there for Payne to deliver the news.

Bad news, Alex found himself convinced.

I'm done with this place.

And with that he hopped off the gurney, bare feet touching down, already in motion for the door.

Alex was late. No surprise, since he was always late.

Samantha shifted the backpack containing the books she needed for tonight's tutoring session from her right shoulder to her left and rang the bell again.

Still no answer.

Sam stepped back, took out her iPhone but saw, strangely, NO SIGNAL lit up in the upper left corner before she could try his number. Then she turned her gaze on the street, wondering if she should wait a bit longer. The fact that Alex was supposed to have been released from CPMC already, of course, didn't mean it had actually worked out that way. But the night air was damp and chilly, and Sam didn't want to linger out here for nothing.

Maybe the bell's broken. Maybe they couldn't hear me knocking because they're in the kitchen.

Worth a try, Sam figured, and walked around to the rear of the Chin family's cozy bungalow in Millbrae, a design better known as "California Craftsman" in this part of the state. A nice contrast to her family's ramshackle, sort of modern Colonial in the hippie throwback town of Moss Beach, farther south on the peninsula. Perfect for her hippie-throwback parents but not always the right fit for Samantha, who felt better suited to a more staid community like Southern Hills.

She reached the back door to find it slightly ajar.

"Hello?" she called softly, eased it inward a few more inches. "Hello?"

Alex's parents were wonderful. Friendly, sweet, open, and caring. They always made her feel at home, enough so that she felt comfortable opening the door all the way but stopped short of entering.

"Mrs. Chin?" she called to Alex's mother, who always offered her tea.

There was no answer. But, as she stood there just inside the kitchen, Tabby, their indoor-outdoor cat, let out a squeal and burst past her, racing through the yard.

Sam reeled backward, clutching her chest. She nearly slipped down off the stairs and found herself back on the grass, heart hammering against her ribs.

Okay, I tried. . . .

Sam walked around the side of the house, readying her car keys. But then she heard voices coming through an open window on that side: muffled, harsh voices. Maybe Alex was inside watching a video or something. That's what the voices reminded her of. No wonder he hadn't heard her knocking!

Then one of the voices she'd thought sprang from a DVD demanded, "Where is he?"

She heard sobs, pressed herself closer to the drawn drapes.

"Not here!" she heard Alex's mother plead. "He's not here!"

An Chin should have been smiling and offering her tea, not sounding so scared and desperate.

Call the police!

Sam fumbled the phone from her jeans. She hit the HOME button to no effect. Pressed it again.

Nothing. Not even a NO SIGNAL warning.

Sam thought of fleeing, of getting somewhere to a phone that worked to call the police. But she couldn't just leave the Chins alone like this, had to help them herself if she could.

And then she heard the crash.

21

WRITTEN IN BLOOD

"Dr. Testoni," Payne greeted, recognizing the area code in the caller ID, "thanks for getting back to me so quickly. . . . Yes, I quite agree. Most unusual, I'd say even unprecedented. . . . Of course. . . . No, we checked the machine thoroughly after the first scan and it was found to be in perfect working order. . . . The second scan? . . . Yes, that was precisely my impression too. . . . I considered that, but the spot appears to be too big. . . . What? No, I never—It's impossible. The boy couldn't possibly live with such a . . . Did you say for—"

A screech of static pierced Payne's eardrum. The receiver with Dr. Testoni on the other end slipped from his grasp and rattled to the floor. Suddenly Payne's head was pounding, as if in the throes of a terrible migraine that left him dizzy and nauseous, the room's light suddenly seeming overly bright even though only the overhead fixture was switched on. He looked up, toward the doorway.

Saw the dark shape of a man standing there, so tall his head stretched to the top of the frame.

"Hang up the phone, Doctor."

Alex passed no one on the trek back to his room, not a single, solitary soul. Sure, it was getting late, but this was a hospital and a busy one at that. Didn't patients need to be checked? Weren't doctors and nurses always about patrolling, the way they did on TV?

Apparently not, judging by the two abandoned nurses' stations and three empty hallways later, including the one on his room's floor. The hall lighting seemed dim, as if the hospital were trying to save money by turning the power down after a certain hour. But as Alex turned the corner for his own room, the dim lighting from a single lamp allowed him to see flickers of shadowy movement inside. Something, someone, was shifting about, the lamp's bulb enough to splash a glimpse of its shadow across the hallway floor.

Alex froze, then ducked back behind the bend in the corridor. If a nurse or orderly emerged, he'd know he was suffering from paranoia at the hands of something no more monstrous than a malfunctioning CT scanner. But no one emerged. The flickering shadow disappeared, no nurse, orderly, or anyone else following it out.

Paranoid or not, he knew now that someone was in there, waiting for him. Not just a shadow this time.

So what now? Where to go?

Not where—to whom: Dr. Payne, he of the absolute worst name for a physician. That morning his parents had told Alex they'd just come downstairs from seeing him, which placed Payne's office on the fourth floor, the one floor in the hospital above this one.

Alex started back toward the elevators, then changed his mind and headed for the stairs instead.

The crash sounded like something hitting the floor hard, and froze her hand on the doorknob. Then Sam heard the front door open and slam.

Someone spoke. At least, it sounded like speech. But, eerie, as if . . .

. . . they were speaking through some kind of tube.

"We wait."

"How long for?" another voice answered.

"Until we get what we came for," said a third voice.

How many of them are there?

Sam wasn't sure, but it seemed as if the voices were coming from the front, outside the house. She padded softly across the grass toward the back door, eased it open, and tiptoed inside through the kitchen, into the murky darkness of the foyer and then the living room.

Stopping cold in her tracks when she saw what awaited her there.

It took a few minutes, but Alex found Dr. Payne's office located along a row of others that were all exactly the same shape and size taking up both sides of the hall. It smelled different up here, less antiseptic and more like stale aftershave and deodorant that had lost its bite hours before. The door was closed, so Alex knocked, first softly and then loudly when the former produced no result.

"Dr. Payne?" he called, when the same held true for the latter. "It's Alex Chin, Dr. Payne. I need to talk to you. It's important."

He knocked on the door again, trying to be patient. It was late, sure, but wouldn't Payne hang around to immediately gauge the results of the myriad of tests he'd ordered? Then again, maybe he had a girlfriend as hot as Samantha.

Whoa, did I think that? I meant Cara. . . .

Alex moved his hand to the knob, surprised when it

turned in his grasp, unlocked. He eased the door open, the hallway light spilling inside.

And capturing Dr. Payne facedown on his desk.

"Oh, God . . ."

Alex realized he'd said that out loud when he was halfway across the office. He reached Payne's desk and gently attempted to rouse the doctor to see if he'd simply dozed off. Alex jostled Payne a bit harder when he failed to stir, then maneuvered him upright when he remained utterly stiff and still.

Dr. Payne rocked backward, his skull smacking the headrest with enough force to tip the desk chair nearly over. It jerked back forward and Alex stilled it with his hands jammed against its arms. Saw Payne's eyes were locked open and sightless. A hole the diameter of a thick pen point—from which a trickle of blood had rolled all the way down his face—appeared to have been drilled into the center of his forehead.

Alex lurched away with a jolt, needing to remind himself to breathe.

My doctor's been killed.

There's someone waiting in my room downstairs.

And then Alex heard the thud of heavy footsteps coming his way.

Sam had taken extra-credit medical emergency classes for which she'd done several ride-alongs with local EMT rescue teams. Some of the scenes they were dispatched to were worse than she could possibly have imagined.

But not as bad as this.

The blood; oh, God, the blood.

Mr. Chin . . . Mrs. Chin . . .

Sam moved closer to see the way that An Chin was sprawled over the floor, her tiny frame so broken in the pool of blood beneath her. And Mr. Chin . . .

He was on the floor too.

His back was all she could see.

Then she noticed that An Chin's arm was stretched out oddly. Her fingers were pointed toward something. Sam moved her gaze forward.

More blood. And something else.

An Chin had tried to scrawl something in her own blood, just a few words drying in splotchy fashion on the dark wood floor. Sam crouched to better read them.

ALEX

The bottom of the *l* and *x* had dripped downward, touching the top of a second word:

RUN

The second word was more scratchy than the first, the letters running close to the Oriental carpet on which the room's furniture was set.

ALEX RUN

Sam was staring at those words written in blood when a hand latched onto her forearm and squeezed tightly. She jerked her arm away, nearly lost her balance and snapped her other hand to the floor to keep herself from falling. She felt An Chin's blood, still warm, soak her palm and swung toward Alex's mother, whose hand was grasping for her anew.

Mrs. Chin's eyes were open. She pleaded silently with

Sam. She was moving her lips, struggling for the breath she needed to form words.

Alex . . .

"It's okay," Sam heard herself say, in what sounded like someone else's voice. "You're going to be okay." Her gaze locked on a cordless phone lying atop a nearby table. "I'll call the police."

But An Chin's grasp tightened on her before Sam could move.

No police, Mrs. Chin mouthed.

Then her trembling fingers dropped down and began scrawling a final word in blood to complete the message:

GET ALEX RUN

22

ESCAPE

The footsteps seemed to slow as they approached the door to Dr. Payne's office, but continued on harmlessly. Alex thought fast, at least as fast as the steady dull throb in his head would allow.

Couldn't go back to his room.

Couldn't stay here.

Had to get out of the hospital.

Alex could have called the police on Dr. Payne's phone now, but what was he going to tell them? That his doctor was dead and he was in some kind of crazy danger? Sounded simple enough to say. Make the call and then leave the building. Anonymous. If nothing else, he could wait for the cops to arrive in force and then use their presence as a distraction to flee. They'd know who he was. They'd protect him.

The harder he thought, the more his head throbbed. He willed himself to be calm, to think one thing at a time. The cops first.

Alex reached down for Payne's office phone and lifted the receiver from its cradle.

Nothing. No dial tone.

He hit a bunch of keys and still got nothing but dead air for his effort. Now what?

Cell phone!

Payne must have had one somewhere, but none was in evidence on the desk. So it must be in a pocket.

Alex checked his lab coat pockets first, then held his breath while he felt around the outlines of the doctor's other pockets in search of his smart phone's shape. Nothing in any of those, either, but one of the pants pockets was turned inside out, as if someone had gotten there ahead of Alex with the same idea in mind.

Calling the police was no longer the goal, with no means to do so. And he couldn't venture back out into the halls dressed in hospital garb with whoever had killed Payne and whoever was down in his room still out there.

So Alex moved to the office closet, freezing when he saw it was already open just a crack, a pair of red eyes staring at him from within it.

23

GET ALEX

GET ALEX RUN

Sam had indeed run after An Chin finished her message in blood. She burst out through the back door, dashing through a line of neighboring backyards to avoid being spotted by whoever had attacked the Chins. Those men whose voices . . .

. . . didn't sound like voices at all.

She peeled back for the street when she hit a fence, trying to get her bearings and realizing she'd overshot the place where she'd parked. She couldn't see the Chins' front porch until she was almost to her car and then everything looked normal. No sign of the intruders or of anything amiss. But she didn't let herself think what she'd just seen was the product of her imagination. It was real, and the Chins needed help. Desperately.

The flickering streetlights splayed shadows about the streets and yards. Trees twisting in the breeze coming to life. Rustling bushes blown up to monstrous proportions and sprouting tentacle-like limbs. Cars with dark shapes flashing shiny eyes hidden behind windows misted over with condensation.

An Chin's message returned to the forefront of Sam's mind.

GET ALEX RUN

Run from what, from *who*? And why no police?

It felt like she'd been dropped into some scene from one of the science fiction tales in which she was so fond of losing herself. Heinlein gone to hell, and now she really had become his stranger in a strange land. The night air that had been cool and comfortable suddenly felt hot and steamy. The moonless sky had clouded over and she realized the streetlights illuminating swatches of the dark world around her were buzzing, flickering, while stubbornly pouring out light Sam sought because suddenly she felt like a little girl again, afraid of the dark. She thought of her own parents, terrified something had happened to them as well. She needed to call them, she needed to go home, settle her thoughts, make sure they were safe.

Sam checked her phone, found it was working again, with a signal to boot. Then dialed, breath caught in her throat.

"Dude!" her dad greeted.

Tonight it was the happiest word she could ever hear. "Dad!"

"That's me."

"Is everything all right? Are you and Mom okay?"

"I'm trimming, she's bagging. So, yes, we're okay."

"Because—"

Sam stopped when the phone vibrated and beeped to signal another call coming in, from a number she didn't recognize.

Alex, she thought.

"I have to take this other call," she told her father.

24

THE CLOSET

Alex pulled Dr. Payne's closet door open with enough force to rattle the hinges. The red eyes he thought he'd glimpsed a moment before turned out to be an old-fashioned pager, twin red lights flashing to signal a dead battery or something.

Beneath the shelf on which the pager rested hung several changes of clothes on hangers. Plastic covered the shirts and even a pair of jeans he quickly stripped free of the covering, along with a pullover short-sleeve shirt. The shirt was a tight squeeze but the jeans fit him well enough. He realized only in donning them that he had nothing for footwear. Another check of Payne's closet revealed a pair of sneakers a full size too small for him, but Alex squeezed into them nevertheless and loosened the laces as much as he could. He could feel his toes pressed up flush against the toe box, no room for give. They were all he had, though, and better than nothing.

There was an extra lab coat hanging in the closet as well, and Alex plucked it from its hanger. It was a worse fit than the sneakers, the sleeves climbing well past his wrists and so tight around his chest and shoulders he doubted he could have buttoned it if he had to.

Before leaving he pressed his ear against the door to listen for anyone possibly lying in wait. All he heard was the creaky, squeaking sound of a cart being wheeled along the tile floor. Alex waited for it to pass, eased the door open, and slipped out into the hall.

He was halfway to the stairwell before he realized he was holding his breath and that Dr. Payne's sneakers were an even worse fit than he'd thought. Forcing himself to breathe normally, Alex never broke stride or looked back, just moved straight through the door into the stairwell. His heart seemed to lurch forward in his chest when the echo of the door sealing behind him seemed to go on forever. But he kept moving, taking the stairs as fast as Dr. Payne's sneakers would allow.

The stairwell spilled out into the lobby, awash in light and people milling about. Knowing as a kid he must've looked ridiculous in a doctor's lab coat, labeled PAYNE, no less, Alex quickly shed the garment, squeezed it into a ball, and grasped it in a single hand as if it were a football. At that point, the exit felt very much like the goal line, promising at least temporary respite until he could get his parents on the phone.

The same parents who'd forbade him to play football. The same parents who'd secretly researched prep schools for a possible fifth year of high school. He'd been so angry at them over that. Now it seemed so small and petty.

Eighteen years old and all I can think of is calling my parents. . . .

There was a café called Rigolo just up the street from the hospital he'd eaten at a few times with them. So, pinched by Dr. Payne's clothes and sneakers, Alex headed there in search of a phone.

25

911

"I'll call you back," Sam said to her father.

"Take your time. The trimming waits for no man."

"But you're telling me the truth, right? Everything's really okay?"

"What's gotten into you?"

Her "call waiting" buzzed in again. "Gotta go. Call you back." She switched to the new call. "Hello?"

"Sam!" Alex's voice screeched. "Sam!"

"Alex, what—"

"I need you. I need you to pick me up. Now! Please!"

Thoughts coursed through her mind, so many and so fast she couldn't keep track.

"At the hospital?" she managed.

"No, not there. I can't reach my parents!"

"This number, I don't recog—"

"I'm at a restaurant called Rigolo down the street from the hospital. I've got to stay out of sight."

Sam felt something sink in her stomach, thinking of the men with the strange voices who'd attacked the Chins. "Out of sight from *what*?"

"Never mind. I just need to get home, think this through, talk to my mom and dad."

She swallowed hard. "Alex . . ."

"Not now. Whatever it is can wait. Too easy to see me

from the street where I'm standing. You know the place?"

"Yes. Sure. But—"

"Hurry, Sam, please."

Sam thought she might pass out, by the time she reached the old Volkswagen Beetle's door.

"Sam!"

"I'm here. Sorry, I—"

"You've got to hurry! I can't stay here. Something's—"

Alex's voice cut off suddenly. Sam looked down at her phone, which felt oddly cold in her hand, figuring the battery had died for real this time. But the icon was almost all filled in.

"Alex," Sam managed. "Alex!"

"Hurry," he responded, his voice returned. "Please."

"Alex, listen. I really need to tell you—"

A *click* sounded before Sam could say another word.

26

RIGOLO

His call to Sam on the old-fashioned pay phone completed, Alex might have called the police then and there, if he hadn't seen the men enter. All dressed in identical dark suits, which seemed odd for a Saturday night. Looking dapper, polished but focused. One of them spoke to the hostess while the others seemed to be glancing about the restaurant.

He stopped peering around the alcove wall for fear of being spotted. Whoever these men were, they didn't look right for the surroundings, totally out of place. He figured it would take Sam at least fifteen minutes to get here and once he left the restaurant, he'd have no way to reach her by phone.

Leaving Rigolo was the problem now. From the alcove of the bright and cheery café that catered to families as well as CPMC doctors and nurses, he glimpsed the four black-suited men being seated at a corner table on the far left offering a complete view of the floor. No way he could reach any of the exits without them spotting him. The only thing preventing that now was the slight angle that kept him from their view when he pressed his shoulders against the wall. Move just a few inches and he'd be in their sights.

Alex had no choice but to wait, taking several deep

breaths to calm himself. No clock was in view and he had neither a cell phone nor a watch to check the time until Sam's expected arrival.

Where were his parents?

And something else: Why hadn't he called Cara when he couldn't reach them? Why had he called Sam instead?

He stood there pressed against the wall trying to remember the last time he'd had a really good time with Cara. Couldn't think of a single one, at least not sober, except when they'd had plenty of fun in large groups over the summer, before football camp started in August and then it was all business. This wasn't a new thought, just one he'd passed off as his own fault, given the demands on his time and energy by the season and a championship run. He thought Cara was leaving him alone because she thought that's what he wanted.

I'm an idiot, he thought.

Alex glimpsed the hostess lead a pair of men past the alcove toward a nest of tables out of sight from it, uniformed men.

Cops.

He could go to their table and tell them what had happened, tell them about the men in suits who'd come into the restaurant just after he had. Yes, that made sense. Best available choice, assessing the situation the same way he did when approaching the line of scrimmage. Alex steeled himself for the task for several moments and slid out from the alcove, turning left toward where the cops must've been seated.

Where one of the black-suited men was standing over their table, smiling and exchanging handshakes.

Were the cops involved in this too, in league with the killer at the hospital and these men as well?

Alex could wait no longer. Had to take his chances

they were looking for a kid wearing hospital garb instead of clothes pilfered from a dead doctor's closet. Swung right toward the main entrance, started walking and didn't stop, didn't turn, half expecting a big strong hand to clamp down on his shoulder. But it didn't and then he was through the door back outside into the cool night.

He looked back only when he was in the darkest part of the Rigolo parking lot, standing beside an older model Lincoln Town Car. Writing stenciled onto the rear window read, WATSON FUNTERAL HOME, followed by an address and phone number. Alex thought of the four men inside wearing identical black suits. They were funeral home workers, coming from a memorial service, probably, and were well acquainted with the complement of local police officers who often provided them a security detail.

Alex started to relax ever so slightly when the screech of car tires snapped him back to reality.

27

LOVE BUG

Sam's Volkswagen Beetle, the old model from circa 1990 had barely come to a halt when Alex lunged out of the shadows outside of Rigolo and jerked the passenger-side door open.

"Don't stop!" he ordered when she jammed on the brakes, his eyes checking the street behind him. "Just drive!"

Sam did, screeching off and bleeding more remnants of rubber from her nearly bald tires.

"This car reminds me of the Love Bug," Alex said, his voice settling. "You know, from those movies we watched as kids."

"Seems like a long time ago now."

"Disney, I think," he continued, running his hand across the plastic over the glove compartment. He cocked his gaze behind him again, out the sloped rear window crusted over with dust and grime. "I think we're safe. No one's following us."

"Who would be following us?"

"I don't know. I don't know who they are, *what* they are," Alex said, his eyes dull with shock as he regarded her from the passenger seat.

How was she going to tell him?

"Alex," Sam started.

He'd turned away, gazing emptily forward. "A funeral home, can you believe it?"

"Believe what?"

"Never mind. Just take me home. My parents aren't answering the phone. I'm afraid . . . I think something may be . . . wrong." That final word emerging with a mouthful of air. "I just have this feeling. . . ."

Sam clenched the wheel tighter as she drove on, afraid to let Alex see the fear, the sadness, in her eyes over what she had to tell him. "What happened at the hospital?" she asked instead.

"I don't know. My doctor's dead."

"*What?*"

"Somebody killed him."

"Did you call the police?" she said, focusing on the road so as not to meet his stare.

"I couldn't find a phone. And when I finally did, I called you. Whoever killed him was after me too. That's why I ran." His eyes tightened their focus, chasing her down. "What's wrong, Sam? You're scared, I can tell."

"Well, you scared me," she said, without looking at him.

"No, you were already scared when I called," Alex said, as if realizing that himself for the first time. "I could hear it in your voice."

She could feel him still staring across the seat at her.

"What's wrong, Sam?"

She swallowed hard. "I need to tell you something."

"So tell me."

"It's not so easy." Trying to look at him now. "It's about your parents."

"My parents?"

She squeezed the steering wheel so tight, her fingers ached. "You're right, somebody did hurt them. I was at your house, waiting for you, and I saw . . ."

Sam's voice trailed off and she couldn't get the words back.

"What? What happened?"

"I came in through the back. Your mother, your father . . ."

He snapped a hand out, fastening on her shoulder so hard she nearly lost control of the Beetle, just managed to hold it straight, its worn tires humming atop the pavement.

"Sorry," he said, pulling his hand away. "I'm sorry."

"It's okay."

"No, it's not. Things are very far from okay." Then, locking his unblinking stare upon her: "Aren't they?"

"I . . ."

"What happened to my parents?"

"Someone hurt them."

"Hurt," Alex repeated. "But they're okay, right? They're alive."

He watched Sam squeeze the steering wheel tighter. "I don't know. We should go to my house. My parents will—"

"No, get me home. Drive faster," Alex said, his gaze going blank and fixing forward as he settled stiffly into the passenger seat.

"The men who did . . ." Sam twisted his way, the spray of oncoming headlights making her face look shiny and reflecting off her glasses. "I think it was about you, Alex."

"Why?"

"Your mother, something she said."

"You spoke to her? I thought you said—"

He was struck suddenly by a wrenching agony centered directly behind his forehead.

"Alex?"

"I'm okay," he said, grimacing.

"No, you're not. And we shouldn't go to your house."

He was massaging his temples now, features starting to relax. "Why?"

"Because they could still be there."

"Who?"

Sam didn't know what to say.

"Who, Sam, *who*?"

"Your mother," Sam said, instead of answering, "she told me to get you, to run."

"Run?"

"That's what she wrote."

"Wrote?"

"I . . . can't explain now. You need to see for yourself."

"Give me your phone. I should call the police."

"No!" Sam blared, remembering. "Your mother said no police!"

"But I'm supposed to run. Like someone's after me?"

"There were these . . . men," Sam said, not bothering to elaborate further. "They were still at the house when I left. They could be waiting for you, probably are."

"Then let's go meet them."

"*What?*"

"Drive, Sam, just drive."

28

WHERE THE HEART IS

"Pull into that gap in the trees by the road," Alex ordered Sam, as they snailed down his street at the far end from his house.

He was out of the Beetle before Sam got it stopped all the way, looking through the trees at his house. The cars belonging to Alex's mom and dad were neatly parked side by side in the driveway. The exterior lights were on, the drapes drawn across both the upstairs and downstairs windows. There were no broken windows or doors and no strange men hanging out on his front porch. The scene couldn't have looked more normal. So maybe, just maybe . . .

"I know what I saw," Sam insisted, as if reading his mind.

"I didn't say anything."

"You didn't have to."

"Pop the trunk."

The Beetle's "trunk" was actually in the front, under the proverbial hood with its engine in the rear.

"You have a spare tire?" he asked.

"Yes, sure, but . . . do I have a flat?"

"Pop the hood," Alex told her.

* * *

They looped around to the rear of the house, Alex holding the old-fashioned tire iron tight by his side. The old Beetles came with a full-size spare and hardware that was ancient by modern standards, but very handy in this case. He noticed Sam was brandishing something too.

"Sam, what the hell?"

"It's a taser."

"Like I said, what the hell?"

"My parents insisted I carry it. I keep it in the car. For those drives back and forth to Ames at night. Makes them feel safer."

"I'm glad somebody feels safe."

Sam ground her sneakers to a halt in the tall grass Alex had neglected to mow. They reached the kitchen door, which opened onto the backyard, the room beyond dark as it would always be at this time of night. Alex eased the door inward, slowly enough not to draw the stubborn creak due to an oiling the brackets desperately needed that he'd forgotten to give them.

"Stay here," he told Sam.

"No."

"It wasn't a request. If you hear . . . anything, run and get help."

"I've already got you," she said, not believing how lame it sounded.

He laid his strong hands on both her shoulders, Sam feeling the weight of the tire iron. "I'm going to check things out."

"Alex—"

He lowered a hand to her lips, shushing her. "I'll be right back."

* * *

And he was, within moments, but they were the longest moments of Samantha's life. She expected his expression to be bent in heartache, in misery, and was surprised he wasn't sobbing audibly or hadn't cried out when he saw the bodies of his parents on the living room floor. Instead, his expression was just blank and befuddled.

"You can come inside now," Alex told her.

29

TO PROTECT AND SERVE

They padded softly toward the opening leading from the kitchen into the living room, still nothing amiss or awry, which should've made them breathe easier, though it didn't in Sam's case. All the downstairs lights had been switched off, bathing the living room in darkness broken by a single lamp shining down from a table at the top of the stairs. Sam's eyes adjusted quickly, still making nothing out until their next stop brought them across the threshold from the kitchen into the living room.

But the living room was empty. No bodies or blood. Everything in place just as it always was. An and Li Chin nowhere to be found.

"Sam?"

"I know what I saw," she said, advancing ahead of him, stiff with shock. "Your father was lying here and your mother here. And right here, in this spot, is where your mother had written the message in blood."

"Blood?"

"I didn't tell you before. Your mom had written this message on the floor. Telling me to find you and run."

"Where is it? Where are my parents?"

"I don't know," Sam managed.

"I checked upstairs. No sign of them there, either."

Alex hesitated, as fearful as he was uncertain. "You're sure about what you saw?"

"Yes; well, no. I think I am, but I don't know. I don't know anything for sure anymore. Like what happened to my phone, those strange voices, that smell . . ."

"What smell?"

"I just remembered it. Like copper wire when it heats up. Something corrosive and . . ."

Sam stopped, trying to figure out how best to describe the scent that enveloped the man who'd stolen her iPad last night.

"What?" Alex coaxed.

"Nothing. I don't know what the smell means. Maybe nothing. Maybe—"

Flashing lights appeared outside before Sam could continue, red and blue splashed against the living room walls from the black-and-white police cars that had parked nose to nose on the curb.

"I thought you said *not* to call the police," Alex said uncertainly.

"I didn't call them," Sam insisted.

By then four officers were approaching the house warily, hands not far from their gun belts. The doorbell rang a moment later.

"Don't answer it," Sam warned, recalling An Chin's warning.

"They're cops," Alex told her, as he moved for the door. "I don't think we've got a choice and maybe . . ."

"Maybe *what*?"

"You're not crazy, Sam," he said, his voice cracking with what might've been fear. "I'm not crazy, either. Something happened at the hospital and something happened here too."

"You believe me?"

"I don't really want to, I'm trying not to . . ."

He yanked open the door to reveal the four cops crowded onto the porch. "Millbrae police, son," the one closest to the door with his notebook out said. "We got a report of a break-in. Is this your residence?"

"It is."

"Are your parents home?"

Alex felt something tighten in his stomach. "I'm not sure, I don't think so, anyway. No, they're not."

The lead cop exchanged a glance with the one on his right. "You mind if we come in, have a look?"

"Not at all," Alex said, stepping aside so they could enter.

"Alex," Sam protested quietly, as the cops slid through the door, one after another.

"It's okay, Sam."

The lead cop's eyes fell upon her. "And who are you, young lady?"

"Samantha Dixon. I go to school with Alex."

"That would be Alex Chin," the cop said, referring to his notebook. Then, to Alex, "Is this your girlfriend?"

"I'm his tutor," she chimed in, before Alex had a chance to answer.

"Tutor," the cop repeated oddly, making a fresh note on his pad. "And that's Dixon with an *X*?"

"Is there another way to spell it?"

The lead cop ignored her and looked back toward Alex. "You mind if we have a look around?"

"You asked me that already. The answer's still yes, feel free."

The other three cops scattered about the house, leaving the lead one with the living room.

"Do you have transportation home?" he asked Sam suddenly.

"I have my car, but I'm not leaving," she told him, feeling her spine straighten.

"It might be best while we sort this out with the family, miss."

"I don't know where my parents are, Officer," Alex said.

"Are those their cars in the driveway?"

"Yes."

"Might they be at a neighbor's house, maybe were picked up by someone?"

"Maybe." Alex shrugged.

The cop eased past Sam, nearly brushing against her, and that's when she smelled it: a faint, corrosive scent she barely recorded. Less like copper than she'd remembered and more like the wisps of the odor rising from a car engine as it cools down. And something else.

Oh, my God . . .

It was motor oil, the same scent she'd caught a whiff of when the man had taken the seat behind her in the bleachers last night, the man who'd stolen the iPad from her backpack. Come to think of it, he looked a lot like this cop.

Could it be, was it even possible that . . .

Her thought trailed off, Alex the only thing on her mind right now. She had to warn him.

"Alex," she managed, fighting back against the grip of panic.

"Have you tried calling their cell phones?" the cop asked him, practically rolling over her words.

"No answer," he reported.

"Alex," Sam repeated, trying very hard not to gaze toward the cop who looked so much like the guy who'd snatched her iPad, which contained all the evidence of her findings she'd intended to share with Dr. Donati. Then those findings had vanished from the Cloud too. "Alex," she said, just a bit louder.

He glanced her way and seemed to catch the fear and apprehension in her eyes. Then she touched her nose. Alex waited for the cop to draw closer to him, and his expression told her he'd caught the same scent in the air she had.

Sam looked back toward where she'd found the bodies of An and Li Chin, goose bumps prickling her flesh and a chill riding up her spine. When she turned around again, the other cops had all returned, seemingly at once, and were lined up in a kind of semicircle behind the lead one. He touched his nose, just as Sam had to signal Alex.

"I see you remember me," he said to Sam. "That's too bad."

30

REAPPEARANCES

"This doesn't have to be difficult," the lead cop continued, turning toward Alex, who, like Sam, was frozen in shock. "Cooperate with us and we'll let the girl live."

"Who the hell are you?" Alex managed, hands tightening into fists by his sides.

"Your family, so to speak. Your *real* family."

"Where are my parents? What'd you do to them?"

"We hoped this wouldn't be necessary. . . ."

Alex started forward but stopped quickly, thinking better of it. "I want to know where my mother and father are."

The man blinked robotically. "Right over there," he said, gesturing with his eyes.

Sam turned with Alex, both of them laying eyes on the Chins lying just where she'd seen them before, as if they'd reappeared out of nowhere. The blood was back too, though no message remained written in it that she could discern.

Alex rushed to his parents, his mother first because she seemed, incredibly, to still be clinging to life.

"Mom . . . *Mom!*"

Sam tried to make sense of what was happening, what she was seeing. She felt light-headed, almost like she was going to pass out. The living room started to spin softly around her. She reached down and groped for a nearby table to steady herself.

Alex rose from a crouch by his mother's side. "You guys aren't real cops."

No response.

"I'm calling the real cops," he resumed, moving for the phone.

Alex picked up the receiver. No dial tone. Dead. Set it back down as Sam watched, remembering how her own phone had stopped working. Neat trick, sure. But how had this guy managed to make the bodies of Alex's parents appear again out of nowhere? And what had happened to the message scrawled in blood?

"Who are you?" Alex asked, a few graceful strides placing him closer to the man, with only the coffee table separating them.

"We already told you that."

"No, you didn't. You're *not* my family."

"In a manner of speaking, we are. We have our orders. You must come with us, Alex."

"I'm not going anywhere with you."

"You don't have a choice."

"Try me, bitch," Alex said, looking just as he did before laying into a rival player with a bone-crunching tackle from his safety position.

The man looked toward Sam while the eyes of the other fake cops, or whatever they were, remained fixed forward, resolutely emotionless. Sam realized the corrosive smell of something almost hot enough to burn had grown stronger. And now one of the fake cops had frozen in place, a hand stretched out before him as if he'd been reaching for something, his eyes dark and lifeless.

"This is for your own good," the lead cop was saying. "You don't belong here, with them."

"With *who*? What the hell are you talking about?"

And then Sam realized Alex had positioned himself just over where he'd laid the tire iron down atop the coffee table.

"We've been looking for you a long time. Eighteen years. Your entire life. You belong with us."

"*Us* as in *who*? You're not cops and I want to know who you are and what you're doing here. Why'd you hurt my parents?"

"You must come with us, Alex."

"That sounded like an order."

"You have no choice."

"Yes, I do."

And then Alex was in motion, like this was football, playing a game. The tire iron was resting on the coffee table and then it was in his hand, coming up overhead as he launched himself airborne over the table, bringing the tire iron downward at the same time.

Thwack!

The tire iron struck home, mashing what should've been flesh and skull. Only, the sound and feeling were more like metal on metal, steel on steel. The head he'd struck whipsawed to the side, canting as if on a piston. Alex glimpsed a huge dent, a divot dug into the spot where skin and blood should have been. The head snapped back, the depression remaining in place like a car dent.

"Alex!"

Sam's scream alerted him to the second fake cop just in time. She'd sliced between them to ward off his attack and ended up being shoved violently sideways straight toward a wall, the impact rattling her enough to tear her feet from under her. She noticed plumes of smoke wafting out of the motionless cop's ears, wisps of it rising out of his skull, as if his hair was on fire, hand still extended as if he'd seized up while directing traffic.

Alex, meanwhile, brought the tire iron straight down atop the head of the second man, not so much caving it inward as splitting it in two right down the middle. It cracked more like an eggshell than a skull, spitting wires like spaghetti in all directions, its eyes still trying to focus on him even though they'd ended up facing opposite directions away from their target with the tire iron itself still wedged into place.

The initial figure was coming at him again and a third figure had emerged from another part of the room holding an odd-looking object that resembled a miniature staple gun. Alex went into football mode, launching himself into a perfect tackle that propelled the third man backward with enough force to crash him through the plaster of the wall. Alex lurched back upright in time to block a blow uncorked by the figure with the impossibly dented face. The man tried to pull his arm from Alex's grasp, tugging hard.

Alex tugged harder.

And the arm broke off from the shoulder in his grasp, spitting more thick, spaghetti-like strands of wire that clung to both the severed limb and the joint itself. Alex gazed in shock at the arm he was holding, and the now one-armed figure who'd just seemed to realize he was missing it.

A crackling sounded and he swung to find the figure pulling itself from the wall through which he'd slammed it, managing a single step forward when Sam lunged and stuck her taser square against its temple. A staticky sound burst from the device on contact and then it flew into the air as a shock from the impact rode up Samantha's arm and drove her backward. But smoke, gray and noxious, was pouring out of the man's nostrils, mouth, and eyeballs, followed by a shower of sparks Alex could only liken to a transformer blowing in an electrical storm.

He swung back around just as the now-one-armed man came at him again, realizing at the very last moment he might not have the tire iron to wield anymore, but he did have something else:

The figure's severed arm.

He used it like a baseball bat, slamming it into the already dented face on that side and then the other. Beating him senseless with it as hot bits of plastic and metal that smelled of burned rubber broke off and flew through the air like fireflies.

Still, Alex didn't stop until nothing in the skull was remotely recognizable, quite fitting, since whatever these things were clearly wasn't human at all. The rage spilled out of him, his mind-set the one he brought to the football field, filled with bone-crunching collisions.

They had hurt his parents. They deserved to die, whatever they were.

He was vaguely conscious of Samantha stirring against the wall down which she'd slumped. The burned-metal scent filled the air and he thought he heard cracking and popping as the things he was killing fizzled and stilled. He realized the single lamp was flickering, creating a strobe effect that allowed him to glimpse the remnants of his handiwork in broken splotches.

"It would seem I underestimated you, Alex," a new voice called from the shadows.

31

THE ASH MAN

Alex whirled toward the fallen bodies of his parents, severed arm still in hand, to find a man standing centered between his mom and dad.

"They were just drones, hastily assembled and clearly unfit for this mission," the man continued, turning his gaze onto the motionless, still standing cop figure with smoke bleeding out of his ears and skull.

He was tall and gaunt to the point of being almost skeletal, his clothes hanging over his body like an ill-fitting curtain. He reminded Alex of the equally tall man from the hospital, to the point where they could have been the same man. At first glance the figure's skin seemed albino white, almost translucent. But now, up closer, in the flickering light shed by the lamp, it looked more gray, as if the man had rubbed ash all over his skin.

"If you leave with me peacefully now, your parents can live," the ash man continued. His voice had an odd twang to it, almost a harmonic echo. Sounded like it was coming from somewhere else, a broadcast of sorts, and the ash man was just mouthing the words. "Come with me, and the young woman can call an ambulance to help them. Choose, Alex, choose."

"Get away from them," Alex said, straightening him-

self in line with the man, who cut a dark, eerie figure
across the room.

"That wasn't one of the choices."

"Who *are* you?" Alex demanded.

"The better question, my boy, is who are *you*? I'm sure
you've been asking yourself that since the hospital."

"You killed my doctor!"

"Because it needed to be done. Because he knew."

"Knew what?"

"About you."

"What about me?"

The ash man's eyes cast Sam a sidelong glance before
returning to Alex. "This is not something to be discussed
here."

Alex sidestepped to plant himself between the ash
man and Sam, brandishing the severed arm amid the
broken pieces of what the ash man had called drones.

"You don't need that," the ash man told him. "I'm un-
armed and have no intention of harming you."

"Guess your drones didn't get the message."

"They wouldn't have hurt you. Their orders were specific."

Alex cast his gaze downward, his father lying utterly
still but his mother's chest still rising and falling in rapid
heaves. "They hurt my parents."

"As mandated by their mission parameters. But you're
in no danger. You see, you have something we want,
something that belongs to us."

"Know something? I think you've got the wrong kid,
because I don't have *anything* that belongs to you."

"Yes, you do; you just don't realize it."

Alex studied the ash man closer. He seemed almost
spectral in form, more liquid than solid, the way he stood
there as if the air moved through instead of around him.

His head came to a peak at the top, where hair shaded with the same grayish tint rode his scalp, so even and still that it seemed painted on.

"Where'd you come from?"

"I was here all along, Alex. You just couldn't see me, like you couldn't see your parents when you first got home. You only saw what we wanted you to—for your own good, to prevent exactly what ended up happening. We've been looking for you for a very long time. This night never should have been necessary, we should never have needed to come for you. But now we must live with the consequences and accept them."

"Good idea," Alex said, pointing backward with his free hand toward the fizzling, hissing, and crackling assemblage of clumps that had been whole just minutes before.

"This shouldn't have been necessary," the man repeated.

"You said that already."

The ash man's gray eyes fluttered. "There is a price for disobedience. Disobedience is what has brought us to this point. It will not be tolerated."

With that, he stooped down on his long stilt-like legs and slid his hand along Li Chin's shoulder then upward, pressing a thumb into his temple like he was pressing a postage stamp into place. Li writhed, spasmed, shook, his feet twitching and pulsing.

"No!" Alex screamed, hurdling into motion just as the man's other thumb found his mother's temple.

The severed arm was in motion before he'd had time to form the thought: *read and react,* just like on the football field, and that's what Alex did, unleashing a vicious overhead blow that should have fractured the ash man's skull on contact.

But it didn't. It cut straight through his head instead and kept right on going, all the way through until the severed arm thudded against the wood floor, forging a nasty gash in the wood.

The ash man separated into two equal halves, each dropping to the floor, landing next to each other without any feeling, emotion or pain, showing in his face. He seemed to fade to black in the room's flickering light before regaining a measure of his gray tone, which continued to drift in and out. The two halves of him had landed six inches apart, but the ash man seemed not to notice, empty eyes glaring up at Alex.

"You must come with me, Alex," he managed, the separated sides of his mouth speaking in perfect unison, as if still whole. "You've evaded us for this long, but you're ours again. We won't stop. We'll never stop."

"Go to hell, asshole," Alex hissed, raising the severed arm overhead again.

"You're not one of them, Alex," the ash man said, one side of his mouth lagging slightly behind and flickering toward black more than the other now. "You never belonged with them. You belong to us. And with continued disobedience comes punishment. We must take back what is ours."

"I don't have it."

"They entrusted it to you. It's why you're here and why I've come to take you back."

"Back where, exactly?"

"Home, Alex, your real home."

Alex wanted to lash the severed arm downward again, but was stopped as much as anything by uncertainty over which side of the ash man to pound first. Then he heard a sound like something scratching and scampering across the floor.

"Alex!" Sam cried out.

He swung around to find severed pieces of what the ash man had called drones moving toward Sam en masse, the broken bodies from which they'd been shed lagging a bit behind.

"Punishment, Alex," the ash man said, his dual voice echoing in a tinny, hollow fashion. "Punishment for disobedience."

Alex launched himself across the floor, yanking the tire iron from the head of a drone thing en route to Sam. She was back-crawling desperately across the floor from the hard wood of the living room to the tile of the kitchen, kicking at the chunks of plastic, metal, and wire that were converging on her to ward them off.

Alex began slashing and hammering at them as if they were an angry swarm of rodents. Tile cracked, pieces sent flying airborne with each successive thrust and blow. Nothing at all left recognizable when he crushed the last creepy-crawly drone chunk just before it reached Sam.

"Alex . . ."

He thought it was Sam's voice, then realized it wasn't.

"Alex . . ."

He spun back around. Because it was his mother calling to him, her eyes weak as they struggled to regard him. The ash man was gone, both pieces, leaving behind what looked like a dark shadow where the twin halves of him had landed.

"Alex . . ."

He rushed to An Chin through the flickering light, half expecting the ash man to reappear at any moment.

32

GOODBYES

"Mom!"

Alex took his mother in his arms. "Lie still. We'll get help."

"No," An cried.

"Yes!" Alex insisted.

Alex cradled his mother's head, supporting it gently. Her lips quivered. The terror in her eyes bled off, replaced briefly by relief until An suddenly dug her fingers into his arm, the nails biting against his skin.

"Go, please! Before they come back."

"I'm staying here with you."

She dug her fingers in deeper. "No. Too late. . . ." She shook her head. "But not for you."

"I'm going to the police."

"No!" she said, the hand holding his arm starting to shake. "Police can't help you. No one can help you. You must go far away, must disappear like you never were because . . . you weren't."

"What?"

"Trust Meng Po. Meng Po has the answers you seek."

Jibberish, making no sense.

"Take her. For me. Take Meng Po and never part with her. She will guide you."

Tears streamed down his face, the flickering lamplight catching his father's face frozen in agony.

Death coming into his eyes.

Across the room, a still-dazed Sam had managed to get her phone out, desperately trying to reach 911.

"I can't get a signal!" she wailed. "Like before!"

Alex felt his mother's hand stretch past him into the air and then toward the kitchen. "Meng Po! Please!"

"Mom, please don't—"

"Bring her to me!"

"Mom, I'm sorry! What, what I said in the hospital, I didn't mean it, I . . ." Alex felt the rest of his words choked off by the clog in his throat.

"I know," his mother said, in the same reassuring voice he'd known all his life.

She tried to smile, failed.

"You were right," Alex heard himself say, rewinding time back a day. "I should do that fifth year. . . ."

"Alex . . ."

". . . get smarter. Go to a better college."

"Meng Po, Alex. Please."

Alex snapped alert, time fast-forwarding back to the present. The reality, the pain . . .

"Alex," he heard his mother mutter again, her voice barely audible now. *Alex* . . .

He heard his name, but this time her lips didn't move, his mother's eyes meeting his as his name sounded again.

Alex . . .

In his mind. Her thoughts speaking to his.

What was happening to him?

He let himself believe it wasn't real, just some horrible nightmare induced by the concussion the CT scan must have spotted. He squeezed his eyes closed, willing himself to wake up from this trance, the same way he did to find fresh pages filled in his sketchbook. When he opened them again, though, it was all still the same, only worse.

Because it was real. All of it.

Alex forced himself to look back toward Sam, who was still frantically pressing keys on her phone. "Sam . . ."

No response.

"Sam!"

She finally looked at him; she was standing now, leaning against the wall for support.

"Grab my mother's keys."

"What? Huh?" she responded dimly.

"My mother's keys. Get them."

"Where are they?"

"In the kitchen. Check the hooks by the refrigerator. Or the table."

She moved tentatively that way, seeming to feel her way through the air.

"Got them," Sam called, and Alex heard jangling as she made her way through the living room toward him, careful to skirt the remnants of what the now-vanished image of a spectral figure colored ash gray had called "drones."

She kept her distance while extending the keys downward, keeping an eye on the still standing, and smoking, drone thing in case it showed any signs of life. An Chin grabbed them out of the air, closing her hand on the statuette of Meng Po. Then she pressed it into her son's hand so the keys dangled over the edge of his palm.

"Take," she said, struggling for air now. "Take. Yours now. For luck, luck you're going to need. Promise me, Alex. Promise me."

"I promise," he managed, choking up again, although he wasn't exactly sure what he was promising.

"I'm sorry," his mother said, eyes starting to fade now.

"Sorry? No!"

"We lied to you. All these years, we lied. This is our fault. Should have told, should have—"

The next words caught in her throat and An heaved for breath, just managing to find her voice again. "Others will come. It will never stop, now that it has begun. I'm sorry, I'm sorry, I'm sor—"

She stopped, just like that.

"Mom."

Alex shook her lightly with no result.

"Mom?"

An Chin's expression had frozen in mid-thought, mid-sentence, fooling Alex into thinking she was just pausing. But her eyes didn't blink, just continued to gaze up at him blankly, Alex afraid to let go of their grasp for fear he'd lose his mother forever if he did.

But she was already lost, her final breath crackling from her lips before fading off to nothing.

"We need to go, Alex," Sam was saying, suddenly hovering over him, having recovered her senses. "You heard what she said."

Alex glanced up at her, still holding fast to his mother.

"Alex, please," Sam begged.

She stooped low by An Chin's body, having noticed the strange bracelet wrapped around An's wrist. Then she glanced toward Li Chin's wrist and saw an identical one fastened to his wrist as well. Sam leaned closer to him and started to peel it back.

"What are you doing?" Alex asked her, his own senses sharpening again.

"This looks like an old-fashioned slap bracelet. Not the kind of thing your father would be wearing, and your mother's wearing one too."

Alex followed Sam's gaze to the black piece of fabric

jewelry, which looked shiny as steel. She had straightened out the one she'd unfurled from his father's wrist.

"See?" she whispered.

But then it snapped back into place with a whapping sound.

Alex took it from her grasp and slid the thing that looked like a slap bracelet into his pocket. He lingered over his mother for what seemed like a very long time, before pressing her eyes closed, sobbing and sniffling loudly.

"Alex," Sam said from above him.

"I know," he managed, rising stiffly but still unable to take his eyes off his murdered parents, who lay adjacent to each other.

"I'm sorry, Alex, I'm so sorry," she said, easing a hand to his shoulder, which felt hot and as hard as banded steel.

Alex realized he was still clutching Meng Po. "You've got to get out of here."

"*We've* got to get out of here," she corrected. "You heard your mother."

"She wasn't making sense."

Sam looked back toward the pulverized remains of the drones littering the floor like children's toys or the parts of some massive, unassembled model. "None of this makes sense."

Alex smelled the noxious stench of burned wires and scorched metal searing the air now.

"I can't leave them," he said, looking back down at his parents. "You go."

"I'm not going anywhere without you. And you heard your mother—more will be coming. This is just the beginning."

"Beginning of what, Sam, beginning of *what*?"

Sam saw the shock and sadness in his wet eyes, wished there was something she could say to make him feel better.

"We have to do what your mother said," she reminded him instead, thinking of the severed arm spewing wires instead of veins, and skulls that dented like car fenders. "*Now*, Alex," she continued. "Please, we need to go."

"Where, Sam, where are we supposed to go?"

She swallowed hard. "I have no idea."

FIVE

TRACKERS

The merit of all things lies in their difficulty.

—ALEXANDRE DUMAS

33

THE BUNKER

Langston Marsh studied the scroll on his computer as he did every morning and whenever time allowed. Hours spent in darkness broken only by the light of the screen, absorbing incident report after incident report into his psyche until he found what he was looking for. In a few minutes, the new man would be ushered into his office, located in the sprawling bunker he almost never left.

There was a war coming, and he needed to be ready for it at all costs. The new man, who came highly recommended, was extremely well versed in military matters, a worthy addition to the army, and the cadre at its top, Marsh was building.

The beautifully furnished office in which he was working offered a magnificent view of the Pacific Ocean through its expansive window-wall of glass. The scene was even more beautiful to him at night, the way the moonlight reflected over the currents lopping over the shoreline and filling the room with the steady crash of cascading waves. Other than the spill of moonlight and a single standing floor lamp, the room's only illumination sprang from the glow off the computer screen through which he continued to scroll.

The complex software constantly scanned the Web sites of every newspaper and television station in the country in search of stories containing several preprogrammed key words and phrases, prioritizing those with the highest concentrations. The software left the most mundane stories in black, ones of some note in green, and those of the highest interest in red, which were accompanied by a pinging sound when his computer received one.

The stories pulled were confined mostly to accidents, crime, and particularly murder, the vast majority of which were mundane and easily dismissed. Disappearances interested Marsh the most, along with sightings of strange lights, machines acting up in inexplicable ways, animals behaving strangely, and other unexplained phenomena. The software organized the most notable among these incident reports by region in search of geographical patterns. Other data banks were searched for patterns as well, including large migrations from some areas and influxes into others.

Marsh knew what he was looking for; he just didn't know how exactly to find it. This war was his life's work, something that had driven him to amass the vast fortune he had for the power that came with it. Power he intended to use to fight an enemy the rest of the world refused to acknowledge. Why should they? After all, that enemy hadn't yet struck at them, as it had at Langston Marsh, changing his life inalterably and setting him down this path when he was a mere child.

A buzz emitted from an unseen speaker built into his desk.

"Colonel Rathman is here, sir," the voice of his assistant followed.

"Send him in."

Marsh rose from his chair, turning toward an elegant section of wood-paneled wall as it parted into a doorway, allowing a huge man dressed in black 5.11 tactical gear to enter. Rathman stood as close to seven feet as six, even without combat boots. He was strangely and utterly hairless, not from birth, Marsh had read in his dossier, but from the heat wave loosed from a terrorist bomb. He had no eyebrows or hair and his arms bared beneath a tight short-sleeve T-shirt looked slathered in oil. The heat had been so intense that it had burned off Rathman's tattoos as well, something Marsh hadn't thought possible, leaving a patchwork of embroidered scars behind.

Then again, Marsh's entire life's work was based around what *nobody* thought possible.

"A pleasure to meet you, Colonel."

Rathman came to a rigid halt ten feet before Marsh, virtually standing at attention. "And you, sir."

"You saw duty in Iraq and Afghanistan."

"I did, sir. Eight tours."

"Which ended rather unceremoniously in your discharge. What was the procedure called again?"

"It was called an Article Thirty-Two hearing," Rathman explained routinely, no trace of embarrassment or indignation in his voice. "I accepted a nonjudicial punishment in exchange for agreeing to resign my commission."

"And this was over the alleged murder of civilians."

"There was nothing alleged about it, sir. But 'civilian' is a variable term. My superiors didn't see them the same way I did."

"But, then, your superiors weren't there, were they?"

"No, Mr. Marsh, they were not. The rules of engagement, apparently, had changed, while I didn't."

Marsh followed Rathman's gaze as it swept the office, his eyes flashing like a camera, seeming to record everything he saw.

"Anything strike you as odd, Colonel?"

Rathman looked toward the sprawling window offering

a majestic view of the sea and waves beyond. "We're inland, sir. The Pacific Ocean is hundreds of miles away."

Marsh waved a hand before an unseen sensor. Instantly the seascape vanished, replaced by a tranquil mountain scene with mist riding the peak.

"Is this more to your liking? You see, Colonel, I don't believe in windows. The ability to see out brings with it the ability to see in. Windows create vulnerability, and against the enemy we face there can be no vulnerability."

Rathman stiffened a bit at that, his expression flirting with a smile.

"How much do you know about what you're doing here, Colonel?" Marsh continued.

"I know you're building a private army."

"And its purpose?"

The big man shrugged. "Armies only have one purpose."

"You believe we're going to war."

"You wouldn't be talking to a man like me, sir, if that wasn't your intention. War is what I do and I do it well."

"As your experience in black ops would definitely attest to. You haven't asked about our enemy."

"Because I don't care. You point me toward them and I do as I'm told. That means people are going to die, since that's what I do."

"You're only partially correct, Colonel."

Rathman's expression narrowed, self-assurance replaced by sudden uncertainty.

"We're going to war, all right," Marsh continued, "but not against people. They may act like us, even look like us but, make no mistake about it, they are not us. Would you like to see how I know that, where it all began? Come, allow me to show you. . . ."

34

GUARDIAN

"Another?" the bartender asked, tipping the whiskey bottle forward as a prod.

Raiff eased his glass out to meet it halfway, a sign of concession as well as necessity. Nothing stood out more than a man *not* drinking in a bar like this, which was short on swank but long on atmosphere. That is, if you considered atmosphere to include warped floors, dim lighting, and the residue of too much hopelessness hanging in the hazy air in the form of a musty combination of odors.

Raiff sipped his drink, thinking maybe he should add some ice this round. The bar featured a mirror back with several cracks denoting a whole bunch of years of bad luck for somebody. A thick layer of grime coated the glass, obscuring the reflections of those caught to the point of muddling their features into unrecognizable. But it was enough for Raiff to track motion, and motion was a better giveaway and predictor of intentions anyway, especially bad ones.

Raiff was a Guardian, or what the Trackers who made it their life's work to find him called Zarim. He'd taken the name Raiff, first name Clay, from a gravestone years before in a town whose name he couldn't recall. The deceased was about his age and clearly in no position to protest. Back then it had been much easier to build entire identities around little more than that; a trip to the local town hall to obtain a duplicate birth certificate was normally all it took. A thing of the past. Computers had changed the world, all right, making it just about impossible to live off the grid because the grid encompassed everything these days.

Raiff had learned that places like this were the best in which to hide in plain sight. He'd watched the way the regulars regarded him, studying and memorizing it so he'd have a match with any similar looks cast by other strangers who may have come here on his tail. His own personal early-warning system.

Raiff cared little about place and only slightly more about time. As a Guardian, he had one task to perform and one task only. Whether he'd ever actually be called upon and, if so, when and under what circumstances, remained the quandary confronting him every day. He knew only that his mission was crucial to the survival of two worlds, not one, but it was this one that was currently facing the most jeopardy.

Raiff took another sip of whiskey and felt the cell phone vibrate in his pocket. The Watchers were the only ones who had his number and checked in normally on a regular basis. So he thought little of it, as he eased the phone out and up, ready to text back the standard reply when he saw the message was anything but standard.

THE DANCER'S IN THE LIGHT

The code was birthed by a Bruce Springsteen song, "Dancing in the Dark." For more days and nights than Raiff chose to count, the Watchers would send him the same message, indicating the subject the Guardians were charged with protecting was safe:

THE DANCER'S IN THE DARK

Of course, it hadn't been a text message at first; that had come later, not quite a decade in the past around the time the Dancer celebrated his eighth birthday. The Watchers didn't watch him all the time; that would be too risky, given the chance they themselves were being watched. But they watched the boy enough to be certain he was safe, the truth of his being and identity secure. Anytime when they weren't certain, a Guardian got the call. Not always Raiff, not even most of the time. Back then there hadn't been any Trackers yet. Or, if there were, they'd yet to begin their murderous purge.

Raiff knew the crazed man who was their leader, at least from sight. All crazy men were dangerous, but the ones with the resources to back up their twisted thoughts and visions promised the worst peril. When the Trackers first surfaced, and both Guardians and Watchers found themselves targeted for summary execution, it quickly became clear that they had a new and equally dangerous enemy. A man committed to eradicating them at all costs, with no sense that he might well be laying the groundwork for the destruction of his own world in the process.

Langston Marsh.

And now the work of Marsh's minions had left Raiff as the only Guardian still standing, placing the responsibility for Dancer's continued well-being squarely with him.

THE DANCER'S IN THE LIGHT

Raiff was regarding that message again when he spotted the figures in the mirror glass.

35

THE MEMORY ROOM

"I call this my Memory Room," Langston Marsh told Rathman, his voice echoing slightly in the larger confines of the sprawling space that looked like an exhibit hall.

He noticed that the big man had a round, soft-looking face. A baby's face riding atop a hulk's body, save for neat, thin red lines crisscrossing both cheeks that looked like nail impressions. Four on each side as if someone had dug all their fingers home at once, clawing at him

"The place where I keep all my pain to remind me of the task at hand," Marsh continued.

Overhead lights had snapped on upon their entry, cued by some sensor. The floor before them, looking to be about half a football field in size and stretching up two stories, was lined with regularly spaced museum-like objects, one of which was instantly identifiable: the wreckage of what looked like an aircraft, a sleek fighter of a kind he'd never seen before. Its reassembled remnants looked similar to a much scaled down version of the old B-52 Flying Fortress, the massive sentinels that had protected the U. S. against surprise attack for generations.

"Recognize it, Colonel?" Marsh asked as they approached the display, which resembled a funeral pyre more than an artifact of military history.

"No, sir, I don't."

"That's because there's no record of its existence. This is one of only three prototypes of the design ever manufactured as part of Project Blue Book."

"Project Blue Book?"

"Goes back to 1947, Colonel. My father was a World War Two fighter pilot assigned to an experimental division in White Sands, New Mexico." Marsh stretched a hand out as if to touch the wreckage, then pulled it back sharply. "He was flying this craft when it was shot down."

"In 1947? Two years after the war was over?" asked a befuddled Rathman.

"Only *that* war," Marsh told him. "My father's division was scrambled. Three of these went up and one managed to shoot down the craft that destroyed my father's plane with a kind of pulse weapon that would still be cutting-edge today."

"I've never heard of any of this, sir."

"Of course you haven't. It took place in July of 1947 over Roswell, not far from the site of what would become Area Fifty-one." Marsh hesitated, holding Rathman's tightly focused stare. "My father wasn't killed by the Germans or Japanese, Colonel. His plane was shot down by aliens."

"That's who the war I've been fighting for years is against," Marsh resumed. "If you don't believe in the cause, then you're the wrong man for the job." He hesitated. "I know that the enemy is among us, impossible to identify visually because they look exactly like us. Do you believe me?"

"I don't need to believe you or in anything, sir. I just need to be given something to kill."

Marsh's lips flirted with a smile. Yes, Rathman was the

right man for the job, all right, carefully culled from dozens of candidates. The one common denominator those candidates held was death, lots of it by their own making. Men who were not only no strangers to killing but had become intimately familiar with the act to the point where no degree of it would trouble them.

Like Rathman.

Marsh stopped before the remnants of his father's plane and ran his hand in tender fashion along it. The steel wasn't just cold, it was frigid. Though Marsh knew this always to be a trick of imagination, he let that same imagination conjure up visions of some alien weapon leaving its icy residue forever embedded in the jagged wreckage.

Explosions were traditionally thought of as hot, searing. But maybe alien explosions were the exact opposite, icy cold. Who knew what their air was like, after all? Their entire world could, likely did, operate on different principles.

"They've been among us since the very dawn of civilization," Marsh told Rathman, not bothering to gauge the level of the man's skepticism. All his troops started out that way and each arrived at their ultimate moment of realization in their own time. "But there is reason to believe plans are being laid for an invasion. Call it a surprise attack, an intergalactic Pearl Harbor."

Marsh held on to the tip of what was left of a single wing of the fighter in which his father had died. It felt like the bottom of an ice cube tray. He thought for an instant if he squeezed his hand, the steel would compress in his grasp, all spongy and soft, the molecular composition altered by whatever weapon the aliens had used to down it. But he shook off the illusion as quickly as it had formed in his mind.

"I call them Zarim," Marsh said, exaggerating the *reem* syllable as he swung around abruptly enough to almost draw a rise from Rathman. "Have you heard the term before?"

"No, sir."

"It's biblical. The general translation is 'outsiders' or 'strangers.' But another interpretation refers to the Zarim more like creditors or criminals known for seizing the possessions of others. Usurping their worlds, swallowing their identities. That's what will happen to us, to our world, Colonel, if we don't act. So we hunt them down. We hunt the Zarim down and kill them before they can kill us. Does that concern you at all? Do my words make you rethink your presence here?"

Rathman seemed to ponder that briefly. "These Zarem—"

"Za-*reem*."

"—do they bleed when you kill them?"

"They do indeed. Just like us. Strangely. They look just as we do. It's how they've managed to walk among us undetected for so long."

"Then how do you—"

Marsh felt his phone vibrating and jerked it from the clip on his belt, the rest of the big man's question lost to him as he read the text message on his screen.

"Ah, it appears one of my teams is closing on the latest target now."

36

A BIG STICK

They'd just entered the bar, dragging the night's chill in with them, something all wrong about their eyes. Not their actual eyes, more the way they looked about. Raiff was a firm believer in patterns, the comfort zones in which the behaviors of people nestled. You walked into a bar, you looked for a table, booth, or stool to do your drinking, and you made a beeline for it.

But the men who entered this bar swept their gazes about without that priority in mind. The four of them were big and broad and wore long, dark coats baggy enough to conceal any weapons held beneath. Trackers for sure, then, as opposed to the other enemy committed to Raiff's destruction. Flesh and blood as opposed to steel and cable, dispatched by Langston Marsh with no clue about the war into which he had inserted himself. If the modern-day Fifth Column commanded by that madman succeeded, they would effectively be ensuring the demise of their own world.

Raiff was considering that irony when he spotted the first pair of eyes falling upon him, lingering there. The man started toward him, the three others quickly falling into step. Raiff was proficient, expert, even, in the use of any weapon, all manner of guns and knives included, but he most preferred the one that had accompanied him here eighteen years before.

Speak softly and carry a big stick.

Teddy Roosevelt had said that, one of Raiff's all-time favorite characters lifted from this world's history. He read a lot, especially loved reading about men he considered heroes for one reason or another. Raiff's stick, meanwhile, was nothing like the one Teddy had been thinking of when he coined his famous phrase. It had been formed of subatomic, programmable particles based on nanotechnological principles. The particles responded to his thinking on command, first lengthening into baton size and then either hardening to the texture and weight of titanium steel or softening to be more like a whip. Raiff's mind could sharpen the stick to a razor's edge capable of cutting a man, or drone, in half.

For now he left it dull and hard, like a cop's nightstick. He continued to follow the Trackers in the mirror, their approach slowing when he failed to respond as uncertainty entered the picture. He was just baiting them, of course, but the Trackers could just as easily have thought they were closing in on the wrong target, in which case the right one could be getting them in his sights right now.

Raiff sprung in the moment frozen between action and doubt. He came off the stool in a blur, stick whipping from left to right and impacting the lead Tracker square in the temple. Taking out the leader first always made for the best strategy. Rudderless, the others would hesitate for the mere seconds Raiff needed to overcome their advantage in numbers.

The second man fell quickly to a lashing blow to the back of a knee that followed a deft feint. Still enough time for Trackers three and four to draw their weapons.

Before they could fire, though, Raiff's blur of motion became a whirlwind. Barely any pause before a blow against the ribs of one and a lighter blow across the face of the other that turned his nose into a bloody memory. The one he'd slammed in the ribs with his stick was trying to right himself, all bent over to one side, while the other, still-conscious Tracker lurched toward him.

Dealing with that one was as simple as kicking the stool over in his path. The Tracker's foot caught within its spokes and he went flying, literally, straight past Raiff. This as the Tracker all bent to one side from his fractured ribs managed to get his pistol out and half steadied. Raiff snapped his stick outward, its composite softening to something like pudding held in a flexible tube. Then he lashed it out in whip-like fashion and spun his hand to twirl it around the man's wrist. He pulled and the pistol came free, a single errant shot taking out one of the cheap light fixtures held to the ceiling by a rod.

The air was raining tiny glass shards and Raiff felt them settle in his hair. The edge of his consciousness recorded the fact that the Tracker he'd used the stool on was lumbering back to his feet, while the final Tracker stood at the far end of the bar. He had a broken bottle pressed against a woman's throat, her head jerked back by the hair to expose her jugular.

"Right there!" the man screamed at him. "Don't move!"

Raiff did as he was told, let his stick that had morphed into a whip dangle by his side.

The Tracker started backpedaling for the door, dragging the woman with him. Raiff had never seen her before but he'd seen a thousand like her in bars like this. Single or long divorced, wearing too much makeup and perfume and letting her gaze drift toward the door every time someone new entered in the hope it would be a familiar face, which it never was.

"Stay where you are!" the Tracker ordered. "Don't come any closer!"

Raiff didn't hesitate, didn't wait. He snapped his stick outward and watched it unfurl, seeming to lengthen through the air as it went, like a disembodied tentacle. It wrapped around the Tracker's throat and Raiff dislodged the man's hold on the woman with a simple yank that further tightened the whip-like weapon in place.

The Tracker flailed wildly, struggling to pry what must've felt like icy rubber from his windpipe. He sank to his knees and keeled over face-first, with his hands trying to wedge their way between it and his skin. Then Raiff lashed it sideways, catching the legs of the Tracker who'd tripped over the stool and yanking violently. The man's feet came out from under him and the back of his skull broke his plunge to the floor.

Raiff retracted the whip back into stick form, seeing no need to kill this Tracker or the others still crumpled on the floor. The force behind them had an army committed to the destruction of the Guardians and Watchers, so killing these four would make little dent in that army's ultimate capabilities. Sparing their lives ensured they would talk, stoke fear and hesitance into the hearts of other Trackers who would follow them into this undeclared war that had so complicated the Guardians' plight.

Because the Guardians had two enemies to contend with, one of which was committed to the Guardians' demise while the other sought to destroy this world as it existed today. Stopping the latter from happening formed the true mission of the Guardians, a mission that just moments earlier had reached its own level of desperation.

THE DANCER'S IN THE LIGHT

Which meant, Raiff thought as he slipped the stick back into his belt, the only real hope mankind had for its survival was in grave danger himself.

Because the real enemy must've found the boy at last.

Raiff stepped back to the bar and finished his drink, then stepped over three of the four Trackers he'd dropped en route to the door, needing to find Dancer before more of them did.

37

THE SCENT

"Is something wrong, sir?" Rathman asked, watching Marsh turn away after reading the contents of his latest incoming message.

Marsh clipped the phone back on his belt, containing his anger over the brief message from his team in the field that minutes earlier had reported a hit. Now they were reporting mission failure with casualties.

"How do you feel about failure, Colonel?" he asked Rathman.

"It's unacceptable under any circumstances. I don't think about the successes very long. I never stop thinking about the failures."

Something about those words relaxed the tension Marsh was feeling. "It would appear I've chosen well."

"I haven't accepted the job yet, sir."

"Yes, you have, because you've done everything else. I've seen your file, Colonel, the parts of it known only to a very select few. You've taken on some pretty bad hombres, some of the worst anywhere, through the course of your career in special ops."

"True enough, sir," Rathman agreed.

"But you haven't come up against the very worst yet, the most threatening, not by a long shot. That's why you decided to sign on before we even met, before you even knew what we're facing. For the challenge, a true challenge."

"These Zarim," the big man started, his bald head looking shiny under the harsh lighting of Marsh's Memory Room.

"What about them?"

"I believe you said they appear exactly as we do."

"I suggested it, yes."

"So how do you track them down, take them out?"

"An excellent question, the answer to which was a long time coming," Marsh explained. "Occasionally, we've been able to take them prisoner. Not often, and when we do they never talk about their origins, purpose, or mission. But we've still learned from them, learned plenty. Autopsies, and other scientific analysis have revealed them to be anatomically identical to us in all respects. We still haven't determined if this is the Zarim's actual appearance or a disguise they're able to utilize in order to infiltrate our species toward eventual assimilation."

"Assimilation?"

"A polite way of saying they're out to conquer our world. But I digress. Getting back to your question, our researchers have managed to isolate the one primary factor that distinguishes them from us. You know all humans give off radiation."

"I knew we gave off electricity."

"Same thing in this case. Call it electromagnetic radiation, also known as thermal, or infrared, radiation. Thermal radiation only transports heat and indicates the temperature of its source. Different people at different times give off differing amounts of radiation. But these differences just indicate who is hotter, and not who is fatter, taller, sadder, or more saintly. Thermal images of a person captured using an infrared camera provide the temperature of the person's skin.

"What we've done," Marsh continued, getting to the point when he saw Rathman's eyes drifting, "is take the principle of this infrared camera one step further. The Zarim, Colonel, give off electromagnetic radiation within a different, a higher bandwidth. Not very dramatic, but pronounced enough to be distinct and detectable to the cameras we've constructed. And they're not so much cameras as sensing devices programmed to alert our Tracker teams in the event the presence of one is identified in the immediate proximity."

"I'm picturing men driving in trucks with mini-satellite dishes on top."

Marsh smiled tightly. "It sounds like you've seen them."

"Have I, sir?"

"In all probability, yes. Everyone has. But our vans are always concealed in the guise of delivery, maintenance, or local cable vehicles."

"And they just cruise the streets, what, listening?"

"More like recording readouts, Colonel," Marsh told him. "It's a methodical, painstaking process, but necessary and well worth the effort. You'd be surprised at the level of success we've managed, less so over the years because there's less of them left to target. But that doesn't make our job any less challenging or important. You know what gets me through, keeps me going?"

Rathman's eyes beckoned him on.

"The possibility that someday, someday, we might lock onto the Zarim who killed my father. I'd like you to be the one to bring him to me, Colonel. I think you're up to that task."

"I need to know what's expected of me, sir, the precise parameters of my mission."

The walkie-talkie feature on Marsh's phone beeped before he could answer the big man and he held a hand up to signal a pause, then turned and raised the phone to his ear. Marsh listened to the report, spoke nothing in response. He swung back around, as he fit the phone back into its belt holster.

"We've got a blip, Colonel."

"A blip, sir?"

"An anomaly suggesting alien involvement. It would seem you have your first assignment. There's a jet fueled and ready."

"Bound for where, sir?" the big man asked, appearing even taller and broader in that moment.

"San Francisco."

SIX

MONTER_Y MO_T_R INN

> In three words I can sum up everything
> I've learned about life: it goes on.
>
> —ROBERT FROST

38

BLUE PLATE SPECIAL

Alex and Sam drove south through the night until the clouds covered the moonlit sky and then broke apart, avoiding the 101 in favor of the Pacific Coast Highway. Fog wafting in from the ocean made the difficult drive even more precarious. But the scenic nature of the PCH belied the fact that it also passed through areas of near-desolation and small, little-known towns all the way to Santa Cruz.

Sam drove with her fingers so tight on the Beetle's wheel her hands began to ache, then her forearms, and finally her shoulders. She kept starting sentences, only to have no words emerge. Just air, which was fine since the drive commanded all of her attention. The road was like a winding black ribbon shifting over a coastline so close below that she could hear the waves crashing against the rocks. She welcomed the sight of her headlights reflecting off guardrails, held her breath through the most dangerous curves when there were no guardrails at all.

Every time she looked toward Alex in the passenger seat, he was staring straight ahead out the windshield as if it were a blank screen. A few times when she looked over, the angle of the streetlights bounced his reflection back off the glass. He didn't seem to be blinking, and Sam couldn't tell if he was even breathing.

"Should we go to the police, FBI—somebody?" she managed to ask finally, her voice trailing off to barely a whisper at the end as the road ahead blackened anew, thick blankets of fog wafting across it.

No response.

Minutes passed.

"Is there somewhere you want to go?".

Nothing.

"Someone you can call?"

Dumb question, and she felt stupid for even posing it. She understood full well Alex had only his parents, no other relatives even in China, for all she knew.

Sam gave up. Just drove in silence, no words and no destination in mind. Finally a fog bank too thick to risk driving through forced her onto a side road, black as tar, that ran perpendicular to the PCH. It seemed as if she had driven into some spooky netherworld of nothingness until she spotted an old-fashioned diner and truck stop off to the side. It looked practically deserted. Kind of place that was long past a prime lived out in an age before superhighways stitched their way in all directions.

"I'm hungry," Alex said suddenly.

Sam aimed her Beetle toward the parking lot.

She watched him eat. A pile of bacon and eggs to go with a double order of toast, while she couldn't even think of food right now. Sam waited for him to speak, tried again when he didn't.

"What do we do next?"

Alex didn't answer right away. There were only a few other customers around them, none at all resembling the drone things dressed as cops or the ash man, who was more of a shadow. Bells hung from the door jangled a few times to announce the entry of new customers, making them stiffen each time. Sam was seated with a clear view of it, and none of those coming and going seemed to even register their presence. This wasn't the kind of place you ate to get noticed or notice anybody else.

"I need to think," Alex said, shoveling the last of his eggs into his mouth. "That's where we need to go, somewhere I can think."

"You think you're still in danger? I mean, you *are* still in danger."

"We can't go to the cops."

"Why?"

"Because those guys were dressed as cops."

"Sure, but . . ." Sam's voice drifted off, her thought incomplete.

"Drop me somewhere," Alex told her.

"Where?"

"I don't know. Somewhere."

"And just leave you?"

He leaned a little forward. "I don't want you in danger too."

"Endangered."

"What?"

"It's how you should've said it. Hey, didn't think you were going to get out of our tutoring session, did you?"

She thought her attempt at humor had failed miserably, but Alex smiled, a tight smile.

"And I'm already in danger," Sam continued.

"Endangered, remember?"

"No, the way I used the phrase was proper."

"Proper? Who uses *that* word anymore?"

"The people who write the SAT and ACT tests."

"Not on my radar right now."

"Tell me what is."

"That," Alex said, pointing over her shoulder out the window.

39

SLEEPOVER

The motel they ended up at wasn't the one Alex had pointed to out the window, because that one and two more located miles from the Pacific Coast Highway had insisted on credit cards.

The fourth one had a clerk who couldn't have cared less, probably as much as he did about the sign that had so many bulbs burned out it was hard to read. The Monterey Motor Inn was one of those places that looked grown out of the landscape instead of built upon it. So old it might well have been held together by the weeds and dead brush that surrounded the U-shaped assemblage of buildings enclosing a crumbling parking lot with ancient asphalt bleached near-white in the sunniest spots. The office was on the right as Sam pulled into the parking lot, the sign flashing amid a nest of bulbs that spelled out only a portion of the letters.

The clerk had Coke-bottle glasses that made his eyes look huge, but he squinted as he looked up from a comic book when they entered. Then looked away again, back at the page, just as fast. Sam and Alex approached the counter to be met with him raising a hand into the air like a stop sign until he finished the page he was on.

"Cash only."

"Fine by us," Alex said.

He noticed a cheap ceramic figurine sporting a boner below the sign KNOCK WOOD and spun it around so Sam wouldn't see it. She forked over the forty-dollar nightly rate, bemused by his gentlemanly gesture.

The clerk took the bills in a hand that was shiny with oil, smirking as he regarded them. A couple of horny teenagers looking to do what horny teenagers did. Cash was the order of the night because credit cards could be traced too easily.

"We're not in Monterey," Sam noted.

"Hey," said the clerk, "you're a smart one, aren't you?"

"So why's this place called the Monterey Motor Inn?"

"Hey, I don't even know why it's called a motor inn at all." The clerk shrugged. "Phones in the rooms don't work and the cable's busted," he added, handing an old-fashioned key with a massive plastic fob shaped like California across the counter, stained with what looked like chocolate. "I called the guy."

Sam didn't care that the phones didn't work; she had her own, but was afraid to use it.

Because what if they knew who she was, were waiting for her to turn her phone on so they could track it? She imagined switching it on and seeing a dozen messages and missed calls from her parents, wondering where she was, why she hadn't come home.

Unless something had happened to them. Unless more drone things had showed up at her house too.

The thought gave her chills, made her shudder. And what would she have told her parents anyway, that these *things* had killed Alex's parents, that they wanted to take him with them?

It would sound like she'd been raiding the weed stash they grew for purely medicinal reasons, distributed among a number of marijuana dispensaries, thanks to their legal status as registered growers. No, not easy at all to explain drone things that refused to die and a spectral being who spoke out of both sides of his mouth after being separated in half.

What do you think of that, Mom and Dad?

Once registered, they climbed back into the Beetle and drove to their room, easing into a parking slot directly before it, each of the rooms boasting their own separate entrance. Sam counted five other cars for the sixty rooms spread over two twin levels.

The room was just what she expected: old and worn, but good enough. A single bar of soap cloaked in an unmarked white wrapper and a pair of plastic cups stacked one inside the other atop the counter. The toilet bowl was stained and the seat wobbly, thanks to a missing bracket. Sam switched the dull bathroom light off, then back on again. Alex was sitting on one of the double beds, staring at the nineteen-inch tube television screen like something was showing other than his own reflection.

Vending machines lined the walkway on the side their room was located, the steady whir of the soda machine and regular *thunk* of the ice dispenser slipping through the walls in the quiet. The motel marquee's stubborn bulbs flickered and flashed, sending an alternating wave of red and blue light pouring through the flimsy window blinds, which were torn at the bottom.

Sam sat down on the edge of her bed, staying there until Alex finally laid down atop the bedcovers, clutching the tiny wooden statue of Meng Po as if it were a teddy bear.

"I want you to leave," he said, breaking the tense silence. "I don't want anybody else I care about getting hurt."

"We've been over this, Alex."

"So we're going over it again," he said, without looking at her. "You got me this far. That's enough. Go home, please."

"My answer's still the same."

"It wasn't a question."

"Would you leave me?"

He looked at her finally.

"You wouldn't, would you?" Sam continued. "No more than you'd leave that kid who was about to get smashed last night."

"He was my teammate. It's what we do."

"Well," Sam said, lying back on the second bed, "this is what I do."

40

JANUS

"I believe we're ready now, Doctor," Donati heard the disembodied voice say and slid his chair closer to his computer.

Six hours had passed since Donati called for an alert, that much time taken to assemble the Janus team—no small challenge given two of the five were in truly remote regions and had to be transported to where service was available. Even with that, one remained out of touch, leaving only four boxes on his computer with bar grids that danced in accordance with which one of the participants was speaking. No names had been exchanged and, for all Donati knew, the voices had been scrambled for security purposes as well.

"We've all had a chance to review your classified report from eighteen years ago on the explosion and its aftermath," the voice, associated with the top left-hand square on Donati's screen, continued, "along with the addendum material filed in the wake of your call for an alert earlier today."

"Most disconcerting," the box immediately beneath that one voiced. "What degree of certainty can you provide as to the validity of your conclusions?"

"One hundred percent."

"No such thing," the box on the lower right insisted.

"There is this time," Donati told him, told all of them.

Janus had begun years before as an amorphous extension of the NEO, NASA's Near-Earth Object office, located at the agency's jet propulsion laboratory in Pasadena, which monitored asteroids and the algorithms of their potential trajectories with regards to Earth. Its mission statement was to function as a kind of extraterrestrial NSA or CIA, responsible for dealing with threats posed to the planet from outer space. Unlike the NEO, however, Janus trained its focus on *hostile* threats, specifically from other life forms. Since its existence had been covertly circulated among the various departments responsible for monitoring space, primarily the Search for Extraterrestrial Intelligence, or SETI, three alerts had been called, all of them ultimately deemed to be false alarms.

Janus hadn't been around eighteen years ago, and Donati was all too aware that it owed its very existence in large part to what had taken place at the lab he'd been working at back then.

"Doctor," the sharp voice of a woman began, from the top box on the right side of Donati's screen, "the purpose of this call is not to rehash your unfounded conclusions from eighteen years ago. Indeed, none of your claims involving the incident at your former workplace were supported by the investigation that followed."

"That investigation was sanitized, covered up, eighty-sixed, deep-sixed, shoved under the rug. Should I go on?"

"Stick to the present, Doctor," from Lower Left.

"Precisely, completely, and inalterably my intention, sir, sir, sir, and madam. Except for the fact that the repeat of the same, or similar, pattern is impossible to ignore."

"You're speaking of this sequence of naturally occurring phenomena," said Top Right, the lone woman again.

"That all depends on your definition of 'naturally occurring.'"

"I wasn't aware there was more than one, Doctor."

"Semantics, ma'am. In both cases, today's as well as eighteen years ago, such phenomena may have been natural, but they occurred as a direct result of outside stimulus."

"Your report on the laboratory explosion from eighteen years ago made that clear," noted Top Right.

"The odds of those particular phenomena following the precise curvature of the Earth were estimated at a million to one. The odds of these similar phenomena today following that same pattern are closer to ten million to one."

Lower Right's voice grid began dancing a beat ahead of the actual sound. "Which in and of itself does not suggest the kind of hostile action your alert specifies."

"At least not directly."

Donati heard the woman in the top right chuckle mirthlessly. "Direct threats, Doctor, were what Janus was created to deal with, not theoretical ones."

"Unless a particular threat boasted as a harbinger geoplanetary disruption. I'm convinced that such seismic disruptions are due to slight alterations to the Earth's rotation, as demonstrated by them occurring along a specific line of curvature in both instances, accompanied by drastic spikes in electromagnetic radiation. So small and minor, infinitesimal, really, as to be completely immeasurable."

"And what," asked Top Left in a flat tone, "would you say was to blame for such disruptions both then and now?"

"Alterations in the time-space continuum."

"Not this again," the woman sighed.

"If you'd read my complete report on the circumstances surrounding the explosion of eighteen years ago," Donati retorted, trying to stay calm and keep his voice steady, "you wouldn't take that attitude."

"But I have read it, Doctor—twice, in fact."

"No, ma'am, you haven't. Because the report I wrote back then was never circulated. It was sent back to me with a request to reissue, redacting certain information not deemed appropriate or professional."

"And what does that mean, exactly?" interjected Lower Right.

"From a 'scientifically enforceable standpoint,' I believe was the phrase that was used. I suppose one purpose was to avoid a panic. The other, more relevant intent was to avoid the shuttering of the division that gave birth to Janus in the first place."

"Am I missing something here?" challenged Lower Right again. "What division are we talking about?"

"Laboratory Z," Donati said, speaking the phrase for the first time in years.

"We're well aware of the existence of Laboratory Z," Top Left reminded him. "The explosion, after all, destroyed it."

"Laboratory Z's existence, yes, sir, sir, sir, and madam. But not its true purpose, what it was chartered in total secrecy to achieve."

"Janus didn't exist then," the woman in the top right added. "But we do now. Please speak plainly, Doctor."

"Suffice it to say," said Donati, "that our experiments were figuratively based on leaving bumps in the night. Until something bumped back."

41

LATE FOR PRACTICE

Alex dreamed of showing up at football practice late. In the dream he could see the field, but no matter how fast he ran he couldn't reach it. Like the world beneath him had turned into a treadmill, making it impossible to get anywhere at all. He kept looking behind him as his legs chugged uselessly, certain each time someone would be there in pursuit, with him powerless to escape them. They'd get closer and closer until they were upon him.

Except there was never anyone there.

The dream then dissolved into a replay of the brutal battle in his house, only his parents were still alive in the end because he had saved them. Then he was explaining to his coach that he was late for practice because he had to fight android-like beings who smelled of burned metal. Only it wasn't the coach he was talking to; it was a life-size version of Meng Po.

Then he woke up and it was all gone, except for Meng Po, still grasped so tight in his hand that the statue's impression was forged into his palm. His mother's keepsake, symbol of luck.

Apparently it hadn't worked very well. His parents were dead. And it was his fault. Somehow.

In other times when stress got to him, Alex focused on football plays. On reading defenses and calling an audible at the line of scrimmage. He reviewed hot reads in his head, being on the same page as his receivers when a blitz was coming. Recognizing a man-to-man defense so the middle would be open and, as quarterback, he'd be free to roam unhindered through the secondary. There was something incredibly fulfilling and cathartic about the sensation of his shoes pounding turf as the thuds of oncoming tacklers sounded in the narrowing distance. Those moments when the field was clear and all his life crystallized into a base simplicity where everything was perfect and nothing could go wrong.

As it had now. Badly. For real. A dream from which he wasn't going to wake up.

"*Alex*," a voice called at the edge of his consciousness. "*Alex*."

A soft voice, soothing. Female. His mother maybe, not dead at all, all of that no more than a nightmare sprung from his getting his head rattled. He was probably still at the hospital, about to wake up in his room there.

"Alex!"

Louder this time, loud enough to rouse him. But he wasn't in bed. He was standing in the shadow of a window covered by a flimsy blind that let the flashing letters of a motel marquee slip through.

"What are you doing?" Sam asked him, eyes moving to the wall crusted with peeling paint. "What did you *do*?"

Alex saw the drawings on the wall before him of monstrous machines rolling this way and that like a scene out of *War of the Worlds*. Like a giant page from the sketchbook still hidden in his bedroom.

42

ARTIST IN RESIDENCE

Alex looked down and saw the motel pen in his hand, ink splattered across his palm and fingertips.

Sam couldn't believe what she was looking at. "I didn't know you could draw."

"I . . . can't."

"But, then . . ." She let her own thought dangle, unsure how to complete it until: "This is what you were talking about in the hospital, when you asked me about not remembering doing something."

Alex dropped the pen, as if it were suddenly hot. Then he sat down on the edge of his bed, grimacing.

"Your head?"

"It's killing me again."

Sam sat down next to him, close enough so their legs were touching. "You don't remember drawing all that?"

"I remember dreaming about football."

She looked toward the wall. "That's not football. And this has happened before, hasn't it?"

Alex followed her gaze. "Not this big, but, yeah."

The flickering lights from the motel sign framed Sam's face in a way he'd never seen it before. Like a posed picture with just the right amount of shadows to make her features glow beneath the colors reflecting off her glasses.

"We need to figure this out," she said.

"Figure *what* out?"

"All of this. Why it's happening. How it may be connected."

Alex's gaze cheated toward the wall again. "To that?"

"You know what I always tell you about math."

"To reason the problem out, to approach it logically."

"Let's try that," Sam told him. She shifted slightly, bracing her hand against the bedcovers and inadvertently running her fingers across his thigh. "Where should we start?"

"You tell me."

"No, you're the quarterback."

Alex frowned, making himself hold his stare on the wall. Sam realized he hadn't slid sideways to put some distance between them, any more than he'd stiffened or recoiled at her touch.

"Okay," he said, focus still locked on his drawings, "what does that remind you of?"

Sam followed his gaze. "The things we saw tonight, the drone things dressed as cops. Machines like nothing that are supposed to exist today. That must be where these sketches come from too. Somehow."

"Except I've got a sketchbook at home I filled with the same kind of drawings *before* tonight."

"Oh" was all Sam could think to say.

"And then there's the ash man."

"Ash man?"

"That's what the guy I cut in half back home looked like to me. Like he was coated in ash."

"How'd he show up the way he did?" Sam interjected. "Where'd he come from?"

"And how could he still talk when he should've been dead?" Alex added.

"But he didn't bleed," Sam remembered. "He didn't

even seem to be in any pain. And then he disappeared. Poof!"

"Like magic," Alex picked up.

"Maybe *exactly* like magic."

"What do you mean?"

"He was never there, not really. Like an illusion."

"You can't cut an illusion in half."

"I said *like* an illusion. Like those fake cops were like robots."

"Androids."

"Huh?"

"What you call a combination man and robot," Alex explained. "An android. Or a cyborg, like in *Terminator*."

"What's that?"

"A movie."

"Oh, yeah. Never saw it. So the ash man wasn't just a projection. He had mass of some kind."

"You're doing it again," Alex said, rolling his eyes as he canted his body to face her.

"What?"

"Saying things in a way I don't understand."

"You don't understand mass?"

"Not the way you said it. We need to make a new rule. Whenever you do that, I'm going to say 'time-out.' Do this with my hands," Alex continued, making a T with his right fingers stuck into his left palm, turned downward.

"'Mass' meaning there was something physical about him, even though he wasn't really there. And something was there, on the floor when he disappeared, remember?"

"Like a shadow." Alex nodded.

"Maybe that's what he was, a shadow. Maybe he was a projection, but a projection with some type of gaseous mass, some type of substance included in the mix."

"But the androids weren't shadows or projections at all. They had *real* mass."

"Until you tore them apart."

"I did," Alex nodded, "didn't I?"

"What was it the ash man said about them?"

"He called them drones."

"That's right," Sam followed. "And something about them being hastily assembled."

"Because whatever brought them to my house must have happened fast, must have been unexpected. Sudden."

"Even though the ash man said something about looking for you for a long time, even since you were born. So what changed? Why tonight?"

Alex shuddered, the memories striking him like an electric shock. "The hospital," he muttered.

"Huh?

"CPMC. My doctor getting murdered in his office. Somebody waiting in my room."

"That doesn't tell us what changed," Sam said, repeating her original point. "How the ash man found you all of a sudden."

"Maybe it does," Alex told her.

43

BY THE NUMBERS

"The CAT scan," Alex continued, shifting his leg now so it rubbed against Sam's. "Payne ordered a second one, remember? He told me the first one showed a shadow, said not to worry. Know what happens when someone tells you not to worry?"

"You worry."

"Of course. Guess I should have figured."

"Figured what?" Sam asked, liking the feeling of their knees pressed against each other.

"That something was wrong. Because of the headaches . . . the ones I was having *before* the game last night. But I was afraid, afraid of somebody telling me I couldn't play football again."

"Like the headache you had when I came to the hospital."

"It doesn't matter now. Just normal shit from playing football."

"You mean, like a concussion?"

"No. Maybe. I don't know. It's football."

"You said that already. But concussions are serious, Alex. Nobody ever examined you?"

"With the play-offs coming, I wasn't about to let them."

"So you didn't tell anyone."

"I'm telling you."

"I meant before."

"'Before' doesn't matter anymore, does it?"

Sam watched the lights of the motel sign flickering through the flimsy blind. She thought she saw an elongated dark shape projected against it, but she blinked and it was gone.

"That shadow could mean the results of the first scan were just inconclusive," Sam said. "Something wrong with the dye or the machine itself, something like that."

"What if it was something else?"

"Like what?"

"I don't know, Sam. All I know is that's when all this started, with the second CAT scan." Alex swallowed hard, fighting to cling to whatever composure he had left. But thinking it out, working the problem, took his mind off what had happened just a few hours before. At home, to his parents.

"Occam's razor . . ."

Alex formed his hands into the time-out signal. "Occam's *what*?"

"Razor. A principle postulating that the simplest answer is often, even usually, correct. That's what you're suggesting about the CT scan."

"Why couldn't you just say it that way?"

"I thought I did."

"What time is it?"

Sam checked the watch her mother had given her a few months back for her eighteenth birthday. "Almost one."

"Tomorrow, then."

"Well, today, actually."

"Sam," Alex snapped.

"All right, tomorrow."

"I've never wanted a day to end more." Alex's gaze turned downward, his bare feet kicking at the worn carpet, faded and stained in as many places as it wasn't. He rested a hand on her knee that had rubbed up against his. "And I need new clothes. I feel like I'm wearing a dead man's."

"You are, but it's not like your doctor was killed in them. Was he?" Sam asked, stiffening so much at the thought that Alex pulled his hand from her knee. She missed the feel of it immediately.

"No, but it still feels weird. I don't know why, but it does."

"We'll get clothes tomorrow."

"Then what?"

"I don't know," Sam answered, trying not to sound as scared as she was feeling again.

"You need to call your parents," Alex said suddenly. "They must be worried sick."

"I know, but I'm scared."

"Those men, the fake cops, came to my house looking for me. Any others, if there are any others, would have no reason to come looking for you."

"I can't risk a phone call giving away our location."

Alex looked at her, swallowing so hard it looked as if the air had lodged in his throat. "You should go home."

"Don't go there again."

"It's too dangerous," he said, looking down once more. "I can't ask you to stay with me."

"You didn't ask me. I volunteered and I'm not leaving you now."

"On one condition."

"Name it."

"We figure out a way for you to call your parents. Tomorrow," Alex said and ground his feet into the worn carpeting.

Sam found herself doing the same, the two of them finding a strange rhythm to the motion, seeming to work in concert.

"And I've got to get new sneakers. Dr. Payne's are killing me."

"You should try high heels," Sam told him.

"I never saw you wear high heels, never saw you, you know, dressed up."

Sam held his gaze. "Maybe you weren't looking."

"Really?"

She shrugged. "Okay, so maybe I haven't been to a lot of the dressy stuff."

"Well, prom's coming up," Alex said, seeming to brighten up a bit, embracing a brief moment of normalcy. "Let's make a pact: we get out of this, we go together."

"It's a date—er, I mean a plan."

"No," Alex corrected, "it's a date. Hey, do your parents really grow weed?" Alex asked her suddenly.

"Not the way you put it."

"How did I just put it?"

"Like it was a crime or something. But it's legal. They've got a license and everything."

Sam's parents had barely been making ends meet by packaging their own line of herbal supplements grown in gardens they tended themselves. For a long time they supplemented this by growing exotic flowers, orchids mostly, that appealed to a specific clientele. And when that proved more costly than it was worth, they began their foray into growing marijuana for a local dispensary.

Her mother approached the effort as if pot were like all the other plants she nursed lovingly from mere seedlings. Making a go at the world of weed meant growing in much larger quantities than her parents had ever taken on before, posing a challenge that left her mother perpetually exhausted and hoarse. Exhausted because of the hours it took tending and trimming such a volume of plants. Hoarse because it was the habit of Sam's mother to speak out loud to her plants, going so far as to read them children's books when they were seedlings. It took hours to manage that task within the hydroponics greenhouse that had once held exotic flowers, their luscious smell replaced by the skunk-like stench of weed. Sam wondered how much weed her parents had smoked as kids, how much they continued to smoke today, often lighting incense in an inadvertently hilarious attempt to keep their habit from her. Once when she was a sophomore they'd even sat Sam down, her father extending a joint toward her.

"We want you to try it with us first."

"But I don't smoke."

"It's safer than drinking," her mother noted.

"I don't drink, either."

"Sam?"

Alex's voice shocked her back to the reality of the present and the plight in which she may have placed her loony, ditzy parents. His hand was on her shoulder, squeezing gently, to bring her back to reality.

"Finally," he continued. "Have a nice trip wherever you went?"

"Doesn't matter. I'm back."

"I wanted to tell you that I'm sorry."

"For what?"

"Getting you involved in all this."

"I don't mind."

Spending the night in a motel room with the boy of her dreams? Not that it had happened the way she'd conjured in this fantasy or that. . . .

"I'm sorry for messing up your life," Alex was saying. "I wish you could just go home and forget this ever happened."

"Then who would I go to prom with? And what kind of friend would I be if I just left you alone like that?"

"So we're friends."

"What else do you want to call us?"

He managed a smile. "Don't give me any ideas."

In that moment, he was charming and charismatic Alex again. But the glimpse of a smile quickly faded, his eyes losing their gleam and glow.

"Just remember I'm still your tutor," Sam said, failing to get another smile out of him.

"But you're forgetting the first lesson you taught me, back to math again."

"What's that?"

"What you said to do whenever I couldn't solve a problem set in calculus or analyzable geometry. Go back to the beginning. Start there and work forward toward the answer."

"Good point, but it's *analytical* geometry."

The tension broke between them, Alex reaching out to squeeze her shoulder again, as if he'd liked it the first time. Even the lightbulbs in the sign outside seemed to catch, however briefly.

"Okay, so start at the beginning," Alex prodded.

44

PROBLEM SET

"We've got androids," Sam said, doing just as Alex suggested, "physical projections and those weird slap bracelets that worked like electronic handcuffs, holding your—"

She broke off, but it was too late.

Alex swallowed hard. "Are we talking about aliens here or something?"

"Theoretically, that doesn't make any sense."

"Theoretically? *None* of this makes any sense, theoretically or not."

"Okay—it's not even logical."

"So what are you now, Spock from *Star Trek*?"

"More like Nurse Chapel."

"Who?"

"Dr. McCoy's nurse in the original nobody ever remembers."

That seemed to pique Alex's interest. "You watched the original *Trek*?"

"Every episode maybe a million times."

"Me too," he told her.

"Really? What character do *you* see yourself as?"

"I don't know."

"Come on, Alex, it's obvious: Captain Kirk."

"I'm no Captain Kirk." He frowned.

"No, you're just captain of the football team, homecoming king, and the most popular kid in school."

Alex started kicking at the worn carpet again, the tension settling back into the room. He slid Meng Po from his right hand to his left. "I never got into all the *Trek* follow-ups, though. A few of the movies were good."

"I like the new ones," Sam told him, "the reboots. Nice to be able to go back to the beginning and start over from scratch."

"Wish I could do that." Alex sighed. "But just tonight."

"I wouldn't mind starting *everything* all over again. Not that it would matter since it would probably all turn out the same." Sam frowned too, not bothering to add how things had turned out when Heinlein's Valentine Smith had tried that.

"That's how you think of yourself?"

"Because it's the way I am."

"Not to me," Alex said, looking down.

"The ash man wanted you to go with him," Sam said, trying to hold on to this moment, whatever it meant.

"So?"

"So why? He said something about you belonging to him."

"Not exactly."

"Okay, but close. That you didn't belong where you were."

Alex thought on that, tapping his head with his knuckles. "Maybe this has something to do with me being adopted."

"I don't see what."

"My mom was apologizing for something she and my dad never told me. She said something like I deserved to know the truth. That's what the ash man must've been talking about. What else sticks out to you?" he asked

Sam, not quite looking at her, again squeezing the statue of Meng Po tight in his grasp.

"My phone not working, then working again as soon as I got away from your house."

"So they were jamming the signal or something."

"More advanced science, *really* advanced, *too* advanced."

"For us. Means it must come from somewhere else."

"So we're back to aliens again."

"I didn't think we ever left them."

"Say they are aliens, Sam. What could they possibly want from me? What's this thing the ash man thinks I have?"

"I haven't got a clue," Sam told him. "But the fact remains they knew a lot about you, an awful lot. And not just stuff you could pick up on the Internet, even though you're famous."

"I'm not famous."

"How many autographs you sign after the last game?"

"None—I was on my way to the hospital, remember?"

"I meant the game before that, Alex."

"I don't remember. A few, a lot, I guess."

"Because you're famous."

"Okay," he shrugged, "whatever you say. But the ash man's going to be back; I know he will." Alex gazed toward the room's wooden door, currently dead-bolted with an old-fashioned chain lock fastened into place as well. "And it doesn't seem like locks are about to stop him."

That thought made Alex think of his parents again. Had his mother really understood how sorry he was for throwing a fit over finding those brochures? Truth was, his grades did suck and washing out of college was a very real possibility unless he got his act in order. So maybe a fifth year wasn't such a bad idea.

If only that was all he had to worry about. . . .

He felt the emptiness again in the pit of his stomach, something seeming to scratch at his insides. He squeezed Meng Po tighter, feeling the tiny statue's ridges digging into his skin. Alex eased off and studied the impression it had made in his palm, watched it slowly fade away just like the life had faded from his mother's eyes.

It was my fault.

Because the ash man and the others had come for him. And with that thought the pangs mixed between rage and grief returned, Alex left alternately trembling and squeezing Meng Po so hard he felt the wood seem to compress in his grasp. Then he felt Sam tightening an arm around his broad shoulders, resting her head against his chest.

"And me thinking you were just my tutor. . . ."

"I am. This is a lesson."

"In what?"

"Psychology. The chapter on methods of reassurance and coping."

"Funny," he said, stroking her hair lightly, "I don't remember signing up for that course."

"Alex," he heard Sam say.

"I'm busy. Doing my psych homework."

He felt Sam ease her head off him. "What's that?"

Alex looked down to see a thin rectangular object that had dropped atop the frayed bedcovers. It had a dull black finish and looked like a piece that had broken off something bigger. Taking it in hand, though, he realized it was a flash drive, the kind you could buy practically anywhere these days. Then he looked back at Meng Po still clutched in his hand and saw the hole in its bottom, revealing the secret slot where the flash drive had been hidden and slipped out of.

"You think . . ." Sam left her thought dangling, eyes rotating between Alex and the flash drive.

He held the flash drive in one hand, Meng Po in the other. "I think it's why my mother wanted to make sure I took the statue with me. Because this may have the answers we're looking for."

SEVEN

MENG PO

The real voyage of discovery consists not in seeking new landscapes, but in having new eyes.

—MARCEL PROUST

45

MESSAGE

Raiff reached Dancer's house in Millbrae three hours after receiving the message.

THE DANCER'S IN THE LIGHT

He'd been waiting for that message for eighteen years now, expecting it to come far sooner than it did. The fact that it hadn't was testament to Dancer's adoptive parents' ability to keep the true nature of how he'd come into their lives secret from everyone, including Dancer himself. Dancer was the only hope, not just for the people of this world but also for the people back in Raiff's.

Raiff parked amid a bevy of police vehicles, both vans and cars, squeezed everywhere on the cordoned-off scene in the shadow of gaping oak and pine trees. He busied himself with a review of what he'd long committed to memory about the town, how it had grown out of a country estate built in the 1860s by one Darius Ogden Mills. The estate combined "Mills" and the Scottish word "brae" to form the town's name. Raiff recalled that Mills allowed local children to swim in three lakes situated on the estate and sell acacias to tourists passing through until his death, at which point his family began to sell off the land for development. The mansion itself remained standing until it burned down in 1954. The town was ethnically mixed, boasting a modest complement from the Asian community along with Hispanics and even immigrants hailing from the Philippines. All the bungalow-style homes on the street were quaint and roomy, if unremarkable, the Chins' looking to be one of the smaller ones on the block.

Raiff reached under the driver's seat of this week's vehicle and plucked free a wooden cigar box he'd taped there. Inside were any number of identification badges and IDs. Originally he'd carried them in doubled-over cases that fit neatly in his pocket. Now he kept lanyards under his seat too, with which to dangle the badges from his neck. Times changed and Raiff changed with them.

He needed to select the right agency cautiously, careful not to duplicate any already on scene. That ruled out local police and the sheriff's department, left him with something federal. The FBI, maybe, but he'd need a pretext for that. No matter. Local cops were inevitably deferential to law enforcement officials higher than them on the totem pole. Perhaps resentful at the outset, but normally cooperative, albeit reluctantly.

FBI it was.

Raiff looped the proper ID over his head and stepped from the car. He passed a number of uniformed cops milling outside Dancer's house, shaking their heads. A few plainclothesmen, police badges dangling from their lanyards, were smoking cigarettes. Raiff watched the wisps of smoke climbing up through the air toward the sky, where secrets abounded none of these men, and a few women, would ever comprehend. His own ID flapped against his chest and he held it steady and forward, out for inspection. It spoke for itself and he need add no words until he was inside. Climbing the steps now, approaching the door, open to let in the late night chill and help mitigate the smells of death that had been present within.

Veering right once inside brought him into the living room. The bodies of Dancer's parents had been removed, but their placement was marked clear enough by flags and blood soaked into the rug.

Lots of blood.

Clumsy work. Amateurish, but not surprising.

It was the smell Raiff noticed next, a burned odor like wires roasted by a power surge. He always put colors to smells, for some reason, and this one was dark, black, even. More bitter and corrosive the deeper he got into the room, as if it were stuck to the air by some cosmic glue. Raiff took a deeper whiff and half expected the sharp and vaguely sweet scent of adhesive to find his nostrils.

But it didn't and he surveyed the scene for the officer who was in charge, spotting a plainclothes cop with a lieutenant's badge dangling on a lanyard and coming to rest upon a stomach that protruded well over his belly.

"Hey, you," the lieutenant cop called to him, before Raiff had a chance to say anything. "Stop right there."

46

DANCER'S HOUSE

Raiff stood still and waited for the cop to reach him. He glanced about the room, still crowded with forensic techs snapping pictures, taking measurements, and collecting blood samples.

"What have we got?" Raiff asked, making sure his FBI identification was in clear view while pretending to study the lieutenant's.

Lieutenant Grimes, according to his ID, paid it only cursory regard. He had prominent cheekbones slathered with flesh that was flushed red, the rest of his face so pale that it seemed those cheeks had sucked up all the blood. Raiff wondered if he'd detected the burned odor clinging to the air. He let Grimes see him running his eyes around the toppled furniture and broken fixtures.

Grimes led him into the recesses of a corner the lamplight only grazed. Kind of place families like this put their Christmas trees.

"Home invasion is one possibility," he said.

"Give me another."

"It's too preliminary."

"That's why I'm here."

"The son of the murdered couple has been missing from the hospital for hours. Nobody's seen him."

"What was he in the hospital for?"

"Head injury."

"Oh," Raiff noted, trying to sound like this could be a major piece of the puzzle. "I hear head injuries can have strange and unusual symptoms."

"I think you're getting my drift here. And, get this, the kid's doctor was found dead too—at the hospital not long after the kid disappeared."

"You keep saying 'kid.'"

"The Chins' son, Alex," Grimes specified. "His parents dead and him missing? You do the math."

"You think the boy killed his parents." Raiff nodded.

"I think it's a possibility worth investigating, that's all."

"Looks more like a war. Two victims?"

Grimes nodded. "Husband and wife. An and Li Chin. Chinese couple."

Something was bothering Raiff about the scene but he couldn't put his finger on it yet.

"What's the FBI's interest in a home invasion?" Grimes asked him.

"Are we back to home invasion again?"

"Never left it. Just a matter of considering *all* the possibilities." Grimes hesitated uneasily. "You see it some other way?"

"If I did, you know I couldn't tell you. . . ."

"Goddamn feds," Grimes said under his breath, just loud enough for Raiff to hear.

"You didn't let me finish, Lieutenant. What if this fit the pattern of a bunch of other, similar incidents, cutting across a whole bunch of states?"

"You mean, like a ring?"

"Or a very busy gang."

"And very thorough, Agent. Forensics tells me the only prints they've been able to make so far are the victims', and two others'."

"What else do you know about the Chins' son?" Raiff asked, getting to the point at last.

"Besides he's missing, the fact that he's some kind of high school football star. Ended up in the hospital after a vicious collision last night. A day later his doctor's dead, he comes home and, boom! his parents are dead too."

Raiff suddenly realized what had been bothering him about the room. All this damage, all this chaos, but where were all the shards, the broken pieces? It looked like someone had cleaned the place up in a manner painstaking enough to leave enough residue behind not to arouse suspicion in the cops. But that wouldn't satisfy someone with a better inclination of who, or what, had killed An and Li Chin.

They wouldn't have needed to come here if they'd found Dancer in the hospital, Raiff thought, meaning he had surprised them here. Him and someone else, if the fingerprints were to be believed. The Chins' killers didn't leave fingerprints because they didn't have any. And if Dancer had tangled with one of the Shadows, there wouldn't be any residue of that, either, because the Shadow had never really been here, at least not physically.

It must've been a hell of a fight. Raiff found himself very impressed by this boy he'd never met and seen only in pictures. It was important to keep his distance, do nothing that might risk exposure.

THE DANCER'S IN THE LIGHT

But where was he now?

"Your turn," Grimes was saying, repeating himself after Raiff had ignored him. "A dead doctor, two dead parents, and a missing kid. Run the numbers for me, the way you see them."

Raiff doubted Grimes wanted to hear the truth: that his entire world was currently hanging in the balance and a missing boy was the only chance it had to hold on.

"I'll let you know," Raiff told him, turning to retrace his steps out of the house.

"Hey," Grimes called, before he reached the door.

Halfway there, Raiff swung back toward him.

"Tell the other guy I didn't appreciate his attitude."

Raiff stopped in his tracks, something seeming to prickle against his spine. "What other guy?" he asked.

47

KNOCK WOOD

Rathman approached the clerk behind the counter of the Monterey Motor Inn, disgusted by the stench of body odor rising off the man so entrenched in a comic book that he didn't even notice his presence.

"Ding-ding," Rathman said, instead of ringing the flimsy bell.

A ceramic figure, being used as a paperweight to keep a stack of registration forms from blowing away every time the door opened, sat next to it. A placard reading KNOCK WOOD was strung across the male figure's chest while his hands were frozen over what was clearly a boner in his pants, which had a chip at belt level.

"You want a room?" the clerk asked, frowning over the interruption.

"Not why I'm here."

"We only take cash."

"That's okay," Rathman nodded, snatching the comic book from his grasp so quickly, the clerk was left grasping air, "because I'm not staying. I'm here to ask you a few questions about some recent guests of yours. A boy and a girl. Would've checked in, er, maybe four, five hours ago."

"Hell, no. I don't rent to anyone under the age of eighteen."

"One of those kids belongs to my employer. He'd be most grateful for your assistance," Rathman said, and slid a twenty-dollar bill across the counter.

The clerk stuffed it in the pocket of his white button-down shirt, which was stained yellow under his arms. "What do you mean by 'belongs'?"

"The money means I get to ask the questions."

"For twenty bucks, no kids checked in tonight."

"How much is a room?"

"Forty."

Rathman slid another twenty across the counter.

"But information's more, say, a hundred."

Rathman made it look like he was going for his pocket again, then grabbed hold of the KNOCK WOOD paperweight in his free hand instead. He brought it down hard enough on the back of the clerk's ink-stained hand to shatter the ceramic figure at the base. Then, instead of pulling it back up, he pressed the jagged shards that began where the figure's feet had been into the clerk's flesh.

"You were saying?"

The clerk was gasping for breath, his now broken hand trembling horribly as he fought to pull free.

"Two kids, high school age, checked in here earlier, yes?"

The clerk nodded.

Rathman pulled a photo of Alex Chin from his jacket pocket. It hadn't been hard to find one, since various shots of the boy were all over the Internet. It was the same picture he'd flashed to a waitress at a nearby diner just off the Pacific Coast Highway who'd recognized the boy and told Rathman he'd been in there earlier along with a girl who looked about his same age.

Which made her a bit too old for him. His tastes ran younger, accounting in large part for the unceremonious end to his military career. Army brass didn't grasp the meaning of fringe benefits and it was only Afghanistan. Rathman was truly shocked anybody cared. No mention of this, of course, appeared anywhere in his record, the army wanting to spare itself the embarrassment. The man who'd turned him in was buried in Arlington National Cemetery now, though Rathman guessed the funeral had featured a closed casket. He also guessed Marsh wouldn't have given a shit, even if he had known. Maybe he did.

"This is the boy, yes?" he continued, enjoying the pain the clerk was in and pressing the jagged bottom of KNOCK WOOD deeper into his skin to bring on more.

The clerk gasped, his knees almost buckling. He managed to nod again, still breathing hard with thick rivulets of sweat now dripping down his face like a bad paint job.

Rathman looked out the office window toward the parking lot where his team had gathered. He preferred handling interrogations alone. More fun that way.

"What room are they in?"

"They're gone," the clerk managed, just barely. "Checked out. Asked for directions before they left."

Rathman pushed the jagged edge in just a bit deeper. "To where?"

48

FLASH DRIVE

The motel clerk had smirked when they turned in their key so fast, figuring whatever business they'd come to the Monterey Motor Inn to do was done.

"We might be back," Sam offered.

"Sure."

"I mean it."

The clerk was back in his comic book, Coke-bottle glasses hiding him from the rest of the world. "Whatever you say."

"Just hold on to the key," Alex added.

The clerk nodded, flipped the page.

"Oh, and, hey," Alex continued, "where's the nearest FedEx Office located?"

The FedEx Office they ended up at was located in Santa Cruz off Route 1 on Front Street near the University of California at Santa Cruz. It featured a sign in the window that read NOW OPEN TWENTY-FOUR HOURS and charged twenty dollars an hour to rent a computer, one hour minimum, and they accepted cash. Sam forked over the cash again, without protest. She always carried plenty of it on her because her parents hated credit cards, in large part because their credit history made it hard for them to qualify for decent ones.

"I'll pay you back," Alex told her, and dropped into the chair in front of the computer.

This time of night only a single clerk was on duty and, other than him and Sam, there were only two other people in the store, both of them making copies. Besides the odorous residue left behind by his chair's last occupant, Alex also smelled overheated machine parts from the pair of copiers still spitting out pages the clerk was busy prepping to be bound. He thought he smelled hot plastic in the air too, something like when you drop a grocery bag into a campfire and feel your eyes burn if you stray too close to the smoke.

Side effect of getting his bell rung, maybe, Alex thought, wondering why everything seemed to have a smell to it all of a sudden. Maybe that's what the mysterious CT scan had revealed, his olfactory nerves growing like weeds inside his skull, accounting for his newfound skill.

"What?" Samantha asked him.

"I didn't say anything."

"Yes, you did. But you were mumbling."

"Just thinking out loud, I guess."

Be nice if I knew what I said, though.

"You're doing it again."

Alex looked away from her.

"We haven't talked about what happened in the hospital yet," Sam said.

"Yes, we did."

"Not everything. You started to tell me about that second CT scan, then you stopped."

Alex took the flash drive from his pocket, not in the mood to describe what had happened while he lay on the scanner table. "The machine went crazy. Now, could you watch the front of the store? Just in case."

He watched Sam glance at the flash drive, understanding. "Sure."

"Thanks."

As she moved away, Alex eased the drive into the USB port and waited for the drive's icon to appear on the screen. He didn't want Sam seeing whatever his mother had left for him on the flash drive, at least not before he did. He glanced toward her standing by the front door, pretending to study some magazine she'd found, and when he looked back at the rented computer's screen the drive's icon had appeared:

FOR MY SON

That's how it was labeled, nothing more. *For my son* . . . Such simple words belying a far more complex story that had led to tonight's maelstrom of violence, still cushioned by the haze of shock. But the haze was receding now, the reality setting in as sharply as the scents Alex grabbed out of the air.

Alex clicked on the icon, revealing a collection of labeled files contained on the drive from which to choose. Their titles banged up against each other in his head, save for one that captured his eye and held it:

ORIGINS

Alex positioned the mouse over that file and clicked. The screen flashed dark, then light again, and Alex found himself staring at his mother as captured by her cell phone in a kind of video selfie.

He watched the screen jitter as she laid the phone down, atop the fireplace mantel, and backed off enough for the camera to capture her, just as Alex had taught her to do. Judging by the length of her hair and bruise on her forehead from where she'd walked into a door, he guessed she'd recorded the video perhaps three months before, late summer, maybe.

"Hello, my son," greeted An Chin, trying for a smile.

Alex turned down the computer's volume so only he could hear his mother's words.

49

ORIGINS

There is no easy way to tell this tale, so I will start at the beginning, before you were brought into our lives.

America was the dream of both your father and I and we worked for years to attain it, ultimately immigrating with little more than the money in our pockets after having our funds bled dry by the corruption it took to get out of China. We would settle down in this land of so much promise and build a family. Try as we may, though, no family came. Doctors explained the problem lay with me; apparently, a childhood fever had done unseen damage to my insides. Your father put up a brave face, not wanting to blame me, but I knew how sick with disappointment he was. When the doctors failed to help us, we sought outlets in San Francisco that offered traditional Chinese medicine, but this proved no more fruitful than traditional medicine.

Then, when neither prayers nor remedies provided the answer, fate intervened and smiled upon us.

By bringing us you, Alex.

You've heard me talk about Laboratory Z to your father, I know you have. I never really knew what went on there. I didn't clean that part of the complex in San Ramon; nobody on the menial staff did, all of us lacking the proper security clearance to even enter that section of the facility. As a maid, though, I kind of melted into the scenery, becoming no different in my dark blue uniform than the artistic tapestries that adorned the walls. I was part of the woodwork and scientists in lab coats whose name tags featured bar codes instead of names spoke without reservation in my presence. Enough for me to discern that something very big indeed was happening here.

In Laboratory Z.

I was working outside the secure entrance to the lab the day fate brought you to me, when a shrill emergency alarm sounded. Drills were hardly unusual, and I assumed this to be merely another until a flood of personnel stampeded past me dragging panic behind them. The open doors let a peculiar smell emerge in their wake. It made my nose feel hot, actually hot, when it reached me. Something metallic and coppery, a combination of something left burning on a stove and spilled blood. Amid the steady flash of the emergency lighting, I heard cries and screams, plaintive wails coming from inside the laboratory.

Instinct took over and I dashed inside into a noxious white mist that burned my eyes. I took it to be some sort of fire suppressant at first, then wasn't so sure. It didn't seem to be coming from anywhere in particular, just seemed like, well, air. As if someone had taken a spray can to that air and painted it. Darker in some places than others, as if it were still drying.

Everyone who'd been inside the lab must have evacuated and I was struck by the awful fear I'd lost my way in the gray air, when I heard something that made no sense:

A baby crying.

I stopped and listened some more, trying to pinpoint

the sound. The noxious odor grew thicker the deeper I ventured into Laboratory Z, intensified the more I sank into a white, dewy mist that felt hot and cold at the same time. Sparks flared, illuminating the semblance of a path for me. Cries and screams sounded, seeming to come from beyond a wall of super-thick glass that was fracturing into a spiderweb pattern even as I neared it. I caught glimpses of motion beyond that glass where the mist thickened the air to a soup-like consistency that formed a curtain over the world beyond.

I did my best to ignore whatever awful toxic thing was transpiring inside that mist, not wanting to picture the product of the leak, explosion, accidental release, or whatever had spawned the disaster. I sucked in mouthfuls of the stench-riddled mist, expecting it to be like smoke when it was more like, well, nothing but stained air, neither hot nor cold. I kept on toward the crying, a whirring sound reaching me then that reminded me of the noise an amusement park ride makes when it reaches the crescendo of its pace.

Instinct, a woman's, drove me deeper inside whatever the mist contained. Tracing a line against the fracturing glass when the thick blanket finally stole my vision, tracing it to the sound of the baby. It stopped crying as I neared where it must have lay.

Please don't stop, I willed, cry so I may find you. . . .

And, as if complying with my unspoken command, the cries started anew and I saw a disembodied shape emerge, a pair of arms with the rest of whoever they belonged to hidden by the mist. The crying, loud enough to stun my ears now, was coming from those arms because, I saw, they were holding a baby, extending it out toward me.

"Take him!" a voice screeched. "Get him out of here!"

I didn't question, didn't argue, just took the infant in my own arms and drew him tight against my chest protectively to shield him from whatever the mist might be carrying.

"Should I . . . ," I started.

But the arms were gone and the shape beyond them was gone too, pulled back inside the thicker portion of the mist. So I turned and did my best to retrace my route from the lab I realized was growing hotter by the second. I felt trapped inside a steam oven until my route got me back to the doorway and outside into the cool, clean air. I took a deep breath, realizing only then I'd been holding it the last stretch of the way that had seen me tuck the infant inside my regulation jacket to further shield him.

Maybe I would've still turned the child over once I reached the triaged chaos of the parking lot. Halfway across the asphalt, though, I was struck by a shock wave equal parts hot and cold that swallowed me up and coughed me out. I felt airborne but when I looked down, my feet had never actually left the concrete, which had cracked underfoot like thin glass. Everyone around me was rushing, the wail of sirens sounding intermittently in my head as if someone was turning them off and then on again.

There was no one to hand the baby I'd rescued to, so I held fast to him, charging through the parking lot I now saw was strewn with cars missing all their window and windshield glass. My own car was parked in a lot reserved for lower-level employees and my breath had long deserted me by the time I reached it, gasping for air with the burned-wire stench stuck in my nostrils that felt as if they'd been zapped by some medical freezing agent.

I got my door open and climbed inside my car with

you nestled in my lap. You'd stopped crying, seemed to be smiling, your eyes meeting mine.

I fell in love in that moment and knew I could never part with you. You were mine and your father's; fate had willed it so. Where the herbs had failed us, destiny had intervened and gave us what we wanted more than anything.

Gave us you, Alex.

50

THE DANCER

Alex realized his eyes hurt; his head too. He'd been staring so intensely at the screen that his neck had knotted. It cracked audibly when he stretched, unable to resist returning his eyes to the screen. His mother's story had brought her back to him during the course of those moments. Alex felt he was with her in Laboratory Z, witnessing her brave actions as they unfolded. Rescuing the baby fate had not allowed her to have with his father.

Both gone now.

And Alex was starting to realize why, the pieces falling together. His eyes had misted up. His lips were trembling and he suddenly felt very cold. He sat in silence, the world narrowed to the scope of the computer and no more.

But that was enough.

Who am I? What am I?

Thus far, the flash drive had offered more questions than answers. Something either terrible or wonderful, maybe both, had been going on inside Laboratory Z. On the day of his rescue, the day of the explosion and fire, his mother had been unable to provide much detail as to the cause.

And there were so many secrets contained in his mother's words. Except his family was gone. Every other relative he had lived in China, and besides an occasional e-mail and rare Skype call, the Chins had maintained no contact with any of them. They were, after all, Americanized and likely thought less of by the folks back home.

So who was the person who'd thrust him at An Chin through the thick mist that had enveloped the lab?

It might have been an obvious question, but no obvious answer was in the offing. Someone trying to protect baby Alex seemed the soundest explanation, but that didn't explain how baby Alex had gotten there or if he was somehow connected to Laboratory Z's ultimate destruction.

Alex felt the rigors of all this thinking making his head throb again, the shards of pain that seemed to radiate out from inside his skull.

I've got a football game to play Friday night. . . .

He tried to distract himself with that thought, but it only made the pain worse. The throbs lasted longer this time, resonating like a dull echo banging up against the sides of his skull. He couldn't bear to listen and look anymore at his mother for now and decided to try one of the other files, focusing on one labeled PICTURES.

Alex opened the file and clicked on the first photo, watched it sharpen on the screen before him.

"Sam," he called, toward the front of the FedEx office, "you need to see this."

51

PING

Rathman had the big SUV's driver cross up and down the street a few times, looking for any changes in the parking lot that fronted the FedEx Office. In his experience, variance was the indicator that set alarm bells ringing in his head more than any other. Two or three cars appearing where there had been none just moments before. So the first order of business, bred by that experience as well as instinct, was to make sure the scene was stable, with no unexpected threat that might catch his team unprepared and waylay their plan.

Plan . . .

Right now he didn't have one. He needed to get a lock on the position of the targets first. Confined spaces like this could be tricky. Too easy for bystanders to get in the way and too easy for witnesses to get a good look at the proceedings. So Rathman's team would go in shooting. Nothing sent potential witnesses dropping for cover and eliminated their seeing what they should not more than gunfire, no matter where it was aimed. His men would shoot upward initially, take out some lights, turn chunks of the cheap drop ceiling to particleboard rain to further discourage those hugging the floor with heads covered up.

This was the place to which the desk clerk had provided directions to his targets. That's what had brought him here, but the rest of the night, his first exposure to the reach and power of Langston Marsh stuck in his mind more.

"Something amiss," in Marsh's words, referred to a "ping" his quantum computer had come up with. The unseen machine was like a technological insomniac, forever scanning police frequencies, wire services, cellular telephone calls, e-mails, and a host of other sources for incidents that stood out for reasons that rendered them inexplicable. Crimes, mostly, perhaps indicative of Marsh's Zarim targets behaving in desperate fashion. Emerging from their anonymity because pursuit was closing in, choice bled out of their lives.

Rathman couldn't say if he entirely believed the man's spiel about the aliens he was committed to exterminating, because he didn't care. The man was giving him free license to do what he did best: inflict pain and kill, not necessarily in that order.

According to Marsh, his supercomputer had pinged a crime in a suburb of San Francisco, something the police were calling a home invasion. But the computer had also found that the dead couple's son was missing from a hospital and a doctor there was dead as well.

Connections, Marsh had explained. His computer was an expert at making them.

The computer was expert at something else as well, that being the capability to process incoming information from over ten million security cameras scattered across the country. One of those ten million had provided the picture of Alex Chin climbing into a canary-yellow Volkswagen Beetle not far from the hospital he'd fled. The driver's face was grainy, mostly obscured, and barely clear enough for Rathman to be certain it was a girl, likely the same girl the motel clerk had told him was with Alex Chin now.

By the time Rathman had reached San Francisco, the computer had found six more instances of the Volkswagen being recorded by security cameras. The last one came at that diner just off the PCH, where the waitress had directed him to the motel. Now that motel's smelly, comic book–reading clerk lay dead behind the counter. Police would think he'd slipped on the floor and broken his neck because that's the way Rathman had made it look after the clerk had provided this address. His death was of no consequence at all, though hopefully the investigation wouldn't make too much about the damage done to the back of his hand and the broken KNOCK WOOD statue Marsh had dumped in the trash before leaving.

There was no canary-yellow Beetle in the FedEx Office's parking lot, but his target and the car's owner could easily have stashed it out of sight somewhere nearby.

"All right," he told the driver, as the big SUV started back down the street again, "pull into the lot and park in the far corner, facing the FedEx Office."

52

CONFESSION

Alex waited for Sam to join him before clicking on the first icon contained in the pictures file. The screen seemed to darken briefly before a grainy photograph took shape.

It was a baby picture, an infant wrapped in a blanket atop a taupe-colored couch. Alex recognized the couch from other pictures he'd seen of his parents' first apartment after they came to America to pursue their dream.

This must have been his first baby picture, snapped as soon as An got him home to the apartment. The other icons offered more of the same, charting his early growth. Stereotypical shots, the kind every family stockpiles.

Only Alex had never seen them before. His parents had always told him all his baby pictures had been lost in the move from the apartment to the Millbrae home where he had grown up.

And just hours before had watched his parents die.

Alex felt himself choking up again, his insides tightening, his throat clogging. He felt Sam stroking his back, trying to comfort him, realized he was sobbing. Then cleared his throat, made himself refocus.

"This is why," he said out loud.

"Why what?" Sam posed tentatively.

"No baby pictures, nothing of me until I was, like,

four or five." He turned from the screen to look at her, words forming with his thoughts. "Because they were evidence of what my mother had done."

"What'd she do?"

"She saved my life. Rescued me from a fire," he said, leaving things there.

"So what's the problem?"

"Let's find out," Alex said, and clicked on his mother's frozen image to pick up the story An Chin had left for him inside Meng Po.

There is little more I can tell you about Laboratory Z.

The media, of course, was filled with news of the strange explosion at the lab. As is customary, people talked of nothing but it for days and weeks and then it, like all else, became old news. There were all kinds of stories and rumors, investigative reports about it being some secret installation probing travel between dimensions, wormholes, teleportation, and all kinds of things nobody really believed were real. Stuff for crackpots and conspiracy theorists.

But maybe not so crazy, after all.

Meanwhile, your father and I waited in fear. Waited for someone to come and take you away. Waited for a story about a missing baby. Someone's tragedy that had become our joy. But no such thing was ever reported and no knock ever fell on our door.

Your father had a friend—an old Chinese man—who was shady in a good way. He'd spent most of his life arranging adoptions for Chinese babies by American parents. He managed to get us all the legal papers for you. As far as the world knew, we had adopted you legally.

All the paperwork was in order, down to the day and time of your birth and signature of a fake birth mother relinquishing all claims to custody.

The documents made me wonder about your real mother. Why she never came back for you, what she could have possibly been doing in Laboratory Z. I considered many explanations and rejected them all. None made any sense, but I didn't care because I had you. That was all that mattered. Sometimes fate must be accepted and not questioned.

But the passage of time brought more questions. Initial reports indicated three bodies had been recovered from Laboratory Z. Then it was reported that all personnel who worked for the company had gotten out safely. A major discrepancy until the newspaper and television corrected their original story, saying no bodies had been found inside Laboratory Z at all.

Your father and I were frightened by this, but also elated, since not one of the reports mentioned anything about a baby. You were ours and nobody was coming to take you away.

Still we worried, every day and night we worried. We feared every knock on the door or ring of the doorbell. We were scared every time the phone rang or when a stranger cast us too long a stare. That happened a lot and we had to remind ourselves that we were a Chinese couple with an American baby. Of course people stared. We learned to just smile at them like nothing was wrong.

Because it wasn't.

Until we felt safe enough to take you to a doctor a few weeks later. A kindly Chinese pediatrician on the verge of retirement who'd made his life here just as we had. Even though all the paperwork pertaining to your

"adoption" was in order, he seemed suspicious almost
from the first moment we brought you into his office.
And that was before he had reason to be, before—

The computer timed out with a *ping*, the screen freezing.

"I'll buy us some more time," Sam said, starting to
stand.

Alex restrained her with a hand to her forearm.
"Maybe you shouldn't. We've been here too long. Maybe
we should just go."

"Alex—"

"And we may need the cash later, right?"

"Alex—"

"We already learned what we needed to. The rest, this
stuff with the doctor, can wait until we get more settled,
figure stuff out."

"You need to know, Alex," Sam said, after he'd finished. "*We* need to figure out why all this is happening."
She glanced down at the screen. "Let me buy us some
more time on the computer."

He nodded, let go of her arm.

Sam slid away, reluctant to leave him, even for a moment. Leave him staring at his mother on the screen.

And that was before he had reason to be, before—

53

WILD CARD

What other guy?

Raiff didn't recognize the man from the description Lieutenant Grimes had provided.

"He was big," Grimes had said.

"What else?"

"Bald?"

"That it?"

"All you feds look the same to me."

Raiff didn't need to know any more than that to know it was bad. His real enemy never announced themselves that way. That meant another Tracker team, led by Big Bald, had found their way to Dancer's house. On his trail now for sure. Which meant he had two problems to contend with instead of one, making his task simple:

He needed to find Dancer before either of the other parties did, either Langston Marsh's Trackers or the androids the boy must have somehow overcome before fleeing his house, before he could be pinned with the blame for the murder of his parents. Hard to say which was more dangerous at this point.

I should've been closer, in position to move preemptively.

But he'd come to fear that his mere presence in Dancer's vicinity could place the boy in more danger, not less. In the absence of protocol, he'd determined that keeping his distance and waiting for word from the Watchers to be the most secure strategy to maintain. Imagine if the Trackers happened to find Dancer when they came looking for him.

All these years of quiet had erupted in this. Like the contents of a clogged drain bursting upward once plunged.

Raiff had made himself learn patience over the years, grown accustomed to a lifestyle off anything remotely resembling a grid. But this kind of frustration was an entirely new sensation and it was chewing away at him.

Where had Big Bald gone after leaving Dancer's house?

Raiff drove around aimlessly as if Big Bald might pop up out of nowhere at any moment. He wouldn't be alone, either; he'd be accompanied by a team likely larger and more proficient than the one Raiff had dispensed with earlier in the night. The incident report would've alerted them and they'd likely left Dancer's house with a reasonably clear destination in mind.

While Raiff had nothing. All he could do was either drive or park and wait for a text message from a Watcher telling him where Dancer could be found. And even then everything would depend on him getting there ahead of Big Bald.

Everything.

Raiff pulled into a McDonald's, the interior restaurant closed but the drive-through advertised on the sign as being open until 3:00 a.m. He found a darkened corner to pull into. The funds that supported him wouldn't last forever, but they'd last long enough. His native world was rich in precious metals, including gold to the point where it was less valued there than here. Decades before, centuries, for all Raiff knew, stores of gold had been brought over and hidden away in anticipation of these times coming at last.

Whenever he ran low on funds, Raiff need only collect some of that gold, never more than necessary, and exchange it for cash. He bought old-model used cars always from private sellers and drove them until they didn't drive anymore. The identity he'd procured was ironclad, but still precluded an actual residence or owning anything that left a trail. He had a single credit card in the name he'd assumed, necessary in order to fly or rent a car, and of all his documents the California state driver's license had been the easiest to obtain.

He lived for his mission, and his mission was to protect Dancer, above and beyond anything else. If and when Raiff was needed, he had full operational authority. Anything within his discretion was permissible.

But discretion was pointless until he located Dancer.

The real problem here was Langston Marsh and his Tracker teams. They were the wild card, the factor never considered prior to Raiff's dispatch because they hadn't come into existence yet and thus were a presence that could not possibly be accounted for. Protecting Dancer against those hunting the boy was one thing. Protecting himself against those who were hunting their very kind, something else again.

No matter how much the Trackers had come to dictate his actions and movements, though, he had to accept their presence in full awareness that the threat they posed was miniscule compared to the threat looming over this planet. Without Dancer, Earth's fall would be inevitable. Few things in Raiff's estimation bore such certainty, or any certainty at all. But that was one of them.

His phone beeped with an incoming text message
from a Watcher, the bright translucent letters piercing
the spill of the parking lot's darkness.

FOUND DANCER. LOCATION FOLLOWS.

54

DIAGNOSIS

"I've got the code," Sam said, retaking the seat next to Alex.

When his eyes remained rooted on the screen, she leaned across and typed in the access code another twenty dollars had bought her. Instantly, the screen jumped back to life, Alex regarding her briefly before returning his attention to his mother.

—until the results of the blood tests came back and Dr. Chu asked us to come back in so he could take another sample. I hated watching him do it, sticking that needle in your arm and filling one vial and then another. He wouldn't tell me why he needed the tests repeated but I feared the worst.

You were sick, with some awful illness certain to take you from us. Why else would someone have abandoned you the way they did? It all made sense now. A monstrous act for a parent to abandon a child, no matter how sick, especially when your father and I wanted one so badly and never could have a child.

But we had you and that was enough. I held you while Dr. Chu siphoned off the blood he needed, swearing I'd always love you no matter what. Even if always was only another week or a month. I prepared myself for the inevitable, for learning the name of whatever disease you'd been born with.

Except it didn't have a name; it wasn't even a disease. The results of the second test came back and Dr. Chu wanted to do a third. I wouldn't let him until he explained why. He showed me the first two blood tests, identical in all respects, with the results all out of whack. Numbers wildly askew to the point where they made no sense. White counts, red counts, T cells, liver enzymes, kidney function—nothing was right.

There must be a mistake, I told him, even as I knew there couldn't be, not two times in a row.

It's impossible, Dr. Chu said, because if these numbers are correct, then your baby couldn't possibly be alive.

But you were, at least for now. Miracles happen, don't they, and the world is held together by fate. Fate dictated that I find you and fate dictated you would survive no matter what the numbers said.

But even miracles have their limits, and I resolved not to rely only on them. I scoured San Francisco for Chinese herbalists, practitioners of the most ancient medicine known to man. None of them would treat an infant. One, a mostly blind man, said yes, but he needed to examine you first, needed to know you by touch.

So I lifted you out of your stroller and placed you in his withered arms with scars from the years he'd spent in a Chinese prison. He ran his fingers over your face, your head, your chest, your arms and legs. I watched him start to quiver, then shake. I barely was able to take you from his grasp before he slammed backward against the wall, looking to be in the throes of some kind of seizure.

No! he spat out. No! Leave, you must leave!

In that moment I met his eyes and I knew he could

see. Impossible, I know, but something had happened. Touching you had triggered something so deep inside him that his sight returned. But then, just as quickly, his gaze hazed over and he slumped down the wall to the floor, pale with shock. I put you back in the stroller and tried to help him but he wouldn't let me. Just pushed me away, screaming in some Chinese dialect I didn't recognize. To this day I don't know what he was saying but I know he was scared, terrified.

I bundled you back in the car and drove straight to Dr. Chu. Night had fallen and he was just closing up his office. I blocked his way, wouldn't let him pass until he told me the truth. I pressed him, left him no choice.

We went back inside, into his office. He only turned on a single light, kept glancing down at you in the stroller, his eyes not terrified like the old blind man's, but wary and uncertain. The results of the third test mirrored the first two. Identical again, leading Dr. Chu to a conclusion that defied his Harvard education and fifty years of medical experience.

Your son is not dead, but he should be, he told me. There can only be one explanation for this. Even if it makes no sense, it's all we're left with. . . .

You're not human, Alex.

55

BLINDS

Rathman's team had the FedEx Office surrounded, all exits covered. He'd been viewing the store's interior through his Brunton Eterna ELO Highpower binoculars ever since arriving fifteen minutes ago. At just thirty-two ounces they delivered a crisp, clear image thanks to a bright fifty-one-millimeter objective and BaK-4 prism glass with fully multicoated lenses. But such high-tech lenses had trouble penetrating even the thin blinds that had been drawn over the store's windows. Maybe they were there all the time, to shut out the harsh afternoon sun. Rathman didn't know, didn't care.

A young man and woman sat side by side behind one of the computers rented by the hour. Used to be hotel rooms were sold like that. Now computers were, cars too. The world had come a long way.

Or maybe not.

Even when Rathman caught a head-on look at the young man and woman, the flimsy blinds obscured their faces just enough to prevent positive identification of his targets.

Well, mostly.

This was the store to which the now deceased motel clerk had provided directions. A young man and young woman matching the descriptions of Alex Chin and the young woman driving the Volkswagen were inside. The only thing that made Rathman uneasy from a planning perspective was the absence of the Volkswagen from the parking lot. It must be parked out of sight somewhere, something that made perfect sense.

What didn't make sense was whatever had transpired in the boy's house.

Marsh had provided no details on the subject. His quantum computer had pinged, because the circumstances of the Chins' murders, coupled with their son gone missing from a hospital where his doctor had been killed, raised flags. But the machine couldn't tell Rathman what those flags were.

He needed Alex Chin to tell him that. Now, while the scene was contained and under his control.

His phone rang.

56

THE IMPOSSIBLE

You're not human, Alex. . . .

Alex and Sam continued to stare at the screen, at An Chin's frozen image.

Her words made no sense and perfect sense at the same time.

"Just like the CAT scan," Alex muttered.

"What? Huh?"

"The doctor ordered another one, because he must've seen something that made no sense, either—that shadow, maybe more. Just like the blood tests Dr. Chu kept doing. Oh, man . . ."

Alex dropped his face into his hands, covering it as if everything might be different as soon as he took them away. But the words, his mother's message, wasn't about to change.

You're not human, Alex.

"Guess I'm an illegal," he tried to joke. "The mother of all illegal aliens. Jesus Christ, what does it all mean?"

He started the video running again, hoping his mother would tell him.

That's why we never let you have another blood test. Your father and I made up the excuse that our Bud-

dhist religion forbade it. Never an X-ray, either, because we didn't know what that might show. Your father and I should have known better than to let you play football. But you loved the game so much and were so good at it. We wanted you to fit in, to blend. Bad enough you were the English son of Chinese parents, but if those Chinese meddled in your life it would be even worse. We wanted you to be happy. That's all we ever wanted.

We never ceased to acknowledge that you were different and we didn't care. You are our son and you'll always be our son, no matter what the DNA says. You wouldn't have been ours if you were human, would you? So what was the difference?

You need to know that Dr. Chu's words made us love you no less. It made us love you even more, in fact. Because you were truly a gift, a miracle, given us by some cosmic force we could never purport to comprehend. The heavens have a strange way of doing things sometimes, and if they heard my prayers and delivered you to us, who were we to think different of you because your blood was different?

But you need to hear what Dr. Chu said. . . .

Alex swiped the tears from his face with a sleeve and sniffled. All his parents had done for him, never stopped loving him even after learning he wasn't human. And his last memory, the thing he would always take away, would be an argument.

And yet, and yet . . .

Who am I?

The most clichéd question ever posed, but so appropriate right now because Alex had absolutely no idea.

"Alex," Sam prodded, fidgeting in her chair. "We've been here too long. We need to hurry."

So he turned back to the screen and listened to his mother again.

57

DR. CHU

He was a saintly man with hair the color of birch bark. An immigrant who'd earned his medical degree and settled amid his familiar native populace clustered around the San Francisco area. That sense of comfort providing the strongest rationale for your father and I to remain in the area even after slowly coming to grips with the truth about you. At least here we'd be able to blend in better; then again, being the Chinese parents of a Caucasian child would stand out anywhere we went.

The day of the "explanation," as I would come to call it, or jiěshì, in Chinese, Dr. Chu asked me to return with your father after office hours. The fog had rolled in off the bay, a perfect complement for the thoughts clouding my mind. I had prepared myself to make a stand, to argue at wits' end for a rational explanation for what we were facing here. Chinese history was full of mysticism, jam-packed with it, but Dr. Chu's claims about you stretched way, way beyond that into a new scientific realm that challenged the very nature of reality as it was currently perceived.

Because if you really weren't human, then what were you?

I clutched your father's hand as we walked up from the parking lot through the fog, with you tucked into your car seat, sleeping soundly. My mind suddenly felt cluttered with thoughts of Laboratory Z. That was the missing piece, whatever the mysterious experiments being conducted there had unleashed, what doorways they had opened. I had never been told a thing about it. As I was part of the maintenance staff, though, people talked around me like I wasn't even there. I melted into the scenery and they spoke in my presence as if I were no more than a wall or a chair. Only one word that made any sense, recalled from half-heard conversations:

Doorways.

Whatever that meant. I have no more idea today than I did eighteen years ago. And from the moment I found you, all that seemed inconsequential. Bringing you home was day one in the rest of my life, all that came before dissipating into memories that were as obscure as any other sight gleaned through the fog wafting over Dr. Chu's office.

He was waiting at the door when we arrived, drawing it open before your father could even ring the bell. The waiting room beyond was empty, a single table lamp illuminating a colorfully painted wall dominated by smiling animal figures with tools in their hands.

"Come," he said, and led us into his office. Closing the door, even though no one else was about. "I know this is hard for you."

He moved behind his desk, but stopped short of taking the chair set there. Your father and I took the matching chairs set before the desk, your car seat resting between us where I could stretch a hand down to gently rock you. I looked down at your sleeping form, feeling uneasy about continuing in your presence, as if not wanting you to hear what Dr. Chu had to say. Might you somehow be able to? I wondered, lapsing into a brief moment where I actually felt uncomfortable around my son.

Stop it! *I scolded myself.*

"When blood test results come back," Dr. Chu contin-ued, "the lab highlights anything anomalous in red." Adding, "Here are Alex's results," as he handed stapled sheets of paper to both your father and me.

Everything, every single line item, was in red. Your readings on the left with the normal baseline reading variances on the right.

"Now," Dr. Chu resumed, as your father mouthed the lab results silently to himself, "the first thing to keep in mind is that functionally, Alex is totally normal."

"What does that mean?" your father asked. "'Normal.'"

"His heartbeat is strong and sound. His lung function is perfect. All his muscle reactions and reflex coordina-tion is textbook. In all those respects, he is a perfectly healthy baby."

"Those respects," I repeated.

Dr. Chu leaned over his desk, sighing deeply as he inter-laced his fingers on the blotter just short of an embossed placard that read TRUST ME . . . I'M A DOCTOR. *"In other respects," he continued, "there are factors the tests revealed that I can make no sense out of, because they don't make any sense. It's why I ordered a new batch of tests, on the chance that the samples I took had been somehow corrupted the first and second times. But the results were the same, identical."*

The results of all those tests Dr. Chu did are here in a file. We never had any more bloodwork done. And the whole time, while you grew up, you know what your father and I worried about the most?

You getting sick.

Dr. Chu never said as much, but it was pretty clear your immune system didn't work like ours, at least not exactly. The first time you caught a simple cold, we were afraid it might kill you. But you hardly ever got sick at all, and never seriously so. I guess the germs and viruses could never find a home inside you because your metabolism worked so different. Not better or worse—just different.

I know what you're thinking right now, my son, because I'm thinking the same thing.

So many questions.

You ask one and a hundred others pour out, each leading to the next. What's your life expectancy? Will there be any changes as you age? I've avoided talking about puberty here for obvious reasons, but your father and I were terrified when it struck you. For how could we know if growing more body hair and your voice changing would be all of it? Maybe something far more dramatic was going to happen. I never speculated beyond that—I was too scared—and then it came and went with only the normal drama.

I haven't got much more to say, my son, but I think it's important I cover one thing Dr. Chu told me: that you are different, different from human beings born on Earth, but you are still Homo sapiens, just like your father and I, just like everyone else. Your DNA strands are the same, just infinitely more progressed. And while there are some minor variances accounting for the issues with your blood, you are most certainly a person.

Which begs the question I know you want answers for just as I always did: Where exactly did you come from? How could you be alien and human at the same time?

I avoid thinking about Laboratory Z as much as I can.

But I can only assume that you came through whatever it was they were experimenting with there, just before the explosion that caused the fire and destroyed the building. Only, you couldn't have come alone. Someone handed you to me. Someone must have brought you through and that same person might well have been the one who triggered the explosion, so no one else could follow them through. I wonder if it was your real mother or father. No—strike that, because we're your real mother and father.

That, though, doesn't change the fact that you were brought here for a reason. And it also doesn't change the reality we must face—well, you must now—that they might come back for you. The most important thing since we learned the truth in our minds has been to keep you safe, to do everything we could to blend in and make sure you did too, so no one would ever suspect. We thought of moving but thought that might be one of the things they'd look for. So we stayed. And let you play football, even though we knew there were risks.

There are risks with everything. Your father and I learned that firsthand back in China before we immigrated.

You immigrated too, Alex. That's the way you must look at this.

I'd love to end this here, but I can't. Because if you're watching this, it means something bad has happened. It means the worst has happened and they came back for you. I wish I could tell you who "they" are, but I can't. But I know they're out there. A few times I thought I could feel them, a mother's intuition. I don't believe they ever totally let go or gave up. Wherever it was you came from, they haven't forgotten you. And I know they'll be back.

If you're watching this, know that it brings me great joy even though it almost surely means your father and I are gone. But your viewing this means you're still alive and now you know everything I do, hopefully enough to help you survive against the ones who have come for you. I don't want to stop talking, don't want these to be my last words to you. You were the light of our lives from the day the fates brought you to us. We knew, your father and I, we needed to protect you, not just raise you as our own. All things come with a purpose and plan. The Chinese believe happiness lies in plugging gaps, having no great chasms into which our lives might plunge. Saving you filled our greatest gap but we knew the day would come when someone would come for you, someone from Laboratory Z or the parties from whom we kept you hidden. Our questions stopped there. You were a gift willed to us by fate and we chose to leave it at that.

There's one more thing you need to know. When you were just starting to speak, sometimes your words came out in an indecipherable language. Your father and I thought it was just jibberish at first, but at night we'd hear you mumbling in your sleep. Your native language, Alex, language of the world from which you came. You must've recalled it somehow. You'd only mumble in the midst of a terrible dream and we thought you might be suffering from night terrors. Then the dreams and the mumbling passed, and we let it go, trying not to wonder what you had seen and experienced before you came to us.

But now we all know those terrors are real, and they won't only come at night.

58

THE CHRYSALIS

"Tell me what happened during that follow-up CT scan," Sam said, after the screen froze on An Chin's sad expression.

"It was crazy," Alex said, when he'd finished the tale of bursting bulbs and fried circuits. "It felt like, I don't know, like I was making it happen."

Sam shrugged, all this a bit beyond even her.

"What do you think it was?" Alex more demanded than asked.

"I . . . don't know."

"I thought you knew everything."

"Something magnetic."

"Huh?"

"A CT scan uses electro*magnetic* waves. Picture what happens when you stick something covered in tinfoil into a microwave."

"Sparks, like miniature lightning," Alex offered. "Come to think of it, yeah, that pretty much describes what happened in the exam room. Only, I wasn't covered in tinfoil."

"You wouldn't have to be, if there was something inside you."

"Inside me? Like what?"

Sam shrugged. "I have no idea."

"Guess."

"I can't. We're in uncharted territory here."

"Then answer me this: Why didn't the same thing happen during the first scan?"

"I can't. More uncharted territory."

"Connected maybe to that shadow Dr. Payne spotted in the first scan?"

Sam shrugged again.

Alex shook his head. "You'd make a lousy football player."

"How's that?"

"You're afraid to take a chance."

"I thought you just wanted me to take a guess."

"So go ahead."

Sam looked around her. "Later. When we get somewhere else."

Alex returned his attention to the screen and clicked on the next file, containing the results from Dr. Chu's tests the recorded image of his mother had referred to. "I want to print this first."

59

THE SIGNAL

"We're prepared to move, sir," Rathman had told Langston Marsh, through the Bluetooth device clipped to his ear. "We have the situation contained."

"You have a positive identification?"

"Yes, sir," Rathman responded, perhaps more surely than he should have. "And my men are in position both front and rear, all exits covered."

"What's the boy doing in there?"

"He's on a computer. The girl's next to him."

"We've got more on him, Colonel. He was admitted to California Pacific Medical Center two nights ago now after suffering a football injury believed to be a concussion."

Rathman was nodding to himself impatiently, wishing Marsh would get to the point. "This would be the hospital where a doctor was found dead around the same time the boy fled the premises."

"We must assume that he's dangerous. You should proceed with caution."

"Understood."

"And we need this one alive, Colonel."

"Also understood, sir."

"Then see it done."

"Yes, sir. Prepare to move on my signal," Rathman said into the throat mic connecting him to his men.

60

THE MEN AT THE DOOR

Alex collected the pages from the printer, the medical tests compiled by Dr. Chu all those years ago filling a few scant pages. But his mind was back at his house, confronting the drone things and ash man who'd killed his parents.

We are your family. We have our orders. You must come with us, Alex.

I'm not going anywhere with you.

You don't have a choice.

But the thing dressed as a cop was wrong; Alex *did* have a choice. They weren't his family. Theirs wasn't his world, any more than China had been his parents' world. They'd fled to America, just as he had, in a manner of speaking. The Chins might not have birthed him, but he was more like them than he could've possibly realized, something he found sadly ironic.

Mostly, just sad.

This is for your own good. You don't belong here, with them.

Words spoken by the ash man before Alex split him in half with one of the cop thing's severed arms, leaving him to talk out of both sides of his mouth.

You have something we want, something that belongs to us.

* * *

Raiff picked up speed as soon as the lights of the FedEx Office came into view, framed by an endless ribbon of empty sky. Sights like this made him wonder what people here who didn't know the truth about the contents of that sky saw when they looked at it. Surely not the same thing he did, his perspective stilted by the knowledge that something else really *was* out there.

But it wasn't that simple.

Not even close.

The truth wasn't something that could be spotted through telescopes or by space stations. The truth was that the boy inside that FedEx Office was the only thing standing between this world and extinction.

Raiff gave the car more gas.

"You remember what the ash man said?" he asked Sam suddenly, feeling her hand tighten around his while they waited to pay for the copies.

"No, not exactly."

Her eyes left his to dart toward the manager, who was busy helping another customer with an order, the harsh lights reflecting off her glasses.

"That I have something he wanted," Alex said, "something that belonged to him."

"I was thinking of something else he said, that this night never should have been necessary, that they shouldn't have needed to come here—something like that."

"They," Alex repeated, "as in *who*?"

"That's what I've been thinking about," Sam said, trying to clear the fatigue from her voice. "I don't know, maybe whoever brought you from wherever you came from to Laboratory Z. Like rebels, going up against the establishment."

"So now I'm a rebel?"

"I didn't say that. But you're obviously important to them, and whatever their cause is, back where you came from."

"My parents told me I came from an adoption agency. They didn't say it was based somewhere in outer space."

"I think you must be part of some civil war," Sam said suddenly.

"That's what you've been thinking about?"

"And it makes perfect sense. The way the ash man talked about disobedience, how it wouldn't be tolerated, that there was a price to pay for it. What did that sound like to you?"

"Is this a test?" Alex asked her, managing a smile.

"Just answer the question."

"I don't know, maybe something like the Nazis would say."

"Exactly my point."

"Go," Rathman commanded and watched his men move.

He'd never worked with them before and the files he'd read on the private jet that brought him from Marsh's fortress in the Klamath Mountains in northwestern California to San Francisco told only part of the story. Their training was rock solid, experience too. But until he saw them in action, he wouldn't know if they were really any good, how they'd respond to such a challenge.

He watched the front team moving with perfect fluidity, avoiding the most direct spills of light so their approach could not be detected from inside, weapons held at the ready.

They were good, all right. Now it was time to see *how* good.

"I'm going in, sir," he told Langston Marsh.

61

MISDIRECTION

Alex tucked the now folded pages containing the results of Dr. Chu's final tests in his pocket, while Sam handed some change to the clerk to pay for them.

"Okay," she said, backing away from the counter, "let's go."

Alex held his ground, seeming to grind his shoes into the floor. "I've already ruined your life enough. I can't drag you into this any more than I already have," he said, his voice warm, gentle, and very sad.

She shook her head. "I'm not going anywhere without you. I can't."

"Why?"

"I don't know, I just *can't*."

"You need to go home, back to your parents. Leave the rest of this to me."

"Alone?"

Alex swallowed hard.

"I go where you go," Sam said.

And then she started to shake and couldn't catch her breath. Like some kind of panic attack had set in, like the past ten hours had been poured into a bottle that had burst apart inside her, all the death and fear spilling out at once. The tears were coming before she could even try to stop them, all the unanswered questions hammering at her mind. She tried to breathe again but managed only to gasp. She'd never hyperventilated before but was pretty sure this was what it felt like.

Then Sam felt Alex wrapping his arms around her, hugging her so close she could feel his heartbeat against her chest and wondered if he could feel hers skittering. The rapid beating slackened as he held her. She could feel her breathing steadying as well, wanted to wipe her nose and eyes but realized she was squeezing Alex too tightly to let go. She felt like a little girl again, weak and helpless. Not the high school girl with the perfect GPA and through-the-roof SAT scores, which were her ticket to the Ivy League and a career with NASA in space.

All that seemed so distant now, so behind her. Tonight had changed everything; no more looking any farther ahead than the next hour, if not minute. Sam started to feel it all overwhelming her again, the same tightness returning to her chest and stomach, and clung to Alex.

The boy of her dreams for as long as she could remember.

Then he was kissing her and Sam felt her glasses push up against the bridge of his nose. In that moment it seemed like everything would be all right, as if nothing bad had ever happened at all. Her glasses shifted again and Sam found movement flash in the mirror placed high by a corner ceiling. Three men wearing matching suits just entering the store.

Three men who looked a lot like the drone things that had killed Alex's parents.

Raiff saw them too, from the street. His mind conjured the corrosive, burned-wire smell that hung in the air of the Chins' home. He wondered why they smelled that way, guessed the internal cooling mechanisms designed to keep them from overheating still hadn't been perfected. To him, this had long before indicated that they were being manufactured here on Earth. So the raw materials had come from here, and the manufacturing process was unable to account for all the variances and variables at once.

Hence the drones smelled like car engines with their temperature gauges flirting with the red. Raiff wondered if they might even spontaneously combust after too much activity. That would be something.

But it wasn't going to happen in time to help Dancer, so Raiff jumped the curb and tore, tires screeching, toward the FedEx Office entrance.

"Alex!" Sam screamed, tearing herself from his grasp.

Alex twisted from the counter, facing the suited figures as they reached the door.

Sam looked at them again, wondered if they were no more than businessmen needing materials for an early morning meeting.

Then where were their briefcases?

They seemed not to see her, focusing on Alex with laser-like eyes as they stormed through the door. Sam swinging around when something rattled behind them.

Rathman caught up with his advance team just after the breach. They fanned out to provide support, while he moved into the lead, the shocked targets out of their chairs now and clearly in view, the team covering his rear flank as he burst in from the door at the store's back that led into a break room.

All exactly according to plan.

Rathman leveled his submachine gun, finger pawing the trigger. Locked and loaded. Ready for whatever came next.

Then he froze.

"You need to pay for those?" the store's shift manager called to Sam, emerging from the part of the store sectioned off by a counter where staff printed jobs that were completed. "Hey, is something wrong?"

An old SUV's headlights flashed through the store an instant before the rest of it followed through the glass, the suited figures swinging toward it.

"Stand down! Stand down!" Rathman had the sense to order, over the staccato bursts of automatic fire driven up into the ceiling.

Also as planned.

Targets surrounded. Targets controlled. Targets captured without incident.

"Cease fire! Cease fire!" Rathman called out next, signal hand flapping in the air.

Because these weren't his targets.

EIGHT

BATTLEGROUND

You may have to fight a battle more than once to win it.

—MARGARET THATCHER

62

DRONE THINGS

Alex grabbed Sam and pulled her backward, up and over the counter, crashing past the shift manager, who'd covered up in a crouch. He'd popped back up again just as a figure surged out of the ancient SUV with pockmarked paint, now bleeding steam from its radiator, which rose toward the drop ceiling like a curtain.

The drone things, near-twins of the figures wearing cop uniforms back at Alex's house, seemed suspended between intentions, their focus divided.

"Alex," one of them had said just before the SUV crashed through the storefront. Same voice as the fake cops too.

Your family, so to speak. Your real family.

No, they weren't and neither were these, no matter what planet or world Alex came from. An and Li Chin were his family.

Alex felt his blood heating up, his skin seeming to bake. But then the figure from the car was in motion, moving as much with the air as through it. He was holding something in his hand, some kind of weapon, lashing it out toward the drone things even before his feet touched down.

* * *

Raiff counted three of them, their positions imprinted on his brain. He'd recognized them as androids immediately, even before he caught that burned odor wafting in the air.

He extracted his stick while hurdling airborne out of the SUV embedded in the front wall. Firearms were fine but not very effective against the androids' steel, maybe titanium, shells. He snapped the stick outward, feeling its connection with his own DNA register like a switch being flipped, elongating the elements, their molecular composition altered by its whip-like form. His whip could cut through anything, and without the randomness of bullets or blasts. Perfect weapon for the kind of in-close maneuvers he'd most likely have to perform.

He spotted Dancer, and the girl the Watchers had informed him about, at the edge of his vision, but she was not yet his concern. Protecting *him* was Raiff's concern. So many years of waiting and preparing, finally coming to this, his purpose fulfilled.

Even now, though, even as the whip whistled through the air, that purpose seemed empty against the bigger picture that Dancer's world would never be the same, any more than Raiff's task would ever be. They had found the boy twice already, not even a day apart, and they would find him again.

Something was coming.

He felt it with a dread certainty in the pit of his soul, the last eighteen years rendered meaningless in the face of such a concentrated attack.

Two of the androids swung toward him in perfect unison, as if possessing the same mind. The third went for Dancer.

So Raiff went for the third.

Lashing his whip outward so it sizzled through the air,

a crack resounding when it impacted the overlayer of skin-like material wrapped around the neck of android number three. Raiff pulled and twisted and the head popped off in a shower of smoke and sparks that intensified the burned odor to the point it hurt his nostrils when he sniffed it.

"Run!" he yelled to Dancer, their eyes meeting ever so briefly for the first time ever. "Run!"

Raiff watched Dancer drag the girl with him out of sight through a door leading out the back, distracted long enough for the android on the right to lurch for him, laser knife in hand. The size of a common kitchen knife but far more deadly.

He saw the first blade as a flashbulb-bright light coming straight for his face. Raiff twisted, feeling the thing graze his shoulder, taking flesh and fabric with it. He smelled his own blood now, the wound as searing hot as the sparks that flew from the first android's head when he'd lopped it off.

The remaining two androids sensed his vulnerability, came in for the kill together and tossed laser blades from twin angles to catch him in the cross fire. Raiff dropped to the ground and rolled, his whip in motion. Low first toward the one on the right, slicing off both its legs at the ankles. Then he snapped the whip with a violent jerk of his wrist, sending it on an upward trajectory from floor level directly between the final android's legs.

Wires, electrodes, and capacitors popped, frizzled, and flamed as the whip made a neat slice upward all the way through the android's metallic skull. Leaving both halves of him sputtering on either foot, somehow managing to retain their balance while the matching eyes on the perfectly symmetrical husks popped out in a final flame burst.

Raiff reeled his whip in, starting to push himself back

to his feet, when a boot clamped down on his hand, the disembodied foot of the android he'd upended. The rest of the thing hopped along on ankles spewing smoke and wire, the burned smell noxious enough to turn Raiff's stomach.

He felt the severed boot trying to crush his hand, the pain starting to shoot up his arm, when he swept it off into the air by whipsawing his own foot across his body. Launched airborne, the booted foot struck the android it had belonged to in the face, toppling the thing over as it continued hopping after Dancer. Raiff got one leg up in front of him, balanced on his other knee, and lashed his whip out from there. The blow struck the thing's face, left it a mass of severed, spaghetti-like wiring with the eyes still attached by clear strands.

It was done. Dancer was safe, at least for now.

Then Raiff heard the scream coming from the back of the store.

63

TRASH

Even as he darted toward the screams and hurdled over the counter, Raiff was aware of the store manager and single other customer cowering for dear life: witnesses to the scene of unprecedented risk and exposure on the part of the enemy he'd been sent here to fight.

Just like in Dancer's house.

Reaching the back door, he spotted another witness, a pimply faced kid wearing a FedEx shirt, with phone pressed to his ear, desperately trying for a signal that was blocked. Raiff burst past him outside into a nest of massive trash bins overflowing with paper, crushed cardboard boxes, and shredded document remains that now blew like confetti across the scene. His feet crunched over the glass shed by outdoor light fixtures the androids had broken, likely to cloak their presence long enough from a big trash hauler with an automated pincer assembly that grasped, hoisted, and dumped the contents of the trash bins. Its engine idled, no driver anywhere to be seen.

Raiff's eyes scanned the scene and saw two of the androids dragging Dancer and the girl off, along the back alley of the FedEx store and the others in the strip mall, barely wide enough to accommodate the trash truck.

The girl's presence here had thrown Raiff a bit. His mission, though, remained unchanged:

Save Dancer, the one and only priority. He could not risk Dancer to save the girl.

Complicated.

Right now it was moot. Right now the androids had both of them in tow, and Raiff couldn't attack without alerting the androids to his presence well before he reached them. They'd be ready this time and, worse, might kill Dancer to make sure the secret he was keeping remained just that.

Raiff's mind was made up in a fraction of a second, the pieces falling into place as he turned and slid off in the opposite direction.

Alex struggled but it was useless. He was a feather in the first drone thing's grasp, being dragged along. The other had Sam by the hair and throat at the same time, dragging her too, her face red from lack of air, mouth gaping for breath.

They'd walked right into the trap set outside the back of the store.

The only working computer at the FedEx Office in Capitola, the one the motel clerk had recommended, was being used, so they'd driven a few miles up the road to this FexEx Office in Santa Cruz.

So how had the drone things found them? And who was the guy who'd driven his car into the store, saving them from the man-like machines, at least for the moment?

Alex couldn't bother considering that or any other question right now. He needed to figure out a way to break free and escape.

And take Sam with him.

"Sam!" he cried out and felt a hand clamp over his mouth, crinkling like a soda can.

Her eyes were gaping in terror.

He needed to do something, but the drone thing was now holding both his hands in a single, gloved grasp by the thumbs. When he struggled, he felt the wrenching pain of the thumb jerked so hard, it strained the bonds of its tendon.

Sam's taser was still tucked just behind her hip in her jeans, hidden by her jacket. If he could reach it, maybe, just maybe . . .

But he couldn't. Only thing that would get him was more pain. He needed to bide his time, wait for an opportunity—which came when a shape lunged out from an idling trash truck, complete with compactor and arm-like assemblages, parked across the alleyway directly before him.

The route out blocked, Raiff projected himself through the passenger window of the garbage truck, having looped all the way around the strip mall to avoid being spotted. He hit the ground tucking, rolled once, and was back on his feet. His whip was useless to him with Dancer pulled in so close to the android holding him. The android didn't let go, pulled Alex in even tighter against it, backed up closer to the trash hauler. Raiff let it, showed the whip he had no intention of using to make the android retreat even farther. . . .

Directly beneath the pincer apparatus's electronic eye.

It had engaged automatically when Raiff had put the truck into "park" and now it lowered with a mechanical whir and captured the android in its grasp at the shoulders, a near match to the width of the trash containers for which it was fitted. The pincer apparatus clamped on tight, lifted the android up and out. The thing desperately tried to free itself, almost managing to when the pincers lowered it into the compactor.

Raiff grabbed Dancer and shoved the boy behind him before he could move to rescue the girl. Above, the android was clawing desperately for anything it could grab, as the compactor sucked it further and further inside, until a crunch sounded and nothing but its hands remained visible. The compactor bucked once, settled, then opened anew.

The other android tossed the girl aside to move for Raiff, who went for his whip, now to find it gone, lost when he'd grabbed Dancer in its place. The android flashed its laser knife, reeled it back to send the first blade flying, Raiff's best hope that it might miss him.

He caught a flash of motion at the android's rear and then the girl was on it, something in her hand coming forward.

A taser, Raiff realized, in the moment before she jammed it against the back of the thing's neck.

A buzzing sounded and kept sounding, as the girl held the taser firm against one of the android's most vulnerable spots, where conduits of wires joined together, all spooling out of its computer brain. The thing lashed out with an arm that sent both the girl and her taser flying. Not a blow so much as a reflexive response.

The thing's arms began to flap about. It spun and smoked and sizzled, but still somehow lurched toward Raiff, blindingly fast.

To Raiff's amazement, the boy—Dancer—broke free and threw himself on top of the android, giving Raiff time to dive headlong for his whip. Taking it in his grasp and lashing it forward to catch the thing hard against the left side of its head, which snapped and lopped to the right. The android beginning to snap, crackle, and pop as sparks flew from its steel neck like Fourth of July sparklers.

Two more down.

Raiff pulled himself back to his feet, feeling pain in too many places. Watched Dancer heaving for breath, steadying himself against the garbage truck's frame directly below the robotic arm that had dumped the other android into the compactor.

Raiff had just started moving toward him when a pair of disembodied hands grabbed hold of Dancer from inside the truck's rear.

Raiff glimpsed what remained of the android still attached to the forearms and hands, which were all that were still intact, the rest of it no more than a flattened husk of steel and wires compressed into a jagged assemblage, still sparking and popping but maintaining enough "brain" function to complete its mission of capturing, or killing, Dancer.

Its hands had found the boy's neck, tugging on it as if to pull his head off, when Raiff lashed his whip into motion and sliced the forearms free of what remained of the thing's body. That, though, made its fingers clamp down, sure to squeeze mindlessly until there was nothing left in their grasp.

Raiff knew they couldn't be pried free, knew he couldn't risk using his whip, either. That left . . .

The girl's taser!

She seemed to read his mind, or form the same thought, located the taser and tossed it to him. Raiff snatched it out of the air and lunged toward Dancer, who was gasping for breath now and fighting desperately to work the hands killing him free as his face purpled.

Raiff touched the taser to one hand, then the other.

Dancer jerked and spasmed both times, but the fingers snapped open and locked there. Raiff peeled the fingers off the boy and tossed the hands into the trash truck's rear, hoisting Dancer to his feet and shaking him to keep the boy from passing out.

"Can you hear me? Can you hear me?"

Dancer managed a nod, still gasping for breath. The red had started to wash from his face, but the bruises left on his neck by the android's grasp were already turning black.

"Can you move, can you walk?"

Dancer opened his mouth to answer but no words emerged, so he just nodded again. His knees buckled as he moved from the truck and Raiff caught him, held him upright while steering for the truck's cab.

"Come on," he said, jerking the passenger-side door open with his free hand, "let's get you inside."

Then Raiff turned his gaze on the girl, who stood silent and still ten feet away, staring at him.

"You too. Hurry," he continued, beckoning her on, "we need to get out of here. Before more of them show up."

64

AC/DC

Raiff reversed, Dancer and the girl squeezed next to him in the cab.

"Tell me this isn't happening!" he heard the girl utter, her words partially drowned out by an AC/DC song blaring over the speakers.

"Highway to Hell," of all things.

The dashboard was too dark for him to find the controls to shut it off, as a raspy voice screeched something about a one-way ride.

"Alex!" he said, calling him by name.

"Who—"

"Am I," Raiff completed. "Doesn't matter. Tell me you're okay, you're not hurt. That you're whole."

"Whole?"

"Intact!"

"I'm not hurt. I'm not okay, either."

Raiff looked at him, then back to the front as he reversed the trash truck around the front of the strip mall and ground the gears into "drive."

"You saved me, us."

Raiff said nothing.

"Who are you? It *does* matter."

"I'm a Guardian, *your* Guardian. Have been for your entire life."

"Then you know who I really—"

"Yes, I do know," Raiff said, completing the boy's thought yet again.

"Then tell me, please, because I don't know shit."

"Yes, you do," Raiff replied, stealing a look at him. "You know *everything*. You just don't realize it."

AC/DC was now headed to the promised land along the highway to hell, Alex sitting board straight against the passenger-side window of the trash truck.

"Am I an alien or not?"

"We both are." Raiff gave the big truck as much gas as it would take. "But we're human too."

"You just said—"

"I know what I just said. We're human, but also aliens. To this planet, anyway."

Sam rotated her head back and forth between the two of them as each spoke, trying to make sense of their words. She reached forward and turned off the radio just as the lyrics "highway to hell" sounded for what felt like the hundredth time.

"You're losing me," Alex said.

Raiff's eyes fixed on the side-view mirror. "It's them I want to make sure I lose."

"'Them' as in the drone things?"

"Interesting term."

"It's what the ash man called them," Sam interjected. "Drones. Back in Alex's house after . . ."

"It's okay, Sam," Alex said, trying to sound reassuring.

"Ash man?" Raiff repeated.

"Before Alex split him in half. He kept talking out of both sides of his mouth."

"That's because he wasn't real," Alex added.

"No, he was a projection," Raiff noted.

"Like a hologram or something?" asked Sam.

"Far more advanced," Raiff said, holding both of them in his gaze. "Holograms don't split in half. Weapons go right through them, for obvious reasons."

"Like a drone's severed arm," Alex told him. "That's what I used."

Raiff glanced over at Alex to make sure he'd heard that right. "Not holograms as you understand them. Next generation, actually about *five hundred* generations. I call them Shadows."

"Shadows," Alex repeated.

"But they're more like astral projections—with actual mass created by a gas and gamma rays; the particular gas is found only on our mother planet."

"What," Sam speculated, "like an out-of-body experience?"

"No," Raiff said, impatient to have to be addressing her at all and aiming his response at Dancer instead. "Our world is so far away from this one, there'd be no way to hold the signal carrying the hologram together. So this projection who spoke to you, the Shadow you call the ash man, is instilled with gamma energy to simulate form and matter in order to maintain structural cohesion during the transmission."

"Okay," Alex managed.

"Like pouring sand into water," Sam concluded.

"Pretty much." Raiff nodded.

"So he was talking to me from your planet."

"*Our* planet, Alex, but yes."

"He said I had something he wanted, something that belonged to him."

"You do, but it doesn't."

"Oh, boy," Alex said, shaking his head again.

"It belongs to us," Raiff told him. "That's why you were smuggled here."

"Smuggled?"

"How many androids, drones, were there in your house?" Raiff asked, hands squeezing the wheel tighter, eager to change the subject.

"Four. Dressed as cops."

"And you killed them all?"

"You can't kill a machine but, yeah, I messed them up pretty good. What are they, exactly?"

"Long story, Dancer."

"Dancer?"

"Your code name. What I've always referred to you as."

"You can call me Alex. Now, tell me about these drone things, androids, or whatever they are."

"They're soldiers."

"From?" Alex demanded.

"From the world you and I come from," Raiff said, then added, "Well, not exactly."

"Not exactly? What, then?" Alex asked.

"The technology comes from our world, but they're manufactured here. Truly made in America."

"Like in a factory?" Sam asked before Alex could.

"Sort of."

"Could you be any more vague?"

Raiff shot her a look. "I don't even know who you are."

"His tutor," Sam said, gesturing toward Alex.

"You'd think I'd be smarter, coming from a world that can manage all this shit. What's your name, anyway?" Alex asked him. "I mean, you do have a name, right?"

"Clay. Clay Raiff. Call me Raiff."

"And why do I need a Guardian, Raiff? Why have I

needed one all of my life? What the hell is going on here—just who, *what*, am I?"

"Tell me what you know, and I'll fill in the rest."

"That's easy: nothing, I know nothing!"

"Wrong. You know *plenty*, lots more than you realize. Think!"

Alex summarized what he'd learned from the flash drive hidden inside Meng Po as best he could, his mother's final message to him, those test results still tucked into the pocket of Dr. Payne's jeans. He hit on all the most salient points, including Dr. Chu's findings, as well as the circumstances of his rescue and "adoption" by the Chins as a baby.

"Guess I'm the ultimate illegal alien," he finished.

"Join the club," Raiff told him.

They'd swung onto the Pacific Coast Highway, heading north, just as Alex began telling his tale to Raiff. The sharp, maddening curves of the PCH were treacherous enough without having to negotiate them in a garbage truck. But Raiff nonetheless gave the truck more gas and its poorly weighted frame instantly began whipsawing from one curve into another. Undeterred, Raiff held his speed steady, settling into the drive despite the truck seeming to protest the effort by bouncing and shaking. Every twist of the wheel became an adventure, the truck seemingly ready to shimmy itself off its frame. The road widened and then straightened appreciably as they wound into the Santa Cruz Mountains, all of them able to breathe easier without the air clogging in their chests.

For Alex, it felt like a roller coaster finally docking at the end of the ride. "I leave you enough to fill in?"

"Plenty," Raiff said, checking the side-view mirror again.

"So start."

"Sorry. Can't right now."

"Why?"

And that's when Alex glimpsed headlights brightening in the side-view mirror.

"Because we have company," Raiff told him.

65

CHASE

"Two vehicles," Raiff continued. "SUVS, or vans, maybe."

Sam instinctively turned to look behind her, forgetting the enclosed cab of the garbage truck had no rear window. "How could they find us so fast?"

"Because they were close all along. Backup for the androids we destroyed. Or the cleanup crew, like the one that erased all trace of what was left of them at your house, just in case."

Alex rolled his eyes. "Well, 'just in case' happened again."

"You need to get out of the truck," Raiff said to both of them.

"We're not finished talking yet," Alex said stubbornly.

"We are for now."

"How are we supposed to *get out*, exactly?" Raiff heard the girl named Sam ask him.

"I slow down as much as I can around the next bend, and you jump, Tutor," he said, coining a name for her.

"Don't call me that. It sounds—Wait, did you say *jump*?"

"Like in the movies," Alex told her, readying his hand on the door latch.

Sam gazed out the window toward the dark swatch of

the coast redwoods forest, over which the mountains towered like giant sentinels.

"People in the movies don't understand the physics involved," she noted. "If they did . . ."

Alex watched the shoulder flashing by through the passenger-side window. "Well, I don't, either, and please don't tell me."

Raiff scanned the road ahead, then looked back at the side-view mirror to gauge how fast the pursuing vehicles were gaining on them.

"Count to ten," he told Dancer and the girl. "Jump out at one." Raiff met Dancer's eyes. "Open the door."

"Not until you tell me what I've got that the ash man wants."

"I told you we haven't got the time," Raiff said, reaching across the seat to thrust open the door himself. "And if you don't get out now we might never have the time."

Alex didn't bother to protest further, just started counting, mouthing the numbers. He eased the door further open, and a cool rush of air flooded the truck's cab.

In the side-view mirror, the dark vehicles were drawing nearer; Raiff realized it was going to be close.

"How do we find you?" Dancer asked, hand moving to the girl's shoulder to ready her.

"Don't worry about that. Just stay out of sight. Don't use any cell phones or computers, nothing that can be traced digitally back to you."

The truck eased into the curve, Raiff slowing its speed as much as he dared.

"Now!"

Dancer had already grabbed hold of the girl, easing her up even with him. Pushing the door all the way open as he tugged hard and drew her out into the night.

Raiff watched them separate in the air and hit the soft

shoulder together: Dancer with grace and his tutor with a thump and a thud. It made him wince as he leaned over and got the door closed, just as bright headlights flashed anew in the side-view mirror. He gave the truck more gas, needing to widen the distance between them but not too much.

Just enough.

Thoughts flooded through his mind in that moment, most notably the fact that all this wasn't just about Dancer's identity being compromised. Something *else* was happening: what he knew was coming now and had sacrificed everything to prevent.

So this world could survive. So its people would not know the pain and hardship his did.

Raiff checked the gap between his truck and the pursuing vehicles. Not wide enough for comfort but as good as he could manage.

He took a deep breath and changed his hand position on the steering wheel.

Alex watched the two big black SUVs speed past without noticing him, already moving to Sam, who lay dazed and bent on the downward slope of the shoulder.

"Sam, Sam! Look at me, can you hear me?"

She looked at him. "Ouch."

"Can you move?"

"I'm afraid to try."

But she did anyway, found herself sore and scraped but otherwise okay.

She managed to sit up. "I just jumped out of a moving truck. . . ."

"Yeah."

They looked down the stretch of straightaway into

which the road had settled. The garbage truck and SUVs shrank in the growing distance, their lights becoming mere specks on the dark horizon, when the garbage truck suddenly twisted round and skidded sideways down the road.

Sparks and smoke erupted beneath its big tires, the SUVs powerless to do anything but surge on. Then the garbage truck was twirling, a giant clock hand spinning in sped-up motion along the center of the road.

The screech of tires echoed in the night air, the first SUV slamming into the truck broadside by its nose and sent rolling, tumbling, across the road. The second SUV rammed it dead center, halting the truck's spin and driving it forward until it toppled over. The contents of its hold coughed into the air in a ribbon of stray refuse and bags, seeming to float down in slow motion, as the SUV pitched over it and spun in the air.

It came down on its side directly in the path of the other SUV, still spinning wildly. The crunching impact showered steel and rubber into the air just ahead of the flame burst that left Alex and Sam covering their eyes, even before the garbage truck erupted in a curtain of fire.

"Raiff . . . Do you think he . . . ," Sam began, leaving it at that.

"I don't know," Alex managed. "I don't know."

66

"Janus didn't exist then," the woman in the top right reminded him. *"But we do now. Please speak plainly, Doctor."*

"Suffice it to say," said Donati, *"that our experiments were figuratively based on leaving bumps in the night. Until something bumped back."*

At that point, the principals of Janus had requested a complete report on what exactly had transpired in Laboratory Z, leaving Donati utterly perplexed. Didn't these people understand the gravity of what was unfolding? Is this how they or their counterparts in the Near-Earth Object office would react if informed that a potential planet-killing asteroid was on a collision course with Earth?

A bad metaphor, really, considering that this threat was potentially just as bad and far more immediate than that one.

Donati, though, had no choice other than to succumb to the bureaucracy, the Janus board not seeing any harm in putting off action for the few hours it would take to consider his full report on Laboratory Z before reconvening. He knew this was a stall tactic as much as anything, since there was really no action they could take if what he suspected turned out to be true.

Indeed, what action, exactly, could the Earth take against a possible alien invasion?

No copies remained of his original report, but Donati was able to re-create the most salient facts from a memory that had never relinquished its hold on them. He kept it short and sweet, not wanting to burden the Janus board with too much technical or scientific jargon. And when they finally reconvened three hours after the initial call concluded, Donati sensed a different attitude and approach from the four voices, which had now been joined by a fifth in the center. More somber and inquisitive, while less confrontational, all the participants' comments and questions laced with something as clear as it was undeniable:

Fear. Of facing an actual threat, at least within the realm of statistical probability, for the first time.

"I think you need to better explain whatever it was that bumped back," said the fifth member of the Janus board, his voice grid dancing in the center of Donati's screen.

"I would if I could, sir," Donati told him. "But I've got to back up a bit more first. Laboratory Z was dedicated to finding more expeditious ways of exploring the universe."

"And by 'expeditious,'" Center interjected, "you mean—"

"Practical, given the limitations of space travel eighteen years ago as well as now. By the time Laboratory Z became operational, the logistics of mounting even a Mars mission were incredibly daunting. If travel to a planet within our own solar system was deemed infeasible, what did that say about the prospects of traveling light-years to reach new and potentially habitable worlds? My question is rhetorical because the answer was and is obvious. Working in conjunction with officials and scientists at both Goddard and JPL, Laboratory Z's purpose was to explore alternative means of space travel."

"Your report goes into some detail about wormholes," said the lone female, still in the top right corner of the screen.

"Because, ma'am, that's where we'd made the greatest degree of progress. Simply speaking, a wormhole is a postulated method, within the general theory of relativity, of moving from one point in space to another without crossing the space between. Picture a typical sheet of paper. Laid flat, to go from the bottom to the top you'd have to travel eleven and a half inches. But fold the paper in half and the top and bottom portions become connected with virtually no space between them. The overarching principle of a wormhole is to displace massive amounts of energy to create the same effect in space along the time-space continuum. To effectively shrink the distance of travel from light-years to distances of time and space that would be quantitatively comparable to the Gemini and Apollo flights to the moon."

"But we can't even approach or envision such technology now," Top Left started, "never mind eighteen years ago."

"Approach, sir, no, but we can envision *anything*. It's what makes us scientists. And envisioning what is deemed currently impossible has defined NASA since the beginning."

"You're not saying you actually constructed a wormhole at Laboratory Z, are you?" asked the new voice perched in the center.

"We started, as we always do, with models. Miniature re-creations and simulations of what we're actually striving to accomplish. It's the way pretty much all of NASA's greatest achievements have begun. And you are most correct in your assumption that we didn't have the technology then or now to fold space over to create a wormhole. Let me explain how you'd build a wormhole if you had absolutely everything you needed to turn theory into practice. First, a disclaimer: Although Einstein's theory of relativity forbids objects to move faster than light within space-time, it is known that space-time itself can be warped and distorted. It takes an enormous amount of matter or energy to create such distortions, but such distortions are possible, at least theoretically.

"So if the sky was literally the limit, you'd collect a whole bunch of super-dense matter, such as matter from a neutron star, enough to construct a ring the size of the Earth's orbit around the sun. Then you'd build another ring where you want the other end of your wormhole. Next, just charge 'em up to some incredible voltage, and spin both of them up to near the speed of light. Of course, we weren't capable of doing any of that back at Laboratory Z, but we were able to construct what was in essence a particle accelerator to at least mimic the effects and experiment with the possibilities. Even then we lacked the ability to generate enough energy to go through the door from the point of origin to the destination, but our particle accelerator proved able to build that door and approximate the aggregate amount of energy it would take to fashion at least one side of the doorway."

"I don't believe I understand the distinction," said Bottom Left.

"Building a wormhole, folding space, essentially creates a tunnel, a void in space—actually, *between* space—that in the theoretical realm makes traversing impossible distances possible. Call it a bridge through space. We were able to figure out how to simulate that void and enter the space bridge, but not achieve the means to actually travel through it."

"Without elaborating, though," inserted the new voice in the center, "your report indicates that Laboratory Z's destruction was directly related to hostile action from beyond our universe, this alien invasion you're hinting at now. That would seem to be a contradiction, a discrepancy at the very least."

"Not at all, sir. The key is the pattern of seismic-type events following an elementarily narrow, even microscopically contained, line of the Earth's curvature. Eighteen years ago I uncovered this pattern but didn't, couldn't, grasp exactly what it meant."

"Which was?" two of the voices asked at the same time.

"Someone had honed in on the precise coordinates of our bridge, essentially followed the directions we provided in quantum space. The pattern of events, I believe now, was emblematic of them breaking through, folding space over from the other side to complete that bridge and erect a tunnel through space."

"But by your own admission," the woman's voice blared in clear argumentative fashion, "the events forming that pattern took place over an extended period of time. How can you reconcile that with the immediacy suggested by this space bridge of yours being completed?"

"Precisely the question I've asked myself a thousand times, until I came up with an answer that made sense. If we accept the pattern as an early warning sign, then we're suggesting the events are directly related to the space-time continuum, which must be manipulated in order to create what is essentially a rudimentary wormhole. And in that continuum, time gets skewed between chronological and effectively practical. In other words, what transpires over a week or a month in our time might only be a blink, a moment or a minute, within the void itself once the door on the other side of the space bridge was opened."

Donati assumed Top Left would offer the first response to that and he was right. "And you believe that's what happened eighteen years ago. Someone or something came through that door you built from the other side."

"I can't say with any certainty that anything came through per se, sir, but I can say they opened the door we'd built from that other side—blew it open, to be more accurate, with enough quantum force to destroy the entire facility."

"Get back to the present, Dr. Donati," said Bottom Right. "You've already detailed your evidence of this pattern reoccurring. But this door you built has been closed for some eighteen years—not just closed, but obliterated when Laboratory Z was destroyed. I imagine you and your director, this Orson Wilder, were lucky to survive."

"Indeed," Donati acknowledged. "Just because we didn't build the door this time, sir, doesn't mean somebody else didn't. And maybe it's taken all of those eighteen years to achieve."

"By which you seem to be suggesting something may indeed have come through that door eighteen years ago and has been laying the groundwork for whatever's coming all that time."

"The thought had crossed my mind, sir," Donati affirmed in obvious understatement.

"The question," said the woman in the top right, "is what, or who, exactly? And where?"

"I can expound forever on who or what, but can speak more authoritatively on where," Donati explained. "See, if you continued along the line of the Earth's curvature as suggested by the original pattern, you'd cross right through Laboratory Z. Follow today's pattern in the same manner and you'll end with a grid that contains the new doorway with a reasonable degree of certainty."

"I'd strongly suggest," said Top Left, "that there can be no degree of certainty of any kind pertaining to this topic."

"We're talking in theoretical concepts here," Donati reminded him, "not absolutes."

"I believe we all understand that much," the lone woman chimed in. "Much harder to grasp is precisely what all this portends and what exactly we're supposed to do about it."

"I don't have answers for either of those questions at this time, ma'am," Donati conceded. "If whoever was on the other side of that door eighteen years ago is coming back, though, I can tell you one thing with a reasonable degree of certainty."

"And what's that, Doctor?"

"That this time they're going to get it right."

NINE

END OF THE ROAD

Blessed are the hearts that can bend;
they shall never be broken.

—ALBERT CAMUS

67

THE WOODS

Alex and Sam huddled against the cold, tucked into the lip of the coast redwoods forest, safe from sight of the road.

"He's not coming back," she said softly between quivering lips.

"I know."

"What are we going to do?"

Alex hugged her tightly in response but didn't answer, because he didn't know. Somehow the canopy provided by the towering redwoods made him feel safer. The trees of this forest were some of the tallest and oldest in the state, but little known to nonresidents compared to the more famous forests farther north. As a boy, he'd often imagined them coming to life, unhinging their roots from the ground and moving en masse to save the world from monsters making war on it.

If only they could do that now . . .

"The sun'll be up soon," he said finally. "It'll get warmer."

"That's not an answer."

"It's something."

Sam continued to tremble against him, whimpering softly.

"I'm scared," she said, voice hushed and cracking.

"I know."

"I mean *really* scared. If they know who I am—"

"They don't know who you are."

"But if they do, my parents . . ."

She left the thought to dangle, hanging in the crisp air.

"When I was a little girl, I'd wake up scared like this some nights and wait for the sun to come up. Because I knew once it did, everything would be okay. But it's not gonna be okay this time, is it?"

Alex eased Sam from his embrace but still held her tight. "I don't know."

"If I got home and found my parents like . . ."

"Mine?" he completed, when her voice drifted again.

She swallowed hard, or tried to. "I'm sorry."

"Don't be."

"I don't know if I told you that, after what happened."

"You don't have to."

He hugged her to him again.

"We have to do something," Alex heard her say in his ear. "We need help."

"Raiff will find us."

"If he's alive."

"He's alive."

"And what if those things find us again first?"

"Then you'll taser them again."

She almost laughed. Almost. "I lost my taser."

"We'll buy another."

"With what?"

"You ask too many questions."

She slipped away from him, smoothed her hair and took off her glasses. "You said that to me in the hospital."

"Because it's true."

"I'm not your tutor anymore, Alex. I think . . . I think it's more like you're mine."

He reeled her back in against him. "Now, that's a scary thought."

Sam smiled and pressed her head against his heart.

Well, she thought, *at least it's beating. That's something, anyway.*

"Alex?"

"What?" he said, stroking her hair.

"It's not a scary thought at all."

Sam tightened her arms around him, feeling warm and safe in his grasp.

68

GROUND ZERO

Langston Marsh walked about the ravaged FedEx Office store in Santa Cruz, awash in the spray of revolving light from the police vehicles still securing the scene with sawhorses. Dawn was just breaking, a beautiful sunrise starting to fill in the sky as if it were a coloring book. Marsh turned his gaze on that sky and envisioned what no one else did.

What was coming.

His identification listed him as Homeland Security, the catchall most guaranteed to keep other officials quiet and deferential. He didn't have much time, knew real agents from Homeland Security would likely be here soon to try and make sense of the evidence and witness statements, which made no sense at all.

To everyone but him, that is.

Rathman trailed him at a safe distance, arriving here what might have been mere minutes after this, whatever *this* was, had happened. He watched Marsh retracing the same path over and over again, as if wondering if seeing the very same things might change his view of them. He let his gaze linger on the security cameras.

"Anything?"

"Just static. Nothing but snow, sir."

"Our enemy is formidable, Colonel. We must give them that much."

Marsh surveyed the scene once more, feeling as if it were the first time again. The shattered remnants of severed robotic parts, with wires running through them instead of veins and current instead of blood, that lay strewn all over the store's interior was final proof, provided undeniable affirmation of the merits of his life's work.

"A war zone, Colonel; that's what this looks like. A war zone pulled from the future."

"A war requires two sides, sir. And these . . . *things* aren't what your Trackers have been pursuing."

"Not at all," Marsh acknowledged, looking at the upshot of the battle that had been fought here, again. "You're reading my mind."

"Just stating the obvious."

"Which would imply these machines came after the boy. Are we to assume, then, that he's the one who did this to them?" Marsh knelt and ran a finger sheathed in a plastic glove along the innards exposed by one of the robot's heads being lopped off. "This cut is totally clean. There's minimal scoring, suggesting the weapon that did it utilized heat or some kind of energy. A laser, maybe."

"I'm seeing something else, sir."

"What's that?"

"A professional, capable of taking out the three in here and two out back. That's not this boy."

"We don't know that."

"I do."

"How?"

Rathman crouched on the opposite side of the robot's remains. "Because I know my enemies."

"We need to collect some of this evidence, Colonel, before anyone is any the wiser."

"Already done, sir."

"And we need to find this boy," Marsh said, his knees cracking audibly as he rose. "He's the key. Find him and we'll find the answers we need. I've already summoned all our teams to the area. Ground Zero—that's what we're looking at here."

Rathman rose too, Marsh not liking something he saw in the big man's eyes.

"What's wrong, Colonel?"

"It's all a bit hard to stomach, that's all."

Marsh knew there was more, even thought he knew what it was, but let it pass. In that moment, he felt like a frightened, bitter little boy again, angry over his father's death and finding solace only in a resolution to seek revenge on his killers. From the first moment he'd glimpsed the wreckage of his father's fighter plane, now displayed in his Memory Room, he'd known his murderer was something from beyond this world. Just as he'd known this day would come, the day for which he'd dedicated his entire life to preparing. Behind the vast success he'd attained, behind all the money he'd made, this day had been lurking. Soon the world would know what he had known for sixty years.

That we aren't alone.

That they were here once.

And would be coming back.

Marsh's mind drifted, leaving him feeling almost disembodied. Trapped somewhere between the past and present. A sad little boy certain of things no one else believed trapped in the body of an old man. As an adult he'd built a private army, a modern-day Fifth Column, tasked to exterminate the vermin but had fallen short. Just like the time as a boy he'd doused his plastic toy soldiers with lighter fluid and lit them on fire, only to have his mother extinguish the flames before they burned.

In that moment Marsh thought he saw something in a corner of the ravaged FedEx Office, trapped between a crevice of shadows and the first of the dawn light sneaking in through the windows. An almost translucent figure that looked ash gray against the white wall: tall and gaunt with an irregular dark seam down its center, as if the two halves of him had been sewn together.

"You were thinking they may not be enough," he said to Rathman.

"Sir?"

"After I mentioned I'd summoned all our teams to the area—I saw it in your eyes."

Rathman stripped off his gloves, surveying the room yet again without denying Marsh's words. "You were more correct than you could possibly realize, sir. The first thing you told me."

"What's that?"

"That we're going to war."

Marsh looked back at the corner where the sad boy inside him had glimpsed the ash-colored creature. But the old man saw nothing now.

"In that case," Rathman was saying, "I'd like your permission to bring in some more soldiers."

"Of course, Colonel. As many as it takes."

"It's not just numbers, it's also experience."

Marsh glanced about the wreckage once more. "With *this*?"

"With anything. That's the kind of men I want to call

in. Special operators who know their way around combat."

"They've never encountered what they'll be facing here," Marsh reminded him.

"Close enough, sir," Rathman said.

69

GONE

Sam awoke hunched against a tree, Alex nowhere to be seen.

"Alex," she said hoarsely through a mouth that felt all dry and pasty, imagining what her breath must have smelled like. "Alex!"

He was nowhere to be seen, having left her sometime in the night. She pulled herself to her feet, found her legs so gimpy she could barely stand.

"Al . . . ," she started to cry out again, but her voice drifted off before she finished.

He was gone. They'd slept leaning against one another and clinging to the warmth that the other's body provided. She'd dreamed of this night for so long, never imagining it would come at so steep a price. But they had slept holding tightly to one another, afraid to let go, as if they might slip away. Or maybe he'd never been here to begin with and this really was all some crazy dream or illusion, an alternate reality starting to clear amid the dewy mist with the sun's touch.

"Hey, you're awake."

Sam spun around so fast, her wobbly legs nearly gave out. She held fast to the tree just in time, as Alex made his way into the clearing.

"Where the hell were you?"

"Had some business to attend to."

Sam realized he was zipping up his fly. "Oh."

"I was up before," he told her, "when the sun first came up. I found a stream, just down a path over there. Come on," he said. "Fresh water, at least."

Alex didn't say a word about how torturous his night had been. Every time he drifted off to what passed for sleep, he saw the ash man, what Raiff had called a Shadow, split in half, talking literally out of both sides of his mouth at once.

You must come with me, Alex. You've evaded for this long, but now you're ours again. We won't stop. We'll never stop.

The ash man wanted something from him, something Alex had no conception of. Raiff thought it might be something he knew instead of an actual object. Maybe the ash man didn't know for sure, either.

"Come on," Alex said, taking Sam's hand, "you look thirsty."

He led her through the trees deeper into the forest. Before long, Sam heard the soft sound of water slipping over rocks and moments later the stream came into view. Thin and shallow, looking more like a man-made drainage culvert than something natural.

Sam dropped to her knees and splashed her face, feeling herself coming back to life. Then she started drinking and couldn't stop. The water was bitingly cold but refreshing and she kept raising her cupped hands to her mouth, as much of it spilling down her shirt as finding her lips.

Sam caught Alex half smiling at her, at least briefly. "What?"

"You should see yourself."

Sam stiffened, only then thinking what she must've

looked like after a night outside in the elements. She sniffed at her clothes, as if they might yield something.

"I said 'see,' not 'smell.' "

"Don't look at me."

"Why?"

"Because I'm a mess."

"Meaning I must be one too," Alex managed.

"It's different for you. You're a guy."

"That would make you a girl."

Spoken as if he just realized it.

"Why are you looking at me like that?" he asked her.

"What, like you're an alien or something? . . . Sorry, that wasn't funny."

"Only because it's true."

Her expression changed, more what he was used to seeing from her. "Then why don't you look any different from anyone else? I mean, I understand DNA, but, hey, we're only a bit off from the great apes as human beings and we look totally different."

"You forgetting the CAT scan that found something in my head? You forgetting all the shit Dr. Chu figured out about me from just a blood test?"

"Neither of those have anything to do with your appearance."

"You mean, like I've got two arms, two legs, two eyes, two ears, two feet, two hands, two—"

"You can stop there. And the answer's yes. The entire study of astrobiology postulates that alien life would develop according to its native environment, potentially so different from us that we wouldn't even recognize or identify it as life."

"So what's your point?"

"I just made it. The odds that an alien species could

develop along parallel or identical lines to our own would be off the charts."

Alex rolled his eyes. "I'm guessing the odds of ever finding alien life of any kind would be off the charts. And you're missing the real point, anyway."

"What's that?"

"Go back eighteen years, Sam. Somebody from that other world hid me here and made sure no one could follow. Raiff's been waiting the whole time in case the ash man and these drones got wise to my presence. And if I've got something the bad guys want, it stands to figure it can help the good guys."

"Which still leaves us with a big question," she told him.

"What's that?"

"Just who are the good guys?"

His expression tightened. "Your parents, Sam, and you need to call them. They'll be going crazy now."

"Call them with what?"

"We'll buy one of those throwaway phones."

"With *what*?"

"Haven't figured that out yet, but I will." He tried to smile, came up just short. "I'm the savior, remember?" A faraway look suddenly filled his sandy brown eyes. "Some savior. I couldn't even save my own mother and father."

"One thing's for sure," Sam told him, trying to bring him back. "We're not going to find the answers we need in these woods."

"I was thinking more like someplace that isn't there anymore."

"What's that?" Sam asked.

"Laboratory Z."

70

MARSHALING THE FORCES

Rathman found Langston Marsh in his Memory Room, polishing the wreckage of his father's plane with a rag dipped in solvent that smelled like fresh lacquer.

"What do you remember most about your father, Colonel?" Marsh asked him, without turning from his toils.

"Getting smacked when he came home drunk."

"For misbehaving?"

"For happening to be there."

Marsh finally looked his way. "Unhappy memories, then."

"I don't think about it much, sir. Not at all, really, anymore."

"They're memories all the same," Marsh said, backing away and regarding the wreckage as if to inspect his own handiwork at keeping the metal as pristine and shiny as he could. "I have very few of my father and that number seems to shrink each year. One stands out, though, one that will never slip away." Still regarding the wreckage, perhaps seeing the plane as whole again, he said, "Not long before that night, he took me flying. Just the two of us. Strapped me into the cockpit in the seat behind his in an old de Havilland Hornet F.1 he'd restored himself and kept hangared at the base. It had that famous Rolls-Royce Merlin engine. It was my first time flying. I remember being scared at first, but I was with my father and so long as I was with him, nothing bad could happen. I'm sorry it wasn't the same for you, Colonel."

"It was a long time ago, sir."

Marsh's eyes remained fixed on the wreckage. "It wasn't long after my maiden flight that my father was shot down. I remember thinking it would never've happened if I'd been with him, because he never would have let anything bad happen to me. I blamed myself, Colonel." Marsh looked Rathman's way, his gaze curious. "Did you blame yourself when your father beat you?"

"I blamed the fact that he was an asshole, a lush, and a loser."

"You joined the army to get away from him," Marsh said, in what had started out as a question.

"I joined the army so I could come back one day and square things. My father was a big man too, sir, a dock-worker and longshoreman who'd put any number of men in the hospital he took on in bar fights. Those were the nights he was the nicest, having already got it out of his system. He beat me because it was convenient."

"And did you?"

"Did I what?"

"Square things."

"He got sick before I had the chance. Cancer from smoking too many cigarettes and inhaling too much asbestos. I didn't even recognize him in the hospital."

"What about your desire for vengeance?"

"Never went away. I hoped he'd get better, go back to being the big strong man he used to be so it would mean something when I took him down. The cancer denied me that. It didn't seem fair, left a hole inside me I've never been able to fill completely."

Marsh was nodding. "Then you know how I feel. This boy, those *things* . . . Fate is granting me the opportunity it denied you. I'm going to get my shot at my father's killers." He started forward, leaving the plane wreckage behind him and seeming to step back into the present. "Tell me about these men you're assembling who are up to that task."

"I was only interested in the ones groomed in the special ops world."

"Your world, in other words, Colonel."

"The kind of men we need. The fees you're offering will definitely get their attention."

"How many?"

"Five hundred, give or take a few, and that's only the ones I share a personal connection with, normally through their commanding officers."

"When can they be on site?"

"Several are already en route."

"I thought it would take longer than that."

"These kind of men are used to rapid deployments, sir."

"What about the enemy they're going up against, Colonel?"

"Need-to-know basis, sir."

"And what do they need to know?"

"What to shoot at and when."

Marsh turned back toward the wreckage. In that moment, its remnants were replaced by the old de Havilland Hornet, and his father was beckoning him forward, ready to hoist him up into the seat that was waiting for him. He thought if he reached out, the jagged husks of scorched, ruined metal would be replaced by the smooth, freshly painted steel his father had lovingly restored to full working condition. But then the illusion passed and

Marsh was again left with only the iron corpse in which his father had died, his body never recovered.

Marsh canted his body sideways, almost perfectly centered between Rathman and the wreckage. "Take a look, Colonel, take a good, hard look. *They* did this the last time they tried to take our world and would have, if brave men like my father hadn't taken the fight to them. Now they've come back, with the same end no doubt in mind. Only this time we're going to wipe them out, leave none behind to fight another day. You hear what I'm saying, Colonel?"

Rathman nodded. "I do, sir."

"You were in Iraq and Afghanistan."

"Saw the worst of things in both. Not so much the front lines, as places where the lines don't exist."

Marsh nodded, liking what he heard. "Men like my father saved the world once, Colonel. Now it's left to us to do the same."

71

ON THE ROAD

"Have you ever hitchhiked before?" Sam asked Alex, as they started down the road.

"Nope."

"I have," she told him.

"You're kidding," Alex said, eyeing her incredulously.

"No, I'm serious. I was with my mom. Her Volvo, the one she had since I was born, overheated and neither of us had our phones. I remembered we passed a gas station a few miles back and started walking. A trucker who saw the Volvo pulled over and gave me a ride."

"That's not hitchhiking."

"I was walking and somebody gave me a ride. What would you call it?"

"Did you have your thumb out?"

"No."

"Like I said."

"It smelled like the drone things," Sam said suddenly, her thoughts veering. "When the car overheated, that burned smell. Like the drone things."

Her gaze tightened on him, just as the sun caught his face, revealing the thin streaks of grime on his cheeks that seemed dragged down by tears. Alex's hair was stringy and mussed, the way it looked when he took his helmet off during a game. She remembered stealing sight of his perfect butt framed by the contours of his form-fitting uniform, leaving pretty much nothing to the imagination, and hoping nobody caught her.

How dumb that felt right now after all that had happened, like her old life was really the dream set against an entirely new reality.

"You were a gymnast once," Alex said out of nowhere. "What happened? Why'd you quit?"

"I got tall," she told him.

"That's not a reason."

Sam hesitated. Why had she quit? She'd been good. Maybe not the best—but good.

"Time," she said. "Time and priorities. I wanted to be a gymnast, but I realized I wanted to be something else more."

"What's that?"

"Promise not to laugh."

"Okay, promise."

"An astronaut."

Alex laughed.

"Hey, you promised!" she said, smacking him in a shoulder that felt like molded steel.

"Couldn't help myself. It's funny."

"What's so funny about it?"

"I'm just trying to picture you in one of those outfits."

Like I picture your butt in your football pants, Sam thought.

"You know how much you love football?"

"Sure."

"That's how much I love science. You think of playing professionally, don't you?"

Alex's shoulders dropped, as if the air had been sucked out of them. "Until yesterday, anyway."

"Well, that's the same way I think about being an astronaut. Not as funny as it is ironic. I so wanted to be an astronaut and find out the truth—like Scully and Mulder said: the truth is out there."

"Who? *What?*"

"*The X-Files.*"

"Oh, the TV show."

"You've never seen it?"

"I've heard of it."

"Not even a single episode?"

"What did I just say?"

Sam shrugged, left it there. "Anyway, being an astronaut, that's what I dreamed of—until yesterday too," she added.

"Because why go to them when they're coming to us?"

"It does change the way you look at things. But I meant it makes me want to be an astronaut even more, because now I know there really is something out there. Sounds silly, doesn't it?"

Alex stopped walking and Sam almost plowed into him. To her surprise, he took her face between his hands.

"Not silly at all." He grimaced. "At least, no more silly than me still thinking about playing pro football. Hey, you know what I'm craving now more than anything?"

"A hot shower?"

"A PowerBar." His eyes widened, expression veering in mid-thought. "Do I smell?"

"Can't tell. I'm holding my nose against the way *I* smell."

"Okay, a shower and *then* a PowerBar."

"You know, this is stupid," Sam found the courage to say finally.

"What?"

"Laboratory Z. Going there. It's been gone for eighteen years."

"According to Meng Po, it was part of a complex."

"Meng Po?"

"The flash drive inside. And the complex will still be there."

"Doesn't mean we'll find anything."

"Doesn't mean we won't." Alex stopped, picked up again with his eyes on the road ahead. "And I need to see it."

"Why?"

"I don't know. I just do. Maybe it'll help me think, sort all this out."

"Anne Frank," Sam said without meaning to.

"You helped me with her diary," Alex recalled. "For history."

"English, actually. You were studying the memoir."

"I thought it was a diary."

Sam let the remark pass. "The book always scared me, her cooped up in that attic with the Nazis outside on the street, sometimes knocking at the door downstairs. Cooped up and surrounded by monsters. That's what made it so scary."

"I think I get the point."

"The story didn't have a happy ending, Alex. They get her in the end. She loses to the monsters."

He reached out and drew her in close against his shoulder, a car engine sounding behind them. "Well, Anne Frank didn't have me." Alex stuck his thumb out too late for the driver to notice and the car, a souped-up Camaro, thundered past. "Damn!"

Sam eased herself away from him. "Let me try."

"Yeah," Alex grinned, "good luck with that."

They heard the squeal of an engine and swung to find a battered old van cresting the hill and rumbling toward them, belching a curtain of white smoke out its backside as it veered to the shoulder with a set of four nearly bald tires spraying gravel and stones into a brief tornado.

"What'd you say?" Sam winked, jogging ahead of him toward the van.

72

T-H-E-N-D C-O-M-E-S

The old van's engine rattled, its front end shimmying toward a stall when Alex yanked its passenger door open to a grinding squeal.

"Where you kids headed?" came a voice as cracked and worn as the van's faded upholstery.

"Back to the city," Alex said, leaving it there while Sam was still composing the answer in her mind.

"Well, climb in," the voice continued. "Meter's running. Let's go."

Alex climbed in first, positioning himself in the middle and ceding the window to Sam. Squeezing inside next to him afforded her first clear look at the driver. He had pinkish, sunburned skin that was mottled and patchy dark in spots. His hair was a splotchy mess of gray spikes and waves. It looked self-trimmed, somewhere between a brush cut and military-style crew cut. The driver's eyes were bloodstained in spidery lines that circled the tired blue pupils, which looked as if someone had bleached the color out of them. The van smelled of old weed and cheap aftershave baked together into the fabric, thinly disguising the musty odor of stale sweat and unwashed clothes.

Sam reached for the seat belt but found no buckle threaded the loop, which was snapped in half. The van had once contained more seats, but they'd been removed behind this single row to make room for a grungy, coffee-stained mattress and boxes overflowing with well-bound books that looked like Bibles.

"The city it is," the driver announced. "The Reverend William Grimes at your service." He flashed a cigarette-browned grin. "But you can call me Reverend Billy."

"I'm Kit," Alex said, beating Sam to the punch again, paraphrasing the name from the imaginary friend to whom Anne Frank had addressed her diary. "And this is Anne, my girlfriend."

The Reverend Billy Grimes reclaimed the steering wheel with his fingers and Sam noticed that a single letter had been tattooed on each of them, just below the knuckle:

THEND COMES

He didn't have enough fingers on his left hand to spell "the end" out all the way, so he must have improvised.

"Let's get this show on the road," Reverend Billy said, jerking the old van into gear and fighting it back onto the highway, where its bald tires stumbled and stammered before finding pavement.

And off they went.

"We shouldn't be here, none of us," Reverend Billy resumed. "We should be in His house on this holy Sabbath, so let's make of it what we will, shall we?"

Alex turned and met Sam's eyes, the message in his matching her thoughts exactly, before finishing in a shrug and a frown that said, *Let's grin and bear it.*

"Are you a preacher?" Alex asked him.

"In a church with no name to anyone with the wisdom to listen to my word. I've seen things, children, things I wouldn't wish on another human being. Things that make you question the very nature of man and humanity, although I don't expect you kids to be able to relate to such a thing."

"Well," Alex began, shooting Sam another gaze that came up just short of a wink, "you'd be surprised."

But Reverend Billy wasn't listening. "See, before I came to be what I am, I served as a military chaplain in war zones. Think of the worst things you've heard about those wars and multiply that by about a hundred and you'll have an idea of what I'm talking about. There's so much of it I'd give anything to *un*see, if that were even possible, and I won't bore you with the details. Suffice it to say, you know when you see all the truth of the world laid bare? When you look into the eyes of a dying man. Lord God, so many of those eyes belonged to mere children little older than you kids. I was the last thing far too many of them saw and I do believe a little of me died each time. So by the end of it I had no choice but to be reborn."

He spoke with his eyes fixed tightly ahead and hands gripping the wheel so tightly that the letters imprinted on his knuckles seemed to stretch. Sam thought she saw the man's eyes glistening with the start of tears and was relieved beyond measure when Alex reached down and grasped her hand in his.

"Problem was," Reverend Billy continued, "the womb of the world had gone sour, so what emerged lacked the normal mechanisms to cope with the awful realities we all must face—that being hope and dreams. I have neither, children, because I've seen the world for what it really is, exposed to the core. I've seen the true depths of depravity to which man can sink, and in the eyes of dying men I saw the world's fate as only they could show it to me."

Sam squeezed Alex's hand tighter, hoping he'd just tell Reverend Billy to pull over so they could start the whole hitchhiking process anew. Maybe land a ride with someone who smelled better and listened to talk radio.

But Reverend Billy cocked a gaze their way before Alex had a chance to say anything. "I saw there is no hope. No reclamation or redemption, either. Wish I could tell you why the Lord chose me to be the bearer of His word, I truly do. Why not the pope or the president, instead of some nobody that no one would ever give credence? The kind of man you stop on a street corner and listen to, only to walk away shaking your head and grinning at his madness."

Reverend Billy sucked in some breath and seemed to chew on his lips.

"Then I realized that was His point. That nobody was going to listen to this truth, this message, anyway, so it didn't matter who was delivering it, did it? So, Anne and Kit, I am indeed a preacher, but one without a flock. I pass out my Bibles to anyone who'll take one in the hope they'll find some message I must've missed along the way. But I know they won't because it's not there, since whoever wrote it only put down what God wanted us to know to spare us the truth of our being and essence. See the dashboard?"

Alex and Sam looked in unison, noticing a patchwork of torn wires emerging from a rectangular slot of a hole where the radio should have been.

"I ripped that out so I could be alone with my thoughts during these drives, hoping maybe, just maybe, He might choose to let me hear the truth of His word. Then I finally realized I never would because that word hasn't been written yet. I wish I could say what this overriding truth truly is but all I see when I ask for divine guidance is the face of man himself, not God. As if we made ourselves, while He sat back and watched. And how can that be, children? I ask you, how can that be?"

His question rang with restrained desperation. Sam realized Reverend Billy smelled vaguely of moss and fresh earth, on top of the weed and dried sweat, and thought she glimpsed strips of vine reeds sticking out of his mismatched hair. She pictured him sleeping outdoors at night, nothing between him and the stars. A man who spent his time digging holes into the earth, never finding exactly what he was looking for.

"You really think the end's coming?" Alex asked Reverend Billy, no whimsy in the question at all.

"I'm sure of it, son, just as sure as I am your name's not Kit and hers isn't Anne. But it's not going to end the way we expect, the one the Bible portends, no. It's like we're still gonna be us but not us, at the same time. It's like it's all gonna change with the turning of the sun, the world a whole different place when we wake up one morning than it was when we went to bed the night before. It's like there's a purpose we've been prepared to fill since time immemorial and everything else, what passes for glory and goals, are nothing more than illusions we've tricked ourselves into believing are real."

Reverend Billy stopped again. The plaintiveness that had ridden his voice like a saddle had spread into his expression, making him look sad and a bit desperate. Sam wondered on what street corner he'd be found today, peddling his free Bibles to anyone who passed and preaching to those who lingered about the meaning of his tattooed knuckles. Then he'd pack up and resume the process somewhere else tomorrow, the cycle continuing with the record player needle stuck scratchily in place.

He resumed speaking, his voice hoarse and cracked with sadness. "I think we're gonna get what's coming to us and the simple fact of the matter is, based on what I've seen, Armageddon is the least of our problems."

73

ALL FREE TOMORROW

Reverend Billy dropped them in the parking lot fronting a Buy Two store in a Daly City shopping center south of the downtown San Francisco area, Sam far more unnerved by his quiet rants than Alex.

"You're shivering," Alex noted, rubbing Sam's arms, the gooseflesh prickling the surface.

She loved his touch but it made her feel no warmer. "Tell me that guy didn't scare the hell out of you too."

"I was too busy holding my nose. You wanna talk about scary? Try sitting next to him."

"I'd rather not," Sam said, watching Reverend Billy's van shrink away down the road before disappearing altogether.

"The guy was harmless. Didn't touch my knee or reach for something higher, nothing like that."

"No offense, pretty boy, but he was looking at me, not you."

"That was my hand on your knee, not his," Alex quipped as they walked toward the Buy Two store, called that since buying two items got you a third, lower-priced one for free. No exceptions.

"Well, that's a relief, anyway."

They entered the store together to the sound of canned music piped in just under the sound of a happy voice singing out the praises of today's specials, which featured no-name jeans to go with no-name shirts, shoes, and underwear. A huge banner, a bit worn and discolored by the sun, hung over the alcove entry, reading, ALL FREE TOMORROW.

"Too bad it's not today," Alex mused, digging a hand through his pockets.

"So let's come back tomorrow, like the sign says. Catch ourselves in a vicious cycle where it's never really today." Sam's features flattened. "Oh, man, I sound like Reverend Billy."

"So long as you don't smell like him," Alex said, passing under the ALL FREE TOMORROW sign to enter the store.

Adding up all their cash, Sam's and what Dr. Payne had tucked away in his jeans, came to a grand total of sixty-one dollars. Thanks to the Buy Two store's mantra, that was enough for a change of clothes for each of them and some food with twenty bucks maybe left over. They filtered through the clothes piles in search of a decent enough fit.

"Be nice if we knew exactly where Laboratory Z was located," Alex said suddenly.

"Well, we've got a general location."

"San Ramon's spread out over a pretty wide area."

"Any other clues you can remember?"

"Horses and cattle."

"Huh?"

"As a kid, I overheard my parents talking about it a few times—at least, I think that's what they were talking about. Anyway, for some reason I remember horses and cattle."

"So we're looking for a farm?" Sam said, laying a decent enough pair of jeans aside.

"I didn't say that."

"No, you said horses and cattle. Maybe Laboratory Z was located near a farm or something, or a ranch. Maybe that's what you remember." She looked across the stacks of clothes at him. "This place is right on a bus route. We can get to San Ramon with only a couple transfers. Man, I hope my car's okay. . . ."

He grinned, started to chuckle.

"Hey, what's so funny?"

"The way you said that."

"Said what?"

"About your car. Hoping it's okay."

"Well, I do."

They steered the cart holding their selections to the food aisles next, starting in the section vaguely labeled "Nutrition."

"Wow, you meant what you said about PowerBars," Sam noted, as Alex dumped a handful of boxes in atop their clothes. "Six boxes?"

"We only have to pay for four, remember? And I went with the generic brand."

"Right, a real sacrifice."

"Come on," he said, holding up one of the boxes. "Food fit for an astronaut."

"All we need is some Tang to wash it down."

"Tang?"

"Never mind," Sam told him.

At the checkout line, both their eyes drifted to the prepaid cell phone offerings while waiting their turn. The best deal was $9.95 for a cheap, knockoff smart phone offering unlimited talk, text, and Web for the first week at that introductory price.

"You should call your parents."

"We already went over this."

"They'll be worried sick."

"I just want them to be safe and sound when I get home."

Alex pushed their cart forward and back again. Two more carts had piled in the checkout line behind theirs, the woman currently at the front paying for her purchases out of a quarter jar, taking forever.

"Maybe they don't know who you are," he said unconvincingly.

"They stole my iPad, remember? And wiped the backup off the Cloud."

"Why?"

"I'm still trying to figure that out. Must've had something to do with the pattern I uncovered."

"What pattern, exactly?"

"It's hard to explain, complicated."

"And I won't be able to understand." Alex nodded.

"Did I say that?"

"You didn't have to."

"It doesn't matter, anyway. Even though Dr. Donati seemed interested in my findings, *very* interested."

"See, you're even smarter than you think." He sighed and blew the stray hair from his face. "I want you sleeping in your own bed tonight. I want to get you home."

"Not if it means leaving you alone."

"Apparently, I've always been alone. I just didn't know it."

"You're not alone now."

"Thanks," he said shyly, gaze tilted downward. "We'll go to San Ramon together. After that—"

"After that," Sam interrupted, "we'll figure out what comes next."

"Your parents. They need to hear your voice, Sam."

"Not over one of those things," she said, eyeing the prepaid phones displayed at the register. "Might as well hold a spotlight on myself."

"I've got another idea," Alex told her.

He leaned against the cart. The woman in front of them had her purse in the child seat—open. Her phone was clearly visible.

Alex deftly slipped it out and handed it to Sam. "Now, be like ET and phone home."

74

PHONING HOME

Sam backed off, noticing the phone's real owner was just then placing her purchases on the register conveyor belt, too busy with that and her two kids to have any idea the phone was missing. Her throat felt thick, her heart hammering against her chest when the phone began to ring and she willed someone to answer.

"Joints Are Us," her mother greeted, Sam realizing instantly that she must have forwarded her home calls to the business line.

"Mom?"

"Honey," her mother's voice came back, "where are you?"

"Well, I—"

"Ronald, it's Sam," her mother called to her father before she could continue. "What's going on? Why didn't you come home last night? The police were here."

"Police?" Sam repeated, feeling something flutter inside her.

"Two of them, asking to speak to you. They wouldn't say what it was about. You weren't answering your cell phone, straight to voicemail. We've been worried sick. What's going on, Sammie?"

"What did they look like?"

"Who?"

"The police."

"Like . . . cops."

"What about smell? Did you notice how they smelled?"

"What?"

"Never mind," Sam said, switching gears. "What did you tell them?"

"Nothing, because there was nothing to tell. That's right, isn't it? I think they may still be parked outside. Let me look—wait, your father just came in. I'm handing him the—"

"Sam!" she heard her father's voice call.

"Hi, Dad."

"Whatever it is, you can tell us, Sammie. Why were the cops here? What's it have to do with Alex Chin?"

"Alex?" Sam posed, looking right at him.

"They asked about Alex too. They were careful to say you hadn't done anything wrong. They didn't say the same thing about him. When the cops come back—"

"They said they were coming back?"

"Maybe. I think so. Strange that they didn't write anything down, come to think of it."

"Did they smell like motor oil, Dad?"

"How'd you know that, Sammie?" her father asked after a pause.

75

THE GENERAL

Raiff dressed his wounds as best he could. His head still felt like a hammer was pounding the inside of his skull and he didn't dare risk taking any medications likely to dull more than the pain.

Because it was coming.

He didn't know precisely where or when, or even what, exactly. Only, the very reason why he'd spent the last eighteen years of his life protecting a child who had no idea of his true being or heritage was about to be fulfilled. It was the sole explanation for the events of the past two days—Dancer's house and the hospital first, then the attack of last night. The appearance of the Shadow that Dancer had called the ash man and the import of the quasi-apparition's words the boy had managed to reconstruct.

"'No, faith, not a jot; but to follow him thither, with modesty enough . . . ,'" he said across the table, where a chessboard sat between him and the General.

Quoting Hamlet, specifically a scene where the doomed prince holds a skull in hand while musing on the inevitability of death. "Inevitability" being the key word because that described the war that mankind had no idea was coming.

"'. . . and likelihood to lead it,'" Raiff completed. "What do you think of that, General?"

The General was actually a marble bust of whom Raiff believed to be Labienus, Julius Caesar's most trusted commander and confidante. Now his one and only of the same distinction, salvaged like virtually all the furnishings in Raiff's underground lair from trash heaps and Dumpsters. The General wasn't much of a conversationalist, of course, which made him a fine companion and even better chess opponent since, of course, Raiff never lost.

"Checkmate," he said, moving his knight in for the kill. "As inevitable as what's coming. I don't suppose you've got an idea of how to stop it. No, only Dancer knows that, the problem being he doesn't know *what* he knows. But it's got to be there. That's why he's here, why I'm here."

Raiff stopped, as if waiting for a response. Some nights, when the light was right, he thought the statue's lips moved. No sound emerged, though, as if its makers lacked the ability to string vocal cords from marble. But not being able to speak didn't mean the General couldn't listen.

Raiff reconfigured the pieces on the chessboard, starting a fresh game from scratch with the dueling armies neatly staged across from each other. "But here's the real problem, General: What am I missing? These androids didn't come from the other world, they came from this one. Built right here. Where? How? How many? You see what I'm getting at? Dancer's the only hope to stop them and whatever groundwork they're laying for the real invasion that's coming. Except that suggests spaceships pouring out of the sky packed with troops and weapons prepared to wage war. But we know they won't be coming that way, don't we? We know they'll be coming the same way I did when I brought Dancer through the wormhole."

But the boy's remaining Watchers hadn't checked in since last night. Could be Marsh's Trackers had got them. Or maybe more of the drones. Either party homing in on metabolic signals and waves, which explained why Raiff had long ago built his lair underground instead of above it.

And in the last place anyone would ever think to look.

"Your move, General," Raiff resumed, when the marble bust made no response. "Oh, that's right," he said, correcting himself. "It's mine."

TEN

LABORATORY Z

Secrets are things we give to others to keep for us.

—ELBERT HUBBARD

76

SAN RAMON

Alex and Sam stopped at an information desk inside the BART, short for Bay Area Rapid Transit, station a few blocks from the Buy Two store. A blue uniformed woman with milk chocolate skin smiled their way when she noticed them.

Alex leaned in toward her, but Sam shouldered him aside. "Let me this time." Then, to the clerk, "This is going to sound crazy, but is there, like, a huge farm around here, something with livestock and cattle?"

"You mean like a *ranch*?"

"Yes, exactly!"

The woman stifled a laugh and shook her head. "Honey, there's a ranch, all right, but you won't find any horses or cows there."

Bishop Ranch, it turned out, was a sprawling office park that ranked among Northern California's most prestigious business locations. On the woman's advice, they'd taken BART to the Dublin/Pleasanton station, where buses were conveniently available to take them the rest of the way to San Ramon in Contra Costa County, where Bishop Ranch was located.

"You can see it now." Alex pointed out the bus's window. "Over there on the right."

Sam followed his finger to the massive interconnected complex of buildings that reminded her somehow of the Pentagon, trying to picture things as they were the day of the fire eighteen years earlier when Laboratory Z had burned to the ground.

Situated in a tree-laden valley dominated by rolling hills and the same oaks, elms, and spruce that grew like weeds over the entire Bay Area, the city of San Ramon sat in the shadow of Mount Diablo to the northeast. A curious mix of urban sprawl enclosed by untouched land that passed as wilderness ruled by grasslands and tree orchards. The dryness of fall had turned the vast planes of grasses a goldenrod shade that made for pleasant viewing outside the window of their BART car in the trek there. They'd had the car virtually to themselves, Sunday marking the return of casual drivers along what is less than affectionately known as "the Maze."

"I can't believe your parents grow weed," Alex said to make conversation, when Sam's gaze lingered out the window a little too long.

"Why?"

"I don't know, it just seems strange."

"No, strange was when they tried to pay the mortgage with a trunk full of homemade jams and jellies."

"A trunk full of jams and jellies? That sounds crazy." Alex smiled.

"Based on the past couple days, I don't even know what qualifies as crazy anymore."

"If I hadn't been born on another planet, I'd wonder if maybe we weren't switched at birth," Alex said. "What with your parents likely preferring a football player and mine wishing they had a kid who actually was good in school."

The smile slipped from his face at that.

"Alex . . ."

"No, don't bother. I'm okay, Sam. Really I am."

She shrugged, leaving things there.

"What are you thinking about?" Alex asked, when Sam's gaze strayed out the BART car's window again.

"You told Reverend Billy I was your girlfriend."

"So?"

She turned back his way. "So what would Cara think of that?"

"What's the difference?"

"No difference. I just . . ." Sam started to turn back to the window, then stopped. "I want to tell you something I promised not to tell."

"That Cara's breaking up with me."

"She told you?" Sam asked, squaring her shoulders with her gaze now.

"No, you just did. Well, not really—I already knew it was coming, was just stringing her along. I mean, did you really think I wouldn't find out about that college guy she's been seeing?"

"So why lead her on?"

"Because she led me on first. And it was the brother of one of the other cheerleaders who told me and I promised to let her spill first. It was kind of fun."

"Leading her on?"

"And seeing her for what she really was. It's like, what was I thinking? How did I not see through her before?"

"You really want me to answer that?"

"I asked." Alex shrugged.

"She was an accessory, like the souped-up wheels on your car or your new leather jacket."

"I don't have souped-up wheels or a leather jacket."

"Figure of speech."

"Yeah," Alex said, "ironic, isn't it? And Cara wasn't always an accessory. I really liked her for a while."

"You didn't say 'loved.'"

"For a reason."

Sam shook her head, frowning. "Someday you need to explain all this high school stuff to me."

"You mean, like be your tutor? Be careful, I'm expensive."

"What happened to 'All Free Tomorrow'?"

"Then we'd face the same problem in twenty-four hours. And right now we've got something more important to do."

"Find Laboratory Z," Sam finished.

77

BISHOP RANCH

"Where do you think it was?" Sam asked Alex, as they walked along the outer perimeter of the sprawling Bishop Ranch Business Park, which seemed to stretch on forever.

"Only wish I remembered," Alex said dryly, sweeping his eyes about. "Maybe I'm a different kind of human, but even my kind doesn't seem to retain much of what happened as an infant."

He tried to keep his gaze indifferent, purposeful, avoiding thoughts of the fire from which his mother had saved him. It didn't work. A coldness gripped him, spreading from the inside out, the chill as bad as any winter could muster. The somewhat cross-shaped spread of interconnected buildings was bracketed at each arm by parking lots that formed endless, glistening seas of steel. But Alex saw only flames and noxious white smoke, more like vapor, overspreading the area like a vast wave. The stench of it was something corrosive and sweet at the same time, and Alex fully believed had he been closer to the buildings themselves he would've glimpsed a tiny but brave Chinese woman lugging a baby from the death trap of flames that burned white hot.

Bishop Ranch had either risen from the resulting refuse or been part of the same complex all those years ago, only to be spared the brunt of the blast that had

leveled Laboratory Z. "Ranch" was the word he'd overheard his parents use. Never any mention of the livestock
Alex's imagination had filled in. An Chin had said nothing of Bishop Ranch in the flash drive tucked inside
Meng Po, which Alex took for a clear sign she never
wanted him to come here. Or an even clearer sign there
was nothing left to return to.

A waste of time. A fool's errand.

Still, all he had right now.

"Alex?" Sam prodded.

"Huh?"

"You didn't answer my question."

"What'd you ask me?"

"What are we supposed to do now?"

"I don't know. Haven't got a clue."

Then his eyes fastened on a lone figure in a sun-
drenched clearing shrouded by a thick umbrella of trees.

"Maybe we should ask him," Alex said to Sam.

The man was seated on a cream-colored blanket splattered with grass stains beneath a frayed and flimsy pop-
up tent. He had long flowing white hair, gnarled and
matted into ringlets in places, blue eyes the color of the
sky, and a bushy beard that looked like cotton candy. The
grounds he occupied alone had a park-like feel to them,
likely still the civic property of San Ramon, which would
explain why the man was allowed to stake his claim here
unmolested. He held an unlit pipe in his mouth and a
small pot hung from a swivel at his side beneath a sign
that read, DEPOSIT A DOLLAR AND ASK THE PROFESSOR A
QUESTION.

But it was a series of larger signs staked in a semicircle
around the bearded man's blanket that grabbed Alex's at-

tention first, among them: THEY WALK AMONG US, TRUST NO ONE, THE WAR IS COMING, and ALIENS GO HOME!

With the exclamation point formed into something that looked like a ray gun aimed downward.

The professor pulled the unlit pipe from his mouth and gestured toward Alex and Sam with it, as they approached. Alex couldn't help thinking of Reverend Billy and THEND COMES stenciled across his knuckles. Maybe they were related or, more likely, keyed in to something on a cosmic level, able to hear and see things others couldn't. Alex remembered a tutoring session during which Sam explained that if humans could see as well as dogs could smell, they'd be able to identify a man clearly a half mile away with the naked eye. Begging the question: Who knew more, things being relative and all?

"You kids lost?" the Santa Claus–like figure asked, uncrossing his long legs and stretching them across the blanket.

"That depends," Alex told him.

"Does it now? On what, exactly?"

"On whether you can help us."

The professor looked toward the small pot swaying slightly in the breeze. "Answers cost a dollar."

Alex unfurled a crumpled bill from his pocket and pushed it into the empty pot. "Where was Laboratory Z?"

The professor looked at them with his sky-blue eyes turning narrow and suspicious. "Take back your dollar."

"You didn't answer my question."

"That's why you get your money back."

"I don't want my money back, I want an answer."

"Then ask a different question."

"Where was Laboratory Z *located*?"

The professor smirked, making him look even more like a mirthful Santa Claus. "Clever, aren't you?"

"Not really," Alex told him. "That's why I've got my tutor, Samantha, with me. I'm Alex."

The professor looked at both of them. "Do you always travel with your tutor, Alex?"

"Only when we're on the run," Alex told him, surprised by his own frankness.

The professor tried to look bemused, but failed. "What'd you do, rob a bank?"

"Actually, we're being chased by really bad guys who killed my parents. Only, they're not 'guys' at all. They're robots, drones, androids—something like that."

"And what's their interest in you?" the professor asked, playing along as if it was something he was used to doing.

"I'm an alien." Alex let the professor see him turn his gaze on Bishop Ranch, taking in as much of the sprawl as he could. "My adoptive mother rescued me from here, from Laboratory Z. The day of the fire. Her name was An Chin and she and my father were the best people I ever knew."

Something had made him tell the professor the whole crazy truth. He couldn't say what, exactly, something that told Alex this man wouldn't be surprised by it. Not at all.

"And I can prove it."

"Prove that your parents were the best people you ever knew?"

"No, that you're right. They really do walk among us and a war really is coming."

With that, Alex extracted the slap bracelet he'd taken from his father's wrist from the pocket of the still-stiff jeans he'd purchased at the Buy Two store. His feet felt much better squeezed into cheap sneakers his own size.

"Alien piece of jewelry?" the professor asked him.

"I guess you can call it that. But slap it on and you won't be going anywhere for a while."

"What do you—"

The professor's words froze in his throat when Alex slapped the bracelet on his wrist. His features seized up and his eyes bulged with fear until Alex stripped the thing off him.

"Where did you get that?" the professor asked, wide-eyed as he rubbed his wrist as if it were someone else's.

"From my father's wrist after they killed him."

"After *who* killed him?"

"Androids, cyborgs."

"We call them drone things," Sam chimed in.

The professor looked at her briefly before returning his focus to Alex, the fear still in his eyes. "You're saying a cyborg murdered your parents."

"'Cyborg*s*,' plural, yes. And we haven't even gotten to the ash man yet, a kind of astral projection. I'm the one he's after because I've got what he wants."

"And what's that?"

"I don't know."

"You don't know?"

"That's why we're looking for whatever's left of Laboratory Z," Alex told him. "Because maybe the answer's there."

78

MR. WIZARD

The professor climbed to his feet, one knobby knee cracking and then the other. He held his ground on the grass-stained blanket as if to keep his distance, then suddenly reached down and plucked Alex's untangled bill from his pot.

"Here," he said, extending it with a trembling hand.

Alex didn't take it. "What's with the refund?"

"You didn't ask a question."

"Yes, I did; you didn't answer it," Alex said.

The professor suddenly looked like a man who badly wanted to be somewhere else. "You need to leave."

"Tell me where we can find Laboratory Z and we will."

The old man's eyes sought him out, seeming to view him differently now, with an odd mixture of wonder and apprehension. "What makes you think I know?"

"The way you looked at me, the way you looked at that bracelet."

The professor sat back down. Alex and Sam joined him on the blanket next to each other, with the older man centered across from them.

"I've been coming here every day for fifteen years," he said, spooning a hand through his beard. "Around the last time I shaved. I don't want to believe you. I want to

believe you're full of shit. I want to believe that bracelet's something your tutor cooked up for a science fair
project."

Alex stuffed the crumpled dollar bill back into the tiny
pot. "Do you think I'm full of shit?"

The professor shrugged. Sam realized the crown of his
scalp was bald and he had a pointy, long nose with a pair
of reading spectacles dangling on the tip. She thought he
looked more like Mr. Wizard, the cartoon character who
invariably rescued Tooter Turtle from all manner of mis-
hap with a wave of his magic wand.

"I paid for an answer, Professor," Alex told him.

"Then do yourself a favor and just accept another
refund."

"That's not an answer."

"Yes, it is." He ran his eyes from Alex to Sam before
settling his gaze somewhere between them. "How much
do you know?"

"I told you what we know. The short version. There's
more if you want to hear it, lots more."

"I meant about Laboratory Z. Let's start there."

"I know about the explosion, the fire, and my mom
rescuing me," Alex said, swallowing hard as he tried to
fit all the pieces of what he'd learned together. "I know
there was some experiment going on there, something
big. I know that had something to do with the fire and
the lab's destruction."

"Then you know more than just about anyone alive,
except for me and one other man."

"You worked there," Sam put forth, "didn't you?"

"Yes, I did, young lady. I had a particular area of expertise the lab was most interested in."

"What's that?" asked Alex.

"We need to back up first, young man. Laboratory Z

was actually a NASA installation, a *secret* NASA installation that had existed already for more than a generation when you were born. Young lady," he said to Sam, "what was the significance of 1960 to the space program?"

"The election of John Kennedy."

"Exactly!"

"Do you owe me a dollar now?"

The professor didn't seem to hear her. "It was one of JFK's personal obsessions, and not just winning the race to the moon, either. But he had the foresight and vision to realize the logistics and realities of deep space travel, anything beyond the moon, really, brought challenges and costs that barely qualified it as a pipe dream. So Kennedy assembled a group of experts to come up with alternatives to rocket ships and star cruisers even as work continued on those as well." The professor paused long enough to meet both Alex's and Sam's gazes. "Here, my young friends. On these very grounds that had been housing an amusement park destroyed by an earthquake. Laboratory Z was built under the cover of a Western Electric company manufacturing plant and continued in operation after the Sunset Development Company created Bishop Ranch in 1978."

"Not exactly the New Mexican desert," Sam noted, contrasting the infamous Los Alamos facility in New Mexico with the million square feet of modern office space before them.

"No, but the scientists who worked here didn't have as clear an agenda, either. We were basically poking at the wind to see if anything poked back."

"And did it?" Alex asked the professor.

"I can safely report that virtually every experiment conducted here was a failure, often abysmal. It's why the government, and NASA, didn't dare show us on the books. We were a financial black hole—no pun intended, since black holes were among the subjects we studied extensively."

"You said *virtually*," Sam noted. "Meaning . . ."

"Meaning all but one."

"And were you involved in that one?"

"Intimately. It was my specialty, accounted for why they brought me and another scientist to Laboratory Z as project supervisors in the early nineteen nineties."

"What was your specialty?" Alex asked him.

"Wormholes," said the professor.

"Let's start with the basics," he continued, turning his focus on Sam. "Feel free to jump in at any time, young lady."

Alex's shoulders snapped erect. "Why didn't you say that to me?"

"Feel free to jump in at any time, young lady," the professor repeated. "But for now all you need to know is that the purpose of a wormhole is to facilitate travel to and from distant areas of space—I mean, *really* distant, as in different universes, potentially. Like this."

The professor reached behind him and grabbed one of the signs staked into the ground that read, LOOK UP AND SOMEBODY'S LOOKING DOWN. He stripped the thin cardboard from its post and turned it over so the blank side, with just a smidge of black washed through, was up.

"Picture this as space," he resumed, "the goal being to get from an originating point at one end to a destination point at the other. Since they could be light-years away, the journey would be all but impossible. Even traveling at the speed of light, you'd be gone hundreds, even thousands of years of Earth time by the time you got home."

"Einstein's theory of relativity," Sam said, just loud enough to be heard.

"I know that," Alex said meekly. "Don't I, Sam? And I even know about string theory and black holes and wormholes." He smiled at her.

The professor half rolled his eyes. "The ability to create a wormhole changes the very nature of the journey," he said, starting to fold the strip of cardboard over. "Notice how close the two points are now, the distance between them shrunk by folding space over. That's what a wormhole is, a theoretical passage through the space-time continuum to create shortcuts for long journeys across the universe. How am I doing, young lady?"

"Perfectly on point," Sam told him. "Einstein and another scientist named Nathan Rosen used Einstein's theory of relativity to theorize that bridges through space-time could exist connecting two different points. A shortcut, like you said, like cutting through the woods instead of taking the long way along the street."

"I'm impressed, young lady."

"I'm interning at Ames."

"Are you now?" the old man said, raising his eyes just enough to make her think his response hid something else. "I'm *really* impressed now. Only the best and the brightest, as they say. And did you learn anything about wormholes at Ames?"

"No."

"They contain two mouths with a throat connecting them together. The mouths would most likely be spheroidal. The throat might be a straight stretch, but it could also wind around, taking a longer path than a more conventional route might require."

"But they're likely to collapse after milliseconds," Sam

noted. "Isn't that the whole problem in conceptualizing them?"

"Challenge, young lady, not problem, but, yes, generally. My specialty, what brought me to Laboratory Z, was an expertise in the more theoretical realms of quantum mechanics, specifically realms dealing with exotic forms of matter. Exotic matter, which should not be confused with dark matter or antimatter, contains negative energy density and a large negative pressure. Such matter has only been seen in the behavior of certain vacuum states as part of quantum field theory. But if a wormhole contained sufficient exotic matter, whether naturally occurring or artificially added, it could theoretically be used as a method of sending information or travelers through space."

"Artificially added," Sam echoed. "That was your specialty, wasn't it?"

"Actually, playing the fiddle was my specialty. But artificially adding exotic matter to the construction of a wormhole, what we called a space bridge, was a close second. Now, I won't bore you with the details of the myriad of development and construction issues we faced in building the particle accelerator we needed. Even you, young lady, wouldn't be able to grasp their intricacies and dynamics," the professor said, as if speaking only to Sam now. "It was, suffice it to say, the most advanced work in applied physics done to this day by the best minds gathered since Teller and Oppenheimer shared the same room in the Manhattan Project. But you'd need a doctorate in quantum mechanics to even begin to understand the principles involved. You know how it began and how it ended. The middle, on the other hand, the middle was wrought with setbacks and misfires. We had some success and in 1997 actually managed to erect a wormhole that remained stable for all of a hundredth of a second. A remarkable achievement in itself that, of course, in no way satisfied us. Instead if left us only after more, seeking something we were hardly ready to find," the professor said, his voice sounding sad and bitter at the same time.

"You caused the fire," Alex blared suddenly, eyes wide in realization. "Trying to keep the wormhole open longer was what did it."

"Not at all, young man. We had nothing to do with the explosion that originated in our particle accelerator. Nor did we have anything to do with the wormhole we'd created actually opening. That wasn't our doing at all."

"Then whose was it, Professor?" Sam asked before Alex could find the words.

"Someone from the other side," he said, folding the cardboard over anew and tapping the top.

79

THE OTHER SIDE

"We were just trying to open a wormhole to space," the professor continued. "No specific destination or designation. Just a bridge to the great out there. But somebody on the other side seized the opportunity to home in on Laboratory Z as a destination point in the fold, home in on the beacon we'd provided."

"Why?" Sam wondered.

The professor answered her with his gaze fixed on Alex. "I had no idea until today, until now. Your story, your very existence, is the missing piece I've been looking for. I don't think this was the first time someone from that other side opened a wormhole to our world, not at all. But it might have been the most important."

Alex leaned over, shrinking the distance between them. "Because of me?"

"Because of what happened after. The explosion and resulting fire, young man. Whatever caused it didn't originate with us; it originated on the other side in a desperate attempt to close the wormhole from that end before anyone else could follow you through. I'm going to assume this makes a degree of sense to you, to both of you."

Thoughts flooded Alex's mind, all the revelations of the past forty-eight hours that had begun with getting wrecked on the football field. He thought of his mother's tale tucked inside Meng Po for safekeeping, proof in the form of Dr. Chu's lab results currently squeezed into the back pocket of his new jeans, all the dots it had left dangling connected by the professor's assertions and Laboratory Z's work on forging wormholes in space.

"You said the people, the beings on the other side, had used wormholes before," Alex said, words and thoughts forming at the same time. "You said they used the one you created to get me through before destroying it. Question being, what were they doing here?"

"Yes," the professor nodded, "that's the question."

"They look like us," Alex continued. "Does that help at all?"

"Wait, there are others? You've actually *seen* them?"

"It's a long story. Might take a wormhole to get from one side of it to the other."

"I don't want to hear it," the professor said, waving him off. "I'm afraid the information might fry my brain, leave me in a white coat bouncing around a rubber room. But this one thing: You say they look like us?"

"Pretty much, yes; exactly, even. Like me."

"Even the drone things," Sam added. "First time we saw them they were dressed as cops."

"First time?"

"Long story, like Alex said." Sam shrugged.

"Cops . . ."

"Is that important?"

"It suggests complete societal immersion, a necessary precondition."

"For what?"

"An invasion," the professor said without hesitation.

* * *

But then he lapsed into silence.

"What is it you're not telling us, Professor?" Sam prodded.

"I've said enough."

"Not even close."

"All I'm going to say, then. My partner warned we were going too far, pushing the envelope too much. Never look for something you're not ready to find, he said. Risk versus reward, the zero-sum game. By the time I finally listened to him, it was too late."

"This partner of yours, did he die with the others?"

"No, we both managed to survive. Otherwise . . ." The professor let the remark dangle.

"So he could still be alive."

"And indeed he is, making a much better account of himself than my daily silent protest against that which I only feared but now know to be quite real."

"Where can we find him?" Sam asked.

And her mouth dropped when the professor told her.

80

ALIENS GO HOME

"I need to see it," Alex said suddenly, after Sam and the professor had lapsed into silence.

The professor's eyes turned quizzical. "See what, young man?"

"Laboratory Z."

The old man's quizzical expression turned caustic. "Then close your eyes and use your imagination. That's as close as you'll ever come."

"I don't think so," Alex said, a mix of suspicion and surety lacing his tone.

"I've given you my company, charged you for only a single question when you asked a dozen. I'd appreciate your respect."

"You said you've been coming here every day for fifteen years."

"Thanks to the courts ruling in my favor, decision after decision," the professor told him. "This part of the complex being public land and all."

"I think you come here every day to make sure nobody else finds it," Alex continued.

"Finds *what*?"

"Laboratory Z."

"It's gone, young man. Burned to the ground in an explosion of white heat. All the records, the readouts that could have provided more specifics of those final moments, lost too."

"But there's something that wasn't lost," Sam interjected. "Alex is right, isn't he?"

The professor looked away, then turned back toward them looking almost guilty. "The past is better left to itself, young lady."

"Not this time," said Alex.

And they watched as the professor yanked the blanket aside beneath the pop-up tent to reveal a strange-looking patch of ground.

The tent cloaked the professor as he felt about the thin ground brush, dried, blanched of color, and flattened by being covered from the sun on a daily basis. His knobby hands latched onto some holds, Alex and Sam watching him pull up on them.

The ground seemed to lift upward, enough of a space created to let a wash of cool, stale air flood outward from below.

"Behold the last remains of Laboratory Z," he said, holding the hatch up.

"What's down there?" Alex asked him.

"Can't tell you that, since I've never ventured down there myself. I know there's an emergency escape tunnel lab personnel caught in the fire never got the chance to use. Beyond that, well, there could be more. What exactly, I have no idea." His gaze turned sad, sky-blue eyes looking suddenly duller. "You have the right, young man, and I won't try to stop you. Just remember my warning about what happens sometimes when you find what you're looking for."

* * *

Alex and Sam found nothing at the foot of the dust-layered ladder, not at first. Just a tunnel that, if their bearings were correct, led underneath Bishop Ranch and the original location of Laboratory Z.

A dull haze of luminescence filtered down from recessed areas of the tunnel's side walls even with the ceiling. Sam figured the lights must be powered by a solar generator or something, to explain how they were still functioning after eighteen years. The tunnel smelled of nothing at all and she felt a constant air flow slipping past her, evidence of massive pumps and recirculators at work somewhere down here too.

She and Alex continued to follow the tunnel's irregular path, the twists and turns likely spawned by the need to dig around deposits of rock and shale that would otherwise have to be blasted through. If this were only an escape tunnel, their trek would end with a pile of earth and rubble at the other end. But both of them sensed there was something else down here, something more. Most of Laboratory Z itself, after all, was contained on subterranean levels beneath one likely reinforced with plate steel and concrete. So it wouldn't just offer escape in the event of an emergency, it might also provide storage for huge reams of records before the Cloud was a thought in anyone's mind along with vital equipment, so they might survive such a catastrophe too.

And, sure enough, they rounded a final corner to find the tunnel continuing in one direction, while a heavy steel door that looked like the entrance to a bank vault seemed to open onto another. There was no visible latch and the steel was cold to the touch, almost icy, forcing Alex and Sam to keep pulling back their hands as they checked for a knob, button, or keypad.

Alex slapped a palm against the cold steel in frustration, and lurched back with a start, dragging Sam with him as the door, incredibly, started to slide open. Both figured Alex had stumbled on something that did the trick, until they spotted a shadowy figure standing just beyond the now open door.

"I thought you might find your way here," said Raiff.

81

PINGS

The machines hummed. The machines whirred. The machines spit out data at speeds beyond comprehension, at least Langston Marsh's.

Fortunately, the same could not be said for his army of technicians, who lived their lives hunched over keyboards in front of LED screens following the constant scroll of readouts. They worked out of a cavernous underground structure amid tons of limestone and shale layered beneath the Klamath Mountains of Northern California, a bunker within a bunker lined with workstations laid out east to west, and north to south, in a manner mirroring the country. So the upper left-hand corner of the room represented the Pacific Northwest, the upper right, New England.

And so forth.

Hits, or "pings," as Marsh preferred to call them, were far too rare and uncommon. When they came, though, as subtle as the blip on an animated bouncing wave, they unleashed a fury of Marsh's making. For just as his monitoring room was laid out according to the geographical composition of the country, so too were the teams of Trackers already in place to hunt every single ping down and shut off the signal.

Every ping that registered on the vast array of monitoring machines tuned to electromagnetic frequency discharges represented another of those in league with the forces behind his father's death. His father had once had a part-time job as an exterminator and Marsh figured he had taken that baton from the great man he barely remembered as well as this mantle of responsibility. His father had fought the aliens in the sky, very likely giving his life to forestall an invasion. Marsh had never flown a plane in his life, but his charge was still much the same: to face down another coming invasion.

Rathman had already departed to the San Francisco area to pick up pursuit of the boy. He was marshaling his supplemental forces, comprised of special operators, and had explained that the arrival of dozens of them was already imminent, just hours off. Marsh didn't know the place of Alex Chin in all of this, only that his presence had unleashed the firestorm that had left severed robotic limbs all over a FedEx Office outside San Francisco the night before.

Ping.

It was Marsh's favorite sound in the world, but right now the chirping of his cell phone claimed his attention, a number given out only to a very select few. Marsh answered and listened to the man's fervent report on what had just transpired.

"I thought you should know immediately," the man finished.

"And right you are, more right than you can possibly realize," he said.

"We're in this together, but it's partially my fault we're in it at all."

"You've more than redeemed yourself, Professor," Marsh told him, hitting END on his phone so he could call Rathman.

82

THE CAROUSEL HOUSE

"This used to be storage?" Sam said, running her gaze along the sprawl of Raiff's lair and his mismatched furnishings.

"For what, I can't say. It was probably emptied out as soon as the site cooled enough after the fire."

"And you turned it into a home," Alex said, as he followed Sam's visual sweep.

"It can never be home," Raiff told them both flatly. "I'll never see home again, Alex. Neither will you."

"This *is* my home."

"I was talking about where you were born."

"Same place as you, right?"

"Same planet, yes."

"Sure. Because that would explain why we both have the same, or pretty similar, DNA to humans, right, Sam?"

"Right," she affirmed. "Almost exactly."

"So how can that be, Raiff?" Alex asked him, his tone making it sound more like a demand. "If we're from another planet, if we're not human."

"Because we are."

"Are what?"

"Human, Alex. We're human too. In every way, shape, and, especially, form."

* * *

"With some slight deviations, of course," Raiff continued, making Alex and Sam think of Dr. Chu's analysis of infant Alex's blood work.

"What," Sam began, "like a parallel world, as in string theory—something like that?"

"No, a parallel world would suggest independent development based on the same environment and conditions, the product of coincidence as much as anything. But there's nothing coincidental about the fact that our species are identical in virtually all respects."

"How's that?" Alex asked him.

"Because millions of years ago this planet was seeded by travelers from mine—ours."

"Seeded?"

"He means they're responsible for our very existence," Sam told Alex, her gaze fastened on Raiff. "Right?"

Raiff nodded, the gesture reluctant, regretful, almost sad. "This planet was a virtual match for ours, the most suitable by far of any of those tried."

"There were more?"

"Dozens. The seeds didn't always take; they usually didn't. And this was going on millions of years before we found Earth and has continued in the millions of years since."

"You used wormholes," Alex concluded, recalling the professor's assertions.

"Or something closely aligned with the same technology, yes. The voyage through space, even for ships capable of traveling at light speed, proved untenable. And the side effects of such travel, well, let's just say it became impossible to find volunteers."

Sam advanced ahead of them deeper into Raiff's lair. She thought she heard music playing softly in the background, something classical. "So you appropriated this for your digs. Nice."

"It seemed to make the most sense."

"I'll tell you," Alex said, "what doesn't make any sense at all. What all this crap is about. Why take over a planet you basically created in the first place?"

"Oh, it makes perfect sense," Raiff countered. "And it was the point all along, explaining what you're doing here." Then, after the briefest of pauses, "What I'm doing here."

"Here's what I don't get," Alex told him. "Why didn't those drones just kill me? I mean, they had their chance."

"You don't understand."

"Then help me to understand. You call yourself a Guardian, right? Well, do your job and tell me why they didn't just kill me."

"Because they need to know what you know."

"I don't know anything," Alex said, studying the way Raiff was looking at him, evasive and uncertain at the same time. "Do I?"

"You know how to defeat them."

"Bullshit."

"It's why you were brought here, why people—good people—on the other side risked their lives to send you through."

"I was an infant at that time. What do infants know?"

"Plenty, in your case. No one, none of them, was allowed to know all the details, to make sure they remained secret, to be revealed at the proper time."

Alex glanced toward Sam, who spoke before he had a chance to. "I think this qualifies as the proper time. So tell us."

"I can't. It was never explained to me. There wasn't time. We were caught breaching the facility back on our side. Everything had to be accelerated. More of us were supposed to go through to join the others already here. But they were on to us and the channel had to be closed to stop them from following us over. At all costs."

"The people who sent you here blew it up," Sam said, realizing now the truth of what had happened. "That's what caused the explosion that destroyed Laboratory Z. It originated on the other side of the field, the other side of the space bridge."

"I was just able to make it through with you in my arms, Dancer, and I mean barely. The wormhole was already closing when we reached the end of the tunnel."

"Tunnel?"

"What we called the route created by the fold in space. We'd just reached the end when it started to close. I honestly didn't think we'd make it. And even when we did, the energy disruption, kind of a shock wave, threatened to tear a hole in the fabric of this world and almost killed us." Raiff's gaze deepened, boring into Alex. "We were trapped in some kind of bubble. Moving felt like trying to fight a rip current. The best I could do was shove you out of it, right into the arms of a woman who happened to be standing there."

"Oh, my God . . ."

"Your mother, Alex," Raiff finished.

83

SHOCK WAVE

"I was supposed to stay with you until the others arrived," Raiff resumed, when he felt Alex was ready. "They're the ones behind whatever it is you don't realize you know."

"Because I don't. I was an infant at the time. It's not like they could teach me anything."

"Since it was clear they weren't coming," Raiff said, not bothering to break his train of thought to respond to Alex's assertion, "all bets were off, and you were better off with the Chins."

"My parents, you mean," Alex said, not bothering to hide the indignation in his voice.

Raiff took a deep breath and framed Alex in his stare, seeming to forget Sam was even there. "I reacquired you shortly after—it wasn't hard once I had a list of facility personnel and connected the dots after learning about your mother. I counted my blessings, knowing this was the perfect scenario to keep you safe, better than any I could possibly have planned. But I never lost track of you and enlisted other refugees from our planet to serve as Watchers, keeping an eye on you as much as possible, Dancer—"

"Alex. Please call me Alex."

"Alex," Raiff tried. "We never let you out of our sight,

knowing this day would come. Knowing the future depended on it."

"Refugees?" Sam posed.

"I'm getting to that. Suffice it to say for now that we knew what those who control our planet were going to do to you because they'd already done it to us."

"Get back to what you said about what I know," Alex prompted. "About how to defeat whoever killed my parents."

But before Raiff could, a bell began to jangle.

"My early detection system," he said, leading them through the sprawl of what felt like a grand loft-style apartment, albeit one that came without windows.

"What," Alex began, "a bunch of tin cans tied on a string?"

"The bells are just the sound I programmed. The system itself is a bit more sophisticated."

The jangling sounded again.

"We need to get out of here," Raiff said, leading them straight toward a wall paneled in rich, dark wood.

Some sort of sensor must have picked him up because the wall slid open. They continued on through it, finding themselves in another cavernous space, blackout dark until Raiff flipped a switch somewhere.

Sam screamed.

It was a dragon. Red and real and fiery with flames shooting out its mouth. As Alex clutched her, she realized it wasn't moving and smelled vaguely of sawdust—and that the flames weren't at all real, but carved out of wood as well.

"Sorry about that," said Raiff. "I should have warned you."

Sam nodded, sucking in big deep breaths to settle herself. Here she was, eighteen years old, and she'd just been scared out of her wits by a wooden dragon perched atop a carousel—called Dragon Wheel, according to the sign she could just glimpse upon a flag-topped cover—and featuring all manner of comparable creatures.

These days, though, who could tell what was real and what wasn't?

Laboratory Z, Sam now remembered the professor had mentioned outside, had been built on the ruins of an old amusement park in the time before Bishop Ranch. Hence the Dragon Wheel and another dozen vintage carousels battling for space, each looking freshly carved and painted.

"Hobby of mine," Raiff explained briefly. "I restore them to working order. Come on, we need to hurry."

But before leading them on, Raiff threw a long series of switches that looked like circuit breakers. Instantly the restored carousels whirled into motion, their horses, dragons, and assorted other creatures bobbing up and down with a chorus of instrumentals dueling to be the loudest and most annoying.

"If it's androids that are coming," Raiff said, "this will throw off their tracking. If it's Trackers, it'll provide cover."

And with that gunshots rang out, echoing amid the spinning thunder of wooden creatures gaining speed with each twirl of their respective circular homes. Raiff pushed Alex and Sam down low, even with the carousel bases, making them almost impossible to spot, as the hundreds of beautifully restored empty mounts sprang back to life.

More shots resounded as Raiff pulled them on.

"Stay low!" he ordered. "See the carousel way off to the right?"

"Painted Ponies?" Alex asked.

"No, the White Castle. There's a door just beyond it. That's our target, an extension of the original escape tunnel. Hope you're not afraid of the dark."

And with a pistol that had suddenly appeared in his grasp, Raiff fired two shots at the bank of switches he'd flipped moments before. Sparks fizzled on the first shot, and on the second the lights in his carousel house died altogether. It was pitch black now except for the eyes of the hundreds of bobbing creatures, all of which were luminescent, providing plenty of light for someone already familiar with the cluttered terrain.

Raiff stuffed his gun back in his belt and led them on through the maze-like confines. Dipping and darting, twisting and turning, and never letting go of either Alex or Sam, as if the three of them were dancing together through the glowing eyes that looked like monsters ready to swallow them.

But these weren't the real monsters, Sam reminded herself. The real monsters were already here, with more on the way.

Raiff found the door, shouldered it ajar, and they slid through as it sealed as quickly as it had opened. They found themselves dashing down a long winding hall that seemed identical in every way to the one that had brought Alex and Sam to Raiff's lair.

"As for where we go from here—" he started, when they reached a ladder at the end leading up to a hatch.

"I already know where we go from here," Sam said, between pounding breaths, before he could finish. "The professor pretty much told me."

84

WAITING

For Dr. Thomas Donati, everything was on hold, including, it seemed, the world itself. He felt as if he'd been frozen in a form of suspended animation, waiting for the phone to ring, buzzer to chime, or team to show up. Of course, he more than anyone should've known this day was coming; its inevitability, he supposed, had been sealed eighteen years before in Bishop Ranch.

He hadn't told the faceless voice grids he'd been speaking with over the course of the past day the entire truth, not even most of it. And now he was left to wonder how much of what was happening, and about to happen, was his fault. Because if the wormhole was about to open again . . .

Donati didn't complete the thought; he couldn't. The prospects were just too real and terrifying. He imagined that's why he'd missed the warning signs a high school student, a NASA intern, had found. He missed them because he'd wanted to, unable to bear the thought that the inevitable was upon him, perhaps ultimately of his own making from trying to reach what no man was ever meant to touch.

He was glad the faceless voice grids couldn't read his mind, couldn't see into his memory to the moments that had followed the first shrill emergency alarm sounding before the destruction of Laboratory Z. How'd he raced down to the basement sublevel containing the massive tubular chamber he and Orson Wilder had constructed, essentially a particle accelerator and mini-supercollider that formed a potential doorway to other worlds. The testing had only been in the most rudimentary and fundamental stages. Expectations were low; in point of fact, nobody knew what to expect and most familiar with the project expected nothing at all.

As a boy, Donati had been obsessed with model trains and, later, with the transcontinental railroad's construction. Even then, before his interest in space exploration had turned obsessively into his life's work, he'd been fascinated by the idea of all that wilderness, all that untamed frontier, being linked together. Worlds connected. Impossible journeys made possible.

For Donati, Laboratory Z was an extension of that same romantic adventure where man expanded his horizons by forging routes between worlds. Back then it had merely been east and west, north and south, while today it involved roads built to connect planets and galaxies. His and Orson Wilder's early work trying to theoretically construct a trans*world* was similarly about creating connections that just a decade or so before had been unthinkable. And they'd been wrong and right at the same time.

Right, because they had indeed opened the door.

Wrong, because something was waiting on the other side.

And now the day of reckoning for their oversight and myopic vision had come. Ever since that day eighteen years ago, he had ceased seeking other life forms in order to build bridges; he sought them instead to prevent those bridges from ever being built. The very real danger the prospects of such contact created had already been demonstrated, proof enough for him.

But that wasn't the problem at this point. The problem at this point was that the signs, the pattern, were re-occurring, which could only mean one thing.

They were coming back, perhaps through a wormhole entirely of their own creation. And right now he had to find Samantha Dixon before someone else did.

Or some *thing*.

But her phone was going straight to voicemail and she'd returned none of his e-mails or texts, the latter being a practice Donati utterly deplored but knew teenagers these days normally preferred.

Donati's phone rang and he jerked it to his ear, answering it quickly.

"Yes. Donati here."

"It's Samantha, Dr. Donati."

"Who?"

"Dixon, Samantha Dixon, Doctor. I think we need to talk."

ELEVEN

REBELS

Awake, arise or be for ever fall'n.

—JOHN MILTON, *PARADISE LOST*

85

PLAYGROUND

"We can wait for the girl to get back if you want," Raiff said, uneasily taking the swing next to Alex in the Live Oaks Elementary School playground, just a few miles from Bishop Ranch.

Alex rocked slightly in his swing, legs scrunched up to compensate for being so close to the ground. "She has a name. It's Sam."

"We can wait for Sam to get back," Raiff corrected, having lent her his phone so she could make a call to someone she thought might be the only person, on this planet anyway, who could help them.

Alex steepened his rock. "No, talk. Just know that whatever you tell me, I'm telling Sam. I'm sick of secrets, starting with the fact that I'm not human."

"You *are* human."

"But I come from another planet. Through a wormhole in space. And a doctor didn't deliver me; you did, to my mother."

"I'm human too, Alex, both of us as much as anybody here."

Alex pushed harder, riding a swing for the first time in longer than he could remember. It seemed to him that Raiff was moving and he wasn't. Raiff had the hard look of a soldier mixed somewhat with the hardscrabble appearance of a fisherman. His face, even in the sunlight, seemed bathed in shadows, all angles and ridges. His wavy hair was untamed, his eyes big and set far back in his face. The kind of guy who didn't care what he looked like and didn't care what other people thought, either.

"So even though I come from another planet," Alex continued, forcing himself to focus, "I'm human because your people seeded Earth millions of years ago to create another version of the human race."

"Remarkable experiment. The most successful the minds behind such pursuits ever encountered by far."

"Okay, Raiff, why? Why bother seeding the planet in the first place? I mean, for what?"

"Go back to your original question."

"I don't remember what my original question was."

"How can you be human and come from another planet? The human race on this planet was created directly from DNA that came from ours and allowed to develop organically, without intrusion or interference. Totally independent of us, which was deemed crucial by those who devised the project."

"What's all that got to do with me, with why those androids and the ash man—Shadow or whatever—killed my parents?"

"They weren't your parents."

"Don't say that. The ash man said that and I cut him in half."

"I'll keep that in mind. But it doesn't matter who your real parents are. What matters is why you were brought here."

"The fact that they think I know how to stop them."

"Because you do, somehow," Raiff told him. "But you're getting ahead of yourself. We need to go back to why this and other planets were seeded."

Alex rolled his eyes again. "Fine, why were they seeded?"

"Because at a certain time the human race you grew up among would be needed."

"Needed for what?"

"To provide things our planet could no longer provide for itself. Back there civilization developed as a single aggregate—no cultural or ethnic disparity. Everyone pretty much the same because of the placement of our land-masses in proportion to our oceans. There, like here, a caste system developed in our ancient times. The difference is we never progressed beyond that two-class system, those who have and those who do not."

"Owners and workers."

"Close enough," Raiff affirmed.

"And a recipe for disaster," Alex said, recalling the lessons learned from history. Thanks to Sam.

Now Raiff started swinging too, holding Alex's rhythm. "How so? Tell me why."

"Well, even a dimwit who needs a tutor like me knows that our history is full of revolutions where the workers, those who see themselves as oppressed, rise up and overthrow the owners."

"Our world anticipated that. Steps were taken."

"What kind of steps?"

"Population control, mostly via sterilization. Control the masses by keeping their numbers from overwhelming the ruling class. Makes revolution unthinkable and escape much more preferable."

Alex nodded, starting to get it. "Escape to Earth, right? That's what brought you and others here. Refugees."

"Me and plenty of others, yes. Even though we knew they'd be coming eventually. But not for me, not even for you, necessarily."

"Who, then?"

"Everyone else."

Alex felt his hair bouncing about as he swung right next to Raiff. It made him remember his father telling him he needed a haircut, giving him ten dollars to get one when it cost almost five times that in the city.

"You've lost me," he told Raiff, and ground his heels into the dirt to stop his swing.

Raiff stopped alongside him. "We had a haves-and-have-nots problem in our world too, but a different one than yours. Thanks to the measures that we enacted ourselves—at least the haves did—we didn't have enough have-nots to power our civilization. They'd essentially been bred out of existence. But there were these several planets we'd seeded in order to claim their resources or turn their worlds into foreign outposts. Planets like yours packed with have-nots."

"Oh, man," Alex managed to say, shaking his head.

"That's what all this is about, why your planet was seeded in the first place," Raiff told him, his breathing gone shallow between his words. "To create a crop of slaves for the taking."

86

FIFTH COLUMN

"And resources as well," Raiff said, when Alex finally looked at him again from his swing.

"Resources?"

"Finite in any world. No matter how infinite knowledge may be, the growth, progress, and very existence of any race is limited to the resources they're able to mine around them. And we vastly exceeded those limitations to the point where the survival of our species was threatened. Air, water—everything."

"So Earth isn't just a breeding ground for slaves, it was also a great big environmental bank where your world could withdraw anything and everything it wanted."

"My world, Alex, but not my doing. The doing of the ruling class that owns and controls everything, and what you were sent here to stop," Raiff continued. "That's why it was so vital eighteen years ago that we get you through the tunnel with whatever it is you know."

"But I don't know *anything*. I'd tell you if I did, Raiff."

"You do—you just don't realize it."

"I draw things sometimes," Alex said softly. "I have this sketchbook. Never shown it to anybody, not even my parents." *Or Sam,* Alex almost added.

"What kind of things?"

"Stuff that doesn't make any sense, stuff that just pops into my head."

"Machines?"

"And buildings," Alex added. "Structures so strange I can't begin to describe them."

"Sounds like the world I came from, both of us came from."

"Except you remember it. This, everything about us, this is all I know. All I've ever known and ever want to know."

"I need to see these pictures."

"Why?"

"Because they may hold the clue as to this knowledge you have but don't realize you've got. They may form some kind of pattern or message, like the pieces of a puzzle. We just have to put them all together."

"I told you, they don't make any sense."

"Maybe not to you. But they must be in your head for a reason."

"Like what?" Alex persisted. "Tell me more about this thing I'm supposed to know. What's coming when that wormhole opens again?"

"You don't want to know."

"Doesn't seem like I've got much choice right now, does it?"

Raiff nodded grudgingly, turning to see if Sam was anywhere about. "Our world's a lot like this one, only millions of years more advanced . . . and older. Cursed by those declining resources with a predicament exacerbated by a longtime disregard for the environment and taking the planet for granted. Sound familiar?"

"I don't know what 'exacerbated' means."

"Made worse or more prominent."

"How do you know so much shit?"

"I read a lot. For eighteen years now."

"While you've been protecting me, even though you have no idea why."

"I know enough. This isn't the first world they've seeded, only to plunder and enslave."

"We may not be the pushovers you think we are, Raiff."

Raiff started to smile, then stopped and started to shake his head, stopping that motion swiftly as well. His expression flattened, all the edges and ridges seeming to melt into a single, processed form.

"Oh, no? You think they come with rockets and ray guns? You think this is like some movie where the world mounts a brave resistance and ultimately triumphs? Maybe until the lights go out and the faucets get turned off and the food supply is contaminated, and all of a sudden the civilized world finds itself losing everything it's always taken for granted. The forces coming across the space bridge don't need to kill, only to control. They fight wars that are won before they're even fought. You can't beat them because they know every move you're going to make before you make it."

"And they know about me."

"The wild card in all this. I think you're finally getting the point. You scare them, because they fear you're the only one capable of stopping them from taking this world. They have the same knowledge I do. And, just like me, they may not know everything but they know enough."

This time it was Raiff who started swinging a bit, but Alex didn't join him. "Just not how what you think I know can stop them."

Raiff braked himself with his feet. "I'm not sure what it is, only that it's the key to defeating them."

"Which you couldn't do up close and personal back home."

"There was no point in trying. The lucky among us made it over to this world. We've been hiding among you for generations."

"Not so lucky, considering there's this guy who's trying to exterminate you."

"Langston Marsh, and his modern-day Fifth Column, is your problem now too."

"What's a Fifth Column?"

"A clandestine group organized toward a singular purpose not in keeping with the greater interests of society." Raiff started to chuckle, then stopped. "I can see why you need a tutor."

"Hey, lay off me. I'm your only hope, remember."

"You might be this world's only hope."

Silence settled between them just as Sam approached and handed Raiff back the cell phone he'd lent her. "So what do you want to hear first, the good news or the bad news?"

87

GOOD NEWS AND BAD NEWS

"Turns out Dr. Donati, my boss at Ames, has been trying to reach me too," Sam continued.

"Is that the good news or the bad news?" Alex asked her.

"Both, I guess. He had to call me back because he said his regular line wasn't secure."

"That doesn't sound good."

"He knows what's happening," Raiff concluded, "doesn't he?"

"Some, not everything. He was trying to reach me about a pattern of events I found, a pattern that mimics another from eighteen years ago when Laboratory Z was destroyed."

"The wormhole," Raiff said.

"Yes. Donati thinks he can figure out where it's going to open this time."

Alex looked toward Raiff. "So it's closed now and has been for eighteen years. I get that. What I don't get is where the androids, cyborg soldiers, are coming from. You said they were being manufactured here, on this planet. So where?"

"If I knew that, I would've already destroyed them."

"So who's building them?"

"I'm not sure. But the better question was your first

one: *where* are they being built, and the answer is probably lots and lots of locations scattered throughout the world."

"Because these cyborgs are going to be the ones doing the heavy lifting when doomsday kicks in, right?" Alex asked.

"I apologize for the crack about you needing a tutor," Raiff said, smiling thinly.

Sam kicked at some pebbles collected on the ground. "So if we can figure out how to shut them off, doomsday gets postponed, maybe for good."

"Maybe that's what they think I know," Alex said to Raiff. "How to turn all these robots off."

"Cyborgs," Sam corrected. "Androids."

"Whatever."

"There's a difference."

"Explain it to me again after we find the switch. We need to figure out what it is I'm supposed to know, so we can stop them in their tracks," Alex said to Raiff again.

"We need those drawings, Dancer."

"There's something else we need," Alex told him. "My CAT scan results. My doctor saw something before they killed him, a shadow, he called it. Now we need to see it too."

Sam studied Alex's wrist, then made a grab for it.

"Hey!" he protested, pulling away.

Not to be outdone, she latched onto his forearm and pulled it toward her. "You're still wearing your hospital bracelet."

"I forgot all about it."

"Good thing."

"Why?"

"Because it's got your patient ID number on it," Raiff realized.

"And that's what the hospital will file all your test results under," Sam told him.

"Meaning—" Alex began.

"Yeah," Sam said, reading his mind. "I've done some volunteer work at CPMC. I know the layout."

"You're crazy."

"Only for the last day or so."

"What about those drawings, Dancer?" Raiff reminded him.

"It's Alex. *Alex*."

"'We know what we are, but not what we may be.'"

"That's Shakespeare," Sam noted.

"*Hamlet*, specifically."

"I know who I am, Raiff," Alex insisted.

"Do you?" Raiff asked him, expression gone flat again. "Do you really?"

"By the way," Sam interjected, squirming a bit, "no, I couldn't find a bathroom. So, if the two of you don't mind, could we get moving?"

88

WILDER

Langston Marsh eased ahead of Rathman and deposited a five-dollar bill in the swaying pot next to the sign reading, DEPOSIT A DOLLAR AND ASK THE PROFESSOR A QUESTION.

"I figured I'd pay for a few extra up front," Marsh told the figure seated on the grass-stained blanket, who reminded him of Kris Kringle, Santa Claus himself. The grass was damp with a mist that had washed in over the water and then washed out just as quickly. But his shoes still left their mark in the form of impressions across the faded fabric, which dried quickly in the brief reemerged late-afternoon sun. He'd skirted the signs reading, THEY WALK AMONG US, TRUST NO ONE, THE WAR IS COMING, and ALIENS GO HOME!, wondering if the scent of lacquer was the product of his imagination or the result of a fresh coat tracing the original letters.

Dr. Orson Wilder cocked his gaze casually from the pot to Marsh and smoothed the tangled hair from his face. "Answers are free for my friends."

"And is that what I am, Professor, your friend?"

"We share the same goals, so I'd say close enough."

"I'd still prefer to pay."

"You failed. You wouldn't be here if you'd managed to take the boy into custody, would you?"

"Should I be charging you for the answer too, Professor?"

"A waste of your money, since I already know it."

"An unexpected development was to blame. No matter. We'll have the boy before long." Marsh glanced toward the five-dollar bill bent into the pot. "So I might as well get my money's worth."

"Okay," Wilder said, squinting up at Marsh through the last of the day's sunlight, which made him look spectral, almost as if he were glowing. "First question."

"Tell me about the boy."

"I already did. When I called in the report. I did my part." Wilder's eyes tried to hold Marsh's gaze longer and failed. "Don't make me regret that."

"As you've been regretting for any number of years now?"

"We make strange bedfellows, don't we, Marsh?"

"Strange bedfellows with a common purpose: forestalling an alien invasion, the kind of invasion your work here twenty years ago proved was possible. The mere proof of their existence was enough for me." He stopped long enough to fasten onto Wilder's stare until the old man looked away again. "Your work validated my entire life's purpose. Now tell me about the boy," Marsh repeated.

"That's not a question."

"What did the boy tell you?"

"That he was an alien. That his mother rescued him from Laboratory Z just before its destruction. That he's being chased by other aliens, or some kind of robots, cyborgs, they've managed to manufacture."

"And you believed him?"

"I believed he believed what he was saying."

"And what did you tell him?"

"The truth."

"Why?"

"Because he deserved it. And that counts as a question. Leaves you one left."

Marsh fished through his pocket, like a man unused to carrying cash, and managed to emerge with a twenty-dollar bill this time, placing it atop the five. "You could have told me that on the phone."

"The boy's not your problem."

Marsh glanced toward Rathman, who was hovering like a statue at the edge of the blanket, so big he blocked a measure of the sunlight from this angle. "I'll be the judge of that, Professor."

"What's coming is your problem."

"And what's coming?"

"They are. Or, should I say, they're coming *back*."

"And you know this how?" Then, when Wilder failed to respond, "I still have nineteen answers left."

"This boy's the key. I don't know how but I know that much. See, I saved you a question."

"He's an alien, like all the others," Marsh said, stiffening.

"He's an alien, but *nothing* like the others, the ones you've exterminated." Wilder's expression changed, almost pleading now. "I came to you because I believed in your cause, believed my experiments had contributed to the problem you were determined to solve."

"They killed my father, Professor. There's no place for them in our world."

"You're missing the point, Marsh."

"And what's that?"

"Eighteen left now. And the point you're missing is that maybe we had things wrong."

"Wrong?"

"Seventeen. Since you asked, I think this kid is some kind of refugee, or was brought here by refugees."

"I didn't ask that."

"Then this answer is for free. I'm afraid the aliens your teams have been tracking are refugees too and that our real problem is not them so much as who they came here to flee."

"Really?"

"I'll give you that one for free too. And, yes, because after meeting this boy it's the only thing that makes sense." Wilder stopped and gave his money pot a shove to start it swaying again. "You said you investigated what happened at his house. What did you conclude?"

"That he killed his parents after they learned the truth about him. Same thing with his doctor at the hospital. He couldn't risk exposure. And you owe me a dollar now."

"The boy said it was these cyborgs who killed his parents, them and some kind of holographic figure."

"You've been out in the sun for too long, Professor. I believe your brain may be roasting."

"How many men have you got?"

"With me?"

"In total."

"Plenty," Marsh said, thinking of the special-ops veterans Rathman was bringing in to rendezvous here in the San Francisco area.

"You better hope so, because if I'm right you're going to need every one of them."

"What I need is to find this boy."

With that, Marsh flashed a nod to Rathman, who moved closer to the seated Wilder, swallowing the old, bearded man in his shadow.

"Tell me how I can find the boy, Professor."

"That's not a question."

"No, it's an order."

"You aren't listening to what I've been saying."

"Because you haven't been saying what I need to hear."

"Which is?"

"How I can catch him once and for all."

"You might start with the girl who was with him," Wilder said, after stealing a glance up at the looming Rathman.

"Tell me more about her," Rathman said.

89

SKETCHBOOK

Night had just fallen when Alex made his way across the adjoining properties into the backyard of his family's bungalow, his home. He tried not to think of it that way, since this wasn't really his home anymore and never would be again; all the crime scene tape and the police cruiser parked outside to keep the curious away was more than enough evidence of that. Raiff had parked down the block, out of sight of the house on the chance either the men he called Trackers or more of the ash man's androids were waiting and watching, his last words weighing heavy on Alex's mind.

"There's something else you need to know, Alex," Raiff told him, before he climbed out of the car. "They think it was you."

"Think *what* was me?"

"They think you killed your parents and probably your doctor too. That's the theory they're proceeding on."

"Nice of you to mention that," Alex said, rolling his eyes.

"I didn't want to say anything in front of your friend."

"Sam. And she's more than a friend."

"You mean . . ."

"No, not like *that*. I mean in spite of everything, she stayed with me. She didn't run. Truth is, Raiff, I don't know what I would've done without her, especially last night."

"All the more reason she doesn't need to hear you're a suspect, on top of everything else."

"Guess that makes me a fugitive too," Alex said, and finally reached for the latch.

There was no one watching the rear of the property, and his parents always kept a spare key inside a fake rock mixed into his mother's flower garden. Her roses seemed to droop, looking almost sad. Alex wondered if it was possible for plants to have some degree of consciousness and awareness of their surroundings. Not here, probably, but who knew on the other planets both like Earth and advanced far beyond it.

Under cover of darkness, Alex used the key to unlock the back door and enter the house where his parents had been murdered twenty-fours earlier. He expected it to smell stale and musty, even faintly of death. Instead, though, the only scents that lingered were from the last meals his mother had cooked. The thought tightened his chest and thickened his throat, making it hard to breathe.

Focus!

That was easy to do on the football field, where moments unfolded quickly and melded into the next. But inside the house in which he'd grown up, everything slowed and lingered. Time seemed to have frozen in the moments before his parents were attacked, beaten by the drone things that had come for him.

Alex padded through the house and up the stairs, careful to avoid looking at the living room, where he'd held his mother's hand as she took her last breath. It felt stuffy, the air trying to choke him as he sucked it in.

He reached the top of the stairs without remembering the climb, stopping when the vision of himself as a seven-year-old boy trampling across the Oriental runner in his football uniform struck him hard and fast. Alex watched his younger version tossing a football lightly enough to dash under it and snatch the ball from the air. Remembered doing just that for hours, conscious now but not then of the concerned voices of his parents coming through their cracked open bedroom door.

"He could be hurt," his father raised in the cautious tone his voice took on when expressing such concern. "Then what?"

"He's a boy," came his mother's retort. "He deserves a normal life."

"If he were normal, you mean. But he's not. And we are fooling ourselves to think otherwise. You knew that when you took him, when you brought him home."

"I knew nothing until we took him to Dr. Chu." His mother's voice hesitated here. "Why do you look at me like that? What is it you're not saying?"

"Dr. Chu is gone."

"Gone?"

"His office is abandoned, closed up. No trace of his nurse or receptionist. He must've gone back to China."

"Without telling his patients?"

"His filing cabinets and desk drawers were empty too—emptied, we must hope, by him."

"He never would've written anything down about Alex. He was too careful a man."

"As I said, that is what we must hope."

Alex wondered if he eased open their door now whether they might be standing there, continuing the conversation. He'd tell them never to let him play football, warn them about what was coming a whole bunch of years down the road. Give them the exact date and time, so they could be someplace else. He'd never thought much about why he could never remember going to the doctor, but realized now it must've been because of Dr. Chu's sudden departure.

Alex continued watching the vision of his younger self tossing the football into the air and running under it. The next toss struck the overhead ceiling fan and light fixture, splaying shadows in all directions until it stopped swaying at the same time his mother peeked out from her bedroom to survey the scene.

Don't hurt yourself, Alex.

Spoken with her eyes seemingly fixed on him instead of his younger self. Then the little-boy version of Alex in football regalia vanished, and the Alex of today pressed on toward his bedroom.

The lump in his throat thickened further as he eased his bedroom door open, stopping just short of flipping on the light. Couldn't do that, couldn't do anything that might alert the cop watching the house that someone was inside. There wasn't much light, but it was enough to move to his bed and clamp a hand onto the sketchbook he kept between his mattress and box spring. He hadn't drawn in it for a while, not since football had started up again over the summer. And because of that the visions he'd failed to sketch out on paper, a kind of relief valve, had begun haunting his dreams. Visions of vast machine-like assemblages strung into barely recognizable forms lurking at the edge of his consciousness.

Just like in the motel room, covering the walls with the ink of a couple Monterey Motor Inn pens he must've dug out of a drawer. Once drawn, the subject of the visions would retreat to the farthest reaches of his mind, where they could not hold him hostage to their whims.

Sliding the sketchbook out in the spill of light coming from a streetlamp beyond, Alex realized very few pages were still blank, his efforts having filled far more than he had recalled. He sat down atop his bed, soothed by the familiar squeak of the springs, and paged to the end as if to refresh his memory.

But none of the drawings touched any chords, as if he'd traced them in his sleep. Had he woken up a few mornings with what he thought might be ink staining his fingers? That thought did strike a chord but he wasn't sure. And what did these drawings mean in any event?

The evening left his room bathed in shadows, sparing him further glimpses of his life until forty-eight hours ago. The pair of jeans hanging off the edge of his bed, collection of sneakers pushing their way out of the closet. He didn't want to think, didn't want to look. But something made him strip off the still-stiff cheap pair of jeans he'd bought at the Buy Two store and slide his old jeans on in their place, careful to replace the folded pages containing the results of Dr. Chu's lab tests into the back pocket. Then he grabbed a pair of sneakers and replaced the cheap ones that were more comfortable than Dr. Payne's but still not right. Alex felt instantly better, himself again. That's what it was—he felt like himself.

Except that person didn't exist anymore; in point of

fact, had never existed. His entire life was a lie and changing his clothes couldn't change that. Still, he fished a shirt from his drawer and pulled his arms through it, the scents of fabric softener and laundry detergent sending a lump up his throat because they made him picture his mother doing laundry, obsessive about adding just the right amount of both.

That lump, and a heaviness that had settled in his chest, accompanied him back to his bedroom door, which he eased open all the way.

"Hello again, Alex," said the hazy shape of the ash man.

90

PRESCRIPTION

Sam crept down the hospital hall wearing doctor's scrubs she'd purchased at a drugstore with the very last of her cash. The outfit at least kept her from standing out. She must've looked like an intern or orderly, the kind of hospital worker who melted into the scenery. Alex had told her where she could find Dr. Payne's office and that's where she was headed now, having no idea if she'd even be able to access it. If it were locked or guarded, her mission would end before it began.

She hated what she was about to do, had to do, in order to create the distraction she needed and give herself time to see if she could find Alex's medical file on Dr. Payne's computer. In school it was always the bad kids who pulled fire alarms as a prank or to get out of class. Normally, they got caught, something she didn't dare let happen here and now.

She also hated being separated from Alex, the intensity of the past twenty-four hours creating a bond with him like none she'd ever felt before. Raiff had driven him to his house to retrieve the sketchbook, while she proceeded to the hospital alone by mass transit with throwaway cell phone in hand to await Dr. Donati's call about where they could meet. The medical tests Alex had endured, especially the CT scan, seemed to have spun these events into motion. So she needed Alex's file to bring with her to Donati to prove to him she wasn't crazy, that all this had really happened, *was* happening. Amazing that barely a day before she'd been agonizing about whether or not to help the girls of the CatPack, who weren't even her friends, cheat on an AP bio test.

Grow up, girl!

Well, she'd certainly done that, going all the way from potentially cheating to breaking into a murdered doctor's hospital office. The fire alarm first, though. Be a lot easier if she could have hacked his computer from an off-site location. Sam knew her way around computers to the point where the keyboard seemed an extension of her hands, but hacking was a whole different discipline she'd never even tried, couldn't even imagine herself trying.

Then again, not too long ago she couldn't envision herself cheating on a test, much less on someone else's behalf. Or triggering a false fire alarm.

Sam waited until she was alone in the hallway and in no one's view before reaching out toward the pull station. She could see herself hesitating, even freezing, but in the end she pulled down on the alarm in a single swift motion and listened to the shrill squealing sound claim the hall, accompanied by the strobe-like flashing of the emergency lights. She had no idea what the procedure was for critical care, ICU, and operating room patients at this point, only that it would take only between six and seven minutes for the fire department to determine it to be a false pull instead of a real emergency.

That's how long she had to get to Dr. Payne's office, too much of the time wasted when the hall filled up almost immediately with hospital personnel spilling out of rooms and stations everywhere. Sam did her best to blend in, pretending to hurry along, shoving an empty gurney before her to avoid being tasked by a higher-up with something else to do.

She abandoned the gurney just short of the bend in the hall around which Alex told her she could find Dr. Payne's office. Sam recognized it immediately from the crime scene tape strung both across the width of the door and in an X pattern covering the whole frame. A now abandoned chair rested outside the office, Sam picturing a cop or hospital security guard on duty there to keep the crime scene secure.

This hall contained only offices, all of them abandoned by the time she reached Dr. Payne's. If the door was locked, she could try accessing the office through an adjoining one on the chance there might be a connecting door. Or she could flag down a janitor in the hope of convincing him to lend her his keys so she could check behind locked doors for any patient somehow left behind.

Such a cover story likely wouldn't have held, but it didn't have to, as things turned out. The door to Dr. Payne's office was unlocked and Sam ducked low and slipped between the dueling strips of yellow crime scene tape to enter.

She eased the door closed behind her, aware immediately that the lamp on Dr. Payne's desk was providing the room's only light. She pictured his body still settled in the leather desk chair, just as Alex had described. It must've been removed from the scene long before, the proper authorities trying to determine how he was killed by something Alex described like a bullet that wasn't a bullet.

Sam breathed a sigh of relief when she spotted Payne's laptop sitting slightly askew of its faded outline atop his blotter. She had to hope Alex's patient ID number would be enough to access his records and started toward Payne's desk, catching a glimpse of her reflection in his bare office window. The sight startled her not just from the simple shock, but because the reflection didn't look like, well, her. It seemed she had changed, and not just because of the hospital scrubs. Everything about her looked different, although she couldn't say how, exactly, and reached the desk before thinking about it any further.

Hoping she could bypass trying the laptop altogether, Sam ruffled a hand through all the desktop clutter, unsure of what she was looking for now. Payne wasn't exactly a study in organization, not based on the clumps of papers and sprawl of files atop his desk. She wondered if he was working on a paper or something, and the unkempt clutter made up the sum total of his research or, perhaps, the result of a fruitless search by police officials investigating his murder. But these files were all labeled with names.

The fire alarm was still blaring when she started thumbing through the folders and random pages containing test results. No idea really of what she was looking for until she found a folder closer to the edge of Payne's desk labeled ALEX CHIN.

He must've been studying its contents just before he was killed. That thought chilled Sam, but the file was hers now so she flipped it open.

And found it empty.

91

OUTER LIMITS

Alex stiffened just short of the doorway. "Get out of my way."

"I just wanted to finish our conversation," the ash man said in a voice that sounded like a car radio station fading in and out.

"We finished it when I cut you in half."

Maybe it was his imagination, or the darkness of the hallway beyond, but it looked to Alex as if a solid black line ran up the center of the spectral figure, tracing the blow he'd struck that had cut the ash man in two.

But he wasn't speaking out of both sides of his mouth anymore. Not too long ago, a couple summers, maybe, Alex had come across the old *Outer Limits* television series, in black-and-white, of all things, and streamed a whole bunch of episodes that all opened with a narrator saying, "There is nothing wrong with your television set," over a jumbled screen. Looking at the ash man's vague grayish shape that kept fading in and out, some kind of astral projection as opposed to a physical being, made him think of the chintzy special effects that dominated *The Outer Limits*.

"There is no reason for all this, Alex. We mean you no harm."

"You meant my parents plenty of harm, though, didn't you?"

"They weren't your parents."

"I'm tired of hearing that. I've got a better idea of what's going on than the last time we talked and it just makes me want to cut you in half again even more."

The ash man seemed to be weighing a response. Then Alex realized from the tightening of his grainy features that there was a slight delay in his words reaching the form, maybe because there were more of them in this exchange. And when the ash man next opened his mouth, no words emerged right away, the lag very slight but present.

"The Chins had no place in your life, Alex."

"What kind of shit are you slinging here?"

"This isn't your world. Your world is with us."

"Who's *us*?"

No response this time, but Alex thought he saw the grainy image swallow hard.

"I think you're scared of me," Alex continued.

He waited for the ash man's response, figured the lag was behind the lack of one, until he stayed silent.

"And I realize now you've got reason to be scared of me," Alex resumed, the spectral shape looming before him suddenly no different than any opponent on the football field.

"This is not your fight, Alex," the ash man said suddenly.

"Yes, it is. I'm going to make it my fight. I know I was smuggled here to stop you. That's why you're scared of me. And know what? I used to be scared of you too, but not anymore. I don't think I'll ever be scared of anything again, thanks to what you did to my parents. And, yeah, they were my parents. They *are* my parents, always *will be* my parents. You get that? Maybe you should've killed me too but you couldn't, could you? Because then you'd never know what it is I know and who else knows about it back where you come from."

"It's where you're from too."

"Home is where the heart is, bro. And how's this for another quote: to know your enemy, you must become your enemy. Sun Tzu said that. And know what? You're right. I already am you. We come from the same place. That's why you're really scared of me, isn't it?"

"You read Sun Tzu?"

"My tutor does."

"That would be the girl I remember seeing."

Alex stiffened. "Leave her out of this."

"It's too late. She's already a part of it, just like your parents."

"You should've left them out of this too. You made a really bad mistake when you killed them."

"What if they're not dead, Alex?"

92

PUSH OF A BUTTON

Sam tried to pause the ticking clock in her head. She'd never expected to find a file folder with the answers she was seeking, anyway, and just had to take her thinking backward to her original intentions in the form of Dr. Payne's laptop.

These days actual CT scan films weren't viewed against a blinding back-lit board. The results and technician's report were e-mailed to the treating physician to become part of the patient's electronic medical records. Armed with Alex's patient ID number, she switched on Payne's computer and waited for the laptop to boot up, counting down the seconds in her head as the fire alarm continued to wail.

The screen came to life and Sam quickly found an icon that looked like a filing cabinet and clicked on it. Sure enough, it opened into the medical records portal through which any physician with the proper patient ID could access a patient's assembled history. The box that appeared on the screen, though, wasn't asking her for that; it was asking her for a physician's user name and password. Even if she guessed Dr. Payne's identification correctly, she'd be no closer to guessing his password. Then in the clutter on the desk she spotted his clip-on

ID badge she recalled from noting his altogether wrong name for a doctor.

And beneath that name was his hospital identification number.

Sam entered JOHNPAYNE in the user name box, then typed in the combination of letters and numbers forming his ID number into the password box, certain it would work. But the machine lit up with bright letters warning that she'd entered the wrong password and did she need help finding it. Sam clicked on "yes" and waited for the next prompt.

Until the medical records doorway closed and the home screen returned, Sam finding herself unable to manipulate the cursor anymore.

What the hell?

She'd done exactly what any thief or hacker would have done, she imagined, thereby activating the system's security override. That was it. She was done here, finished.

Except . . .

Sam yanked the power cord from the laptop and folded its top back down. Wasting no further time, she tucked it under her arm and headed back into the hall, turning toward the gurney she'd abandoned and tucking the still faintly humming machine under the top sheet.

Then she started pushing the gurney along the freshly polished floor, moving with apparent purpose. Reaching the elevator just as the fire alarm stopped wailing.

93

DIVIDED LOYALTIES

Alex continued to stare at the ash man, more through him than at him, really.

"That's bullshit."

"Is it? Can you really be so sure? Do you really think I'd squander the best leverage I had over you?"

"I watched them die."

"You saw what I wanted you to see, Alex," the ash man told him, through a mouth that looked like a gaping black hole. "Just as you're seeing me now."

"More crap," Alex persisted, not so sure anymore. "And you're just a projection who's full of it."

"I'm not just a projection. I'm standing here right now. Go ahead, reach out and touch me."

"I'd rather cut you in half again."

"I'd welcome you trying. Stronger signal this time so I can take you with me. Not your physical form, just the part that matters, the part that knows the secret of why you were brought here, the knowledge you've been entrusted with. You didn't ask for this, boy. It's not your doing. You don't belong here; you never did. Come back with me so I can reveal the truth of your identity, introduce you to who you really are and your true fate."

"And my parents?"

"The Chins? They will be waiting for you, just as promised. Part of the deal."

Alex felt himself weaken, seeing the easy way before him, the route to end this nightmare from which there otherwise seemed no end.

"What's my name?" he heard himself ask.

Something changed in the ash man's hazy visage, the dark holes that rode his face for eyes seeming to narrow, suddenly evasive.

"What's my real name?" Alex challenged again.

"Alex—"

"Stop! You don't know, do you? You can't tell me because you don't know."

The ash man's broadcasted face flattened. "But I know where to find the girl, Alex. We didn't kill her, we only left her alive because of you. Cooperate with us or she dies. Join me now or she dies. Go ahead, take my hand. . . ."

Alex saw a semi-translucent hand stretching out for him, the arm seeming to lengthen as it came forward, slow enough for Alex to stretch a hand into his pocket and come out with the thing that looked like an old-fashioned slap bracelet that had restrained his father. He snapped it forward in line with the gray-toned wrist coming his way, felt it lodge over air and energy. Watched the ash man's liquidy eyes bulge.

"Take that, you son of a bitch!"

"*Nooooooooooooooo!*" the ash man screamed, frozen in place as Alex burst past him like the spectral shape was a linebacker keeping him from the end zone.

94

THE EMBARCADERO

Sam sat among all manner of tourists and locals enjoying their evening meals at outdoor tables in the Embarcadero's Justin Herman Plaza, conspicuous in her mind because she was alone in clear view of the bustling Ferry Building marketplace. A concert had just wrapped up in the area that would be dominated by an ice skating rink during the winter months. She sat a bit isolated in the shadow of Vaillancourt Fountain, a modernistic water-spraying sculpture that many local purists hated but she actually loved for its symmetrical form, everything seeming to belong just where it was placed.

Unlike life.

Dr. Payne's laptop tucked under her thigh, she'd taken the BART and then a streetcar, of all things, to the Embarcadero Station, satisfied that she hadn't been followed from the hospital. Night had fallen and with that all manner of new options for anyone watching her to stay out of sight. She felt like a little kid, having dreaded its fall and now hating the way darkness made the world feel scary and her more vulnerable, to boot.

One of the few things she and her parents actually agreed on was a love for this part of the city, its great history, color, and vibrancy. The Embarcadero in general and this section of it in particular were the encapsulation of everything that made San Francisco special, featuring an easy mix of the old and the new, of history and modernity. That probably explained why she liked the Vaillancourt Fountain in spite of its perceived affront to the area's more classical sensibility. Its presence made her appreciate that sensibility even more and highlighted the area's historical nature by contrast. The Ferry Building had been a pier before being converted to house an assortment of high-end shops and restaurants comparable to an upscale mall, its majestic facade watched over by a huge clock tower.

Alex and Raiff were headed here now, having recovered the sketchbook just as she'd absconded with the computer containing Alex's medical file.

What does it say? What had Payne seen in the CT scan results that had ultimately led to his death?

Sam realized she'd been peering downward and jerked her gaze back up, finding Justin Herman Plaza to be the same. No one amiss in sight, no one seeming to have any interest in her.

She regarded the laptop again, wondering what secrets it held, when a hand grasped her shoulder.

95

BOAT RIDE

"Sorry to startle you, Dixon," Dr. Donati greeted her.

"You . . . I . . ."

Sam tried to stop stammering but couldn't collect her thoughts. Donati noticed the laptop.

"I assume that's . . ."

"Yes, Doctor. But—"

"Not here, Dixon. I think someone's coming."

It was Alex, moving with the same grace and agility he always did. Sliding through the crowd so easily no one even seemed to notice him. But he looked different to Sam from this distance, older somehow and sadder, his shoulders still squared and strong but burdened, as if something was weighing him down. And he wasn't smiling like he always did. Looked grimly determined instead.

Donati looked from Alex to her and then back to Alex. "That must be . . ."

"Yes," Sam confirmed.

"He's just a kid."

"We're in high school. What were you expecting?"

Dr. Donati looked hurt. "I don't think of you as a high school student, Dixon. You should know that. Especially now."

"Those findings I shared with you . . . ," Sam thought out loud.

"Long story. Well, actually, a short one. You were spot-on. Picked up just where I left off and went further. All that was missing was a final dot on the map. But no more, because I've figured out where the wormhole's going to open."

Sam's throwaway cell phone rang. She snatched it from the pocket of her jeans and recognized the number Raiff told her to look for.

"I'm waiting for you now."

"Where?"

"Fisherman's Wharf," he told her. "Pier Thirty-nine. We're going on a sight-seeing tour of the bay."

"Raiff?" Donati asked, as they moved among typically heavy pedestrian traffic for Fisherman's Wharf.

"I thought I told you about him."

"You probably did, Dixon, but my mind's swimming in the shallows, so much sticking to it that I can't sort through it all."

"He saved us," Sam elaborated, edging farther forward. "A couple times."

Donati's gaze remained rooted on Alex, as if wondering if he were real or just some imaginary figment. "Yes, I recall that now. The other alien, your boyfriend's guardian or something."

Sam looked toward Alex, expecting him to correct Donati. But he didn't.

"You were there," Alex said to him instead, "at the very beginning, weren't you? You and the old guy we met at Bishop Ranch."

Donati was still staring at him, almost through him, the way Alex could see through the ash man. "Extraterrestrial life . . . I've waited my entire life for this moment and I find myself at a total loss for words."

"Maybe this will help," Alex said, handing Donati the folded pages containing the tests conducted by Dr. Chu.

Raiff was waiting with their tickets at Pier 39, where a long line of people slowly boarded a tour boat docked there. Donati shook hands with him, stiffly, as if unsure what Raiff's grasp might yield. Then he went back to clutching Alex's pages tight against his body. They reached the front of the line, an attendant waiting for them to hand over their tickets. They did and stepped off the gangway onto the tour boat.

"Let's go below," Raiff said.

Sam showed him the laptop. "It's password protected. We've got a problem."

He flashed a wink. "No, we don't."

The cruise, a last-minute addition to the Blue and Gold Fleet schedule, was only about half full with almost all the passengers perched on deck, where they could better hear the tour guide's narration. That left the tables making up the enclosed area below, featuring a snack bar, virtually abandoned. They chose one against the wall that featured plenty of light for Raiff to hack into Dr. Payne's laptop in record fashion, hardly even a challenge for him.

"How'd you do that?"

"Where I come from such skills are as natural as walking." He plugged in Alex's patient ID number, opened the file, and turned the laptop toward Donati.

But Donati was currently entrenched in reviewing the findings accumulated by Dr. Chu first, focusing on the blood tests. He peeked over the pages at Alex several times while reviewing them, once and then again to make sure he was reading the results right.

"You know my specialty," he said suddenly to him.

"Sam told me it was astrobiology."

"Which makes me rather expert on regular biology as well, enough so I can tell you that if I didn't know better, I'd say these blood tests were the result of a hoax instead of actual samples. The astrobiologist in me passes that off to what must be subtle differences in the atmosphere of your home planet, leading to different levels of oxygen and CO_2, just for starters."

"This is my planet," Alex corrected. "Just like you."

"I was speaking of your *native* planet," Donati corrected quickly. Then his gaze moved to Raiff. "Unbelievable," he said, shaking his head, trying to process everything at once. "All this is truly unbelievable. I've spent my life trying to prove what I always suspected to be the case. And you've validated everything I've ever believed, and instead of being joyous, I find myself terrified. Not of you, or the boy, but of what's coming."

"I wish I could be more helpful," Raiff told him.

"Perhaps you can," Donati said, leaning forward. "Tell me more about this world you come from."

"Virtually identical to your own, just more advanced. Our landmasses are smaller. As a result, our population is substantially smaller. And there's no famine or poverty."

"But there will be, won't there?" Sam interjected. "That's why you came here in the first place. To plant us like crops to be harvested when you needed us to handle the heavy lifting."

"Not me," Raiff corrected, "or those like me. But, yes, human life on this planet owes its existence to the same forces that want to enslave you the way they enslaved us."

"You came here as refugees," Donati concluded, utterly transfixed, hanging on Raiff's every word. Still having only skimmed Alex's medical records.

"There were others who knew more, who preceded Dancer to this world, but they're gone now."

"Gone?"

"Eradicated, exterminated."

"I don't understand."

Raiff crossed his arms and laid his elbows on the table as the boat engines began to rumble louder. The tour guide's voice continued to blare through the speakers on the deck above, echoes merging by the time the sound reached down below.

"Have you ever heard of a man named Langston Marsh?"

"Should I have?" Donati asked him.

"He's built a private army whose sole purpose is to track down and kill every alien they can find. His soldiers have been hot on Dancer's trail since his parents were murdered last night."

"Murdered?" Donati asked, eyes widening.

"Maybe not," Alex interjected tentatively. "The ash man told me they were still alive."

"You saw him?" Sam exclaimed in disbelief. "He came back?"

"He appeared at my house when I went to pick up my sketchbook," Alex responded, leaving out the ash man's mention of her.

"Speaking of which," said Raiff, extending a hand toward Alex.

Alex handed the sketchbook to him. "Not sure if this is going to mean anything to you."

"Let's take a look and see."

* * *

There was a slight jolt as the tour boat eased away from Pier 39 and angled toward the bay. Raiff scanned the contents of the sketchbook quickly, shaking his head in silent amazement at some of the drawings, the ones featuring the most detail. Donati had come around to the other side of the table to study the pages as Raiff flipped them.

"I don't remember drawing those," Alex told them, breaking the silence and feeling the ship being jostled by a combination of waves and the rolling wakes of the big freighters and cargo carriers clinging to the center of the channel. "It was like I was in a trance or something."

"Machines," Raiff explained. "Machines from my world, that practically ran my world. That's what most of these pictures are of."

"But how would I know about them?"

"Let's see if this might help tell us," Donati said, moving back to the laptop to view the results of Alex's initial CT scan.

96

CT SCAN

Donati squinted to better view the laptop screen, scrolling through the various images. "Come have a look, Dixon. Your boyfriend has something tucked in his head besides his brain."

This time Sam didn't even think of correcting him. They'd just passed a family of sea lions nesting on a rock assemblage sticking out of the bay. The boat turned so they had a brilliant view of both the San Francisco waterfront and the city's striking, if irregular, skyline. Nothing like a large city framed by the water at night.

Sam positioned herself to better see the screen Donati had tilted toward her. The object to which he'd referred was oblong, almost egg-shaped. What looked like small hairs of varying sizes jutted out from it at irregularly spaced intervals.

"You're looking at a microchip formed of organic molecules instead of silicon, fully capable of interfacing with the human brain."

"And these tendrils?" Sam posed, referring to the wispy, hair-like things protruding from the organic chip.

"Neuron storage would be my first guess, along with expansion capabilities. If the chip requires additional space, it simply sprouts another. We already know that DNA can reliably store data for two thousand years or more. My guess is the microchip you're looking at has been genetically engineered to interface with Alex's DNA in order to cram an incredible amount of information into an infinitesimal physical space." He moved his gaze to Alex. "Looks like we found the reason you were brought to this planet."

"Then the secrets we're looking for," Raiff interjected, "the secrets to stopping this invasion . . ."

"Might well be stored on that chip." Donati completed the thought for him.

"Why not just bring it over in somebody's pocket?" Sam wondered.

"My guess would be the electromagnetic displacement inside the wormhole," Donati theorized. "In all probability that would cause severe damage or degradation, if not outright destruction, of anything stored on a microchip." Donati reviewed the CT scan images again to make sure what he'd noted the first time was accurate. "I think the chip was installed while your boyfriend was still in utero, Dixon," he added. "Have a look. You can see in some of the scans how the brain has grown over a portion of it. You can also see how the soft tissue has virtually melded to it, no attempts at rejection, which can only mean one thing."

Donati stopped, as if waiting for a response, then continued when Sam, Alex, and Raiff remained silent, as the boat headed straight for the Golden Gate Bridge. "It was manufactured to be able to interface with the human brain and keyed to the subject's DNA to avoid rejection."

"You're talking about boosting brain function the same way you might add RAM to a computer," Sam theorized.

"Indeed I am, Dixon. But in your boyfriend's case the chip isn't connected to any part of the brain. That would seem to suggest it's an independent body implanted by this means to avoid detection."

Alex was massaging his temples. "Until I got my bell rung the other night, you mean, and the CT scan revealed it."

Donati nodded. "Your doctor's report here notes his utter befuddlement at its presence. There's a record of him making a call to a neurological specialist, probably to inquire about his experience with such things."

"That man has been eliminated as well, in all likelihood," Raiff said flatly. "Anyone who could expose or uncover the truth behind Dancer's presence here."

"Which is?" Alex snapped. "I mean, please tell me, because I'd like to know. What is the truth behind what I'm doing here?"

"We've got another problem," Donati said, studying Dr. Payne's report again. "It appears the chip is now leaking."

97

ATTACK MODE

"You really shouldn't be accompanying us, sir," Rathman said to Langston Marsh, as his thirty commandos packed into the Zodiac rafts. "This is going to get messy."

"Nothing you can't handle, I trust."

"We're about to sink a civilian vessel. That's a new experience even for me."

"But necessary in this case. I'm sure you understand that now."

"I do."

"Then you should also understand why I have to be here. Something about this young man is different from the others we've hunted. He must be disabled and taken into our custody, not exterminated like all the others. And I have to be on site to interrogate him immediately—myself."

"Yes, sir."

"What about the insurance policy I asked you to take out?"

Rathman checked his watch. "En route now. Ten minutes or so out, depending on traffic."

"We'll take them with us, then. As leverage."

Marsh gazed out into the bay, toward the lights of the Blue and Gold Fleet tour boat that had now crossed under the Golden Gate Bridge. "I often wonder what my father was feeling as he took off on that fateful flight. Did he know what he'd be facing? What was he thinking when he climbed into that cockpit? Did he somehow sense he was about to confront his own mortality? Did he realize he was among the first men at the front in a war I've been fighting ever since? That's the kind of moment I believe this is, Colonel. That's why I have to be there, just like my father was."

Marsh spotted a dark van slide to a halt up the hill from which the private dock was located.

"I believe," he said to Rathman, "that our insurance has arrived."

98

LEAKAGE

"Leaking?" Alex wondered. "What's that mean, exactly?"

"It explains the contents of your sketchbook, for one thing," Donati told him. "Each of those images you drew represents something your conscious mind couldn't possibly have knowledge of. But if the image leaked out from the chip hidden in your head and was somehow processed by your subconscious, you'd have an explanation for how you could draw things you'd never seen with no memory of imagining them. It explains *everything*."

"Including my headaches?"

"You mean the ones you've been getting since Friday night?" asked Sam.

"And before." Alex nodded. "Only, they've gotten a lot worse since Friday night. But it's not just the pain. It's also, I don't know, kind of a pressure, like somebody squeezing my skull. Seems to originate just behind my eyes, but I'm not sure."

"I thought you were lying about them, to get out of tutoring sessions, so I'd give up and leave. Like you always being late."

"I never told Dr. Payne about the headaches," Alex said, addressing them all, "not a single word."

"You didn't have to," Donati said, still scrolling through the images. "Your CT scan spoke for itself, only your doctor didn't understand the language well enough. That's why he called in a neurological expert, someone who could tell him what it was he'd found. A foreign body that looks implanted in the skull? A foreign body that by all indications has ruptured and is leaking something dangerously close to the brain? I can only imagine what he made of that."

"But how can you tell it's leaking?" Sam asked him.

"I can't, based on these still shots. I'm proceeding from the anecdotal evidence you've provided that further suggests that the concussion Alex suffered altered the chip's positioning which accounts for the worsening of his symptoms. As for the leakage, well," Donati continued, moving a finger from one of the tendril-like things to another, "I believe we have these to blame. Each time a new one sprouts, it weakens the chip's molecular integrity and creates space for neurons to escape and interface with his brain."

"So whatever it is I'm carrying in my head," Alex picked up, "all these secrets about how to win the war that's coming . . ."

"Are stored molecularly inside this chip, essentially within strands of your own DNA," Donati completed. "Its organic nature indicates it could only be implanted in utero to avoid almost certain rejection, explaining why you were smuggled here as an infant."

The tour boat was steering toward Alcatraz now, the island a blotch on the dark, fog-drenched horizon through the big viewing window. They had entered "the Gap," passing between hills on either side that forced the air lifting off the ocean into a kind of wind tunnel. Normally, such thick fog was more of a summer phenomenon, but the unseasonable warmth had left it lingering well into the autumn months.

"There's something else," Alex told them all, "something that happened in the second CT scan."

"Obviously called for since Payne didn't believe the results he got from the first," Donati replied. "Probably suspected a machine malfunction or something like that."

"What happened during the second scan, Dancer?" Raiff asked him.

"The machine went crazy, I mean flat-out nuts. Sparks were flying in all directions, things popping and crackling. How does that jibe with your theory, Dr. Donati?"

"Well, not being a medical doctor, I couldn't say for sure. I'd start from the fact that no such occurrence marked your first scan and that tells me something may have changed before the second one."

"The leakage?" Alex barely managed to ask, as if afraid of the answer.

"More likely related to the effect exposure to such a powerful magnetic field had on the chip itself. It could be that the chip, being an organic entity, was simply defending itself against what it perceived to be a threat. That's something of a stretch, but then so is everything else we're facing here," Donati finished, turning his gaze on Raiff as if to make his point. "And this leakage the first CT scan detected does not bode well for any number of reasons."

"Like?" Sam asked, when Alex couldn't bring himself to speak.

"I'm an astrobiologist and a physicist, not, as I just said, an MD—or a witch doctor. But the first thing I'd say is that the chip you're carrying in your head may be killing you. And the second thing I'd say is that the degradation of the chip, as represented by the leakage, could mean it can no longer fulfill the purpose for which it was implanted inside you."

Alex looked toward Raiff. "You didn't know anything about this chip?"

"Not until tonight, no."

"And what's your thinking now that you do?"

"That the intent was always to drain the information off it."

"How, exactly?"

"Either through some kind of interface or . . ."

"Or what?" Alex prodded.

"Surgical excision," Sam said, when Raiff hesitated.

"You mean open my head to get it out?" Alex exclaimed, his voice growing angry. "No way that's happening, no way!"

"It may be your only chance to live if the leakage worsens, even in the slightest," Donati interjected. "You're carrying a foreign body around in your head that, organic or not, is spewing something that might ultimately be toxic. Radioactive, perhaps, or worse."

"It's a good thing you're not an MD, Doctor," Alex told him. "Because you've got a lousy bedside manner."

"How about 'radiation or something just as bad'?"

Alex shook his head and turned back to Raiff. "You're supposed to be my Guardian. So what's the playbook say for this?"

"To save your world, I'd have to find a way to transfer the information the chip is carrying. To save you, I'd have to find a way to get it out of your head."

"But you can't do both," said Sam.

"I don't know," Raiff admitted. "With the technology available here, in this world, I just don't know."

"The devil's alternative," muttered Donati.

"In other words," Alex said, face starting to tighten into a scowl before going utterly flat, "I'm totally screwed."

"No," Sam insisted stridently, when the others didn't respond, "you're not."

"Huh?"

"Remember when you told me you never let the first tackler bring you down?"

"Sure, but what does that have to do with anything?"

"This is the first tackler."

"No, the first tackler took down my parents, my mom and dad."

Sam's eyes searched his, as if they were alone, nothing and no one else mattering. "You said they might still be alive."

"That's what the ash man told me. I think he wanted to make a deal, maybe bring me to them if I stopped being a pain in his ass."

Sam looked toward Raiff and Donati now. "Is it possible? Could they still be alive?"

"Alex just described a second encounter with an astral projection from millions of light-years away," Donati noted. "I'd say that suggests we shouldn't discount or dismiss anything whatsoever out of hand."

"How's your head feel now, Alex?" Raiff asked, sounding more like a parent.

"Not so bad." Alex frowned. "Nothing I can't handle."

"One other thing," Donati said suddenly, "if there's some kind of invasion planned, if this enslavement is about to commence, they'll have to open another wormhole, won't they?"

Raiff nodded. "One way or another, yes."

"Because, thanks to Dixon here, I think I know where they're going to open it. I could be wrong, but—"

And that's when the first explosions rocked the tour boat.

99

A SINKING SHIP

The first blast rocked the boat, left it teetering in the water. The second blast sent it listing heavily toward starboard, en route to toppling over.

Raiff had moved from his seat instinctively to protect Dancer, but the boy had already moved to grab Samantha just before she hit the floor, cushioning the blow enough to avoid any injury.

Langston Marsh . . .

A single blast could have resulted from something random and mechanical. But two spaced this close could only be sabotage, and professional at that. Raiff came to this conclusion in the moments just before the power died, replaced only by emergency floodlights that did little to break the darkness. The harsh stench of oil and the sight of thick clouds of black smoke flooding the tour boat's covered area told him the bomber, or bombers, knew exactly what they were doing.

As he moved to help Dr. Donati, who'd slipped out of his chair, Raiff also registered the fact that the explosions had been triggered in the hull, well below the waterline. Divers, then—commandos, in all likelihood, well versed in such things—which again suggested the work of Marsh's modern-day Fifth Column. Clearly he was upping the ante and, just as clearly, enough information had reached him to suggest that Dancer was no ordinary target.

"What happened? Are we sinking?" a ghost-white Donati managed to ask, as Raiff helped him back to his feet.

"We were attacked," Raiff said, leaving it there. Then, swinging fast, "Alex?"

"I'm fine."

The smell of oil was already stronger, the smoke thickening, when the covered area of the boat began to take on water. Raiff couldn't tell where it was coming from, meaning it was coming from lots of places at once, which suggested a catastrophic hull rupture.

"Lifeboats!" he called out.

But Alex had already surged ahead of him for the stairs, joining those who'd chosen to enjoy the tour without the bother of the biting wind or cool mist rising off the sea. They pushed up the stairs in a pack, needing to cling to both railings with the boat now listing at what felt like a forty-five-degree angle and increasing. Raiff clung as close as he could to Alex without shoving the other passengers forcefully aside. Keeping the boy safe had been his sole purpose for eighteen years, hyper-exaggerated over the last forty-eight hours. So strange to think of little else for so long without needing to act, only to have the tables turned so suddenly and violently.

Once on deck, Raiff had no choice but to forgo his attempt at restraint. An all-out panic had set in, exaggerated further by the boat's desperate, dying keeling. For all Raiff knew, Marsh's men had infiltrated the tour and had waited for just these moments of chaos to strike, when their target would be most vulnerable. So his rapid scan of faces focused on eyes filled with precision instead of panic. In the process, Alex drew too far ahead of him in the direction of the life rafts, which the crew were doing an incredible job of readying to abandon ship.

"Stay with me, Alex!" Still holding fast to Donati so as not to lose him to the crowd, Raiff's gaze captured Samantha as well. "Both of you!" he added, leading them away from the cluttered mass of humanity funneling toward the aft side.

"But the life rafts are there!" Alex protested, holding his ground.

"Not all of them," said Raiff.

100

LIFEBOAT

Their life raft hit the water hard, Alex tensing and instinctively taking a deep breath when it seemed certain to topple over from absorbing the initial brunt of impact solely on its nose. But the raft flattened out quickly, melding with the waves instead of fighting their swell, and it was just the four of them sliding about the soft bottom and going for the life vests clasped to the sides.

Except Raiff, who went for the oars instead, to get them clear of the tour boat before it keeled all the way over.

"Is everyone all right?" he cried out, as he began to row, alternating the oars to turn the raft away from the listing boat.

"Oh, my God," Donati cried out.

"Alex, talk to me!"

"I'm fine!" Alex called back to him, as he tightened the straps on Sam's life vest for her.

"Oh, my God," Donati said again.

A big swell tossed a gush of water over the side, the raft feeling weightless against the power of the wave rocking it. Alex didn't ski much but he'd taken to it quickly, as he took to pretty much anything athletic. He recalled the sense of "getting air" off a mogul jump or natural hump in the trail. That's what this felt like, the whole raft getting air. He felt Sam throw herself against him and captured her in his grasp, hugging her tight. She clung to him, trembling horribly from the cold and shock. Alex ran a hand through her hair, tightened his grasp.

All he could do.

"Oh, my God," Donati repeated.

Raiff had somehow managed to get the raft righted, the waves still fighting him every inch of the way, but now he seemed to be winning. Angling them for the nearest landmass, which was little more than a dark blotch set against the mist and the night.

"That's it!" Donati cried out, rising in the raft to point in the direction Raiff was steering.

"That's *what*?"

The next wave pitched Donati down into the water pooling at the raft's bottom. "The wormhole! Dixon's pattern plugged into an elementary algorithm to determine the location from which it's going to be opened!"

"Where?" Sam yelled to him.

Donati pointed again, soaked now. "There!"

"Alcatraz," Alex realized.

TWELVE

ALCATRAZ

We shall require a substantially new manner of thinking if mankind is to survive.

—ALBERT EINSTEIN

101

ZERO-SUM GAME

For Langston Marsh, life was a zero-sum game. Somebody won and somebody lost, which must be the case in a time of war.

And in war there were casualties, many innocents inevitably among them. A necessary sacrifice, the level of life lost measured against the rewards that could be gained as a result.

A zero-sum game.

And the stakes here couldn't be higher. Whoever and whatever Alex Chin really was, he represented the highest threat assessment Marsh had ever faced. Something was building, something was coming; he could feel it with the same cold pangs that had left him certain that his father would never return from his mission that fateful day. He had already cried for hours when the man in uniform rang the doorbell with cap tucked stiffly under his arm. His mother had taken on the crying duties at that point, Marsh unable to comfort her because he was too busy staring at the sky, picturing himself soaring up there in a jet suit to destroy whatever had killed his father.

Sometimes life really is that simple, he thought, as the Zodiacs clung to their position in a fog bank a half-mile off the aft side of the now fully toppled tour boat. The fog bank was thick enough to conceal them but thin enough for Rathman's high-tech night-vision binoculars to clearly see the world ahead.

Marsh already knew this wasn't going as planned. There were supposed to be four explosions and only two had gone off, accounting for survivors who should've been victims. Had things gone according to plan and Rathman's divers done their job, the occupants of the Zodiacs would be steaming their way toward the chaos now to find the boy. If that meant killing any number of others in the process, so be it. Victims were far easier to deal with than witnesses.

The zero-sum game again.

As it was, though, the life rafts were filled with survivors fleeing the very chaos Marsh had planned to use in his favor. No sense exposing themselves now, not until they'd reacquired their target and moved to intercept him. Out here, in the bay at night with a suitable Coast Guard response still minutes out, his men still held a distinct advantage once they had the target in their sights.

"I've got him," Rathman said, binoculars still pressed against his eyes.

And moments later the Zodiacs burst out of the fog bank on a direct course for Alcatraz.

102

BEACON

Raiff managed to steer their life raft through the final swells toward the dock used by tour groups to access the island.

"What do you mean, Doctor?" he said, supporting Donati as he tried to grab the ladder despite the lurching craft. "About the wormhole, the pattern leading *here*!"

"That's what I said."

"I know it's what you said, but what does it mean?"

"The wormhole! Dixon's pattern plugged into an elementary algorithm to determine the location! Just like Laboratory Z eighteen years ago! It's going to happen here, the place they'll be coming through from your world on the other side, hordes and hordes, I'd imagine."

Donati was breathing hard by the time he reached the dock, his glasses fogging up from the ever-present mist over Alcatraz.

"Can you be more specific?" Raiff asked him, noticing the slightest flicker of lights and motion growing toward them out on the bay. "Because we're about to have company."

Alex reached the dock next, lowering a hand to help Sam up. She held fast to him when her feet touched down on the moist wood of the dock, felt his knees buckle and clung harder to keep him from spilling over into the water.

"My head," he managed to say, squeezing his temples as he sank into a crouch.

Donati crouched alongside him. "Is this what the headaches feel like?"

"No, this is worse, different. Deeper, more throbbing." Alex winced in pain. "Like every time my heart beats, which is a lot right now. Wouldn't happen to have any aspirin with you, would you, Doc?"

Donati helped Alex back to his feet. "I'm not that kind of doctor, a good thing since I think I've got the right prescription," he said, then turned to Raiff. "I think I know how to find what we're looking for."

The Zodiacs slowed as the dock to which the life raft was tied came into clear view. The kid's protector, the man who'd thwarted the efforts of the men Rathman had deployed to the former site of Laboratory Z, had laid waste to all three ladders leading up. No bother, since Rathman had come prepared.

"I'm not comfortable with you being here, sir," he said to Marsh.

"Nonsense. I've been waiting for this moment since I was seven years old."

"Then wait here. I'll leave two men with you."

"To keep me safe, Colonel, or to prevent me from following you?"

The three Zodiacs slowed further and Rathman turned his gaze out into the bay, as if to look for a fourth one. "To serve as a last line of defense, sir, just as we discussed."

* * *

Raiff brought up the rear, keeping his gaze peeled behind him for their expected pursuit. The twenty-two-acre island seemed like the only chance they had upon skirting away from the toppled tour boat, but now he wasn't so sure. They'd docked on the far side of the island, directly below the infamous prison, that was now part of the national parks system, and across from the relic of a hospital on the other side, facing east.

Donati remained tight-lipped about what he expected they were going to find inside the prison. The island's small size when viewed from the water belied its true scope and the difficulty of the climb, especially amid the chill and biting wind rising off the bay.

"What are you looking for, Doctor?" Raiff asked finally.

"It's not what I'm looking for, it's what Alex here is looking for."

They'd reached the downward-sloped patch of land that rode the island's middle. Not much besides dirt and brush; Raiff realized they were square in the open. He'd moved ahead of Sam to reach Donati and express his concerns, when Alex dropped to the dark earth like someone had ripped the world out from under him.

"Alex!" he said louder than he'd meant to, kneeling on one side of the boy while Donati knelt on the other. "Dancer, can you hear me?"

The boy turned his way, his eyes wandering and skin suddenly pasty pale. "It's my head."

"Worse?"

"Better. The headache's gone."

"We're here," said Donati. "According to the beacon, anyway."

* * *

"An excellent strategy," Marsh said, after Rathman had laid it out for him.

"I was hoping it wouldn't be necessary."

"You're as good as advertised, even better."

"Then you'll stay behind with a pair of my men. And our hostages."

"Of course. Just in case."

Rathman had turned his gaze back on the bay. "That's good, sir, because they're almost here."

"What do you mean, a beacon?" Raiff asked, as Donati kicked at the ground with his feet.

"The chip in the boy's head," Donati told him. "Something in the electromagnetic waves and energy emanating from the place where we'll find the wormhole channel. Like a pair of magnets, the one near Alex's brain and the other somewhere in this area where they're re-creating the wormhole."

"Where *who's* re-creating the wormhole?" Sam challenged. "The androids we call the drone things?"

"Which were clearly built on this planet as well."

"Again, Doctor," Sam persisted, "by whom?"

"Hopefully, Dixon, that's what we're about to find out. But first we have to find the entrance that will take us, I fully expect, into Fort Alcatraz."

A few years before, researchers using the same kind of seismic sensors as the oil industry had uncovered the remains of an old military fort named after the island itself in the mid-nineteenth century. Their work had revealed fortifications extending down farther than the machines' ability to measure and jutting out into the bay as well. It had been built as a Civil War facility from which no shot had ever been fired and upon its ruins the prison itself had been constructed. No excavation work had been conducted and the researchers could not explain why their studies had revealed a far more sprawling underground structure than that believed to be the original footprint of the fort.

"Here," Alex said, his ear literally to the ground as he grimaced again from a sudden jolt of pain. "It's right under us."

"We need to find the doorway," Donati replied, eyes sweeping about as if expecting the entrance to magically appear. "It's got to be around here somewhere. . . ."

"There's a doorway, all right, but we won't find it here exactly," Raiff told him, eyeing the shape of the prison.

103

THE FORT

They traipsed up a path toward the prison entrance, having it all to themselves since no public tours were available on Sunday nights. They ignored the warning signs credited to the National Parks Service and reached the big double doors through which some of the most notorious criminals of all time had been paraded. Raiff extended what looked like a baton that had been wedged through his belt into a whip-like device that cut straight through the middle of the doors, allowing them to sway inward.

"Welcome to Alcatraz," he said, leading the others inside the prison.

Almost ten minutes had passed since Rathman had left the area of the dock with the bulk of his men, leaving Langston Marsh with two of them for his own protection and, Marsh suspected, to make sure he didn't follow. Not that he would have, now that Rathman's "insurance" was arriving in a small launch as opposed to a Zodiac.

Marsh studied the couple handcuffed in the craft's open rear, shivering from the cold. Obviously their abductors hadn't let them dress appropriately.

"I'm sorry this was necessary, I truly am," he called to them.

"Eat me," the man said.

"And choke on it," the woman added.

"Douchebag."

"Asshole."

"I can see where your daughter gets her spunk, Mr. and Mrs. Dixon."

His life had changed a great deal in an incredibly short period of time, but Rathman gave that little thought as he watched four figures, including one he was able to identify as his primary target, enter the prison complex, the big doors left ajar behind them. He also tried not to think too much about this pending "invasion" to which Marsh kept referring, convinced now that the boy was a key cog in its implementation. The group could have simply ventured inside the prison to hide, the connection between the explosions that had toppled the tour boat and pursuit by a committed force an easy one to make.

In this case, though, Rathman found himself agreeing with Marsh at least in principle. There were other strategic places to hide on this cluttered island that made far more sense than this one. For that reason, together with a nagging sense he couldn't let go of, Rathman believed the boy and the others had a different purpose for entering the prison. But his was a soldier's mind-set. He had a job to do and needed only to know where his target was, not why he was there.

"Target acquired," he said into the Black Ops 2 Throat Mic connecting him to all his troops. "The entrance to the prison is our zero. Follow my lead."

*   *   *

The inside of the prison was laced with a peculiar combination of scents ranging from cleaning solvent to musty mildew to cold, cracking concrete. The tile floors were chipped and dull, but slippery as if freshly waxed or finished. Raiff led the way, Alex professing to have no idea where to go from here now that his head was no longer throbbing. All Raiff knew was that they were close to whatever the boy's chip had honed in on.

The accessible prison halls were cavernous and serpentine, eerie in their desolation. The kind of place that left Sam wishing she had someone's hand to hold while traversing them. Made her feel like a little kid, afraid of the dark. But there were plenty worse things to be frightened of than the dark.

"Hard to find something when we don't know what we're looking for," Raiff noted, his voice echoing in a tinny fashion through the abandoned confines.

"A doorway, an elevator shaft—something, anything," said Donati.

"Wait," Sam said, sneakers grinding to a halt. "That elevator we just passed for the second time."

"What about it, Dixon?"

"It's key operated. Did key-operated elevators exist back when Alcatraz was built?"

The doors parted with a *whooooooshhhhh*, after Raiff managed to work a twin-set of precise tools into the proper slots of the keyhole to twist it from left to right. He peered inside, hand on his pistol now.

"No buttons, no controls," he reported.

Alex slipped past him, inside. "Then what's the worst that can happen?"

"Nothing," Sam ventured.

"I can think of plenty worse than that," said Donati, joining them inside and leaving Raiff blocking the door from closing.

"I'm supposed to keep you safe, Dancer."

"Then you better step inside," Alex told him.

The old cab descended slowly, creakily, its ancient hydraulic system an odd match for technology millions of years advanced.

Raiff slid forward as the elevator squealed to a grinding halt.

"No," Alex said, holding a hand against him, "stay behind me."

Raiff's chest felt like banded steel, hot to the touch. "Why?"

"A feeling."

"You'll have to do better than that, Dancer."

"I'm one of them."

Raiff relented and backed off, as the elevator settled into place with a final jolt. The doors opened slowly with another soft burst of compressed air.

"My stars," Donatti uttered.

"Exactly," said Raiff.

Rathman's team advanced on the prison and reached the front steps in assault formation with strict military precision. He wasn't used to leading men he'd never worked with before; on missions like this, familiarity

was *everything*. But the skill and experience of the men
Rathman had brought in showed themselves now. These
were seasoned operators who knew their way around
combat and killing, understanding that having the back
of the man on one side of you ensured that the one on
the other side would have yours. It almost made Rathman smile reflectively, nostalgically, knowing combat to
be the greatest of all unifying experiences. And these
were men who wouldn't hesitate to shoot and kill. Men
who understood the mission parameters and were all
about doing their job.

Normally that job was in service to God and country.
In this case it was in service to Langston Marsh and the
almighty dollar. But once the shooting started, such
things wouldn't matter to men like this.

Only the bodies dropping to their bullets would.

Hey, Rathman thought to himself with a satisfied smirk,
it's not rocket science. Just Combat 101.

Alex moved to the front of the elevator cab, finding
himself just short of a steel catwalk that overlooked a
seemingly endless sprawl of interconnected assembly
stations. Essentially an entire world constructed beneath
Alcatraz Island, built outward from the remains of the
Civil War fort on which the prison complex had risen.
His mind naturally measured things in terms of football
field size and he estimated the sprawl to occupy what
appeared to be five or so fields laid side by side three
stories beneath the catwalk.

It was, for all intents and purposes, a factory. The re-
verberating sounds of heavy machinery and the grinding
staccato-like din of conveyor belts reached his ears, emanating from the vast expanse of interconnected stations.

The smell in the air was oddly familiar, a combination of motor oil, rubber, and superheated electrical wiring. He recalled it, painfully, from the battle against the drone things in his house before the ash man had killed his parents.

Or had he?

Raiff started to edge out of the cab, but Alex grabbed hold of his jacket and slid ahead of him.

Finding a drone thing on either side of the elevator.

Pressed tight against him, Sam dropped her mouth to gasp, maybe scream, until Alex covered it with a palm, his other finger held to his lips.

"Shhhhhhhhhhh . . ."

Something, some inert instinct born of his true breeding, told Alex he had nothing to fear and neither did anyone else as long as they remained tucked tight to him.

"It's okay," he said to Raiff and Donati over Sam's shoulder. "Just stay close to me."

Still, Raiff remained ready with his whip until the cyborgs failed to even acknowledge his presence. They lacked the flat, featureless faces Alex remembered from the drone things he'd destroyed back in his house, lacked any faces at all, their finish work incomplete but good enough to serve this purpose, as sentinels guarding against unwarranted entry to the facility.

"The boy's right," Donati whispered. "They don't see him as a threat."

Alex tapped his head. "Thanks to the chip. They must be sensing it. Maybe it's communicating with them somehow."

"What about us?" Raiff asked him.

"Just stay close, like I said."

Alex taking charge now, the quarterback again albeit on an entirely different field. He watched Raiff pull his stick back, not entirely comfortable with Alex taking point, but knowing he had no choice.

"What is that thing?" Donati asked him.

"Hopefully you'll never get a chance to see."

Raiff left it there, not bothering to elaborate on the fact his stick was formed of subatomic, programmable particles based on nanotechnological principles. He wedged the stick back in his belt and continued along the catwalk in a tight pack clustered behind Alex. His breath caught in his throat at what lay before them, at the cavernous expanse that extended both out and downward, as far as the eye could see in the dim lighting.

It wasn't a factory so much as an assembly plant responsible for building cyborgs nonstop for who knew how long. But there wasn't a person, at least the flesh-and-blood version, in sight anywhere. The entire process looked completely automated, various stations manned only by drones sized and shaped to tasks specific to them.

"Machines building machines," Sam noted, completely awestruck.

"Very good, Dixon," complimented Dr. Donati. "The principle of self-replication, a core element of nanotechnology."

"They don't need a wormhole," muttered Raiff, seeing it all from an entirely different perspective. "They're building an army out of steel and wire. Or arm*ies*. Imagine a hundred of these plants, imagine a thousand."

Sam started to do the figuring in her head, plugging in the years, locations, units produced per—She gave up. Too many variables to consider in the equation, and she was already scared enough. She realized she was clinging to Alex's arm, realized he was letting her. The sight was mind-numbing, its very impossibility too surreal even to contemplate.

As near as she could tell, the farthest section of the plant was churning out finished limbs and steel body parts imitating the human endoskeleton in the tradition of the *Terminator* movies, which scared her no matter how many times she watched them. The next sequence along the line was responsible for assembling the pieces in a fashion akin to the automated car factories she'd seen, with robotic arms swaying about soldering, screwing, affixing, and clamping. And when one broke down she pictured some robotic drone sweeping into repair action, designed and built expressly for that purpose.

Machines building machines.

A machine army to be commanded by whoever came through the wormhole channel, which must have been somewhere else in the complex, out of sight from this vantage point, if Donati's conclusions about her findings were correct.

The pale surface flesh was sprayed on the fully assembled cyborgs in thick sheaths at a final station before they dropped down a conveyor through the floor, likely toward another assembly line where their unfinished chips would be programmed to enable them to spring to mechanical life at the flip of a switch. Capable of accepting complex instructions and fulfilling assignments as detailed and specific as the one that brought four to Alex's house in the guise of fake cops. Looking, talking, and acting almost entirely human.

Then Sam remembered the strange language she'd heard them conversing in outside Alex's house. Obviously the language of their home planet, the programming performed by designers limited to expertise in that language. She guessed the cyborgs were equipped with learning chips capable of cross-converting one language instantly into another to the point where they would always "think" in their native language but speak in the language of whomever they found themselves among. No reason to do that when they weren't aware anyone else was listening, to save functional RAM and power.

Machines indeed. If only she could find the plug and pull it. If only it was that simple.

"I should've brought explosives," Raiff said, still straight and stiff as steel.

"You'd need a boatload to make an impact here," Donati told him. "And that says nothing about the God-knows-how-many other facilities like this that are out there."

"I'll find them," Raiff said, but his voice lacked the surety his words implied. "I'll find them all."

"Right now, this is the one where they're going to open the wormhole," Alex interjected. "This is the only one that matters. For now, anyway."

Raiff ran his eyes along the endless expanse around him. "Now's all we've got, Dancer."

Alex led the way down the catwalk, bringing them to the midpoint of the massive underground assembly line beneath them. They rounded a corner and came into clearer view of the next stage of the process, where the unfinished cyborgs were sprayed with flesh-colored tint, had glass eyes fitted over their swirling orbs. It looked also like the assembling mechanism fit them with distinguishing features, like various hairstyles and facial lines, scars, flesh tones. This suggested the assemblers built each unit with infiltration in mind, as well as assault.

And speaking of assault, another assembly station that had just come into Alex's view was making stubby, rifle-like weapons with short, thick barrels. He had no idea what they fired but doubted very much it was bullets as he, or anyone else, understood them. He thought of all the science fiction movies he tried to watch after Sam boasted enthusiastically of their classic nature. He'd never finished a single one, but remembered enough of what he had seen to realize that this scene could have been lifted from any number of them, in one way or another. Art unknowingly imitating life that was much too real.

"Still no trace of the wormhole mechanism," Sam noted.

"It would almost surely require its own level," Donati explained. "The energy required to open the wormhole, formulate the space bridge, at this end would result in incredible, even immeasurable heat transference from radiation that would require a particle accelerator on the level of Cern, Brookhaven, or Tevatron."

"Or Laboratory Z, right, Doctor?" Alex asked him. "What would it look like?"

"A tunnel, long and tubular. It would have to be tubular to properly use electromagnetic fields to propel charged particles to high speeds and to contain them in well-defined beams. The very definition of a supercollider. It would use oscillating field accelerators to generate radio-frequency electromagnetic fields to achieve the particle acceleration."

"If we can't see it now," Alex picked up, when Donati seemed to run out of breath, "it's got to be beneath us."

Almost on cue, a steel spiral staircase that looked like a massive drill bit forging deep into the bowels of the Earth appeared before him. Alex never hesitated. Still holding Sam's hand tight, he started toward it, forgetting all about the invisible safety line the chip in his head formed around the four of them.

"I'm not sure that's such a good idea, Dancer," Raiff said, holding his ground. "At least let me—"

A shrill, piercing alarm swallowed the rest of his words.

"Raiff!" Alex yelled to him, realizing he and Sam had strayed a dozen feet ahead, clearly too much separation to continue projecting a protective shroud over them.

"Keep going!" Raiff shouted. "Go!"

Alex yanked Sam on toward the exposed stairwell, her eyes having trouble breaking their hold on Donati's.

"Move!" Raiff wailed. "Don't stop!"

And they hurtled toward the stairwell drilled down farther than the eye could see, while Raiff swung toward the cyborg guards converging on him.

104

DESCENDING SPIRAL

"Don't look back!" Alex yelled over the incessant wail to Sam. "And don't leave me!"

"Don't worry!"

She clung to him, not about to let go. The stairwell spiraling downward was closer to them than it had seemed. They stepped onto the platform at its top, even with the floor of the catwalk, together.

And then the stairwell started to move.

At first, Sam thought it was an illusion, then she realized, no, this was really happening. The stairwell was indeed churning, picking up speed on a descending spiral that pushed the air past them in gushes.

"Close your eyes!" Alex ordered, hugging her tight against him.

The spiraling descent continued, everything around them visible only as a whirling blur. Sam opened her eyes. She'd always imagined she could see the miniscule particles that made up air rippling before her and that's what this felt like now, as if she were watching the air itself swirl around them.

She was still hugging Alex when the swirling seemed to slow, an entirely new phenomenon starting to sharpen around them. She recalled Donati's and the professor's descriptions of the particle accelerator they'd constructed at Laboratory Z and realized she was looking at what could only be a far more sophisticated and technologically advanced version of that.

Enabling the wormhole that would open again from the other side. A cylindrical, tubular channel of black steel interlaced with thick glass panels, fifteen feet or so in height and wide enough for a car to pass through. It reminded Sam of the Chunnel, which ran beneath the English Channel connecting Britain and France. If she remembered her lessons correctly, once activated a particle accelerator of this size and magnitude would generate power on a millisecond level equal to that of the grid powering an entire city or even state.

"Oh, shit," she heard Alex say, figuring he was seeing the same thing she was.

Until her vision cleared, settling on a shape standing before them that wasn't totally there.

"Hello again, Alex," said the ash man.

Raiff felt the handle of his stick weapon heating up and thought it into its whip form as the first wave of cyborgs descended upon him and Donati. Keeping the NASA scientist close behind him on the catwalk, Raiff lashed the whip out, up and down, side to side, slicing through everything in its path. The air filled with a baked-rubber-and-hot-steel scent, mixed with the corrosive odor of burned wiring. Residue of what his cuts with the whip-like weapon had left in its path: broken machines collapsing in heaps to the ground.

Raiff continued retracing their steps back to the elevator, a junkyard left in his wake. The first wave of androids weren't equipped with weapons but the second wave, reinforcements surging up from the levels below, carried plasma rifles every bit the equal of his whip and capable of working at much greater distances. Up close, along the narrow width and close confines of the catwalk, which forced the cyborgs into a virtual single-file attack, Raiff's whip proved enough to hold them at bay all the way back to the elevator.

Raiff shoved Donati into the open cab ahead of him and pressed the "up" arrow. The door slid closed just ahead of the cyborgs opening fire, their plasma rounds boring effortlessly through the elevator's old-fashioned heavy steel door as the cab shook into hydraulic motion.

"Are we supposed to outrun them?" Donati managed to say between gasps.

"I haven't figured that part out yet," Raiff told him.

"What about—"

"He'll be fine. The girl too."

"You can't know that."

Raiff's stare bore into Donati's. "Yes, I can."

The elevator trembled to a halt, squealed into place. The door slid open.

"Don't goddamn move!" ordered Rathman.

The ash man's voice sounded like pieces of ground glass rubbing against each other. Utterances somehow stringing themselves into words. He stood before them maybe a dozen feet in front of the entrance to the particle accelerator, which once activated would trigger the sequence ending the world as it was known today. Maybe ten feet before Alex and Sam.

"I didn't give you enough credit, Alex," the ash man continued. "I never thought you would get this far, especially so fast."

"I had help," Alex told him, stepping protectively in front of Sam.

"You don't understand."

"What don't I understand?"

"The truth, who you really are. Have you stopped to think why you, why an infant, was made guardian of knowledge vital to our civilization?"

"I haven't had a lot of time to think lately."

The ash man seemed to move, or float, closer, looming larger in one moment than he had in the last. "I should have told you the truth of your identity the first time we met."

"After you killed my parents, you piece of shit!"

The ash man looked utterly unmoved by Alex's feisty show of emotion. "The truth of who you are and why you were taken through one wormhole lies on the other side of this one," he said in that ground-glass voice, tilting his gaze toward the tunnel, which weaved its way beneath Alcatraz Island. Then he extended a grainy hand forward, the palm seeming almost translucent. "Join me on that other side, Alex. We can take the girl with us if you wish."

And with that the cylindrical entrance to the accelerator opened, disappearing into the thick steel walls to reveal a brightly lit tunnel that seemed to stretch emptily forever.

"Embrace your true identity and take the place that is rightfully yours," the ash man continued, stretching a hazy hand forward. "Come back to your world."

"This is my world!" Alex screamed at him and, for the first time, Sam realized the shrill alarm wasn't sounding down here. "This is my world!"

"It won't be for very much longer."

* * *

"Drop the weapon!" the big bald man wailed on, Raiff watching his eyes, sizing up the situation. "Where's the boy? What have you done with him?"

The hall beyond him seemed dimmer to Raiff than it had when they'd first traversed it, as if power were being pulled away from down below. The overhead lighting faded, flickered, and Raiff realized a power drain wasn't to blame, that something else was . . .

coming . . .

"The boy," the giant standing before him resumed, "where is he?"

Raiff never had a chance to answer. A rumble seemed to pulse through the whole of the prison structure before the floor broke apart along an endless cascade of crisscrossing fault lines. Gaps opening in the cracking tile through which the cyborgs burst with their plasma rifles at the ready.

Raiff shoved Donati against the elevator's far wall, covering him protectively as the battle erupted beyond. The plasma rifles made a pinging sound, something like a toy weapon might, white heat erupting from their barrel bores instead of a muzzle flash. All this in eerie contrast to the steady *rat-tat-tat* of the human force's assault rifles, their fire deafening in the narrow confines of the hallway.

Raiff watched the soldiers of Langston Marsh's Fifth Column being slaughtered in virtually effortless fashion by an army that provided the ultimate vindication of Marsh's obsessive crusade. The sounds of screams and the incessant barrage of fire continued to hollow their hearing, and Raiff realized Donati was screaming in cadence with the constant cacophony of gunplay.

Marsh's forces tried to make a stand while seeking some form of cover, only to have the plasma rounds fired by the cyborg army trace their trails wherever they darted. The rounds flared in the semidarkness like streams of light, darkening only when they hit their targets and obliterating whatever lay in their path.

Raiff had been in this world so long that he'd practically forgotten the fearsome impact of the weaponry from his world. As advanced beyond this world's as virtually every other form of technology. Strangely, the plasma rounds ejected with only that soft *pfffffft*, just a hissing in the air as they sizzled through it en route to their targets.

The big bald man who was obviously the leader of this phalanx of Marsh's Fifth Column managed to hang on to the last, amid the sprawl of spilled bodies around him. He was holding a pair of M4 assault rifles in hand, firing them while wailing himself and managing to take down a few of the cyborgs in his relentless spray. His eyes locked briefly with Raiff's when he crossed even with the elevator cab, sweeping his assault rifles toward him, when a series of plasma rounds tore into the man and blew him apart, pieces scattered all directions.

The damn machines saved us, Raiff thought, but only for the moment.

"How good are you with that thing?" Donati asked, eyeing the stick into which the whip had receded.

"I guess we're about to find out," Raiff said, his whip flashing to life again.

"You must believe me, Alex," the ash man continued, as a hot, static-riddled wave blew out from the entrance of the accelerator, like a wind-powered magnet drawing them toward it. "These aren't your people, that isn't even your name. Come with me now, so I may show you the way, the truth. Come with me to the other side, millions of light-years from here where your true destiny awaits."

The ash man said something else, but Sam didn't hear him. She looked at his spectral image superimposed against the particle accelerator tunnel behind him, began to consider the incredible amount of energy it would take to fold space over to create a pathway between these two worlds.

Positive energy.

That took her to the projection of the ash man, transmitted almost surely by some sort of electromagnetic energy. And yet Alex had cut that transmission in half, implying the projection must be some hybrid or held together in all likelihood by an excess of electrons.

Negative energy.

The ash man was talking again, Alex still listening, when Sam crept closer to him.

"What causes a spark?" she said softly, hoping he recalled the lesson of their last tutoring session.

Alex cocked his gaze toward her.

"What causes a spark?" Sam repeated.

His eyes widened, realizing what she was getting at, what happened when positive and negative charges collided.

"I'm offering you a chance," the ash man was saying, "I'm offering you the future."

"Here's your future, asshole."

And with that Alex was in motion. To Sam he looked just as he did on the football field, barreling forward to take down a ball carrier. Only this time it was the ash man he barreled into, slipping partially through his spectral image on contact even as the image was driven backward.

Straight for the entrance to the particle accelerator.

The ash man seemed to float through the air, slipping through the entrance, where his form stretched out to the length of the ceiling, elongated, as if it were made of rubber. Then Sam watched a shower of lightning bolt–like sparks erupt, firing and dancing everywhere, seeming to both strike and emanate from him at the same time.

"*Noooooooooooooo!*" the ash man wailed.

And then he was gone.

What causes a spark? Sam thought, recalling her lesson with Alex about just this time yesterday in the hospital. *A collision of positive and negative energy.*

"Come on!" Alex said and tugged her away from the scene unfolding before them, back toward the spiral stairwell that had brought them down here.

Sam rushed toward it with him, aware of the sparks both increasing and thickening, hopefully doing their part to short-out the entire mechanics of the wormhole itself. She ducked into the spiraling stairwell with Alex, felt it starting to spin wildly around them as the glass and steel forming the particle accelerator began to rupture and crack near its entrance and then along its endless reach, faster than her eye could process.

Along with the ash man himself, his image looking like crack lines spreading across fine porcelain.

"*Alex!*" he screamed. "*Allllllexxxxxxxxxx . . .*"

His voice crackling in the last moment before the accelerator exploded silently in a final gush of blinding white light and the stairwell sucked them back upward.

Alex gazed about him. He felt exactly as he had the moment before, but this moment found him outside in another place and time entirely: standing with his parents in

San Francisco's Chinatown, celebrating the largest Chinese New Year festival outside of China itself. People packed both sides of a street cluttered with an endless display of colorful floats and displays crawling along.

It had always been one of his parents' favorite days of the year, the one that still brought a connection to their homeland. But this was different than a dream, since Alex was well aware he couldn't possibly be here. This was just a transitory illusion of some kind triggered by a boyhood memory.

Except when he looked down he found himself still wearing the jeans, shirt, and sneakers he'd changed into back at his house.

What's happening?

Alex had no idea, except that it felt real. Like some cosmic trick the wormhole's destruction was playing on the whole space-time continuum. Like he was in some kind of an alternate reality, where he might be able to remain if he chose. Turn his back on all of it, make believe none of it had ever happened. His parents would be alive again and he with them. Who could blame him?

He felt an incredible surge of relief, happiness, as if he'd woken from a terrible nightmare to the realization everything was fine and good after all. How much he wanted to stay with his parents and just watch the floats passing by on the street before them.

But then the ash man slid by, riding a diesel-powered fire-breathing dragon, seeking him out amid the crowd viewing the parade and pointing a translucent finger Alex's way.

Was this his doing, his way of trapping Alex? Or was it truly a quantum anomaly a million times more powerful than the destruction of Laboratory Z?

The answers didn't matter, because Alex didn't belong

here. As safe and secure as he felt on that city street with his parents, his world was still a millisecond behind him, where this scene had never really happened. And if he stayed here, if he stayed, then Sam could be lost forever in some celestial ether, trapped literally between worlds, as represented by the spiral stairwell spinning so fast that the world ceased to exist beyond it.

Sam! Alex called in his mind. *Sam!*

She wasn't there at all, then very far away but drawing closer, until she was back in his arms and he was hugging her tight.

The cyborgs were still converging on the elevator, just seeming to take note of Raiff's and Donati's presence, when something that looked like an electrical storm burst upward through the floor. The machines froze in place, locked up solid, as if frozen by a frigid blast of ice.

"Raiff!" the Guardian heard, recognizing Dancer's voice from the area of a nearby stairwell.

Then he watched the boy lead Samantha through what looked like a tunnel carved out of the increasing shower of sparks and flames. It rocketed up and through the ceiling, churning its displaced energy toward the sky. A vast, swirling whirlpool that Raiff imagined, like a vortex, would suck everything within its reach into its field.

"Don't look at it!" Alex cried out, clutching Sam so close to him they seemed extensions of the same person. "Follow me!"

Raiff did, dragging Donati along with him by one hand and retracting his whip in the other, weaving his way through the seized-up forms of the androids, the light gone from their eyes, starting to stink of burned metal and rubber. For a long moment he couldn't breathe and thought he was holding his breath, until he realized there was no air to breathe, no air at all. Nothing but a vacuum they seemed to soar through, Raiff having no sense of his feet touching the floor as he moved all the way to the main entrance to the prison.

The door had already collapsed before them, the walls cracking in lines widening enough to let the blackness of the night pour through. They rushed through what had been the prison yard, surging downhill without ever looking back, Raiff nonetheless struck by the sensation that the vacuum was on their tail, trying to suck them into the vortex.

They tumbled down the slight hill as a group, fearing the world beneath them had been pulled out like a rug, until all their gazes fixed on the crumbling remnants of Alcatraz prison as it vanished in a blinding burst of white light.

105

MELTDOWN

It felt for a moment that the very night had been sucked away, trapping them in a kind of vacuum where they felt weak and weightless. Their clothes alternately billowing and then sticking to their skin, the color seeming to blanch from their faces, only to return in the next instant as the world kept jumping from color to black and white and back again.

Alex was squeezing Sam's hand so tight it actually hurt. She thought her lungs should have been burning from lack of oxygen, but it didn't seem like she needed to breathe, felt as if she were floating over the ground instead of standing on it.

Back beyond them, up the slight hill half a football-field length away, what was left of the prison building didn't explode or burn so much as melt. Its shape receded in the blinding light, and when the light finally began to dim the entire structure was gone, just a sprawling expanse of scorched ground left in its place, minus any char or smoke.

Sam felt buffeted by a thick wind and just like that the air was back along with the sky, which, she realized, had seemed to vanish as well, stolen from the world in those brief moments along with everything else. She looked down, expecting to see her clothes melted or torn free, but found them still in place, soiled but not shredded and smelling of something that reminded her of the scent that lifted off a campfire to cling to fabric like glue. And the air felt . . . well, funny. Kind of staticky, a vague hum that reminded her of a swarm of insects buzzing about coming from inside her head.

She turned and saw Dr. Donati picking himself off the ground, too busy checking his watch to realize blood was running down his face from where he must have struck his head when he fell.

"It . . . stopped," he said dazedly.

Sam rotated her gaze about, the San Francisco skyline having gone utterly dark as well. Then it sprang back to life, the entire world returning.

"Hey, it's working again," Dr. Donati said, still eyeing his watch.

Something told her that it had been actually working all along, that what just happened had transpired somehow between the passage of seconds. Or perhaps the destruction of the particle accelerator that would have opened the wormhole on this side had frozen time for the briefest of moments, the world, or at least this part of it, needing to catch its breath.

"My head," Alex said suddenly.

"Is the pain bad again?" Donati asked him.

"No, it's . . . gone. I mean really gone. No trace at all."

"Meaning . . . ," Sam began, and they all turned back toward the empty patch of ground where Alcatraz prison had stood. She realized the humming in her ears was gone, but the air still felt strange, like poking at it might give her finger a shock.

"Do you know what that was?" Donati said, almost squealing in excitement. "Do you know what we just saw? A black hole! A black hole, I tell you! It's the only explana—"

Donati stopped short, the brakes slammed on his sentence. Then he fell over like a severed tree, straight down to the ground.

Raiff rushed to him, hand pressed against the head wound from which the blood was spilling. "There's a first-aid kit back in the life raft," he called out to Alex and Sam. "Get it."

But Alex moved toward him first. "Let me borrow your whip thing. Just in case."

"You won't be able to make it work."

"I just saved this world, Raiff. I think you can trust me."

Raiff handed his stick over reluctantly.

Sam and Alex started off, moving as fast as they dared. They took a circuitous route to keep them as far as possible from the empty, dead patch of ground that had been Alacatraz prison.

"Did that," she murmured, clinging to him, "did we . . ."

Alex didn't answer, just held her close and felt her breathing return to normal. His, too, as they neared the dock, the lights flickering over the San Francisco skyline showing him the world was, in fact, intact, and whatever hole punched deep below the island must have closed.

Then he felt Sam stiffen against him, heard her mutter, "Alex."

And saw the gunmen holding pistols to the heads of Sam's parents.

"You're coming with me, boy," said an older man standing slightly in front of them, his eyes rooted on Alex. "You're coming with me or the girl's parents die."

Alex shoved Sam behind him, thinking fast. Read and

react, just like on the football field, where decisions were made in the time between seconds.

He eased Raiff's stick from his belt and held it low by his hip. "Tell your men to lower their weapons."

"Maybe you didn't hear what I said."

"I heard. But let me repeat what *I* just said: tell your men to lower their weapons and let the girl's parents go."

"And if I don't?"

Alex snapped the stick forward and up, felt it turn into a snake in his hand, slithering out through the air, following the picture he made in his mind. It twirled through the air, finding the gunman holding Sam's father and then the gunman holding Sam's mother. Impacting with a snap against both their skulls, their legs left to crumple as they dropped to the ground.

He retracted the whip and walked straight toward the man who could only be Langston Marsh, as Sam rushed to her parents, the three of them clutching each other in a tight ball.

"Leave," Alex told Marsh.

But Marsh stiffened instead of moving. "This isn't over. Not even close. You'll regret not killing me when you had the chance, when I exterminate the rest of your kind, Alex."

"Call me Kit," Alex said to him, again using the name of Anne Frank's imaginary friend to whom her diary was written. "And you know who you remind me of?" And when Marsh remained silent, Alex snapped his free hand into the air. "*Heil*, Hitler!"

Marsh snarled, starting to back away now. "You, your kind, killed my father. And someday you'll all pay, each and every one of you."

Alex made sure Marsh could see him raise Raiff's stick

again. "Remember how you said I'd regret not killing you?"

Marsh moved faster and lumbered down a rope ladder leading into a Zodiac raft. Alex heard him fire up the engine and watched the raft speed out into the bay, where it disappeared into the darkness. Sam was back by his side by then. She pressed up against him, holding him tight.

"You can ace history now. I really mean that."

Alex held his gaze on the bay, so she wouldn't be able to see the sadness in his eyes. "Guess we'll never know, Sam."

EPILOGUE

THE ROAD AHEAD

The future is no more uncertain than the present.

—WALT WHITMAN

Sam knew she had to go home with her parents, just as she knew she couldn't explain all that had happened to them. Impossible. When they pushed, she kept her answers just vague enough and never said a word about Alex's true origins.

Alex . . .

She hadn't heard from him since he'd taken the first-aid kit back to Raiff to tend to Dr. Donati. Donati had tried to reach her several times, but she kept putting off returning his calls.

When she awoke Monday morning in her own bed, her first brief thought was that maybe it had all been a dream. When that quickly passed, she moved to the window and was relieved to find no police car parked across the street or cruising slowly by. But she knew any ring of the bell could mean the drone things dressed as cops had returned to her door, and she felt anxious and uneasy over the fact that they knew where she lived, who she was.

Only then did she realize she was late for school, very late, so late that she'd missed her AP bio exam and could only imagine how Cara would react to her failing to produce the answers she and the rest of the CatPack needed. Maybe she'd just tell her the truth.

*Yeah, we spent the weekend being chased by aliens.
We saved the world, at least for the time being. Oh, and
by the way, Alex thinks you're a bitch too.*

That had been hours ago and the rest of the day had
passed in slow motion, nothing happening at all, until
dusk bled the light from the sky.

Sam stared at the throwaway phone, willing it to ring,
with Alex on the other end. The old-fashioned flip had
been behaving very strangely ever since exposed to whatever had laid waste to every bit of Alcatraz prison itself,
black hole or something else, leaving behind nothing
other than an empty patch of ground with the color and
life bleached out of it. She stared at it, wondering if she'd
ever hear from Alex again. Had he gone off with Raiff?
Was he going to disappear, living off the grid and everyone's radar for years to come?

Too many questions. Sam spared any further ones when
her phone rang.

Alex walked along the shoulder of the 101 freeway
heading south, nothing but the contents of his backpack
weighing him down, hoping to snare a ride before dark.
It wasn't safe for him to stay in an area where he was so
recognizable, and Raiff knew as well as he did that what
had happened last night changed little, if anything.

Langston Marsh was still out there, more of the drone
things were still out there, and neither was about to give
up the hunt for him. There was the chip in his head to
consider as well, still slowly killing him even if it did
somehow contain the secrets to winning this war in the
long term and not just the short. Raiff was working on
finding the best solution to save Alex from the leakage

while coming up with a way to make sure the chip remained intact so the secrets it held could be revealed.

He missed Sam, missed his parents, did his best not to think about either since it hurt too much, leaving him near tears and unable to focus on anything else.

Like staying alive.

Raiff had given him an address in Los Angeles and nothing more, becoming very cryptic when Alex pressed him on that.

"You'll understand when you get there," was all he'd said.

So Alex trudged on, walking backward as he hitch-hiked down the shoulder of the 101. He only wished he could do the same with his life, walk backward until his parents were alive again and he was in a position to change everything. But the ash man had said An and Li Chin weren't dead, and what did that mean, exactly, for where the road ahead might take him?

As he began to ponder that question, an old battered white van pulled to a stop ahead of him on the shoulder. Alex jogged up to the passenger door and watched it pushed open by the driver's hand.

"Where you headed, friend?" asked the man Alex recognized as the same guy who'd picked Sam and him up yesterday. "The Reverend William Grimes at your service. Call me Reverend Billy. But you knew that already, didn't you?"

Alex climbed in and closed the door behind him, eyeing Reverend Billy's pinkish skin and mangy hair and let his gaze wander to THEND COMES tattooed across all ten fingers. The back of the rusted-out van was still packed with Bibles, but the stacks seemed to have come down a bit since the day before.

"What are the odds, son, the odds of me being fortunate enough to pick you up off the road two days in a row?"

"Not very good."

"No, they are not, unless it was no accident, no coincidence at all."

Alex's hand strayed to the passenger door, ready to pop it open and drop back to the road.

"Bet you're wondering whose side I'm on," Reverend Billy continued. "Bet you're wondering how it is I'm able to show up like this yet again. Bet you're wondering what I know that you need to."

Alex eased his hand away from the latch. "Wondering and listening, sir."

Reverend Billy almost laughed. "I'm no 'sir,' 'less you got the worst set of eyes in God's creation. If all this is happening, it stands to reason it's according to His plan. I'd ask you to consider that, for starters."

"Little difficult under the circumstances."

"Then let me explain what I'm getting at . . ."

Sam saw UNKNOWN light up in the caller ID but answered the phone anyway.

"Hello," she said, hearing the hum of a vehicle whirring on the other end of the line.

"You're not safe."

"Alex?"

"It's okay. I'm headed back there now. There's still time."

"Time for what?"

"Same thing, Sam, to save the world," Alex told her. "But we need to save you first."

FROM AN ANONYMOUS JOURNAL

When I look back on those days, I try to remember when I actually realized my life was never, ever going back to normal. That the routine that had so long defined me and provided a respite for my dreams was finished, that those dreams were over too. A door had been opened that could never be closed.

Langston Marsh and his Fifth Column weren't going anywhere. Alex had destroyed the ash man's projection, but back from wherever it emanated, he and countless others like him were still there. Beyond that, Alcatraz was hardly the only place they were building their army to turn us all into slaves. We'd managed to destroy one wormhole, but others were certain to open, bringing with them the means to enact a destiny mankind had been created to fulfill. They looked at us as the only means to ensure their own survival, prisoners, in that sense, of the way they'd built their world. So they couldn't stop, would never stop.

The means to defeat them, the mystery in all this that remains unsolved, lies in the chip inside Alex's head. That is, if it doesn't kill him first. We need to harvest the data contained upon it, we need to stop the leakage before it kills Alex.

But what did the ash man mean when he told Alex his

parents were still alive and where would that lead? What did he mean about Alex's true destiny and that we had far worse things to worry about than the threat from his planet?

So much we didn't know, couldn't see yet. . . .

My family went to Florida on vacation once. We rented a car and my dad was driving on one of the big interstate highways when we got caught in the smoke from one of those brushfires that had drifted over all eight lanes. The road was there and then it wasn't. All my dad could do was throw on his flashers and cut his speed to a crawl. That's what my life turned into. I couldn't see anything in front of me, had no idea what lay ahead in the next day or even hour.

The life we'd led up until just a few days before was over and there was no going back. We'd won a battle, not a war. I never wanted to become a hero and don't consider myself one now. I look back on all of this a lot, looking for something I could've done differently, but there's nothing. My decisions weren't really conscious ones; I did what I had to do in each respective moment and regret none of those decisions. So if I had it to do all over again, would I?

The answer is simple: I didn't have a choice then, any more than I've got one now. Not if the rising of a new world, committed to the destruction of the old, is to be stopped.

You don't know who I am, and you don't need to. This isn't my story.

It's Alex's, because he's our only hope.

The survivor.